"John Lutz knows how to make your heart er."
—Harlan Coben

"Lutz offers up a heart-pounding roller coaster of a tale."
—Jeffery Deaver

"John Lutz is one of the masters of the police novel."
—Ridley Pearson

"John Lutz is a major talent."
—John Lescroart

"I've been a fan for years."
—T. Jefferson Parker

"John Lutz just keeps getting better and better."
—Tony Hillerman

"Lutz ranks with such vintage masters of big-city murder
as Lawrence Block and Ed McBain."
—*St. Louis Post-Dispatch*

"Lutz is among the best."
—*San Diego Union*

"Lutz knows how to seize and hold the reader's imagination."
—*Cleveland Plain Dealer*

"It's easy to see why he's won an Edgar and two Shamuses."
—*Publishers Weekly*

ALSO BY JOHN LUTZ

*Pulse

*Serial

*Mister X

*Urge to Kill

*Night Kills

*In for the Kill

Chill of Night

Fear the Night

*Darker Than Night

Night Victims

The Night Watcher

The Night Caller

The Ex

Single White Female

*featuring Frank Quinn

Available from Kensington Publishing Corp. and
Pinnacle Books

THE NIGHT CALLER

JOHN LUTZ

PINNACLE BOOKS
Kensington Publishing Corp.
www.kensingtonbooks.com

PINNACLE BOOKS are published by

Kensington Publishing Corp.
119 West 40th Street
New York, NY 10018

All Kensington titles, imprints, and distributed lines are available at special quantity discounts for bulk purchases for sales
promotions, premiums, fund-raising, educational, or institutional
use. Special book excerpts or customized printings can also be
created to fit specific needs. For details, write or phone the office of the Kensington special sales manager: Kensington Publishing Corp., 119 West 40th Street, New York, NY 10018, attn:
Special Sales Department; phone 1-800-221-2647.

This book is a work of fiction. Names, characters, businesses,
organizations, places, events, and incidents either are the product of the author's imagination or are used fictitiously. Any resemblance to actual persons, living or dead, events, or locales is
entirely coincidental.

PINNACLE BOOKS and the Pinnacle logo are Reg. U.S. Pat.
& TM Off.

ISBN-13: 978-0-7860-3199-3
ISBN-10: 0-7860-3199-9

First printing: August 2013

10 9 8 7 6

Printed in the United States of America

First electronic edition: August 2013

ISBN-13: 978-0-7860-3281-5
ISBN-10: 0-7860-3281-2

For Jacob (Jack) Murray

What Do Readers Want?

The question confronting writer and editor was whether to update this novel, and the answer wasn't obvious. On one hand, leaving the book as is and simply regarding it as set in 2001 seemed the best approach. But on the other hand, things are moving swiftly these days, and the zeitgeist has been altered more than many of us might imagine. If, while reading a contemporary novel, the reader is informed that one of the characters boards a TWA flight, suspension of disbelief could hit an air pocket.

Stopping by Kinko's to have something copied might also seem downright archaic to some readers. Then there are those scenes that might find the reader stopping and wondering *Why doesn't he use his cell phone?* or *Why doesn't she just Google that?*

Writers try to avoid anything that might jolt the reader out of the story and out of the alternative world we attempt to create. Technology isn't just advancing; it's on a rampage. That can be to our advantage—or not.

The Night Caller was first published in 2001. Long before that, when we saw the movie titled *2001*, we thought it was set safely in a far future where just about anything would be believable. We thought the same thing about *1984*. That devious computer, Hal, would be amazed by my iPhone. As I am.

We tried to maintain a balance in this novel that would make for a smooth read. Sure, there might be cell phones, e-books, and texting. But still around are landline phones, rubber-banded paper manuscripts, and telephone answering machines. A jogger mesmerized by a Sony Walkman? A stretch, but maybe. There must be plenty of folks with cassettes still jogging to Madonna, not to mention Bill Withers and Eric Clapton. Super sideburns? Leisure suits? Not a chance. And yet . . .

Whatever the choices, the goal is to lay out a smooth road for the reader, paved with memory in ways barely noticeable. But memories seldom coincide. In a way, there are as many worlds as there are people. It's a fuzzy line that separates past and present.

Wide lapels, narrow lapels, long hair, short hair, wide ties, narrow ties, hems up, hems down, neighborhood bars, coffee shops. Pardon me while I watch a great 1939 movie on my high-definition flat-screen TV, starring people long gone. It's the stuff that dreams are made of.

Clocks, and some poets, would have us believe that time is a meted-out constant. Not so, not so . . .

—John Lutz
Sarasota, Florida
Sometime in 2012

In ancient shadows and twilights
Where childhood has stayed
Great human tragedies are born and heroes made.
In the lost childhood of Judas
Christ was betrayed.

—Author unknown

Sleep, the fresh dew of languid love, the rain
Whose drops quench kisses till they burn again.

—Shelley,
Epipsychidion

CHAPTER ONE

S ue Coppolino was young, pretty, and nervous.

Her painted nails drummed on the steering wheel as she drove her red Sebring convertible toward the Siesta Key drawbridge in Sarasota. It was a hot and humid Florida night so she had the car's top down, and the wind caressing her face felt like warm liquid. The convertible's tires thrummed over the steel mesh of the bridge, and within seconds she was off the mainland and on the key.

She turned north on Midnight Pass Road, then veered to the right instead of going straight toward the public beach.

Wealthy estates and condominium complexes lay out of sight beyond thick foliage and palm trees on her right, overlooking calm, moonlit water. Because the night was bright, she could see the brilliant oranges and reds of the hibiscus and bougainvillea blooms. It was almost midnight and there was no other traffic, and with the top down the racheting scream of cicadas was sometimes deafening when the car glided past densely wooded areas. To the cicadas the desperate continual scream was a mating call. Right now, Sue heard it the same way.

She was up to no good. At least. some people would see it that way. Not that she was going to commit a burglary or anything. In fact, she made more than enough money in her job with a surveying company. It was just that—

The angular white buildings of Bay Vista condominium with their red tile roofs weren't visible from the road, but there was an ornate wrought-iron steel gate painted bone white just up ahead. Sue slowed the car but drove past the gate. The security guard wasn't on duty in the small air-conditioned booth, but anyone entering needed a resident's plastic card to insert in a slot that would trigger the gate to open.

No card for Sue. And she didn't need one. A few hundred feet down the road, she turned the car onto an unmarked and unpaved side road that ran parallel to Bay Vista's manicured grounds. Then she killed the headlights, letting the light from the bright crescent moon guide her.

She parked where she usually did, off the side of the road behind a tight grouping of date palms. As she turned off the idling engine, her heart seemed to take up its fast and rhythmic beat.

Sue didn't like sneaking around this way. Or did she? On a certain level it was exciting. Like being in a movie. She checked herself in the rearview mirror, then put on fresh lipstick and smoothed back her wind-mussed dark hair with her hand. Excitement aside, she did wish Marlee wouldn't force her to go through these subterfuges every time they met. It wasn't as if this was the love still afraid to say its name.

But she knew Marlee was right; it would be foolish for Sue to use the main gate. Marlee could easily obtain an extra card that would permit Sue's entering and leaving, but a video camera would capture her image and record times and dates of arrival and departure. That would never do.

Marlee Clark—long-legged, lithe, tanned, and muscled—had been a teenage tennis phenom only a few years ago. The experts made her the choice to within a short time be the top-seeded woman player in the world. Marlee had come close, winning major U.S. tournaments, making the semifinals at Wimbledon. But the pressure of high-level competition and glaring publicity had gotten to her. Drugs, first taken at the urging of her coach to ease the pain of injuries, then taken by Marlee despite the coach's warnings, had led to sloppy play on the court, then sloppy play off, with the media. A public shouting match at the U.S. Open, followed by a drugs-and-drink binge and an auto accident that had put her in the hospital for a month, started her real and undeniable decline.

Burned-out, she retired early and used some of her winnings to buy a luxury condo on the key, complete with private boat dock and her own cabin cruiser.

Marlee still needed income, and because of her pretty face and long red hair worn in her trademark braid, she was in demand as a television sports commentator and commercial pitch-woman. But if the public found out about her romantic life, she would lose many of her endorsement contracts.

It didn't seem to hurt her popularity that she'd once been into drugs. She'd been through a very public rehab, even told Barbara Walters how sorry she was.

But if word got out that the pristine Barbie doll of tennis was a lesbian, and an unrepentant one, it would destroy the image that was worth big money to her. Sue argued that Marlee was simply acting paranoid; they were, after all, in the twenty-first century. But Marlee wouldn't budge, quoting her agent's figures on how much other women sports celebs had lost in dollars when they came out of the closet.

So Sue sneaked.

Once on the grounds of Bay Vista, she walked along the powdery white sand beach. There was no one in sight other than a couple strolling along the mystical border of the glittering surf line a hundred yards away. They seemed interested only in each other, but Sue turned her face away anyway as she crossed a narrow expanse of closely mown grass, then walked along a crushed shell path toward the rear of Marlee's building.

Careful not to brush against any of the aluminum-framed loungers that might scrape metal on concrete, she skirted the swimming pool, then approached the sliding glass doors to the ground-floor condo.

The drapes were open, and Sue stood for a moment looking in at the luxurious interior with its plank floors and thick area rugs, cream colored walls, and soft beige leather furniture. On the wall behind the sofa was a grouping of museum-quality oil paintings, all still lifes of fruit or flowers. It was an expensive world so unlike Sue's, and one that Marlee allowed her to share. Nothing in the room suggested its occupant had ever played tennis.

The sliding door was unlocked, as Sue knew it would be. That was part of the arrangement. The soft rumble of the door sliding in its track was barely audible over the collective shrill scream of the cicadas.

It was much cooler inside the condo. As soon as Sue slid the door shut to keep the conditioned air in and the mosquitoes out, she spotted Marlee where she'd fallen asleep in the leather recliner. Her head was canted back and her braid was undone, allowing her long red hair to fan out gracefully on the chair back. She looked so beautiful, doll-like, and peaceful. What were her dreams? Sue wondered. She approached the chair softly so she wouldn't awaken her, then reached out gently to touch her lover's shoulder.

Her hand came away wet.

Crusted scarlet.

Stunned, Sue ran her fingers over Marlee's pale face, her mind still unable to compute what was going on here. Was Marlee drugged? Asleep? Unconscious?

Still rejecting the dark and terrible fact before her, she gently cupped Marlee's cool, lovely face in her hands and slowly lifted her head.

Sue gagged and backed away, absently floating her red hand up to her mouth.

Marlee was dead. The back of her neck had been viciously hacked.

Sue couldn't bear to look at the gaping wound, but she couldn't look away even as she began to scream.

CHAPTER TWO

Two years after Marlee Clark's murder, and two thousand miles to the north, a middle-aged man named Ezekiel Cooper was sitting alone on the outdoor deck of a seafood restaurant. He was over six feet tall, built rangy, with light brown hair straight and combed to the side from a neat part. It was the kind of hair that looked ragged even after a fresh haircut. His lunch companion had been called away, but he didn't mind. These days he ate most of his meals alone, and he'd gotten to like it. When Coop (as his friends called him—even his enemies didn't call him Ezekiel) didn't have to converse, he could concentrate on the simple pleasures of the meal. At this stage of his life, he no longer let the simple pleasures slip away.

Like the sun on his face, still warm even though it was mid-October. And the breeze, bringing him the salt tang of the nearby ocean and the yelps and cries of gulls. The restaurant's deck overlooked Shell Bank Basin, with a clear view of Grassy Bay and a marina lined with pleasure boats. This was Howard Beach, way down in Queens. You couldn't even see the skyscrapers of Manhattan from here. Only the roar of a jet, descending toward nearby Kennedy Airport, broke the peaceful mood.

The restaurant, Seconds, belonged to Coop's friend Arthur Billard. They'd met at the police academy more than a quarter century ago and stayed friends as they made the long, hard climb to lieutenant. Unlike Coop, Billard was still active in the NYPD, but that hadn't kept him from buying this restaurant. He was always starting small businesses, Coop recalled. Seconds seemed to be doing better than most of them had. Every table on the deck was occupied, and there were plenty of customers inside, too The staff was bustling. In fact, Billard had been called into the kitchen "for a minute" when they sat down, and that had been half an hour ago.

Billard came through the swinging doors, mopping his brow. His broad face was flushed from the heat of the kitchen. He was a man of medium height, bald, and so wide in the middle that he didn't even try to button his suit coats anymore. He and Coop were the same age, forty-eight, and over the years Coop had watched Billard's hairline recede and his stomach expand—both at a faster rate than was the case with Coop himself. Coop had taken a secret satisfaction in that. Congratulated himself on aging well. Funny to think of that now. Few things were surer than that his old friend would outlive him.

"Sorry, Coop," Billard said as he settled heavily into his chair across the table. "Problems with the steam table."

"That's okay."

Billard gestured at Coop's bowl of Manhattan clam

chowder, which was still mostly full. "I told you not to wait for me."

"I didn't. I'm just taking it slow."

"Something wrong with it?" Billard was already turning in his chair, looking for their waiter. "Jeez, it must be cold by now. I'll get you—"

"Art, relax, it's fine."

Billard turned to face him, squinting in the bright sunlight. He hesitated, then said, "Nothing—uh—nothing wrong with your appetite, I hope? You're feeling okay?"

"My appetite's fine, too." Coop took a spoonful of soup to prove it. The chowder had a rich tomato flavor, and the clams tasted fresh. "The food's great, Art, really. You have a nice place here. Congratulations."

Billard relaxed. The waiter brought him his plate of fried calamari, and he opened his napkin and dug into it.

For a while they ate in silence. Then Billard began again. "We're doing real well here, Coop."

"I can see."

"In this neighborhood, if you can keep a restaurant going through the first couple years, build up a regular clientele, you're set. Place'll do a steady business for decades."

"Then I hope your luck holds."

"I don't want to trust to luck, you know? I'd like to be here all the time, keeping an eye on things. But I gotta put in two more years in the Job to get full pension. Can't quit now. I'm being pulled two ways here." Billard hesitated. "I hope maybe you can help me out."

Coop was aware of Billard's eyes on him as he took another mouthful of chowder. He swallowed and said, "Well, Art, 1 don't know what I can do."

"I want to bring you in as my partner." Billard held up a hand as if he were directing traffic, a sign to Coop to put on the brakes and hear him out. "I don't want you to put in money. Hell, we don't need money. What we need is a—a managing partner. A guy to be here, greeting the customers, keeping an eye on things."

"I know from nothing about the restaurant business, Art."

"You'll pick it up. What I need is someone I trust to be on the spot."

"Thanks for the offer. But I don't think so."

"Think about it, Coop, at least. This is perfect for you. You're retired. You got loads of time."

Coop set down his spoon. The bowl was a quarter full but he wasn't hungry anymore. He looked away from Billard, out at the line of docked boats in the basin. "Loads of time," he repeated. "Well, I don't know about that, Art."

Billard didn't say anything for a moment. Then: "But you're cured, right? They told me—"

"Not cured. They don't say cured about cancer. They say in remission."

"But it's gone, isn't it? They got it in the chemo. Burned it all out of you."

"Oncologists don't give guarantees, Art."

He could feel Billard's eyes on him but couldn't meet the look. Instead, he studied his chowder.

"You're looking good now, Coop. You've put back some of the weight you lost. And your hair grew back. Hey—that's something I wish would happen to me." He laughed, running his hand over his bare pate.

Coop made an effort and smiled. Then he checked his watch. "Look, Art, I better be going. My daughter's

expecting me down at Breezy Point." He pushed back
his chair and stood up. He'd gotten used to doing that
slowly, during his chemotherapy, because otherwise a
wave of dizziness would sweep over him. And the nausea might follow. The nausea might come anytime. But
he felt all right now.

Billard rose with him. "At least think about my
offer, will you?"

"It's not a time for me to be starting new projects."

"Come on, Coop. You don't wanna assume the worst.
You could live for years. Decades."

"Possibly," Coop said. He held out his hand. Billard
took it. Seemed reluctant to let it go. He said he'd walk
Coop out to his car, but just then a waiter came up to
say they had another problem in the kitchen, so he had
to go.

Coop made his way through the crowded restaurant
and out onto the sunny sidewalk. His car was parked
half a block down. He headed for it. There was a time,
a few months ago, when he wouldn't have been able to
walk half a block. When he wouldn't have been able to
keep down a bowl of clam chowder. Now he was feeling fine.

But decades?

Possibly.

But he didn't believe it.

The guard on duty at the entrance to Breezy Point
recognized his old Honda Accord and raised the bar-
rier, waving him through. Coop rolled the window down
so he could smell the salt air as he drove through the
narrow streets. They were lined with one-story wooden

bungalows set close together. As he got closer to the beach, he passed larger, newer houses. There were some rich people in Breezy Point now. Times had changed since the days when everybody was either a fireman or a policeman. It had been a long time since the community was jokingly called the Irish Riviera.

The Honda hummed smoothly along the road, its tires singing steadily and ticking at regular intervals when they rolled across seams in the pavement. As usual on a weekday in autumn, Breezy Point was quiet. That was what Coop's daughter Bette had told him she needed. Normally the beach house Coop and his former wife Maureen had bought and rehabbed in happier times was vacant and secured for the coming winter, but it was little trouble to ready it for Bette.

She'd been there almost a week now, but Coop hadn't seen her since dinner the night she'd driven into town.

Bette lived and worked in New Jersey, holding down a high-pressure job with a real estate company. Last week she'd called Coop and said she was taking a few weeks off from work and wanted to spend them at the beach house. That was fine with Coop. He missed her increasingly infrequent visits, and she sounded anxious and worn down.

He knew better than to question Bette about her troubles. When she was younger he was an overprotective parent, as cops tend to be. Her mother, strong willed and with her own set of demands on her daughter, hadn't helped matters. So Coop didn't blame Bette for guarding her privacy. He was just grateful she'd invited him down today.

He parked in the drive of the small clapboard bungalow and climbed out of the car. There was raw wood showing where some of the white paint had worn off on the structure's windward side, and the green shutters were starting to peel. The entire place would need painting soon. Usually Coop did that sort of job, but with his illness he found himself wondering if he should take the time. Painting a summer cottage was a productive project only for a man who had enough life to carry him into the next summer. He wasn't sure if he qualified.

He pressed the doorbell button and waited, but got no answer, heard no sound from inside. He pressed the button again and listened closely, sure that he heard the faint doorbell chimes from the cottage's interior.

Nothing else broke the silence.

After a few minutes, Coop tried the door and found it unlocked. He stepped inside and called his daughter's name. There was no answer. The only sound was the refrigerator's low hum, along with a faint shrill vibration of something glass dancing inside it on a wire shelf.

Then he saw Bette lying on her back on the couch, her dark hair spread on a pillow.

Most people would have assumed she was asleep, but not Coop. He'd visited too many homicide scenes and knew death when he saw it. When he smelled it and felt the solemn eternal hush of its presence.

He stepped numbly to the side and saw Bette's face, and he knew she'd been strangled.

Death had come for the daughter of the man who so feared death. And with it a future for Coop that he couldn't have imagined.

CHAPTER THREE

The mourners who'd accompanied them to Maureen's home after the funeral had all gone. Only the flowers were left. Coop sat and looked at them. There were bouquets of roses and carnations in many colors, as well as big, exotic blooms whose names he didn't know, arranged into elaborate horseshoes and wreaths. People had gone to a lot of trouble and expense, he thought dully. Thank-you notes would have to be written.

Maureen prowled the room, hands on her hips. She kept glaring at the flowers.

"I don't get it," she said. "Why do people send flowers?"

"They're our friends. They're trying to console us."

"Watching something beautiful wither and die is supposed to make me feel better?"

Coop sighed. "I'll take them if you like."

"I don't see why people ever thought of cutting flowers in the first place. Why bring them indoors and watch them die? Go to a garden if you want to see them."

Coop repeated, "I'll take them if you like."

"It's the waste I can't stand. If only people had given

money to her favorite charity instead of sending flowers. You should have put that in the newspaper."

He didn't reply. He felt drained of all energy and emotion.

The funeral had been a horror. All through it Coop had held his pain at a distance. An odd sense of guilt had crept into his grief, as if he were somehow to blame for Bette's death. He was her father, a cop, and had protected her all her life.

But not this time. Not against this killer.

Now he and Maureen were alone together with their new burden, the mutual loss they would take with them to their own graves.

They hadn't gotten along after the divorce, which itself had been less than amicable. Along with the recent direction Maureen's life had taken, this could only make things much worse.

She had become an activist, dedicated to environmentalism, animal rights, and natural everything. Not that anyone would call Maureen touchy-feely. She upheld her gentle, holistic principles with a ferocious rigor. Coop's efforts to comfort her had met with polite but sullen withdrawal. Her daughter's murder had stunned her. And made her even more angry.

They were in the living room of her small co-op on a quiet street in New Rochelle. He was sitting in an uncomfortable beige upholstered chair with cold wooden arms. She came to sit directly across from him. He raised his eyes to find her staring at him with her lips pursed, as if waiting for something. She hadn't aged well. Her once lithe figure had become somewhat stocky, her brown eyes dim and haunted. And she'd dyed her hair dark and cut it short so that it added weight to her face. Yet she might still be attractive if she made a minimum of effort. But she didn't.

Voices sounded outside, someone giving directions. Then a car door slammed, and the last of the departed mourners drove away. From across the ensuing silence Maureen stared at Coop bleary-eyed, as if through water.

"How could you have let her stay in that house alone?" she demanded to know. "How could you keep it a secret from me that she was in town?"

Coop sighed and dragged his hand down his face, as if trying to rearrange his features so he could be someone else. He'd known the question was coming, had plenty of time to think about it. But there was only one honest answer, and it wasn't going to satisfy Maureen.

He said, "She would have called you if she wanted to see you. What she wanted was peace and quiet."

"Why? Was she having problems?"

"I felt I shouldn't question her," Coop said miserably. "I was wrong."

"Were you ever!" Maureen sat back, crossing her legs. He found himself staring at her shoes. They were heavy-looking pumps with a dull black finish. Maureen was against using animal products, including leather. Coop was never sure what her shoes were made of. He remembered how good her legs used to look when she wore high heels.

"Everything I heard about her life in New Jersey was positive," she went on.

"Same here."

"You sure? She was always more willing to confide

in you than me. The two of you were always so close. You even told her about the cancer before you told me."

He didn't reply to that. After a while he said, "You were always a good mother to her."

"I was. That's why we weren't close. There were old grudges. I was the one who had to say no, enforce curfews, dole out allowances. You'd arrive on Saturday afternoon and take her to a soccer game. Easy for you to be her pal. So what's she been telling you the last few months?"

"Everything was going well. She was busy at work. Feeling tired. That's all she said." Coop paused, then added, "Believe me, I've thought about this."

Maureen let it drop. There was silence. He kept his head down, watching as the squared-off toe of her shoe turned in a slow circle. She asked, "Do you know a Detective Mackey?"

"Mackey? No."

"He was the one who interviewed me. Asked me one totally insensitive question after the other for an hour and a half. Then you know what he did? Fingerprinted me." She was examining the tips of her fingers as if to make sure she'd gotten all the ink off. "Wouldn't give a reason why he was doing it, of course. You cops hate giving reasons. All he'd say was it was for purposes of elimination."

"That was the reason. They dust the house for fingerprints. Next they eliminate the people whose prints they'd expect to find—you, me, Bette. If they find anybody else's prints—"

"They could be the killer's?"

"Could be."

"Well, did they find anybody else's prints?"

"I don't know."

"What—they didn't talk to you, either?"

"I don't call them. When they have something to tell us, they will."

"Oh? Are you sure about that?"

"I don't understand you."

"Suppose they're covering up. Suppose it was a cop who killed her."

Coop looked up at her face. She stared fiercely back at him, her lips drawn taut. He said, "That's ridiculous."

"Is it? Practically everybody in Breezy Point is NYPD."

"That's not true anymore."

"Our neighbors on both sides are NYPD."

"You think Judy and Kent Mallon are murderers? Or Edna and Ron O'Brien? We've known them for years."

"Why didn't they hear anything, then? Why didn't anybody hear anything? The houses at Breezy are about six feet apart. Thin wooden walls. Open windows. How could someone get into our house and—and do what they did and leave, and nobody heard anything?"

Coop sighed heavily. The question had occurred to him, too. He'd tried to dismiss it, but it kept coming back. He said, "I don't know."

"You don't? Then how do you know witnesses aren't keeping quiet? Protecting somebody. Cops protect each other no matter what. The blue line that never breaks. You're not going to deny that."

"It happens. But not in this case."

"You don't know about this case. You've already

admitted that. Why don't you ask a few questions? Shake things up a little? For God's sake! You're a lieutenant, NYPD, and this is your daughter!"

She was leaning forward now, shouting at him. Coop said, "Easy, Maureen. Try to calm down."

"Don't give me that condescending male crap! If you think I'm wrong, argue with me." She bit hard into her lower lip to keep from crying.

"Maureen . . ."

"Leave me the hell alone!"

"I don't think you're wrong." He stood up from his chair. "I'll make some calls and let you know."

Maureen remained seated. As he let himself out she said something that might have been "Thanks, Coop."

Might have been.

When he got back to his efficiency apartment on New York's Upper West Side, Coop peeled off his suit coat, loosened his tie, then opened a cold bottle of Beck's dark. The apartment was two rooms and a small bathroom. What passed for a kitchen was behind a tall folding screen in a corner. The walls were a mottled cream color, as were the drapes over vertical plastic blinds in the single window. Framed museum prints hung on the walls, modem ones that were like dreams with sharp angles. Coop didn't understand them. The furniture had been in the apartment when he moved in and was the best thing about it.

He sat down on his sofa that at night unfolded and became his bed.

Why shouldn't he look into his daughter's death on his own? Some in the department might not like it, but what could they do to him at this point in his dwindling life? And what kind of life was it? He'd become a disconsolate recluse in his tiny apartment, roaming the neighborhood on late night walks, a man without employment, social life, or purpose. Now he had his grief to keep him company and turn him in on himself even more, along with his self-pity. Better to do something— to use what time he had left to learn who had killed his daughter, and why.

He took a sip of beer, slouched down, and leaned back against the sofa cushion, thinking on what he did know about Bette's murder.

He'd been the first cop on the scene, had seen things fresh. That was always an advantage. He steeled himself and tried to picture it in his mind.

The cottage door had been unlocked, but it didn't seem to have been tampered with. No scratches on the lock or scrapes on the door. The killer had either used a key or been let in, and Coop could account for all the keys to the cottage except the one he'd given to Bette.

Nothing in the house seemed to have been disturbed. Nothing that Coop could recall might be missing. There had been no sign anyone had smoked in the house, no drinking glasses or anything else indicating a visitor. Had Bette talked to anyone on the phone shortly before her death? Coop wished now he'd pressed the redial button before calling for help. But he'd been in shock, disoriented by the sight of his murdered daughter. If only he'd had the presence of mind to treat the situation like any other homicide, to examine the crime scene without touching anything and determine some basic facts. The first building blocks for constructing a case must have been there, but he'd ignored them.

There were so many questions, and no way for him to know the essential answers, or to learn them without help. He couldn't take seriously Maureen's suspicions of a police cover-up. That was paranoia talking. But that didn't mean the detectives investigating the case would speak frankly to the victim's father, even if he was a retired cop.

He decided to go see Billard. His old friend in the department ought to be able to fill him in. Tomorrow, though. Right now he was exhausted from the funeral, from Maureen. He wanted to take off his shoes, lie back on the sofa, and rest.

No, he told himself, not tomorrow.

He made himself stand up and shrugged back into his suit coat.

Not tomorrow. Today.

He couldn't rely on tomorrows.

CHAPTER FOUR

Billard's office was at the other end of Queens from his restaurant at Howard Beach. To Coop it felt like another world. This was Long Island City, a crowded, noisy district of old warehouses and factories and row houses that had been occupied by working people until yuppies moved in during the eighties. The skyscrapers of midtown Manhattan loomed just across the East River.

The dense, mixed population of the area kept the precinct house busy.

As he walked down the hall toward his former patrol car partner's office he could hear the background chatter of a police radio, the earnest pleadings of a man and woman at the booking desk, bursts of muffled, outraged shouting from the holdover cells on the second floor. Two plainclothes detectives he didn't recognize passed him, grinning and chattering about something other than police work, but the suit coat of one was unbuttoned and with each step flapping to afford a glimpse of the checked butt of his belt-holstered 9mm handgun. Coop had loved it all and still did, the sounds and sights, and the scent of desperation on the not so fresh air.

The sergeant on duty was a grizzled old warrior named McCreary. Coop remembered seeing him in Seconds. McCreary remembered Coop, addressing him as "Lou," department slang for "Lieutenant." Making him feel at home. McCreary called Lieutenant Billard to notify him that Coop was in the building.

Billard's office door was the only one in the hall that was slightly ajar, as if he wanted to make sure Coop could find it.

Coop knocked as he pushed the door open farther and stepped inside.

It was a small office with plaster walls painted a dull green. A lot of greasy cobwebs were stuck to and moving around the rectangular heating vent up near the ceiling. The room's one window had a wire grille over its dirty glass and looked out on the precinct house parking lot. A row of gray file cabinets lined one wall, a table with a computer on it sat against another. About a dozen yellow Post-its were stuck haphazardly to the frame of the computer monitor. Coop wondered why people never arranged them symmetrically, the way they did postage stamps.

Billard was seated behind a cluttered gray steel desk. He stood up, came around the desk, and the two men hugged.

When they stepped apart, Billard gave Coop's arm a pat.

"I feel like crap not making it over to Maureen's after the funeral," he said. "I was on my way, but all hell broke loose here this morning and . . . well, you know how it is. The Job never lets up."

Coop nodded, feeling awkward, thinking maybe Billard should have come no matter how much hell had broken loose. But he knew he was being unreasonable. "It's all right, you were at the cemetery." He waited while the bulky Billard, his girth testing the seams of his blue uniform shirt, moved back behind the desk and sat down with a sigh. Billard motioned for Coop to sit in the uncomfortable oak chair set at an angle in front of the desk. Coop sat, thought *the hell with it,* and stood back up. "I'm here because of Bette," he said.

"I kinda figured you would be."

"How close are they to making an arrest?"

Billard hesitated long enough to give him the answer. "Don't guess it'd do much good to tell you we're doing all we can, and we'll keep you apprised of developments."

"No," Coop said. He drifted over to the window and looked out at the rows of patrol cars and assortment of officers' personal cars in the graveled parking lot. Sunlight glanced dully off dusty windshields. "What've you got so far, Art?"

"You know Queen's South Homicide has the case."

Coop watched two young uniformed officers climb into a patrol car, the way he and Billard had done years and years ago. Young knights of the law. "I know, Art, but word gets around."

"I made sure it found its way here," Billard said. He shrugged and ran a hand over his bald pate. "So what do you want to know?"

Coop sat down in the hard chair. He'd expected a little more resistance. Maybe even wanted it. Because the first question was going to be hard to ask. He swallowed and said, "They find any sign of sexual assault?"

"Traces of the sort of powder used to keep latex gloves from sticking together during packaging were found on her body. All over her body."

"But she was dressed."

"Maybe undressed; then her clothes were put back on her. Or maybe they were never fully removed, only unbuttoned and rearranged."

Coop spoke through clenched teeth. "Penetration?"

"Not much."

"What do you mean, not much?"

"There's something we're not telling the public, Coop."

"But you'll tell me, Art. You'll tell *me!*"

"I didn't tell you," Billard said reluctantly. "But if I had, I'd make sure you knew that this one is a tight. small-circle secret even inside the department. The public's not to know—just a very few NYPD personnel, and the killer. Understood?"

"Understood," Coop said.

"A small plastic saint was found wedged in her vaginal tract."

"A *saint?*"

"Augustine," Billard said. "The sinner who found salvation. It's the sort of cheap statuette that can be bought almost anywhere that sells religious items. The ME says it was placed in her after her death. There's that, anyway."

Coop bowed his head. *That, anyway.* He got on with it, calling on professionalism, hiding behind it. "Death was by strangulation?"

Billard nodded. "Killer used some kind of ligature he took with him."

"They turn up any witnesses?"

"Not yet."

Coop felt his fist clench in his lap. "That's hard to believe, Art. Assuming they did a decent canvass, they should've turned up somebody by now who saw or heard something."

"What can I tell you? They're doing their best."

"Suppose they're not trying hard enough. Or people aren't talking."

Billard leaned back and folded his hands over his broad stomach. There was a subtle shift of mood in the room. Coop wasn't surprised. Billard gave him the shades-down look cops give civilians. "I'm not following you."

"What if a cop was the killer? And he's being protected?"

"You don't really believe that, Coop."

"It's Maureen's idea."

"Maureen. Well, she's a piece of work." Billard had never liked Maureen.

"I can't prove her wrong. She's asking how come no one saw or heard anything, and I don't know what to tell her."

"This was a weekday in October, Coop. Not many people around down at Breezy."

"My neighbors—"

"The Mallons were at their apartment in Jackson Heights. The O'Briens were at their jobs in Manhattan. The nearest people were three houses away."

"They still should have heard something," Coop said stubbornly.

Billard unfolded his hands and placed them on the desktop. He hesitated a moment, then said, "There probably wasn't much to hear, Coop."

"What do you mean?"

"Forensic guys have been over the scene thoroughly. No sign of forced entry. No sign of a struggle."

Coop dropped his gaze to the worn, clean linoleum floor. Why should he be surprised by what Billard was telling him? His own thoughts had been running this way earlier. He just hadn't wanted to take the next logical step.

"She let the killer in, then," he said slowly. "It was somebody she knew."

"Looks that way." Billard hesitated again. "It may have been somebody she was very close to."

Coop looked at him.

"The way she was laid out afterward, her hair spread so carefully around her head. The killer wanted to make her look like she was asleep. When you see that at a crime scene, it usually indicates remorse."

Coop realized he'd been holding his breath and there was a lump in his throat. He swallowed a bitterness that had collected at the base of his tongue, and made himself breathe evenly.

"You okay, Coop?"

"Sure." *Except for the fear.* "Go on."

"Lots of prints in the house, most of them Bette's. We checked them out through NCIC and VICAP and came up empty. Several were untraceable, which only means our killer might never have been fingerprinted— no military service or arrest record. The only physical clue is the footprint."

Coop sat up straighter and looked at Billard.

"We found a shoe print in the dust on the floor right inside the front door. If Bette knew him and let him in as we suspect, it might well be the killer's." He reached into a desk drawer and laid a photograph on the desk.

Coop leaned over the desk and examined the photo. The footprint was only a partial, the sole of a large shoe. The design on the sole was a series of crisscrossed indentations reaching to the shoe's edges.

"Distinctive sole tread pattern," Coop said.

"We haven't been able to trace it yet. We're still trying, contacting foreign and domestic shoe manufacturers. We'll match it eventually."

"Can I have a copy of this, Art?"

"Take that one. We got more."

Coop slipped the photo into a side pocket of his sport jacket.

"Not much more to tell, Coop. Whatever Maureen thinks, Queen's South Homicide has been doing a thorough job on this investigation. They've interviewed people all up and down your street, all over Breezy Point. Nobody looks even remotely possible for this crime. They'll keep trying, of course, but they're talking now as if it was somebody from the outside—somebody Bette invited down to see her. Who else knew she was staying at the cottage? Apart from you?"

Coop shrugged hopelessly. "She told me she wanted peace and quiet. It sounded like I was the only one she was telling."

"I know you two were close. Any idea why she wanted to stay out there alone on Breezy Point?"

"Not much of one. She told me she was feeling stressed and wanted to get away for a while and relax."

"She say why she felt stressed?"

"No. I got the impression it was her job, but I could

be wrong. She sounded a little nervous, but not like she was anywhere near some kind of breaking point."

"What it all probably means, Coop, is nobody but an intimate would have known she was staying at your beach cottage. Someone she knew and trusted killed her."

"It looks that way."

"Was there anyone—"

"She wasn't in the habit of telling us about her boyfriends. Maureen or me."

Billard started to say something more, then changed his mind and clamped his lips closed. Old cops knew where not to trespass.

"Do you mind if I look the place over later today?" Coop asked.

"The beach house? Sure. Hell, it's your place. Crime scene people are done with it."

Coop moved toward the door. "If you learn anything new, will you let me know, Art?"

"Sure." Billard tilted his head to the side and re-garded Coop with his cop's flat eyes. "You're planning on getting active in the case, aren't you?"

Coop looked back at him, knowing that his own eyes were just as flat, just as unreadable. "No. I'm only asking."

Billard ended the staring contest, shaking his head and looking away. "You know as well as I do we can't stop you from going around asking questions, as long as you don't cross certain lines. You sure that's what you want to do, though?"

Coop didn't reply.

"How're you feeling, Coop?" Billard went on after a moment. "I mean, how's your health?"

"Still like I told you at Seconds. I'm okay."

"But you also gave the impression you don't believe . . . that it's gonna last. You get into real stress,
you might shorten what time you have. Maybe, you
stay stress free, you got years. You might even change
your mind, go in with me at Seconds."

"I'm not going to count on years, Art. I'm not going
to leave things undone."

"They've got good people down at Queen's South.
They won't let this drop."

"The case is getting old. We both know the clear-
ance rates drop with every hour that passes after a
homicide. And this one was four days ago."

"Yeah, we both know." Billard looked at the floor.
"And we both know what we'd say to a homicide victim's father, if he talked about investigating the murder
himself."

"I won't fuck up the case, Art."

"That's not what I'm worried about. There are emo-
tional dangers when a cop gets involved in an investigation of the murder of someone he loved. You're
bound to find out things you don't want to know. The
truth can be like a bullet to the heart."

"I've never been afraid of the truth," Coop said,
knowing as he spoke the words that they were a lie.

Billard didn't press him any harder. He gazed out
the dirty window at nothing. "Okay, old friend. I'll
keep you apprised of any new developments in the
case. But it should work both ways. What you learn, we
need to know."

"That isn't any problem," Coop said. "I want to nail
Bette's killer."

"We all do," Billard said. "But you're the one who better be the most careful."

Billard sat at his desk thinking for a long time after Coop had left. Thinking about what he hadn't mentioned to Coop. That the tacky plastic saint, about five inches tall, had been inserted in Bette's vagina to a depth made possible by a strategically placed knife cut.

St. Augustine. Billard the lapsed Catholic was pretty sure St. Augustine was the saint who had a lengthy and illegitimate carnal affair with a woman before seeking the solace and wisdom of the church. What if anything that might mean, Billard didn't know. Other than that St. Augustine was the department's ace, an aspect of the crime that, outside a tightly knit group inside the NYPD, only the killer would know.

What Billard knew was that this was one of those times he was glad he didn't have a daughter.

CHAPTER FIVE

The first potential witness Coop talked to was the rent-a-cop manning the kiosk at the entrance to Breezy Point. It didn't go very well. Yes, the police had already interviewed him, and no, he didn't have anything to tell them. He didn't remember any suspicious vehicles or any strangers passing him on the afternoon of the murder. And as Coop knew, there were ways to sneak onto Breezy Point without passing him.

Coop thanked him and drove on to park across from his beach cottage. He sat in the car for a while. The narrow street lined with one-story wooden cottages was as quiet as it had been last week. Only a few houses had cars parked in front of them. An old neighbor named Jack Reynolds, who never remembered Coop's name, sat on his deck, reading the *Daily News*. He didn't look up when a couple passed by, heading for the beach. They were well bundled, for the wind was strong and chilly. Coop sat and watched for several minutes without seeing anybody else.

He supposed he had to accept it: someone could

have come here, killed his daughter, and gone without being seen or heard. It was possible.

He got out of the car and crossed the street. Jack Reynolds didn't look up from his paper.

Coop was braced for the silence inside the cottage but it still took the breath from him. Violent death did that, left a vacuum in its wake.

There was an empty feeling in the pit of his stomach, and his head felt the way it did when he was on airliners dropping fast in their final approach to land. The silence persisted. He coughed for no reason other than to break it.

As if cued by the abrupt sound, the refrigerator motor clicked on and droned in the kitchen, the way it had been droning when Coop discovered Bette's body.

He wasn't surprised to see the faint, dusty footprint on the tile floor just inside the front door. Drawing the digital photo from his pocket, he stooped and compared image with reality.

The computer had done a good job. The enhanced likeness of the print was doubtless a perfect match with the actual shoe sole.

The print had been made because Bette hadn't gotten around to cleaning up the place, including sweeping away accumulated dust on smooth surfaces. That kind of untidiness wasn't like her.

But then it wasn't like her to be murdered by someone she knew.

Coop felt as if the world had been rearranged like a kaleidoscope. Previous patterns seemed to mean nothing.

If a similar print had appeared in soft earth outside,

Billard would have told Coop. But he went back out and looked around the perimeter of the house anyway, making sure.

Back inside, he kept his eyes averted from the couch where his dead daughter had reclined, and he went about duplicating the NYPD's efforts. It was always possible he'd find something they'd overlooked. He knew they'd been professional and thorough, but he cared more.

Aware that he was probably wasting his time, he examined the soles of the two pairs of shoes Bette had brought with her and made sure neither was a match for the dusty half footprint. Then he checked the cottage's closets to see if anyone had left behind shoes that might make similar prints. He found none.

In fact, there wasn't anything very revealing in the cottage. Bette's clothes, still hung in the closet or folded in dresser drawers, were all casual; she hadn't planned on getting dressed up while in New York. Beneath a folded sweater in a bottom bureau drawer was a penis-shaped rubber vibrator. Coop didn't like seeing it but knew he shouldn't be surprised. In another drawer was a packet of condoms. Okay, no surprise there, either. Bette was—had been—an attractive and vital twenty-seven-year-old woman.

He wondered how thorough the Queen's South detectives had been. Was there a list in a file drawer somewhere, an inventory of his daughter's possessions? Probably. He didn't like thinking about that, either.

There was nothing in the desk or her luggage that was connected with her work. She'd meant it when she'd told Coop she wanted to get away from her job for a while, from the small town of Haverton, New Jersey. He wasn't sure exactly what she did in her job at Prudent Stand Real Estate, but apparently it had been getting to her. Or maybe something else entirely had been upsetting her, and only incidentally making it difficult for her to concentrate on her work. Coop wished now their conversation had been longer, that he'd asked more about her, how she was, what was bothering her, did she know he loved her and did she love him? . . .

A lump had formed in his throat. He pushed away thoughts of Bette. Those kinds of thoughts. He was on the job now, with added purpose and more than a little rusty, but on the job.

He felt unexpected great relief when he closed and locked the cottage door behind him.

He wasn't sure if he'd ever stay there again.

The Night Caller watched Georgianna Mason trudge up Vector Street in downtown Seattle. She was breathing hard, not in very good shape to live in such a hilly part of town.

Not aware that she was being observed, Georgianna, a slim, attractive woman in her forties, had met two friends for lunch at a hotel restaurant. She and the other women talked incessantly through lunch, exchanging stories and laughing. Then all three women lit up cigarettes. The Night Caller disapproved.

Georgianna had walked to the restaurant from her apartment ten blocks away, possibly because the day was so beautiful and without a hint of rain.

When she was halfway up Vector she turned on a

side street and entered a large business building. She was going to do what many savvy Seattle residents did to avoid walking the downtown hills, where the buildings were built into the grades; she would take one of the elevators up several floors and use an exit leading out to the next, higher block.

The Night Caller walked faster, breathing harder and feeling the strain from the climb in thighs and buttocks, and reached the end of the block soon enough to see her walk from the building's glass revolving door. Back on the sidewalk, Georgianna hesitated. Instead of continuing in the direction of her apartment, she crossed the street and entered a department store.

The Night Caller didn't bother following her. This was fortunate. She'd be occupied for a while. Her time shopping would create opportunity.

Fifteen minutes later, in a room at the Holiday Inn, the Night Caller used a notebook computer to go on-line, accessing Georgianna's service by typing her password.

The cursor darted, the built-in mouse clicked, and Georgianna's e-mail files were read, her on-line banking and brokerage accounts were examined, and the log of her most recent Web site visits was called up.

Back to the e-mail. There had been something there. The Night Caller's breathing became deeper, more rapid. He felt the familiar tugging, subtle but there, like intimations at the very outer edges of a whirlpool. Georgianna seemed to have a new boyfriend, one she'd encountered on-line but never met personally and who lived in San Francisco. Backtracking through e-mail and message boards led to a pattern of increasingly sweet and soulful exchanges between the two cyber-lovers. Some of them were absolutely cloying.

This was tragic and wonderful. So intimate and re-vealing. Georgianna merited closer and more frequent contact. The Night Caller liked to keep in touch.

CHAPTER SIX

Coop had never been to visit Bette in the town where she lived and worked during the last months of her life. He drove the Honda into Haverton just before noon the next day. He'd exited the Holland Tunnel hours before, and he kept thinking he was about to leave the suburbs and enter the country. But though the roads got narrower, the traffic didn't diminish. He continued to pass malls and new subdivisions where huge houses were springing up close together on treeless flatland.

In Haverton, waves of development were lapping at the edges of a quaint old town that reminded him of New England. A white, steepled Congregational church faced a gray stone city hall across the town square. From the center of the square, a statue of a Union soldier kept watch.

Coop drove slowly around the square and turned onto Main Street. The home of Prudent Stand Real Estate, where Bette had worked, was a brick building with white columns. It had probably been built in the forties or fifties, but the architecture made it look older.

He drove around to the side of the building and parked. It was a sunny day but cool, so he left the Honda's windows up. There was an expanse of still-green lawn in front of the building, and the heavily tinted glass entrance was flanked by tall pine trees. A rectangle of brick bearing the company's name, like that of the deceased on a tombstone, was surrounded by low shrubbery.

For the next ten minutes Coop watched people walking in and out of the building, until one of those leaving was Hillary Bland, a young woman who had identified herself as one of Bette's best friends when she'd introduced herself to Coop after Bette's funeral.

Coop got out of the car and stood leaning back against a front fender with his arms crossed. He could feel warmth rolling out from beneath the car. The cooling engine ticked slightly in the brisk fall air.

He'd phoned ahead and Hillary had been expecting him. She was a petite woman, about thirty, with dark eyes and a magnificent head of auburn hair. She'd worn dark clothing and her hair had been pinned back at the mortuary and funeral; now she had on a white blouse and flowered skirt and her hair flowed shoulder length and bounced slightly as she walked. As with many small women, her walk was precise, high heels clacking with perfect rhythm on the sidewalk. When she saw Coop she smiled and picked up her pace.

"You should have come inside," she said.

"I like it out here," he told her. "And I wanted to get a look at the company's clientele and employees."

"When they weren't aware they were being watched," she said.

He smiled. "An old detective habit."

Hillary hesitated. "Is that all it is? I mean, when you called and said you were coming out, I wondered if you were—I mean if you had suspicions—"

He interrupted her. "The deal was, I offered to buy you lunch while we talked about Bette. Is there a place around here where we can do that?"

"Not without possibly drawing attention to what you're doing. We need to drive a few miles out of town for that."

Smart woman. He opened the car door for her and held it while she got in.

Within fifteen minutes they were seated in a back booth of a roadside bar and restaurant called Bentley's. The place considered itself a pub, and the walls were covered with photos and drawings of classic British cars: MGs, Bentleys, Morgans, Rolls-Royces, Jaguars. . . . Coop always thought that if he ever won the lottery he'd fancy a Jaguar.

"Bentley's is owned by Anglophiles," Hillary said. "I went to school with the owners."

"Here or at Oxford?"

"You're joking."

"Sure."

"The only time any of us ever left the country was on our senior trip to Canada. I'm an actual native, born and raised in Haverton. I remember when it was a quiet town and New York seemed worlds away."

"You resent all the development? The strangers moving in?"

Hillary grinned. "Not all of them. Not Bette. She was no stranger after five minutes. She could have adapted wherever she went. Everyone liked her. I mean that."

"Here's where I say 'Not everyone,'" Coop told her.

Hillary's dark eyes went sad as her smile disappeared. "Yeah, that has to be true, I guess. You think the—the crime is connected to her life here?"

"What do you think?"

"Well, the police were here, of course, asking questions, but I didn't think anything of it. I figured, you know, in New York bad things happen all the time."

"Generally not without a reason, in New York or elsewhere."

A blond waitress dressed like a serving wench came over and took their orders for bangers and mash. Hillary ordered ale. Coop asked for decaf coffee, caught the waitress's arch look, and changed his order to tea.

"How long can you be away at lunch?" Coop asked, when the wench was gone and out of earshot.

"I take long lunches. Don't have to be back in the office until one-thirty, when I'm supposed to discuss Bette's murder with some woman named Deni Green. Probably a local reporter."

"The press been on this big in Haverton?"

"Oh, sure. It's a major story here. I can e-mail you back issues of the papers, if you want."

"I'd appreciate it," Coop said. "Did Bette tell you where she was going before she left for my cottage?"

Hillary didn't have to think it over before answering. The police must have asked her this already. "No. She didn't even tell me she was going to New York. Just that she was going away for some peace and quiet."

"Did you think that was odd? That she should want to be alone, I mean."

"No. That is—" Hillary's brow furrowed as she chose her words. "She'd been a little down the last few weeks."

"Pressures at work?"

"There was that. They've been restructuring her division and a lot of work got dumped on her desk. But I think the real problem was the breakup with Lloyd. She told me it was a mutual consent thing, but it still hit her hard."

"Lloyd is? . . ."

"Her boyfriend she was always trying to get up the nerve to introduce to you. You didn't know about him at all?"

"Bette kept her intimate life private. There was nobody named Lloyd at the visitation or funeral."

"I tried to get him to come but he couldn't. He was shattered by the news of her death. Absolutely shattered."

"When did you talk to him?" Coop asked.

"Right after the police called at work. That's how we found out about Bette. Lloyd is a commercial real estate appraiser at Prudent Stand, in the separate appraisal division. That's how he and Bette met."

"He was at work when the police called?"

"Yep. Happened to be in the office. That was about ten the night after Bette was—after they found her. He was so broken up by the news he had to go home." The serving wench brought the ale and tea. Hillary took a sip from her glass and wiped foam from her upper lip. "I know what you must be thinking, you being a former policeman, but Lloyd couldn't kill anyone or anything. Besides, he has an alibi."

"How do you know?"

"Well, the police were here questioning people. Everybody talked about it for days afterward. The afternoon Bette—died, Lloyd was with clients all day, appraising a factory site, or he was at the office. After work, he was with a bunch of us who went out to dinner. Then two people from work went with him to a bar and they drank and talked until past midnight." She caught the way Coop was looking at her and took another sip of ale. "Yeah, I remember all that. I always wanted to be a cop," she said with her bright smile.

"Then why didn't you apply for the job?"

"Hate guns. Hate violence."

"Me, too," Coop said. "Will you give me Lloyd's address?"

"Here are a list of Bette's friends and acquaintances," she told him, pulling a folded sheet of typing paper from her purse and handing it to him.

He gave her another look.

"Like I said, as soon as you called I had a pretty good idea why you were coming out here."

"Thanks," Coop said, as he folded the list.

"Let me know if I can do anything else. Bette really was a wonderful person. We were close." A hardness came into her moist dark eyes that surprised Coop. "I want to see the bastard caught!"

After dropping Hillary back at Prudent Stand, Coop drove to Bette's apartment and let himself in with the extra key she'd left with him last year.

It was a small one-bedroom unit in Beau Jardin, a newlooking condo project just east of town, possibly built by a Francophile who had remained in Haverton. All of the buildings were two stories, constructed of white or tan brick with mansard roofs.

The silence here wasn't as bad as in the cottage, but it still stopped Coop just inside the door and seemed to drain his energy. He wondered sometimes if silence might be the language of the dead in a lament to the living.

The apartment had about it the look of a place that a woman had left hurriedly and expected to return to soon. The closet door was still open and a few clothes, probably considered, then rejected for the trip, lay folded on the bed. A pair of red high-heeled shoes sat near the dresser as if they'd just been slipped off, one of them lying on its side. Coop figured the Haverton police might have searched the place and left it as they found it, but more likely someone from NYPD Homicide would be showing up soon to search more thoroughly. He knew that when he was finished he'd better leave things pretty much as they were.

He put on the tight latex gloves, just as he'd done countless times before beginning a search. Then he went to work.

It saddened him to find so much of what he remembered about his daughter there, the compulsion for order along with a sort of frenzied impatience that left order frayed at the edges. Though clothes had been left on the obviously hastily made bed, the clothes remaining in the closet were hanging by category—dresses, slacks, blouses, casual, more formal—and the bed *had* been made. Her shoes were arranged in a compartmentalized hanging plastic holder in the same fashion— other than the pair left lying haphazardly on the floor, the pair that tore a hole in Coop's heart. Neatness tainted by carelessness. It was a contradiction in Bette's personality that had long intrigued him, and he wondered if in some way it had led to her death.

Nothing in the apartment provided any clue as to

why she'd been murdered. The usual household bills were in her desk, and her checkbook pads revealed no irregularity in her spending habits. The few work papers in the desk were amortization tables and routine business correspondence that seemed innocent enough. There were postcards from vacationing friends, a birthday card from Coop himself, a few newspaper clippings Maureen had sent, about bioengineering and animal rights, with her fierce red felt-tip scrawl in the corners: *Can you believe?* or *Here's progress for you!!!* Maureen was always sending people clippings that reflected her interests rather than theirs. He found no personal letters. That was no surprise. He couldn't remember when he'd last written a real letter to Bette, or to anyone else. The phone was so much easier. Or e-mail.

That reminded him to look for a computer. He couldn't find one, and there hadn't been one in the cottage. Bette was always carrying around a laptop; she might have left it at work. He'd check.

One interesting item in the apartment was the framed photo on the nightstand near Bette's bed. It was of a smiling, dark-haired man in his early thirties, reasonably handsome but for eyebrows too bushy for him to play the leading man, and with a deep dimple in his chin. The photo was signed *Love you, Bette. Forever, Lloyd.*

Coop drew from his pocket the folded piece of paper Hillary Bland bad given him on which were written the names and addresses of Bette's friends and acquaintances. Lloyd Watkins was first on the list, at 2733-1A Rue de Montre. Coop remembered seeing the street name on a sign recently, and since he'd never

been to France, it figured to have been in the Beau
Jardin condo complex. Lloyd Watkins lived very close
to Bette's condo.

Coop took a last, lingering look around, then left the
condo as he'd found it. He couldn't shake the feeling
that he was leaving Bette, or something of her. So palpable had seemed her presence in the condo that he
wouldn't have been surprised to hear her say his name.

It didn't take him long to drive around and find 2733
Rue de Montre. It was a white brick, mansard-roofed
building much like Bette's, landscaped with low-lying
shrubs. Coop remembered Hillary telling him Lloyd
was too upset to have returned to work yet. Maybe he'd
be home.

Coop parked at the curb in front of the building,
then made his way along an unnecessarily curved walkway to its entrance. The foyer provided access only to
the units on the second floor. Ground-floor units bad
separate, private entrances.

Coop went back outside, found 1A, and knocked on
a white door faintly gilded in gold enamel. Within seconds he heard the muted rustling sound of someone approaching from inside.

The door opened, and he was looking at the man in
Bette's bedside photo.

CHAPTER SEVEN

Lloyd Watkins was shorter than Coop imagined he would be, and not nearly as handsome as his photograph. He was wearing baggy dark sweatpants and a red T-shirt with small white lettering too faded to read. His hair was mussed and he appeared tired and grief-stricken, with eyes that seemed to see miles beyond what he was looking at.

"Lloyd Watkins?" Coop asked, making sure. When the man nodded, Coop introduced himself as Bette's father.

The mention of her name seemed to strike Watkins like a physical blow. His eyes teared up and he backed away a step. "Jesus! It was . . . I mean what happened really got to me. I guess you know Bette and I were close."

"I heard."

"I tried to make it to New York to . . . the funeral, but I couldn't bring myself to do it. I mean, I was so sick about what happened."

"That's okay," Coop said, "I understand."

Watkins shook his head, seeming to awaken from a

trance. "Didn't mean to leave you standing out there." He offered his hand and the two men shook. "Come inside and sit down."

The place was a mess. Magazines and newspapers were scattered over the floor. A blanket and pillow were rumpled on the sofa, and half a dozen empty Budweiser cans and a partly eaten sub sandwich sat on the coffee table. The cans were arranged in a circle, and the sandwich lay on top, spanning two of them. It reminded Coop of Stonehenge. Next to one of the beer cans was a coffee cup, still steaming.

Watkins must have noticed Coop looking at the cup. "Want some coffee? I've been drinking it a lot to keep awake during the day. All I want to do is sleep. Been sleeping too long, too late. It's an escape, I'm sure. Gotta get back to work soon, get on with life. Can't be a wreck like this forever."

"Yes."

"Huh?"

"I'll have a cup of coffee, black."

Watkins nodded and trudged toward the kitchen. He was muscular and moved like an exhausted athlete, slightly bow-legged, elbows out and arms swinging in abbreviated tight arcs. While he was gone, Coop looked around and saw cheap framed prints on the walls, a bookcase that held mostly stereo equipment, and a few books on computers. Watkins didn't seem like Bette's kind of guy, but love was a puzzle. There was a framed photograph of Bette on a table near the TV, with a wilted single red rose lying in front of it. Coop felt a pang of grief and looked away from the photo. He cleared some newspapers off a chair and sat down.

"Bette tell you much about me?" Watkins asked,

when he returned and handed Coop coffee in a white plastic mug. On the mug was a likeness of the Three Stooges in wacky golfing outfits. The unexpected touch of levity made Coop angry all out of proportion. "Sorry, but it was my only clean cup," Watkins said. Intuitive bastard.

"No problem," Coop told him. "And I found out about you just today from someone at Prudent Stand. Bette didn't mention you to me, which shouldn't be surprising. She kept her personal life to herself."

"Yeah, I guess that's so." Watkins seemed to be pondering this for the first time. He sat down absently on the sofa, on top of a *People* magazine. "And it isn't like we were planning on getting married or anything. At least not yet. In fact, we had a big argument about a month ago and broke up. I'm sure we both knew it was temporary."

"How can you be sure how she felt?"

"Well—I wasn't. I guess I should have said I was hoping it was temporary."

"What grounds did you have for hope, exactly?"

"I didn't think the trouble was between us, if you know what I mean. Bette was under a lot of pressure at work. She just didn't have time for me. We didn't go out anymore, only saw each other at the office. That's what the argument was about, really."

"Did she tell you she was going to New York, to my beach cottage?"

"All she said was she was going away for a rest. She thought it was going to do wonders for her. Even hinted that when she got back, we'd make a fresh start. Or maybe I imagined that part." He fell silent for a long moment, thinking that over. Then he said sadly, "Bette was a wonderful person, Mr. Cooper."

"She mention I was an ex-cop?"

"Yeah. She talked about you some. She worried about you. You were . . . um, in poor health for a while last spring, weren't you?"

Coop was surprised. Bette was as careful of other people's privacy as of her own. If she had told this man about his illness, they must have been close. He said, "I'm better now."

"Are you investigating her death on your own?"

"What makes you ask that?"

"I suppose because if I were you, that's what I'd be doing. But maybe that's impractical, like something out of a book or movie. I don't know anything about police work."

"I am looking into the matter some," Coop said. "To satisfy my curiosity."

"If you find out anything, will you satisfy mine? I'd like to know who killed her and why." Watkins sipped his own coffee and studied Coop over the rim of the cup. "I guess I'm a suspect?"

"Why do you say that?"

"If I were you, I'd suspect me. Especially since Bette and I had the argument and temporarily split up. To tell you the truth, I'm glad I've got an airtight alibi. It was a chance thing that people were with me most of that day and that evening, when she . . . died. Normally I'd have had enough time to drive into New York and back. I might have had dinner alone after work, maybe watched some TV, then gone to bed."

If this Watkins was guilty, Coop thought, he was

really something. "I'll check everything out. Don't worry about that end of it."

"I won't," Watkins said. "It's hard enough to deal with the rest of this shit, believe me. Well, I guess you know."

"Yeah, I do."

Watkins noticed the sharpness in his tone. He said, "Go ahead, ask people anything about me. Come back and question me, if you feel you have to. I'll understand."

"You seem like an understanding guy," Coop told him.

This time Watkins didn't pick up on the irony. "My friends say that. People tend to spill their guts to me. Maybe I should have been a cop."

"Everybody thinks that at one time or another." Coop set the mug on a table and stood up to leave. The NYPD had asked Watkins the obvious questions; Billard could show him the file or fill him in. "It's not like they imagine."

"That's what Deni Green said this morning about being a writer."

"Deni Green?" The woman Hillary Bland had mentioned.

"Yeah. She said she was a book writer, doing research on Bette's murder. So I talked to her awhile, answered some of the same questions you asked." Watkins raised his thick eyebrows in sudden concern. "You think I shouldn't have talked to her?"

"I think you should have consulted a lawyer before talking to either one of us," Coop told him.

Honesty deserved honesty in return.

* * *

Honesty with each other was dear to both of them. Sitting outside in the cool Seattle night, each with a mug of light beer, Georgianna Mason and Cindy Romero waited for their vegetarian pizza to arrive. Though they were virtually on the sidewalk, the restaurant had see-through plastic curtains and overhead heaters that produced plenty of heat.

Georgianna and Cindy had been roommates years ago at Kansas State, and had remained friends after graduation. They had few secrets from each other. Now nearing middle age, they were still a striking pair, Cindy with her dark hair and eyes, and the fair-skinned and sandy-haired Georgianna, who possessed the delicacy of a porcelain ballerina that had just stepped down from the lid of a music box.

They both knew the pain of terrible marriages and bitter divorces, but both still held hopes for romance and permanent relationships.

"So you only met this guy on the Internet," Cindy said. "You've never seen him face-to-face."

Georgianna fluffed her long hair back in place where it had come loose in an outdoor heater's warm breeze. *Hard on the ends,* she thought. "I've seen his digital photo."

"If it *was* him. Some guys will lie to you about their digitals."

Georgianna smiled. She'd expected skepticism. But if Cindy had read Bret's (she'd discerned his name when he slipped up and used it) e-mail, she'd feel differently about him. From the first few exchanges of messages in a political chat room, both she and Bret knew something was going on between them. They not only shared liberal politics and a concern for the planet's future, they liked the same books, movies, and food. They both worked out regularly and believed in alternative medicine. Cindy, along with the rest of the human race, would have to learn that electrons could carry first love. Georgianna had revealed her real name to Bret, but she understood his caution, why he still preferred to use only his screen name in correspondence. You could meet all sorts of people online, some of them pests that were hard to get rid of later.

Cindy took a swig of beer and smiled at her. "Don't mind if I'm jealous and bitchy. I truly hope you'll get on famously with this guy if you really meet."

"Oh, we'll meet. He's down the coast in San Francisco. And he owns a new BMW he's dying to test on the highway."

"My, my. So he's rich."

"No, it's a new *used* BMW. He emphatically told me he wasn't rich. He has something to do with software development in Silicone Alley."

"Then he'll be rich."

"Rich isn't necessary," Georgianna said. She took a sip of beer and lowered her frosted mug, grinning. "But it wouldn't hurt."

Cindy leaned toward her across the table. "Seriously, I know you've been down for a while. I hope the future is good for you."

"Thanks," Georgianna said, squeezing her friend's hand. "At least now I feel like I've *got* a future."

CHAPTER EIGHT

Coop remembered seeing a small bookshop, Long Goodbye Books, on First Street as he was driving into Haverton. After leaving Lloyd Watkins he drove there, found a parking spot immediately in front of the shop, and went inside.

The shop's interior was small with narrow aisles, packed with books new and used that were mostly paperbacks. It was warm inside, and had a pleasant musty scent, the way Coop thought all bookshops should smell.

The cash register was on the right but no one was behind the counter. At a small round table at the back of the store sat a slender woman with straight blond hair and squared bangs. She glanced up from paperwork she'd been engrossed in and smiled at Coop. "Let me know if there's anything I can help you with."

"There might be," Coop said, careful not to brush against books as he made his way to the back of the store.

"We're a mystery bookstore," said the woman,

"named after a Chandler novel. I can help you with mysteries."

"That I need," Coop told her. "Ever hear of a writer named Deni Green?"

The blond woman put down her pencil and stared up at him. "The Maltese Kitten?"

"Pardon?"

"That's the title of Deni Green's latest Cozy Cat mystery. She was in here this morning and offered to sign whatever copies I had. Fortunately I had three of them."

"Do you still have a copy?"

The woman smiled. "All three. Cozy Cat is an old series and getting kind of stale."

"What's it about?"

"What they're all about: a woman who has a cat and solves crimes." She got up and went to a crammed bookshelf, then pulled out a hardcover copy of *The Maltese Kitten*. "It's a parody of the famous Dashiell Hammett novel, *Maltese Falcon*."

"I like Hammett," Coop said.

"More's the pity," said the woman, and handed him the book.

The dust jacket illustration was of a gray cat sniffing at a smoking revolver against a field of blood red. Coop looked at the back of the book and there was Deni Green's photograph. She was a slightly overweight woman with short hair and dark ringlets on her forehead. Her features were symmetrical and strong, with arched eyebrows, a broad jaw, and thin, slightly curled lips. Coop thought that if she were a man she'd be described as looking like a corrupt Roman emperor, maybe Nero.

"I'll take this," he said to the bookshop woman.

"You won't like it if you like Hammett."

"You don't seem eager to sell it."

"I suppose I'm not. I'm more interested in my customers believing my recommendations and coming back to buy more books. You want a cat mystery, there's always Carole Nelson Douglas, or Rita Mae Brown. They haven't used up all nine of their lives."

"It doesn't matter with me, I'm from out of town."

"You're still a customer."

Coop studied the expression on her lean, pale face. "What was your impression of Deni Green when she was here?" he asked. "I mean, as a person?"

The bookshop woman gave him a gentle smile. "I didn't like her much. She seemed arrogant and insecure."

Coop went with her to the register at the front of the store and paid for the book. "I can't wait to get into this," he said.

She looked at him as if he were about to start down a ski jump without skis.

The Night Caller snapped on his latex gloves and explored. He saw that holistic medicine seemed to have caught Georgianna's interest. There were various self-help medical books stacked in a bookshelf, and new wave posters on the walls espoused the benefits of various diets and exercise regimens. Some of the posters were political, about corporate greed and global warming. The posters, and the lineup of herbal food supplements in the medicine cabinet, left little doubt as to her newfound direction. She wanted to save herself and the world. Now, there was a tall order.

The refrigerator and a check of her various Internet visits and bookmarks on her computer revealed that she'd become a vegetarian. Magazine clippings, stuck to the refrigerator with magnets, explained how such a diet could virtually guarantee a longer life. The Night Caller smiled. More than most people, he knew there were few reliable guarantees in this world. Fate was unpredictable and sometimes sadistic.

Then the smile faded and was replaced by a thoughtful expression. Georgianna's Internet lover was a worry and a risk. Something had gone slightly wrong and there were things she remembered even if only hazily—he was sure of it from their talks afterward. Things the soul searching of love and lovers' talk might bring to the surface. The series of e-mails suggested that the cyberlover and Georgianna would soon meet face-to-face.

Perhaps they'd have lattes at Starbucks, share a bed, then decide that would be the extent of their affair. The simple rutting of fools.

But perhaps they would be delightfully compatible and their relationship would deepen, the way Internet romances were supposed to work in the second stage. True lovers had no secrets. Sin eating was one of the great benefits of passion, and one of the great dangers.

Each time before, the Night Caller's visit had terminated long before Georgianna returned home, and she had entered an unoccupied apartment.

This time would be different. He wasn't ready, didn't have the terrible, wonderful need, but this time it was necessary in order to ensure his survival. That was his right. It was ordained out of darkness and insects.

She would enter confidently, locking the door and thinking she was separating herself from the perilous outside world. The Night Caller knew what an illusion that was for everyone. Locks were simply distractions to lovers and demons, who were usually on both sides of them anyway. Georgianna remembered that from the time of reptiles but denied it, like everyone else. Almost everyone else. The Night Caller knew how they thought and how they didn't, all of them. He listened to their secret voices and knew their muted screams. They heard none of it, confident they were someone else. Someone safe.

Once inside, the click of the lock still in her mind, Georgianna would glance about, wary and vaguely aware. But there were places in the apartment where she wouldn't look before lowering her guard even more, places where she didn't really want to look. She would instead occupy herself in the way of women living alone, preparing a snack, taking a shower, reading, getting ready for bed. Thinking she was alone, protected by doors and locks and odds. Aware that no one could enter the building without the knowledge and approval of the doorman, or enter the underground garage without punching in a code on a residents' keypad that would raise a gate. The code was also needed to use the elevator from the garage level. Very tight security in this building.

But hardly tight enough.

When all of his senses told him it was time, the

Night Caller would approach Georgianna gradually but surely, closing the distance between survival and death until he was one with her.

Like the others, she wouldn't hear a thing until it was too late.

It was his game, moving silently as time.

And he was on his game.

CHAPTER NINE

Coop awakened rather late—he could tell by the brightness of the room—and found that he didn't feel like getting up. It had been a tiring day yesterday in New Jersey, and traffic delays bad made the drive home twice as long as it should have been.

He thought about breakfast. His recommended: grapefruit juice, Cheerios with a banana, skim milk. Coffee, black. He wasn't particularly hungry, but he wasn't turned off by the thought of food.

Good sign. According to Dr. Gregory, anyway.

He lifted a heavy arm, threw back the covers. Then he pulled himself upright and swung his legs to the floor. His head felt woolly, but that wasn't unusual first thing in the morning. The transition from sleep to wakefulness seemed to be getting more difficult. He'd just sit on the edge of the bed for a while.

The Maltese Kitten was resting on his nightstand. He picked it up and thumbed through the first few pages. The publisher's Web site was listed, but not their phone number. He opened the drawer and took out the

Manhattan phone directory. Already his arms felt stronger, and his head was clearing.

He found the number, then picked up the bedside phone and punched it out on the keypad.

A recorded voice gave him his options and corresponding numbers to press. None of the options quite fit trying to get in touch with the author. Maybe that was on purpose.

Coop hung up the phone, flipped open the novel's cover, and read the first few pages.

Nothing like Hammett.

As he was closing the book he noticed the lettering on the dedication page: *This Cozy Cat adventure is for the purrfect editor, Alicia Benham.*

Coop lifted the receiver and hit REDIAL to get the office of Whippet Books again. This time he managed to talk to a live person and asked to speak to Alicia Benham. "I'm calling in regard to one of her authors, Deni Green," he said.

"Oh!" said the woman on the other end of the line. "Are you with Smurger and Bold?"

Coop didn't hesitate. "Yes, I am."

"We asked you not to call here again," the woman said, and hung up.

Coop wondered if it was even possible to get in touch with an author.

The phone rang a second after he'd hung up.

He lifted the receiver and said hello.

A woman's voice: "Mr. Cooper?"

He said that he was. "Is this the Mr. Cooper who's the father of Bette Cooper?"

"Who is this?" Coop asked.

"My name's Deni Green, Mr. Cooper. I tried to

catch up with you in Haverton but kept just missing you. I think we need to talk. I might have some information about your daughter."

"What kind of information?"

"The papers said you were an ex-cop."

"That doesn't answer my question."

"It's the kind of information a cop would be interested in."

"That was the right answer," Coop said. "When and where?"

"How about the Sapphire Coffee Shop on Amsterdam? Say, half an hour?"

"Fine. I live a ten-minute walk from there."

"I know, Mr. Cooper. Coffee and bagels are on me."

Coop got to the Sapphire Coffee Shop first. It was a narrow diner with a long counter, booths opposite by the windows that looked out on Amsterdam. Swinging doors led to the kitchen in back. Two bored waiters slouched whispering to each other like conspirators near a pass-through serving counter where the orders were posted and filled.

Right now there were no orders on the steel-spiked carousel. Coop already had his black coffee in front of him, and the breakfast crowd was long gone. The only other customer was a man in a tweed overcoat, perched on a counter stool and forking in an omelet while reading a *Village Voice*.

Among the people walking past the window by his booth, Coop thought he recognized Deni Green from her dust jacket photo.

Sure enough, the woman in the black coat, wearing

the squarish black hat, black slacks, and black boots, carrying the thin black leather briefcase, entered the coffee shop.

She saw Coop right away, strode over, and whipped off her hat and grinned. "Deni Green," she said.

Coop stood up and they shook hands.

"So, Ezekiel Cooper. Anybody ever tell you you look like Gary Cooper the actor?"

"Now and then."

"What do they call you? Ez? Zeke?"

"Everyone calls me Coop," he said, "like the actor." He studied her. Stocky build beneath the oversize coat, features as strong and empirical as in her photograph. One of those women who would have been attractive thirty pounds lighter, but who had been thirty pounds overweight all her adult life. Her flesh-padded dark eyes were bright and voracious and projected an eagerness bordering on obsession. "Why were you looking for me in Haverton, Ms. Green?"

"Call me Deni, Coop."

He smiled. "Same question, Deni."

"Let me fill you in before I answer." One of the slouching waiters unslouched and sauntered over to take her order. "Coffee and a bagel with schmear," she said. "Want anything else, Coop?"

"Just a topper on the coffee."

The conspiratorial-looking waiter nodded and went away.

"I'm a mystery writer," Deni said, "and a pretty well known one at that."

"The Cozy Cat series," Coop said.

She grinned fiercely, pleased. "You a fan?"

"Sort of."

"Then you know the Cozy Cat books are fiction. Now I've decided to branch out into nonfiction, try my hand at a true crime book."

Coop didn't like the way this was going. Already burdened by his grief and what he might find out about his daughter, the last thing he wanted was some pesky writer telling her secrets to the world. "Are you saying the crime you're going to write about is my daughter's murder?"

"Not exactly. It's something more. Something much larger."

The waiter brought her coffee and a toasted bagel sliced, with a slab of cream cheese on each half. While he was setting the food on the table and topping off Coop's coffee, Deni was digging in her black briefcase. She got a dab of cream cheese on the edge of her hand, noticed it, and licked it off. Like a cat, Coop thought

"Here's part of what I have," she said, when the waiter had faded away and was again slouched with his fellow anarchist at the back of the diner. "Through my sources on the NYPD, I obtained this crime scene photo." On the table she laid a photograph of the dusty partial footprint on the tiles inside the door of Coop's cottage. "Notice the distinctive crisscross design on the sole."

"I have," he told her. "How is it you have sources in the NYPD?"

"I've done plenty of research there for my mystery novels, made plenty of good contacts."

Coop noticed she hadn't said *friends*. Well, he knew the difference himself.

"Here's what else I have," she said. Next to the first photo she laid another.

At first Coop thought it was just another shot of the footprint in his cottage, only from a different angle. Then he realized that the crisscross-patterned sole print was on a marble floor and in a layer of what might have been finely granulated sand. The metal tracks of a sliding door ran across the top of the photo. This one hadn't been taken in his cottage. It was only a partial, and faint, but it did look similar to the footprint found at the cottage, the print probably left by Bette's killer.

He looked up at Deni. "Where was this taken?"

The startled expression on his face must have been just what she was hoping for. She grinned and said, "Long ago and far away. At another homicide scene."

"Give me the facts and save the hype, will you?"

"Sorry, but you'll admit this is pretty dramatic." She was still smiling, aiming the bright ferocity in her dark eyes at him. "Same shoe, same killer."

"Same *kind* of shoe," Coop said. "Maybe. Neither footprint is clear."

"Clear enough," Deni persisted.

Coop knew she was right. Or maybe he wanted to believe that. It was at least something that had to be considered. "Where was the second photo taken?"

"Two years ago in Sarasota, Florida, at the scene of Marlee Clark's murder."

"The tennis star?"

"The same."

"Then the Sarasota police are aware of the footprint."

"They saw it, all right But they didn't think it was important. And it didn't fit their theory of the crime, or the person they arrested and who was later convicted."

It was coming back to him now. The case had been

widely covered in tabloid newspapers and the more sensational TV news shows, which had played up the sex and scandal. Deni Green was probably planning to give the Clark murder more of the same treatment in her book. What did she have in mind for Bette? Coop's stomach tightened. He asked, "Wasn't Marlee Clark killed by a woman?"

Deni Green nodded, keeping her chin down and grinning up at Coop in a way that made her look especially malicious. "Clark supposedly was killed by Sue Coppolino, her lesbian lover. They arrested her even though her shoe soles didn't match the footprint. They had plenty of other evidence against her, the way she'd been sneaking on and off the property, conducting a secret affair with Marlee Clark. The prosecution said the murder was the result of a lovers' quarrel. Coppolino was convicted."

"Then most likely she did the deed."

"Typical cop thinking," Deni snapped, irritated. "Tell you one thing—she didn't kill your daughter. She's in the penitentiary in Florida. Your daughter and Marlee Clark were killed by this guy, the one who left these footprints." She tapped the two photographs with the back of a knuckle, but Coop didn't look down at them. He was draining his coffee, thinking he might be leaving soon. He was about through with Deni Green.

"You're building a lot on this similarity. What possible connection could there be between my daughter and Marlee Clark?"

"I thought maybe you could tell me."

"There's none that I know of," Coop said. "Bette wasn't even a tennis fan."

"I still think they were killed by the same person."

"On the basis of a similar footprint?"

"And the fact that in each case there was powder residue that was most likely from latex gloves."

"Latex gloves are worn for everything from cleaning the sink to brain surgery, by millions of people. And whatever brand shoe made those prints, there were probably thousands of them sold."

"They look to be pretty much the same size," Deni said.

"The approximate size millions of other men wear. Including me."

"There's something else," Deni said.

Coop was sliding out of the booth, but her tone stopped him. He watched her open a briefcase and take out an envelope from which she drew an eight-by-ten photo. Her movements were slow, grudging almost. He realized she hadn't intended to show him this. Not yet. Coop's heart began beating faster as she laid the photo down in front of him. He had to make an effort to look at it.

It was a photograph of Marlee Clark's body as it had been discovered in her condo, laid out as if asleep. The eyes were closed and the young, pretty face looked peaceful. The long red hair that had been the tennis star's trademark was fanned out carefully as if to frame her face. Only the bloodstains on the fabric, crimson in the police photographer's flash, showed she was dead.

Deni was talking. "The prosecutor said the way she was laid out was additional proof she'd been killed by her lover, who was sorry for what she'd done. I expect NYPD is saying the same kind of thing about your daughter."

Coop didn't reply. He was jolted by the photo but he

resisted the implication. "Bette was strangled. If I remember correctly, Marlee Clark was hacked at the base of the neck."

Deni shook her head as if firmly denying the sophistry of a recalcitrant student. "It doesn't matter. The point is that no wound shows when they're laid out. The killer had closed your daughter's eyes, right?"

"Yes." *As well as her mouth with its swollen tongue.* He fought back the image forming in his mind.

"He doesn't want anything to spoil the peaceful effect."

"He's a psycho, a serial killer," Coop said. "That's what you think, isn't it?"

Deni nodded.

So this was what Deni was after, he thought. Another blood-soaked madman who would be her own personal discovery. With luck he'd make her rich and famous. As far as she was concerned, Bette was only a number. Victim number two.

If she was number two. "Have there been other, similar murders?"

Deni sighed. "You drive a hard bargain, Coop. You're making me show everything and we haven't even struck a deal yet."

Coop waited.

After a moment she shrugged and opened her briefcase again. "Oakland, California. Thirteen months ago. Her name was Ofelia Valdez."

The photo showed a woman lying on her bed. In the background was a nightstand covered with small framed photographs of smiling people. The victim was young, pretty, not particularly Latin-looking in spite of the name. The hair spread on the pillow was light brown.

The eyes were closed. She was wearing a long frilly nightgown. It was impossible to tell how she had been killed.

"Her neck was broken," Deni said. "One sharp twist from behind. Our killer's strong."

A different method again, Coop noted. But that was only his professional mind talking, while he stared helplessly at the photo of the woman who had been posed much as he'd found his daughter. Deni held out another photo. She was quickening the pace now, sensing that she was winning him over. "This one's from five years ago on Long Island. Ellen Banta."

This woman was lying on a sofa. Its tan suede looked expensive, as did her gray silk blouse. The hair spread around her head was black tinged with gray, this time. Ellen Banta had been about forty, he judged, and she hadn't worried about dyeing her hair. It was a strong-featured, vital face that seemed to retain life. She looked as if she were going to wake from her nap any minute and exercise or go sailing.

"The method?" he asked.

"Knife. The wound's at the back, of course."

Coop stacked the pictures and pushed them away. He'd seen enough. "So why isn't the FBI looking for this guy?"

"Because in each case the local cops made the same mistake the NYPD is making in Bette's case," Deni replied. Knowing she'd hooked him, she was paying attention to her food for the first time. She used the flat of her knife to mash and spread the cream cheese on her bagel. "The Oakland cops arrested Ofelia Valdez's ex-husband. They had to let him go because they didn't have enough evidence. But they were sure he did it.

When he died in a car accident three months later, they closed the case."

"And Ellen Banta?"

"She was a Wall Street hot shot who'd made a fortune and retired at thirty-five. Never married or had kids. Her younger brother inherited everything. Naturally the cops liked him for the murder, especially when they found out he was chronically unemployed and had a couple of drug arrests. Again, though, they were never able to make a case."

"Were both victims killed in their homes?"

Deni raised her eyebrows. "You ask all the right questions. No, neither one was. Ofelia Valdez was at her ex-husband's house. They still slept together sometimes. A lot of divorced couples do, but most don't like to talk about it. In fact the cops couldn't find anybody Ofelia had told. That's why the cops arrested her ex. Who else would have known where she was staying the night? But he'd gone to work at three A.M., loading trucks at UPS, and they could never figure out how he snuck home to kill her."

"And Banta?"

"Well, Ellen was a sports nut, but she really liked to eat. Every few months she'd sneak away to a fat farm, live on rice cakes and carrot juice, and sweat the pounds off. She didn't want anyone to know. Always told people she was off scuba diving in the Bahamas or someplace."

"So let me guess. She was at this fat farm when she was killed, and only her brother knew where she was?"

"Actually, they were never able to prove he did know. But he was her closest living relative, so they figured he'd be the one she told." Deni paused. "You see the pattern? Five years ago, two years ago, thirteen months ago, and then your daughter. There's the shoe print in the cases of your daughter and Marlee Clark, and latex glove powder all over the bodies in all the murders. Like most serial killers, this one is compelled to kill with less time between victims. And of course there are probably more victims we don't know about, and he's operating on an even more accelerated time-table. In each case the local cops assumed it had to be a lover or family member or close friend, because the killer showed such an intimate knowledge of the victim in the way he got at her."

Coop nodded. He saw the pattern, all right. Both patterns. "Valdez was sleeping with her ex-husband; Banta didn't advertise the fact she was going to a fat farm; and Marlee Clark was in her high-security condo, so it had to be somebody who knew how to sneak past the alarms and cameras. And my daughter was at my cottage, and the only way for the killer to know that was if she'd told him."

"Exactly. That's why you went to Haverton yesterday, wasn't it? To find out who she'd told? Did you have any luck?"

"According to your theory, how do you—" Coop began.

"You cops. Ignore the question and ask one of your own. Is that something they teach you at the police academy?"

"According to your theory, how do you figure the killer learned his future victims' secrets?"

"My guess is he's a Ted Bundy type, a charmer who insinuated himself into the victims' confidence and affection."

"That's only speculation."

"I'm going to test it, though. If Marlee Clark knew someone like that, her lover Sue Coppolino probably also knew him, or at least met him. I managed to arrange an appointment to question Sue Thursday in Florida. Want to come along?"

Coop wasn't sure of his answer. "You're doing all this because you think there's a book in it."

"Of course. I'm a writer. Are you afraid of what we might find out about your daughter?"

A woman who sensed weakness. And exploited it. "It isn't that," Coop said. *Not entirely that.*

Deni's lips curled into a half smile. "Then come along." It was a challenge. "It's in both our best interests to work together on this. We can be a team, pool our resources and talents. You think like a cop, and I think like a writer. You have cop connections, I have connections that aren't all cops or criminals. My guess is you're not exactly computer literate. I can work the Internet like a wizard and find out anything."

Coop knew she was being reasonable, but he didn't trust her. She was hoping to write a sensational bestseller, and she wouldn't care whom she trashed along the way.

But maybe she *was* on to something, and had information he wasn't aware of. He had little choice but to team up with her, at least until her avenue of investigation arrived at a dead end.

"If we're going to work together," Coop said, "I want to know everything you know. Organize it and make copies, put it in a file folder and get it all to me; then we'll meet and discuss the case."

"Will I know everything *you* know? I have to point

out that so far I've been very forthcoming with you, Coop, and you've told me diddly-squat."

"Am I right in assuming you need me more than I need you?"

"I get the point," Deni said, making it clear that she didn't like the point or maybe didn't even necessarily agree with it.

"I might be retired, but I can't go around blabbing certain police business or I'll lose my credibility and sources. You should understand that."

"I do," Deni said. "We've got ourselves a deal." She extended her hand and they shook on the agreement.

Coop noticed her hand, broad with blunt fingers, nails chewed almost to nonexistence. And with the strength of a man's.

"There's something else obvious about this killer," Deni said. "Ellen Banta was killed in New York, Marlee Clark in Florida, Ofelia Valdez in California, and your daughter was killed in New York. This killer began in New York, though he probably killed elsewhere for years, and now he's come home."

Coop was afraid she might be right.

"See," she said, guessing she'd been a step ahead of him, "you'll find that I'm an asset."

As well as a liability, Coop thought.

He watched her grin and tear into her bagel as if it were alive and might escape.

She hadn't mentioned any plastic saints. And he couldn't.

CHAPTER TEN

The Night Caller had read all the available material on the subject, how law enforcement defined serial killers, how they divided them into "organized" and "disorganized" types by analyzing crime scenes, how they worked up psychological and physical profiles that usually turned out to be amazingly accurate. Or so they said.

From the much maligned point of view of the killer, there were, of course, some common denominators that simply couldn't be avoided. But there were others that were controllable. Variables could be introduced, as well as misleading consistencies. Then the threads the police sought, the compulsions that must be served, would be lost in the maze of conflicting and misleading information.

It was not, for instance, always necessary for a serial killer to use the same sort of weapon or dispose of bodies the same way, to be known as "the .44-Caliber Killer" or "the Hillside Strangler." How many different types of firearms there were! How many different ways and places to dispose of bodies!

How many different kinds of cutting instruments.

Cut to the chase. Shortcut. Cutlery.

The Night Caller opened Georgianna's kitchen drawers until the overhead fluorescent fixture's pale glare glinted off a clutter of bright steel blades.

What would it be? A chef's knife? No, that was too similar to a previous deletion. A paring or steak knife? Their blades were short, flexible, and uncertain. An ice pick? Possibly, possibly . . . But what was *this?* A sharp edge that cut, a cutting instrument, a cutter that could cut through metal—a hand-operated can opener. Here was a change yet not a change in modus operandi. Once a manual can opener snagged skin, entire sections of flesh could be peeled off, in layers if necessary, vital organs exposed.

Messy? Of course messy. But controllable. The victim could be unconscious in a bathtub, heartbeat and blood flow minimal. Initial cutting could be done underwater. If she regained consciousness, shock would immobilize her. The face needn't be touched. That was important. And when the moment was right and true, a dull but sufficient consciousness could be induced, and the union and instant would occur even through the paralysis of shock. All pain, all destruction, would be beneath the surface, leaving the ritual intact and the moment complete.

Georgianna would suffer, but that was a necessary variation on the theme. It would appear to the police that her murder was the work of a vicious sadist, yet she would be perfect and at peace beneath the time and above the blood.

The Night Caller lifted the can opener from the drawer, then experimented with its long lever, observing its clamping action at the cutting wheel. Excellent. And there in the drawer was a heavy steel mallet for tenderizing meat. Perfect! Not for tenderizing, but for effecting unconsciousness with a precise and single blow. After unconsciousness, and what followed, the cutting and misdirection could begin, the creation of a truly red herring. The police would never have seen such a red herring!

But it would all happen under careful control. None of the red must get on clothes. The basin would be for washing away minor stains afterward.

The Night Caller carried the can opener and mallet into the bedroom and laid them on top of the bureau, then began to undress.

As time passed, this seemed a better and better plan. Since this murder was one of practicality and precaution rather than urgency, and out of sequence, it would serve well to divert the authorities. Not only would the MO be altered, but the assumed motive as well. The Seattle police would see the murder as impulsive rather than logical and systematic, or a combination of both. The police would be searching for a mindless ghoul, not a killer who was educated and sophisticated. Nobody liked being cubbyholed. Compulsions could be harnessed. Needs could be met without categorization.

The plastic St. Augustine left last time in the still warmth would divert the police. St. Augustine the forgiven. The Night Caller had come across the cheap souvenir saints in his travels and decided to use one. Yet he had bought a dozen. Eleven more were at home. No, ten. Seattle was a long way from New York.

Nude, the Night Caller padded barefoot into the bathroom and removed the plastic shower curtain so it wouldn't be in the way, then ran lukewarm water into the tub and began to arrange towels.

Anticipating. Smiling.

Everything under control.

Dr. Rainier Gregory leaned back in his black leather desk chair, a green folder containing Coop's charts open before him. Behind him were framed certificates attesting to his qualifications and expertise, family photographs taken at various vacation spots, attesting to his professional success.

Coop hoped the certificates and photos meant something. Dr. Gregory was the surgeon who'd removed the part of his colon that was cancerous, and had, in a series of minor operations and chemotherapy, eliminated what cancer had spread. Once metastasized, the blood-borne cancer from the colon might turn up in any part of the body. It had to be dealt with in a way redolent of putting out brush fires. What was hoped for, prayed for, was the magic word: *Remission*.

"Your numbers look good, Coop," Dr. Gregory said. He was a man in his early forties, younger than Coop. His hair was dark and he'd grown a raven-black Van Dyke beard since Coop had first met him. "Blood count steady. PSA holding." He put down the folder and sat forward. "So how are you feeling these days?"

"Not bad. Tired sometimes. I think more in terms of rationing my energy instead of my time."

"There's obviously been some stress, considering what happened to your daughter. Are you coping with that all right?"

"I think so."

"I know it isn't easy, but it would help if you managed it as well as you can. There are anecdotal data correlating stress with cancer."

"I'm dealing with it as well as could be expected," Coop said.

"Do you need anything?"

At first Coop didn't understand.

"Perhaps something to help you sleep," Dr. Gregory said, seeing his confusion. "Or to relieve anxiety."

"No, I want to keep thinking clearly. Stay active."

"I guess you know, from your profession, that everyone deals with grief, with stress, differently."

"True enough," Coop said. *Some of them murder women.*

"We'll keep an eye on things," Dr. Gregory said, standing up. "Continue your diet, Coop, and get at least some regular exercise. Let me know immediately if you perceive any change in yourself."

"I will," Coop said, also standing, shaking the doctor's hand. "Thanks," he said simply, as always after an appointment. *Thanks for saving my life.*

"Sure," Dr. Gregory said, almost casually. "Don't forget to stop and see Mary on the way out, set up an appointment for your next blood workup. In these cases, the tale is in the blood."

Balancing a box and two paper sacks containing her shopping bounty, Georgianna unlocked the door and entered her apartment. Once inside, she set her burden on a small table, carefully relocked the door, then fastened the chain lock.

She got out a peach-colored blouse from one of the

John Lutz

paper sacks and held it up to herself, beneath her chin, checking her image in the mirror. She was pleased. The blouse's color was right for her, as it had appeared in the harsher light of the department store. That lighting could fool you when it came to color. She hadn't been so sure in the store.

She lowered the blouse but kept looking at herself, at the image of an attractive and confident woman with a mischievous grin. Somebody on the way to somewhere important, if looks and grooming were any indication.

Georgianna tossed the new blouse over the back of the sofa and started toward the kitchen to get a glass of water.

Then she stopped and stood still, feeling chilled and as if every fine hair on her body were standing on end.

She had heard nothing but somehow knew that someone was standing behind her.

Close.

She made herself turn and look, and gasped at what she saw.

Instinctively she whirled to run.

She managed half a stride, hearing or imagining a single, whispered word, *Julia,* as the mallet fell.

CHAPTER ELEVEN

Coop met Deni Green at the Sapphire Coffee Shop after she called the next morning telling him she'd organized the material he wanted. When he walked in, he saw her seated in the same booth where they'd met the last time. She was wearing black again, a baggy dress of some sort of crinkly material. Coop wondered if she always dressed in black.

The Sapphire was more crowded this time, with office workers taking brunches or early lunches, but Coop and Deni could still talk privately. He said hello and slid into the booth so he was seated facing her. Before Deni on the table was a plate of fried eggs, sausage, and buttered toast. Late breakfast, delayed because of Coop and his request for information.

"It's delicious," Deni said. "I eat here all the time and I know. I recommend you order the same."

"I'll just have coffee."

"Sure? It's my treat again," she said. "I have an expense account."

"I'm sure."

She let it drop and went back to her meal while Coop ordered a cup of coffee from the same waiter as before, the guy who looked like an anarchist poisoner. With her free hand Deni removed a fat yellow file folder from the black briefcase on the bench beside her and laid it on the table in front of Coop. "Here'sh the shtuff you ashked for," she said around a mouthful of egg. "Photographsh an' all."

He opened the folder and studied its contents, aware of Deni washing down the bite of egg with a long swig of coffee.

The waiter had brought his coffee and glanced over Coop's shoulder. "My God!" he said.

"We're writers," Deni told him.

He nodded and hurried away.

"So what do you think?" she asked Coop.

"I'll take it home, read it all, and get back to you."

"But your first impression?"

"My first impression is we have a long way to go before we can convince any law enforcement agency we're dealing with a serial killer." He'd asked Billard to contact the police departments in the cities where the other murders on Deni's list had occurred and inquire about plastic saints. None of the departments had such information and was withholding it from the public.

"What about the footprints?" Deni asked.

"What about the fact that the women were murdered in different cities, with different weapons, in different ways, and that in one case an arrest and conviction was obtained, and in two others the police think they know who did it?"

"Well, that's how it works: He kills in different states and jurisdictions because he knows the local police won't run everything through national computer banks and make the connections."

"Don't be too sure you can read his mind," Coop told her. "You have to guard against making too many assumptions or you'll head off in the wrong direction."

Deni stared at him. "I could have sworn you were trying to tell me there was nothing there." She pointed her egg-yellowed fork at the file folder.

"There might be something there," Coop assured her. "Just cool your jets so we don't make a mistake."

Deni grinned. "I'm rocket powered, haven't you heard?"

This woman was beginning to irritate him. "You and Cozy Cat."

"Cozy Cat's not the main character in my novels."

"So what is your detective's name?"

"Deni. I'm the main character. Deni Green. Like Ellery Queen's character was Ellery Queen."

As Coop closed the file folder and moved it aside so coffee wouldn't dribble on it, he noticed Deni staring beyond him. He turned and saw a frail, fortyish woman, whose prettiness prevailed despite a militarylike buzz cut, approaching them. What was left of her hair was red and she was wearing light makeup and bright red lip gloss. She had on a black blouse and black jeans, a men's oversize black blazer, black platform shoes. Coop wondered when they would get over dressing in black.

"Alicia!" Deni said, grinning broadly. "How funny running into you here!"

"I came to get some takeout so I could eat in my office," Alicia said.

"Alicia's my editor at Whippet Books," Deni told Coop. "Coop, Alicia Benham."

Coop reached across the table and shook Alicia's delicate hand gently. "I figured that."

She looked at him with emerald eyes made to seem huge by her frailty and close-cropped hair. "Oh?"

"I tried to call you at Whippet yesterday," he explained. "You aren't easy to get in touch with."

The glossy red lips arced up in a slight smile. "If you met some of the people who try to get in touch with me you'd understand why."

''Coop's helping me on *The Killer Inside,*'' Deni said. She glanced at him. ''That's only our working title.''

"You're a writer?" Alicia asked.

"No. Former cop, NYPD."

"Ah! Well, whatever you are, if you're collaborating with Deni I suppose we do need to talk."

"We're not exactly collaborating," Deni said. "This is my book."

"I can come by your office this afternoon," Coop told Alicia.

"That'd work. Know where it is?"

He nodded. "The address is in Deni's previous book."

Coop continued looking at Alicia. "Who's Smurger and Bold?"

The question seemed to take her by surprise. "My husband's attorneys. I'm in the process of getting a divorce."

"I'm sorry."

"Not necessary. You know Smurger and Bold?"

"Only their names. They came up when I was getting the brush-off on the phone from the receptionist at Whippet Books."

"Oh. I thought for a moment you were going to hand me some sort of summons or court order."

"Not my game. Two o'clock okay?"

The counterman called Alicia's name to let her know her order was ready. She said good-bye and it was nice meeting Coop, not answering his question.

"At your office," he reminded her.

''Two's fine," she said over her shoulder, headed for the register.

He watched her walk away. He'd sensed a glint of dismay in Alicia's eyes when Deni had called her name. Maybe the editor and the famous author weren't all that compatible.

Coop thought it couldn't hurt to have an ally at Whippet, to know what Deni might be writing about Bette in her book.

"She's going through a horrendous divorce," Deni said. "Her husband is an abusive son of a bitch."

"He abuse her physically?"

"Worse than that—psychologically."

Coop remembered some of the women he'd seen on domestic violence calls after physical abuse. Did people like Deni think that kind of damage left little psychological effect?

"The world can be a shitty place for women," Deni said.

"For men, too. For cats."

Deni smiled around a bite of egg. "I betcha we get along just fine, Coop."

CHAPTER TWELVE

Coop had done his research. Whippet Publishing was an imprint of a larger publisher that was a division of a major publisher that was owned by a French conglomerate specializing in commercial concrete applications. All of this resulted in Alicia Benham having an office on the fifth floor of a building on Hudson Street.

After a brief wait in a quiet, carpeted anteroom done in shades of blue and gray, Alicia had appeared and led Coop to the office. It was Coop's idea of an editor's office, small and book-lined, with a window that afforded a distant view of the Statue of Liberty. Alicia sat in a gray upholstered swivel chair behind a gray desk. There were a few yellow file folders on the desk, a gooseneck reading lamp, a stack of robber-banded manuscripts, and on one corner a notebook computer with the lid raised. It was a prewar building of generous construction; no sound from the street made it all the way up five stories, through the thick walls, and into the office. All in all it was a good place to work, to ponder punctuation.

Coop sat in a gray chair in front of the desk. Alicia leaned back in her chair and smiled at him. The harsh sunlight pouring through the window revealed fine lines in her face but seemed only to add to its delicacy. She seemed to have had pain in her life and dealt with it in an objective way that hurt all the more and left its imprint.

"Know anything about commercial concrete applications?" Coop asked.

She laughed, surprised. "Should I?"

"Guess not." He nodded toward the stack of manuscripts. "Those what authors hope will turn into books?"

"By the time they get to me it's already been decided that they'll be books." She motioned with her right arm. "Like those."

Coop followed her glance and saw a lineup of about a dozen Cozy Cat novels on one of the bookshelves. "If Deni's such a successful mystery novelist," he said, "why does she want to try writing a fact crime book?"

"You asking as her collaborator or a cop?"

"Former cop," Coop reminded her. "And more of a researcher than a collaborator. I'm also the father of one of the victims who'll appear in Deni's book."

Alicia's expression changed. Crows'-feet deepened around her blue eyes. "I'm sorry. Really." Then another, more subtle expression entered her eyes. "Is that why Deni? . . ."

"It's how she got me to help her," Coop said.

Alicia clasped her hands together and leaned forward. "Listen, Mr. Cooper—"

"Coop."

"Okay, Coop. I asked Deni to venture into the field of true crime. There's pressure on me to provide Whippet with writers who sell. Her Cozy Cat series has gotten stale and sales are slumping."

"Why?"

Alicia regarded him carefully, weighing whether she should confide in him further. "The book business being what it is, you could get a lot of different answers to that. Frankly, I think it's because the main character is becoming rather unlikable."

"Isn't the main character Deni?"

"That might be the problem. Too much of the real Deni is creeping into the books. You might have noticed she's somewhat self-involved."

Coop nodded. "I figured what the hell, she's a writer."

"Do you know many writers?"

"None other than Deni."

"Well, she's only typical of today's writers in some ways. The fact is, Deni's an egocentric, devious opportunist who's constantly calculating what she can do for herself at anybody else's expense."

Coop stared at her. "You *are* her editor?"

"Sure, but I don't have to be her friend." She squinted up her eyes and regarded him. "Whatever the reason, I decided to warn you about her."

"You haven't asked me not to repeat any of this."

"My feeling about you is that I don't have to ask."

"And you are going to buy the true crime book if she writes it?"

"Sure, I have no choice. But I wouldn't tell her that. And if she doesn't make deadline, my replacement will buy it. If Whippet doesn't publish it, someone else might. And the way things are going, if nobody buys it, it might still turn up on the damned Internet. Be assured, when an author like Deni writes a book, it will be read. The only question is, how many copies will it sell? Make no mistake, Coop, I'm acting out of self-interest here. I need a big seller from Deni, and I'm going to make sure she delivers the manuscript on time to save my job."

"You've been candid," Coop said. "I appreciate it, but I'm wondering why you're talking this way."

"Deni's not the gentle soul some of her readers still think she is. She isn't to be trusted. I learned that the hard way in my dealings with her over the years. She uses people. I don't want to see her use you, especially under the circumstances."

"Would you be talking this way if Cozy Cat sales weren't slumping?"

She smiled. "Of course not."

One of Coop's reasons for wanting to talk to Alicia was to get added insight into Deni Green. He'd sure gotten that in a hurry. His other reason was to feel out Alicia to see if she'd become his ally and source of information if Deni proved to be a problem. To have some idea if she would squelch whatever defaming passages about Bette might be in Deni's manuscript. He now had a pretty good idea that she'd cooperate. Out of self-interest if not because she was basically a pretty decent sort.

He stood up.

She seemed a bit surprised, maybe slightly disappointed. "Interrogation over, Officer?"

"Only for the moment, I hope. Your husband . . ."

"My soon-to-be ex."

"It's none of my business, but I understand he mistreated you. If there's an ongoing problem with that, I have friends in the department."

"Deni tell you he mistreated me?"

"Well, yes. Abused you verbally."

"Deni doesn't know."

"No, I suppose she doesn't." He shrugged, embarrassed. "Sorry. You were candid with me, so I thought I'd be candid back. But I shouldn't have gotten into anything so personal." He moved toward the door.

"You be careful, Officer Coop."

"Of Deni?"

"Her, too."

He wanted to say more to her, but she'd turned her attention to her work.

CHAPTER THIRTEEN

Coop knew Sue Coppolino was twenty-three, but she looked too young to be in a women's prison rather than a juvenile detention center. She was about twenty pounds heavier than the attractive woman in her newspaper photos taken shortly after Marlee Clark's murder. Her face was pale, with cheeks reddened and puffed slightly by acne, and she wore no makeup. A ruined child. Her dark hair was cut short in a way that reminded Coop of Alicia.

From the moment a guard had brought her into the interviewing room, her eyes had been fixed on Deni Green. She paid no attention to Coop.

"I thought you forgot about me," she said to Deni, as soon as the door closed behind the guard.

"No chance of that," Deni said. She put her hand across the table and Sue grasped it with both of her own. "I told you, you're the main reason I'm writing this book. You don't belong in here."

Coop was sitting next to Deni, facing Sue Coppolino. They were alone in the small, pale green room, at a wooden table bolted to the floor, with three wooden chairs. That was the only furniture. One wall was a mirror that was probably two-way glass. An overhead fixture encased in a wire cage provided the only illumination. The locked door had a tall window in it, outside of which stood the guard, who appeared disinterested even though he glanced into the room every four or five seconds. The room held the scent of stale sweat and desperation that Coop recognized from his days in the department. Hopelessness had seeped with tears and perspiration into the scarred wooden table.

"Have you got any news for me?" Sue asked. "What did your friends say—the ones you were going to talk to about my case?"

Deni hesitated.

"You know," Sue hurried on, "your friends at NBC News and *Time* magazine and—"

Deni smiled and shook her head. "You're going to have to be patient, Sue. I know it's hard. But all that has to wait until my book comes out. That's the time to start beating the drums. To raise a media outcry about correcting this miscarriage of justice and freeing you. Remember some time ago that convict Hurricane Carter, how he was finally freed after years in prison? Well, I'm going to make freeing you my personal crusade, I promise you."

Sue's lips tightened. She blinked back tears.

Deni freed her hand from Sue's and reached for a notepad. "Right now, though, we have to ask you a few questions."

Sue's face hardened. "I've heard that so many times. . . ."

"You have nothing to fear from questions, Sue. You're innocent. I know that."

"What about him?" Sue asked, seeming to notice Coop for the first time.

Deni looked with Sue at him.

"Do you know I'm innocent?" Sue asked Coop.

"No. But I think there's a chance you are, or I wouldn't be here." It had sickened Coop, the way Deni was playing this young woman's hopes to get information out of her. He was going to be straight with her.

"Deni said on the phone you were an ex-cop. I don't trust ex-cops."

Coop smiled at her. "You're right in that. Most of us don't have much compassion for the bad guys."

"She's not one of the bad guys," Deni said. She sounded exasperated. Coop wasn't buttering up Sue enough.

"I'm being honest," he said. "Most ex-cops are that, too."

"I haven't noticed such a trait," Sue told him.

"You can start noticing it. If I think you're innocent I'll do what I can to help you. If it looks to me like you're really guilty, I'll work to leave you right where you are."

"Take it easy on her," Deni said. "She's been put through a horrible ordeal and there's no justification. She's completely innocent."

Sue's eyes drifted back to Deni. She could never hear that word *innocent* from her supposed savior often enough. She must have spent hours every day thinking about Deni, imagining what Deni was doing for her in the outside world. Prisoners were so helpless, so easily manipulated by the unscrupulous.

Like Deni Green.

The writer was all business now, opening her notepad, fixing a cool, appraising gaze on Sue. "You've told me Marlee showed you a route into her condo complex that would keep you from being seen. And when she was expecting you, she left a gate open and deactivated an alarm."

Sue nodded. "Right. Marlee was so paranoid about anybody finding out she was a lesbian. She didn't even want her neighbors to set eyes on me."

"But the killer got in completely unseen. He must have known about your route in. Could Marlee have told anyone she was expecting you that night?"

"No," Sue said quickly. She'd been asked that question many times and was bored with it.

"Sue—" began Deni.

Sue squirmed in her chair and made pale fists of her slender hands and fingers. "That's all I've been thinking about in here, and I can't come up with an answer."

"She must have let it slip to somebody. Must have. let her guard down sometime. Think, Sue, did she mention anyone—"

"No," said the prisoner stubbornly. "She didn't let her guard down. Couldn't. She was a wealthy and famous person. You have no idea how people tried to take advantage of her."

"But if she met someone who was charming and easy to talk to—"

"You've told me about your Ted Bundy theory," Sue said, "and I'm sorry but I just can't believe it. Marlee was a public person with a secret she thought could destroy her, or at least cost her a fortune. She would have been very suspicious of a charming stranger trying to worm his way into her confidence. She'd assume he was a reporter."

"If there had been some man she was close to," Coop said, "would Marlee have told you about him?"

"Of course! We didn't have any secrets. She told me often enough I was the one person in the world she trusted. Anyway, she'd had enough of men and simply wouldn't have been vulnerable in that way to one of them."

Coop had to ask. "What about another woman?"

Sue stood up from her chair. The guard outside the room caught the sudden movement with one of his sidelong glances and stiffened and stood square to the window in the door.

"I'll never believe that!" Sue hissed.

"Sit back down," Coop said. "I told you I'd be honest with you. You're no fool, and you know I had to ask that question."

Sue settled back into her chair. "Now you know the answer."

But Coop wondered if he did.

"We did have to ask you about the possibility of someone else," Deni said.

Sue shook her head. "Not another woman."

Deni looked her in the eye. "I told you the footprint we found was made by a man."

"The man who killed Marlee," Sue said.

There was another question Coop had to ask. "Did Marlee ever mention a woman named Bette?"

Sue looked down at the table. This question was new, and she gave it careful thought. But in the end she shook her head no. "Not that I can recall." She looked up at Coop. "Who is she?"

"My daughter. If she and Bette were killed by the

same person, I thought there might have been some sort of connection between them in life."

Sue looked at him for a moment in silence. "Deni told me about that on the phone. I'm sorry."

Coop smiled at her and nodded, believing her. She *was* sorry, and that more than anything else made him think there was a real chance she was innocent.

"Had Marlee done any traveling in the weeks before her death?" Deni asked.

"Oh, sure. She was always flying somewhere or other to film a commercial or do commentary on a tennis match. She got back from the U.S. Open only a few days before she died."

"Sometime, someplace, Marlee met her killer," Deni said. "And so did Bette Cooper and a lot of other women. We have to find the connecting thread."

"I wish I could help you!" Sue said, sounding as if she might begin to sob.

Deni smiled beatifically at her, the way Nero might have smiled gazing at a fire. "You are helping, dear! Just keep trying and you'll remember something critical. Keep thinking about what happened the night of the murder and before."

Sue didn't look at them as she said sadly, "Don't you know that's all 1 do think about?"

Outside again, in the bright sunlight, Deni looked at Coop. "I suppose you think I'm an asshole after the way I questioned Sue."

"You're using her," Coop said.

"No more than I have to."

"For what? So you can write a best-seller?"

"A best-seller that will reveal she didn't kill Marlee Clark, and set her free," Deni said.

* * *

During the flight back to New York, Deni sat quietly beside Coop. They were flying first class, paid for by Whippet. Deni had made a show of that and reminded Coop of it three times since they'd boarded. But that was all she'd talked about. He knew she was disappointed by the way the interview with Sue Coppolino had gone. Despite the careful preparation Deni had obviously made over the phone, no new ground had been broken.

Somewhere over the Carolinas, Coop noticed Deni staring at the flight steward who'd brought her her third Bloody Mary. The man was handsome in a clothes catalog way and well into his forties. He moved about the cabin smoothly and professionally, smiling warmly, making sure passengers' needs were being met.

Coop knew Deni was aware he was watching her, but he didn't ask her why she was observing the attendant so closely. She told him anyway.

"See that attendant?" she said.

"Sure. He's six feet tall, the only one standing up, and wearing a uniform."

She ignored his sarcasm. "Consider the opportunities somebody like that has."

"It's no way to make pilot."

She looked pityingly at him and shook her head. "You're making a joke out of a very serious matter."

"Only because I think you're about to make a digression. You remind me of a partner I worked with in the department a long time ago. He'd always look for clues outside if the weather was good, inside if it was raining. And always where the light was best."

"I know what you mean, but that's not what I'm doing here. That's a good-looking, personable guy."

"It's part of his job to make people like him."

"So he's good at it. That's my point. On a long flight, in a half-empty plane, he could chat with a woman for a long time. He could give her drinks, make them stronger than she suspected. He could work on her, all seemingly very innocent. People will talk freely with a flight attendant, thinking they'll never see him again."

"True enough," Coop admitted. He knew it was a fallacy that people opened up the most to friends and family. Some matters were more freely discussed with bartenders or even perfect strangers, anonymous confessions that were like trial balloons in the face of God.

"Did your daughter fly anywhere recently?" Deni asked.

He thought back. "She went to California on business a few months ago."

"Uh-huh." Deni took a sip of her Bloody Mary. "I bet I'll find that all the victims took flights not long before their deaths."

"You may well, but it won't necessarily mean anything."

"If there's any correlation, I'll find it. You'd be surprised what I can find online. I'll cross-check victims' flights with airline personnel records and crew rosters. I'm a dedicated hacker, Coop. I don't give up."

This new sense of direction had jolted Deni out of her uncharacteristically quiet mood. She talked the rest of the way to La Guardia.

She was still hot on her theory when Coop's cab dropped her off in front of her Manhattan apartment.

As the cab pulled away, he watched her enter her building. He thought of his own apartment, his own bed, only twenty blocks away. He wondered if he could stay awake until he got there.

He felt utterly exhausted. And he felt like a criminal himself, after the way he and Deni had worked Sue Coppolino, held hope in front of her nose like a carrot. There was actually little hope. It saddened him that a young, vital woman like Coppolino would probably spend the rest of her life in prison, where she would die.

In the dim backseat of the cab rocketing through Manhattan, a mood darker than the night took him over. "Where we goin' now, buddy?" the driver asked over his shoulder.

I wish I knew, Coop thought, and recited his address like a lost child.

CHAPTER FOURTEEN

Coop sat in his car waiting for Maureen to emerge from the office building in midtown Manhattan where she worked. Her employer was Allied National, one of the giants of the insurance business. Coop wasn't quite sure what her job title was these days, but she'd been with the company a long time. Insurance seemed to suit her; she was the sort of person who always dwelled on the worst possible outcome.

A steady stream of people issued from the revolving doors of the skyscraper. Maureen stepped out of the crowd, glanced around, saw Coop's Honda, and headed toward him. Coatless despite the cold, she was wearing a plain gray dress, ugly ankle-high socks, and the usual clunky shoes made, probably, out of old tires. Her bra strap that was barely visible at the shoulder was the light tan color of natural cotton. Her slip and underwear, he knew, would be the same color. Maureen refused to wear chemically dyed clothing next to her skin. Yet she had dyed her hair red. Well, everyone had inconsistencies, but Maureen was so blissfully unaware of hers. He'd learned not to mention them to her.

She had become stranger and stranger to him during the final year of their marriage as the stress of being a cop's wife ate away at her. Never a religious person, after the divorce she had adopted causes as a spiritual substitute. They were mostly causes of concern and gentleness, as if she wanted to distance herself as far as possible from Coop's violent world that had pervaded and poisoned their married life.

She didn't smile as she approached the car and got in beside him, bringing a swirl of cold air with her. It was Maureen who had called him and suggested lunch so they might discuss their daughter's murder.

After saying hello to him she stared glumly ahead. He considered again that if she thought more of herself, took better care of herself, she would still be attractive. But that wasn't the new Maureen. She had no makeup on today and was wearing her gray mood as she was her gray dress. Coop didn't blame her. He wasn't looking forward to lunch either. He had a great deal to tell her, but he didn't know how she'd react.

He checked traffic and gunned the engine, pulling out in front of a lumbering Madison Avenue bus. "There's a nice place around the corner," he said, "called Ferrante's or something like that."

"Ferado's," she said. "We're not going there."

They were getting off to a good start.

"Ferado's has Italian subs for me," he said, "veggie pastas for you. I thought it would be a nice compromise."

"Nice for you, maybe. They use the same pans and utensils, so the vegetarian dishes get tainted with meat. I can't go to any restaurant that serves meat. I get sick afterward."

"Okay," Coop said. "How about the vegetarian restaurant on Fifty-second?"

"No. They use butter, milk, eggs."

She suggested a place called the Common Carrot, and Coop capitulated, even though it was way down in the East Village.

Traffic was bad and the drive turned out to be long. Maureen was silent. Coop considered beginning his report on the investigation, then thought *Not yet.* Instead he asked, "What do you believe is wrong with eating dairy products?" She didn't answer. He looked over in time to see her lips tighten. He thought he'd used a respectful tone. "I can see where you think it's cruel to kill animals and eat them, but shearing a sheep or milking a cow doesn't harm it."

"People have no right to enslave animals, to keep chickens in tiny pens and cows in narrow stalls all their lives."

"Well, we can agree that nobody should be unnecessarily cruel to animals."

"You're being sarcastic. You'd like to think I'm just a sentimentalist, weeping over brown-eyed bossy, wouldn't you? But I'm worried about people's health, too. We're violating the natural order more and more and we'll pay the price."

"I wasn't being sarcastic. I actually admire your concern for fellow creatures, human and otherwise."

This was like when they were still married, the verbal duelling, the disconnection, the cold space between them ever widening. He decided to give up the conversation and concentrate on his driving.

When they reached Thompkins Square, where the restaurant was located, there were no parking spaces.

Coop doubleparked and flipped down his visor with the NYPD OFFICIAL BUSINESS sign he'd forgotten to turn in when he retired. He expected Maureen to make a comment about the arrogance of power, but she let it pass.

The Common Carrot occupied the ground floor of an ancient row house, between a store that sold old records, the vinyl kind, and a tattooing and piercing parlor. It had sidewalk tables, empty because of the chilly weather, and a big window giving a view of the square.

The restaurant was crowded, but Coop was the only man wearing a tie. Maybe the only person wearing leather shoes. He was relieved to sit down and get them out of sight. The table was wooden, unstained and unpainted. At least the walls were painted, the same drab green that had been in his office at the precinct. It didn't matter, because not much of the paintwork could be seen. Political posters championing animal rights and environmental causes took up most of the wall space. Across from their table hung a large poster of a bulky woman wearing dark, turn-of-the-century clothing and a white sun bonnet. She looked as glum as Maureen, only more fierce.

"That's Mother Jones," Maureen said, noticing him examining the painting.

"The labor leader?"

She raised her eyebrows, also dyed the new red color, and looked surprised that he'd heard of Mother Jones. And a little resentful. She obviously considered Mother Jones hers. Coop didn't see any connection between Mother Jones and natural products, but he didn't push it for fear of further raising Maureen's hackles.

Instead he opened the large, thick menu. *There must be a tremendous variety of entrées,* he thought. In fact the menu was more of a manifesto. He had to go through pages of political statements before he got to the food.

A waiter so thin and pale he might never have experienced solid food approached the table. Maureen ordered bottled water and a salad without dressing. Coop wondered how she maintained her thickened build, eating that way. He ordered the veggie burger, french-fried sweet potatoes, and a draft beer. This might not be so bad. The waiter smiled wanly and departed.

"Should you be drinking beer?" Maureen asked.

"Probably not."

"You think it's none of my business," she muttered. "Private, secretive, just like you."

Maybe she's right, Coop thought.

They were halfway through an unpleasant lunch before their dead daughter was mentioned. Coop realized neither of them had wanted to bring up the subject, though Bette was the reason they were there.

"You wanted my report about Bette," he said

"You can call it that if you like," Maureen said, expertly folding and spearing dry lettuce with her fork.

She continued to eat while he recounted his talk with Billard and his trip to Haverton. When he started talking about Deni Green, though, Maureen put down her fork. She said nothing but listened intently.

"Do you agree with this woman that a serial killer murdered our daughter?" she asked, when he was finished.

"I don't know. And I can't promise you that we'll ever know."

She used her fork to toy with a tomato wedge, then looked up at him. "What would be the motive of such a man?"

"Maybe nothing we'd understand," Coop told her. "Compulsive serial killers are moved in ways that normal people aren't. They have certain hang-ups at times impossible for us to know about, or to understand even after we do learn about them. Almost all of them were mistreated as kids."

"They hate their mothers."

Coop thought that was a strange thing for her to say. "Sometimes. Often."

"What about female killers? Do they hate their fathers?"

"There aren't many female serial killers," Coop said. "Women don't react to certain kinds of adversity the same way as men."

"A nice way of saying you're the violent gender. Lots of women are molested by their fathers, but they don't go out and kill men. Why not?"

"I don't know. Maybe you're the forgiving gender."

"No," she said sharply. "Some things can't be forgiven."

He looked at her, wondering. "Were you molested by your father, Maureen?"

She flinched and glared at him. "What makes you think you have the right to ask a question like that? Think you're still my husband? Think you're still a cop?"

He realized she hadn't said no, but he let the subject drop. She was right, he shouldn't have asked the question. "Getting inside the thought processes of this kind of killer can be impossible at times," he said. "Sometimes they themselves block out the horror of what they were compelled to do. They've been known to pass lie detector tests."

"Are you saying the killer himself might not even know he committed these crimes?"

"It's possible. It's happened before."

"That's absurd. Cop talk to excuse the fact that they never catch some random killers."

Coop decided not to argue. Cop talk had always been a language Maureen didn't understand.

"Deni Green," she said. "What do you think of her?"

"I'm not sure I trust her."

"Why is that?"

"She takes advantage of people's vulnerabilities or their inattention."

"She sounds smart. Insightful."

"I suppose she's both those things."

"I want you to promise to stay with Deni Green on this, even though her motives might be selfish."

"I already decided to do that," Coop said. "If we can come up with some solid evidence that this killer exists, I'll take it to the NYPD or the FBI. Then we'll get some action."

"How you love a bureaucracy with a set of initials. A lone woman has a better chance of catching Bette's killer than any male-dominated bureaucracy."

He was careful to keep his voice neutral. "How do you figure?"

"Women understand men who kill women. That's because you all do it, in all kinds of different ways, either slowly or quickly. Probably Deni Green has experienced that, just as I have. I'm inclined to trust her."

"Remember I was Bette's father," Coop said.

"What's that got to do with it?"

"I care about her. Deni Green doesn't. She's working against a deadline to write a sensational best-seller. Bette is just another victim to her."

"I'm still not getting you."

"Investigations are hard to control—even when you haven't got an ambitious writer in on them. Facts about Bette may come out that we don't know—maybe that we don't want to know."

"You're talking about yourself. Men are obsessed with hiding their vulnerabilities, stifling their emotions. That's what makes you afraid of the truth. There's nothing about Bette that I'm afraid to find out."

She returned to her salad.

Coop realized they were through talking. He took another bite of his quasi hamburger. It was surprisingly good, but he'd lost his appetite.

Maureen finished her salad, then dug in her purse and laid a handful of one-dollar bills on the table. She clutched her half-empty plastic bottle of water and stood up. "It's a nice day," she said. "I'll walk for a while, then catch a bus uptown."

Coop picked up the bills and tried to hand them back to her, but she'd turned and was stalking toward the exit. She rounded a corner into the vestibule and he didn't actually see her leave, but a minute later her stolid form in the gray dress passed by one of the windows. She was walking with her head bowed, frowning and gnawing her lower lip.

She does hate me, he thought. *She really does hate me. For someone to hate me that much,* I must *deserve it at least a little bit.*

He wondered, though. When they bad gone into counseling together in an attempt to save their marriage, it had been suggested to Maureen that the hatred she directed toward others was really of herself. He recalled the pang of pity he'd felt for her when he'd heard that. Conveniently, she would say. Maybe she was right. She hated him and he deserved it.

Complicated, Coop thought. People were so damned complicated. And more exposed to danger than they imagined. That was why they were easily victimized. Just when they thought they were secure, that's when they found they were most vulnerable.

He sat for a while, munching the few remaining french-fried sweet potatoes without really tasting them. His gaze fell on his glass of microbrewery draft. It was untouched, which surprised him. Had Maureen's conversation about diet and health gotten under his skin? Did she actually care about his health? Were there still remnants of affection?

Complicated

He picked up the glass of beer and drained it.

CHAPTER FIFTEEN

The Night Caller knew Ann Callahan.

Knew everything about her.

Almost.

There was her familiar head, visible at times when the bus she was riding turned a corner. There was her firm chin and slightly uptilted nose, her dark hair arranged to fall lightly about her narrow shoulders. A sharp and distinctive profile.

The bus lumbered and belched fumes from stop to stop through Queens, along seemingly endless Northern Boulevard. The Night Caller's car stayed well behind the bus. Other cars got in the way, but he didn't worry. You couldn't lose a bus, if you knew the route as well as he did.

The bus would turn soon, and Ann Callahan would emerge at her regular stop and walk to the apartment in Flushing where she lived with her father and mother. When the weather was clear, like tonight, the Night Caller would park across the street and observe her lithe figure cross back and forth at the apartment windows. First she would be in the dress she'd worn to work; then he might catch a silhouetted glimpse of her changing clothes in her upstairs bedroom, then in casual clothes, blouses or sweaters, with slacks or jeans. A fashion show. A doll in a dollhouse.

The Night Caller found a certain charm in that. Steering with his left hand, he slipped his right into his pocket and closed it about the plastic saint.

Ann sat staring idly out through her reflection in the bus window at the cars keeping pace with or edging past the lumbering vehicle. Hers was a cheerless existence, especially since her older sister Cara had moved out, gotten a place of her own in Manhattan. That left only Ann and her parents. The Callahans had emigrated from Belfast when the sectarian terrorism was at its worst. Ann's father, Kevin, had brought his strict Catholicism with him. And his fear.

Sometimes Ann thought her father ought to be grateful to New York. The city had employed him for decades in the sort of arid clerking job that suited his crabbed nature. Instead he railed against New York, regarding it as the worst possible place for his two daughters, a city that was both a garden of temptations and a jungle of danger.

He and his wife had raised their daughters strictly, hemming them in with rules and prohibitions, punishing them severely for any transgression. Even now he kept them on a short leash. He couldn't spank them or put them to bed without supper anymore, but he could work on their guilt. He'd had a triple bypass two years before, and he made it clear to the girls that any lapse,

any resistance on their part, might bring death for him—
and decades of recrimination for them.

Ann had discovered, with wonder and admiration,
that Cara had a stiff enough spine to resist the old man.
When she moved to her own place, though, he took it
out on Ann. Each day she made the long trip to a mid-
Manhattan skyscraper, where she worked in a teller's
cage or sat in a cubicle and tapped on a keyboard at
Mercantile Mutual Bank. And each evening she made
her way home by subway or bus, in time to set the table
for the family dinner her mother had prepared. It was
entirely clear to Ann that she was supposed to stay at
home until it was time to take her mother's place, to be
the spinster daughter who looked after her father until
he went to his eternal reward.

Even knowing this, Ann couldn't stand up to her father. She was a mild, sweet-natured girl. She had love
in her. And hope. And ambition, sometimes. Only sometimes.

She was trapped, and she accepted her fate.

Which was too bad not only for her but for the Night
Caller. Ann Callahan's drab life was so circumscribed
that it created only limited opportunity for him. She
left home only to commute to work, or attend church
with her parents, or on rare occasion go to a shop or a
movie. If she stuck to her routine, it would be difficult
for the Night Caller to have a private session with her.

He glanced at the dashboard clock. Tonight, at least,
Ann wouldn't have to make any apologies or excuses.
She was going to arrive while her father's favorite

newscast was still going on and he hadn't begun to worry about her. She'd have plenty of time to set the dollhouse table. The bus was pulling up to her stop.

It had become dark, and the bus's brake lights were dull red stars in the haze of its exhaust fumes as it slowed and pulled to the curb. Half a block behind it, the Night Caller's car also pulled to the curb and sat with its engine idling.

Two extremely fat women stood politely to the side at the bus's front door while an old man with a cane climbed gingerly down to the street. Two teenage boys in Knicks warm-up suits jumped from the rear door and went swaggering down the block. A woman emerged from the rear door after them, just as the fat women were climbing into the bus. Not Ann Callahan, though, an older woman carrying a shopping bag. *Not Ann Callahan.*

The Night Caller's heartbeat quickened as the bus rumbled and accelerated back into the sporadic stream of traffic.

So Ann was going to make it one of *those* rare nights. Once in a great while she would steal a little time for herself. Her usual practice was to call in the afternoon and say that she had to work late. Her father would put up with that, if she didn't do it too often. Ordinarily she waited two weeks or more. But this time it had been only a week. The Night Caller had followed her on Wednesday. And here it was Wednesday again. No doubt about where she was going, then.

The Night Caller's car jumped away from the curb and caught up with the bus, passed it smoothly to pull in front of it before the next traffic light.

The bus didn't make the light.

No matter.

The Night Caller knew its destination, and Ann's. The end of the line. He drove along slowly, just keeping the bus in sight in his rearview mirror. The mirror framed the bus, made it real. The Night Caller's car was only one of many, sometimes nothing but taillights like the red eyes of a demon among other demons. Unnoticed. Unreal. The future looking into the past. Mirrors could do that.

Gradually, electric signs gave way to trees. The traffic thinned and streetlights dimmed as they neared the border between Queens and Nassau County. The bus pulled up to its last stop.

Ann stepped down from the bus and stood in the darkness beneath the trees, watching the vehicle's box-like bulk recede down the street. She didn't move until its twin taillights drew close together and disappeared as it turned a corner.

She looked around, took an obvious deep breath, and strode through a small parklike area onto the campus of a community college.

Ann had considered registering for classes here some time ago but had changed her mind. Perhaps because she was shy, or she simply couldn't afford the meager tuition. Possibly she'd been considering classes simply as a way to meet men. True, she was an adult and her father couldn't stop her from dating, but he did arrange his periods of ill health to coincide with her dates. She'd never been able to talk him out of waiting up for her. And cross-examining her. And pestering her to invite the young man to a family dinner. Eventually she'd given up. She hadn't dated or even been to a party in months.

The Night Caller followed her at a distance along winding sidewalks, past unlighted brick buildings, until she came to a building whose lobby and windows glowed. The Fine Arts Building, according to the lettering over its entrance.

She entered as she had before and walked along the hall, past a cluster of night students sitting on the stairs and talking. One of them, a handsome black man with a shaved head and an earring stud, smiled at her as she passed, but Ann didn't pause. Her father would be proud, the Night Caller thought wryly. He followed as she climbed the stairs and turned down a dimly lit hall. Most of the doors along the hall were open to dark rooms.

As she approached a narrow rectangle of light cast through one of the doors, Ann slowed her pace. There was a small window in the door at eye level.

With deliberate slowness Ann walked past the door and glanced in through the window. In the light that suddenly transformed her face, the Night Caller saw her slight smile. It was the sort of smile not meant for others to see.

Ten paces beyond the door she paused, turned, and repeated the procedure, moving in the opposite direction.

The Night Caller didn't have to look in the room to know what was going on inside. He'd checked last week. This was a class in figure drawing. The model was a man. A young and rather muscular young man. The Night Caller had been a bit startled when he'd glanced in last week; not so many years ago male models in college had worn jockstraps. Not anymore. Luckily for Ann.

This time the Night Caller, ducking back into the shadows of one of the darkened classrooms, didn't see Ann's secret smile, but it was certainly there. He smiled as she walked past unaware of being observed. Ann did this almost every week. It was the repressed young woman's little thrill that she thought was harmless and private. It was a safe bet that she'd be back next Wednesday.

She would retrace her steps to the street now, and catch the inbound bus. Back home, in maimed love and light, her mother was no doubt keeping her dinner warm in the oven, and her father was watching the clock. They were calling her, making no sound, but she heard them. Lonely calling lonely.

The Night Caller waited until her footfalls echoed up the stairwell before following. It was an art, maintaining a proper distance when shadowing, interpreting body language and anticipating the subject. But it was easier if you were already inside the mind and skin of the person you were following. If you knew her apartness and desperation and galaxylike pattern of tiny moles on the inside of her right thigh.

Once they were outside the building, Ann seemed preoccupied, not at all on guard, for an attractive young woman walking alone across a dark campus. Not that it mattered. She was safe tonight.

For the Night Caller this was merely an exercise.

Practice and prelude.

CHAPTER SIXTEEN

It was the kind of unseasonably warm October afternoon that made everyone wish at least for the moment that there were no winters to come. Coop sat at an outdoor table at Seconds, just beginning to feel a fall chill creeping in from the bay. On Billard's recommendation, he'd ordered the crab bisque and wasn't disappointed.

Billard had something going here, Coop decided. He'd hired the right chef, composed the right menu, and chosen a beautiful spot overlooking the inlet. The restaurant might make for a good retirement for Billard, and department politics being what they were, maybe sooner than he suspected.

Billard appeared on the wooden deck and talked briefly with a table of about six diners who were oohing and ahing over their lunch; then he walked smiling over to where Coop sat at a corner of the wood railing. He was still smiling as he sat down opposite Coop in one of the green plastic chairs. Behind him Coop could see the white hulls of pleasure boats bobbing in the marina down the shoreline, the fall sunlight sparking silver off the water. It was a world he didn't want to leave.

"So did I steer you right on the bisque?" Billard asked.

"It's delicious, Art," Coop said honestly. "I was just thinking, you've got something here to retire to when you're ready."

"Yeah. I like the restaurant business, and if this place flies it'll take up more and more of my time. But I'm not quite ready to retire. I'm still a cop at heart."

"Aren't we all?" Coop said.

A waiter arrived and placed a glass of white wine before Billard, who waited until the man had departed before answering Coop. "I've got a feeling you didn't come here just for lunch, old friend."

Coop took a sip of the Beck's dark he was having with his lunch, enjoying it all the more because of Dr. Gregory's advice to limit himself to one glass. "No, I came to fulfill my part in the bargain about Bette's murder. Remember, I promised to keep you posted."

He filled in Billard on his visit to Haverton and his arrangement with Deni Green. He was glad to see that Billard was listening closely; he'd even pulled out a pen and was diligently making notes on a napkin.

"Will you see what information you might have on Lloyd Watkins?" Coop asked, when he was finished and Billard had clipped his pen back in his shirt pocket.

Billard nodded. "It'll be done." He took a slow sip of wine and swished it around in his mouth before swallowing. "Listen, Coop, I don't much like this deal you have with the writer. Think you can trust her not to royally screw up the investigation?"

"No. And that's pretty much the way I'm going to deal with her. I don't want Bette's . . . I don't think my daughter's private life should be in a book."

"Nobody's should," Billard said. "Not even the ones who want their private lives there and think everybody else'll be fascinated reading about them."

"Deni Green might prove useful, though. She's not stupid, and she brings her own slant on things."

"She given you a new slant on the case?"

"I don't know for sure, Art. There's the interview with Sue Coppolino. It wasn't what I expected."

Billard rolled his eyes. "She's the only one in the place who's innocent, right?"

"Sure. That I expected. It was more how she acted. Her attitude toward Deni Green. Toward me."

"You think she might not have killed her tennis star lover?" Billard sat back and watched Coop, knowing a cop's answer to that kind of question about a convicted killer wouldn't be given lightly.

"I'm not sure she's guilty," Coop said.

Both men sat silently and watched a small pleasure boat carrying a man, woman, and teenage girl set in at the restaurant's dock. It was a fiberglass fourteen-foot runabout with no closed cabin and no room below the deck. Though the day was warm, it must have been cold out on the water. All three of the boaters were bundled in sweaters and wearing baseball caps pulled down tight above their ears.

"What about you?" Coop asked, as they watched the three leave their boat tied at the dock and enter the restaurant.

"Me?" Billard asked.

"What are the developments on your side of the bargain?"

"The truth is there are none," Billard said. "Not that we haven't been working. There's nothing on the plastic saints. And there doesn't seem to be any way to match the partial sole print with its manufacturer."

"Maybe the shoe was made by a foreign manufacturer."

"Probably it was. Most shoes seem to be made overseas these days. We're still checking and might come up with a match. But I have to stress *might.*"

Coop paused with a spoonful of bisque halfway to his mouth. "You still don't think the two prints in those photos were made by the same shoe?"

"C'mon, Coop, you know the prints aren't all that conclusive. If they were, there'd be no doubt we'd have the same doer in both crimes."

"What about the powder from latex gloves?"

"Latex gloves were probably invented in prison. Plenty of bad guys see them as part of their wardrobe these days."

Coop knew Billard was right, but he didn't like it. He placed his spoon back in his bowl. "Maybe Maureen's on target."

Billard glowered. "Don't give me that bullshit. You really think a cop might have killed Bette?"

"I didn't mean about a cop being the killer, or any kind of police conspiracy. I mean about police apathy."

"I'm going to let what you said pass, and remind you I'm not the one in charge of the investigation."

Coop pushed his anger, his frustration, to a far part of his mind, but it still roiled in his belly. What he wished was that SID, the NYPD Special Investigation Department, would recognize that a serial killer might be active and take over the case. "I didn't mean you personally, Art. We both know crime doesn't take a break just because a murder is tremendously important to anybody. There's only so much time and so many cops. But that means it's possible Bette's murder's not getting the attention it deserves."

"I can't deny that's true, Coop. That's why I haven't asked you as a friend to butt out of the case. She was your daughter, and I understand how you feel. But be careful of your dealings with this Deni Green character."

"That you can count on, Art."

Billard forced a smile. "So finish your bisque."

Coop lifted his spoon again and started to do as Billard suggested, putting on an act to preserve their friendship, trying to change the mood.

"Speaking of Maureen, how's she doing?" Billard asked. "How's she handling her grief?"

"She's mad as hell," Coop said.

"Anger can be part of the grieving process."

"She was mad as hell before Bette's murder. Now she's got some direction." Billard stood up and patted Coop's shoulder. "Time'll pass. Things'll get better for both of you."

"Thanks, Art."

He knew Billard was right about Maureen's anger. She grieved, but she'd do anything now rather than reveal her emotions to Coop. Her anger, her causes, masked a great deal of pain.

Coop watched Billard walk back into the restaurant,

pausing to talk again to the diners who'd praised his food as he came out onto the deck. Politician, homicide detective, restaurateur.

In the interest of friendship, he finished his crab bisque before it got cold.

CHAPTER SEVENTEEN

"Georgianna?"

Cindy Romero, Georgianna Mason's friend from her college days, knocked again on Georgianna's apartment door, then pressed her ear against the cool wood. She and Georgianna were members of a book club that met once a week. Georgianna hadn't attended last night to discuss the mystery novel they'd all read. She hadn't answered her phone this morning. And when Cindy had called her office number at Northwestern Centre Imports, she was told Georgianna hadn't reported for work the last two days and hadn't called in. The company had tried in vain to contact her, and would Cindy please call them if she found out where Georgianna was, to reassure them that nothing was wrong.

Cindy hadn't felt so reassured after that conversation. On her lunch hour, she'd taken a cab to Georgianna's apartment to see if her friend was home, and to slip a note under her door if she was out.

It was when she stooped to slide the note beneath the door that she first noticed the odor.

She leaned farther forward. supporting herself on one elbow, and sniffed where the door didn't quite meet the threshold.

Cindy recoiled immediately and stood up, swaying and trying to steady herself with a hand against the door. She swiped her free hand across her face as if she could wipe away remnants of the stench seeping out of the apartment.

Backing away, she leaned against the opposite wall of the corridor, staring at the blank face of the closed door. It was a long time before she was reasonably sure she wasn't going to vomit. She tried her cell phone, but its battery was dead. Still walking unsteadily, she made her way to the elevator. On the ground floor, she hurried to the door she remembered marked BUILDING MANAGER. The police! Someone had to call the police!

The harder Cindy pounded on the building manager's door, the more upset she became.

"I probably oughtn't have left her alone," said Ida Kling, the Ardmont Apartments manager. "Soon as she came down to get me, I could see how upset she was. So I went upstairs with her right off to see what she was talking about. She sure was right—there was a hellacious odor coming outta that apartment." Ida paused, made a face, then swallowed. She was a stocky, fiftyish woman who might have been playing Russian peasants in the movies if her life had taken another path. She was as strong a person as she appeared. But what she'd seen today had gotten to her in a familiar way, and one she never wanted to experience again. She'd been affected this way ten years ago when she found her first husband after he'd killed himself with his twelve-gauge shotgun. Waves of nausea, waves of disbelief. *Again!* she'd found herself thinking when she'd gazed at what was in the apartment's bathtub. *Please not again!* But there were the images bright in her mind, so vivid with color and horror.

"Mrs. Kling?" Seattle Detective Sergeant Roy Lyons asked her. "Want to sit down?"

"I'm all right," she assured him.

"You let yourself and Miss Romero in with your master key?"

"Yes, but you could smell the stench some even out in the hall. Then when we opened the door it was awful, the way it hit us. Wasn't no doubt where it was coming from. We cupped our hands over our noses and went into the bathroom, and we . . . saw it and both gagged and backed right out. We both almost fainted. Well, Miss Romero there did faint. I had something to lean on." She pointed toward a high-backed chair near the bathroom door. "She looked okay enough curled up like she was on the carpet outside the bathroom. I thought she'd stay fainted while I went downstairs to my place to call you. I didn't wanna touch the phone here, didn't wanna touch anything. You don't have to be no cop to know that's what you're supposed to do at crime scenes."

Lyons, a muscular man in a brown suit, nodded somberly, letting her know he thought she'd been wise.

"When I came back up here, Miss Romero was sitting up, and when she saw me she started in screaming. I quieted her down and helped her to her feet, held on to her tight, then got her out into the hall quick as I could."

Lyons nodded again. Very wise.

After a few more preliminary statements, he thanked Ida Kling and sent her out of Georgianna Mason's apartment. The crime techs and medical examiner were still crowded into the tiny tiled bathroom, examining the scene of the murder, examining what was left of Georgianna in the crusted brown soup in the bathtub. There was no room for Lyons. He was glad. He didn't want to go back in there. But he knew he would. Then he would again, in his dreams.

He turned to his partner, plainclothes detective Marty Sanderson, and glanced at what was inside the red smudged plastic bag Sanderson was holding in his right hand. "A can opener," he said. "Jesus!"

Sanderson, a calm, stocky man with a bushy head of hair still black despite his forty-five years, said, "The bastard kinda skinned her. I bet she died of shock." Not much got to Sanderson. The dead woman's features had been incongruously peaceful and composed in her discolored bath, but they'd soon discovered that beneath the water's surface she'd been reduced to exposed bone and shreds of free-floating flesh. The sight seemed only to have sobered Sanderson somewhat. At least he wasn't cracking his usual sick jokes the way he often did at murder scenes.

"I hope to God she died fast," Lyons said.

"Me, too," Sanderson said simply. "But I bet she didn't. Whoever killed her probably closed her eyes, too. Maybe her mouth. Ever seen this kinda thing before?"

"Not like this," Lyons said, purposely veering his thoughts, any mental images, away from the cramped tile bathroom with its palpable horror.

"You can't smell her so much out here," Sanderson remarked. "Or else we're getting used to it."

"Jesus, Marty!"

"Yeah, sorry."

"She musta been dead awhile."

"Yeah. We'll see what the ME has to say."

Lyons flipped open the leather cover of his note-book, more for something to do than for any other rea-son. "The Romero woman said Georgianna had an ex-husband, lives right here in Seattle."

"I hope it's him. "

"Why's that, Marty?"

"I don't want to see this kind of thing again, ever. And the way I figure it, when you see this sort of killing, the hate and rage it must have taken, always look to the spouse."

Lyons agreed, knowing that in fact they always did look first to the spouse in these kinds of cases. He reached into a pocket and got out a roll of mints, used his thumbnail to peel one off, and slipped it into his mouth. It was his third since entering the apartment. The strong scent of the mints took the edge off the stench of death and helped hold nausea in check.

"Sure wouldn't want to see this one develop into us having a serial killer on our hands," Sanderson said.

The remote possibility made Lyons wince. "There's no reason to think we have to worry about that." For the first time, Lyons was aware of traffic noises filter-ing up from down in the street. He was glad to hear them, reassured that there was a normal world out there beyond the hell of Georgianna Mason's apart-ment. He closed his notebook and tucked it into an in-side pocket of his suit coat, then glanced around at ground already covered. "No sign of forced entry or a struggle. She probably knew and trusted whoever killed her."

"Like he was family," Sanderson said.

"Family," Lyons agreed. He placed his fists on his hips and shook his head in disbelief. "A goddamn can opener! And maybe while she was still alive. What must *that* have been like? Only a flaming psycho could have done such a thing!"

"Look to the spouse," Sanderson advised again. "You got another one of those mints?"

CHAPTER EIGHTEEN

A cold November wind rattled the windows of Deni's East Side apartment. Coop was seated in a chair, looking out the window at a tall rectangle of gray sky visible between the buildings across the street.

The apartment smelled as if Deni had been frying bacon. It was a cluttered mess, with a layer of dust over everything that wasn't moved often. Last Sunday's *Times* was tented and scattered on the floor next to the sofa. There were overlapping rings from glasses and bottles on the coffee table, a sweater draped over the back of a chair. On the carpet near the front door, Deni's green parka lay where it had fallen from a hook. Dead geraniums were brown corpses in ceramic pots lining the sill of the window near Coop.

"It's been almost a month," Deni said, in a voice to match the mood. She was wearing ill-fitting black sweatpants and a baggy pullover, sprawled awkwardly in a padded swivel chair by her computer. There was a cork bulletin board hanging crookedly on the wall by her cluttered desk, with photos and news clippings about Bette's murder and that of Marlee Clark pinned to it along with favorable book reviews and a black and white publicity photo of Deni that made her appear thinner and younger.

"Homicide investigations can take a long time," Coop told her. She ran a hand through her short-cropped and uncombed hair. "We don't have a long time."

We don't, Coop thought. He considered his cancer, still in remission. Deni was probably considering a publication date.

He'd gone over everything at least twice, gotten information from Billard on Lloyd Watkins, and checked him out thoroughly. Every avenue became a narrow street that became a path that disappeared.

Coop had been particularly disappointed that the check on Watkins had been unproductive. Watkins was alibied up to his eyeballs and seemed innocuous enough. Thirty-five, grew up in Haverton and went away to college in Iowa, came back to Haverton ten years ago and worked his way up in Prudent Stand Real Estate from salesman to chief industrial property appraiser. No police record, no money problems. A social drinker, but nothing to suggest he was an alcoholic or into drugs. By all accounts he'd been genuinely in love with Bette, and some said she with him. It had been one of those star-crossed but inextinguishable affairs that often led to the strongest relationships if mutual accommodation could be made. Coop found himself thinking Watkins would have made an acceptable son-in-law if things had worked out differently.

Deni leaned forward in her chair so she was sitting up straight. "Coop, we've got to get this thing off its dead ass and push this investigation."

"You sound like you've been watching *Law and Order* reruns."

"I've been listening to Alicia. She wants words from me, says that's what Whippet's paying for."

"Makes a certain amount of sense."

"Yeah, doesn't it?" An expression of panic came and went on Deni's face. Coop found himself feeling sorry for her. Time was running out for her. He knew how that felt. "The cops aren't going to solve anything," she said, "that's for sure."

He had to admit it looked that way. The case remained open, of course, as did all unsolved homicides, but the deluge of crime in and around New York continued, demanding manpower and hours and police dedication to other, more immediate investigations where the trail hadn't cooled.

It began to rain outside, drops striking the windows like hard pellets. Mother Nature irritated. "Maybe we oughta talk to Sue Coppolino again," Deni said.

"Why? She'd tell us the same story."

"You have a better idea?"

"I know somebody in the FBI. An old friend who might be able to help us if he buys into the idea there's a serial killer at work."

Deni appeared dubious. "I don't know, Coop. I'm not sure we can trust the FBI in this matter."

"The Bureau can collate our information, and it has access to more national databases than the NYPD. If there is a nationwide pattern of homicides by the same killer, the FBI might be able to detect it."

"Being able to get into more databases isn't the same thing as trust. FBI agents are rigid thinkers, more concerned with their careers and the Bureau's reputation than in solving crimes."

Coop wondered where she got her ideas. "Don't swallow stereotypes whole. The FBI agents I know aren't that way. Especially the one I have in mind. His name's Fred Willingham. He works out of the Bureau's New York field office. I think we oughta talk to him, tell him what we have, and see what he thinks."

Deni lifted a pudgy knee and clasped her fingers around it while she sat thinking. She used the toe of her foot planted on the floor to move the desk chair near her from side to side on its rollers. That took some leg strength, Coop thought. She said, "I wouldn't want the FBI taking this case away from us."

"I would, if they can find the killer."

"Let's be crass for a moment, Coop: we need to be the primary investigators because we've got a book deal going here."

"Career first. Isn't that how you just told me most FBI agents thought?"

She flashed him the rapacious grin she didn't reveal in dust jacket photos. "Yeah, it is. And you can be a real bastard."

"When it's necessary," he said honestly.

"I guess that's part of being a cop."

"It is. You can put that in your book. Along with a meeting with Fred Willingham. I think we oughta see him. It might get the investigation off the dime, like you suggested."

Again the grin that would have made Nero proud. "I love it when you speak cop talk."

"Cop talk is reading people their rights," Coop said. "I'll call Fred Willingham and set up a meet."

"Set up a meet," Deni repeated. "I'll make a note of that." And she did.

Coop guessed it would make better reading than the Miranda warning.

Fred Willingham agreed to meet with them the next afternoon at the Sapphire Coffee Shop, where Coop had first met Deni. And Alicia Benham.

Before going to the Sapphire, Coop subwayed downtown to the offices of Whippet Books on Hudson Street.

The receptionist, maybe the one who'd hung up on Coop when he'd said he was with Smurger and Bold, called back to Alicia, then told Coop he could go back to her office.

The office door was open. When he gave it a perfunctory knock and walked in, Alicia was standing behind her desk. She was wearing black again today, a sweater and slacks, and looked even thinner than when he'd last seen her. Her smile was the same, though, and one he enjoyed having beamed his way.

"How's the book going?" she asked, when they'd exchanged greetings.

He smiled back at her. "That's sort of what I wanted to ask you."

"Sort of?" She waved an arm at the chair in front of her desk as an invitation for Coop to sit, then sat back down herself.

He settled into the chair and looked beyond her out the window. The Statue of Liberty was still out there, far enough away to look like one of those cast-iron miniatures sold in Times Square souvenir shops. He said, "To be honest, I guess I'm here to find out what if anything Deni has written about my daughter."

"Aren't you always honest?"

Odd question, Coop thought. "Most of the time," he said. "It's the easiest way to live."

"Tangled webs and all that," Alicia said. "I suppose you learned that from interrogating suspects."

"That brings it home to you," Coop told her.

"Can you tell when someone is lying?"

"Not always right away. But there are telltale signs. And lies tend to become obvious eventually. They're more consistent than truth in the short run, less consistent in the long run."

"And always less honorable."

"Most of the time," Coop said, remembering the lies he'd told family members about whether their loved ones had suffered before death.

"The truth this time, long and short term," Alicia said, "is that Deni hasn't turned in any pages yet. Not even an outline. She says there's no way to know where the investigation will take her, so an outline would be impossible. That simply doesn't wash with me. She'll have to get something to me soon that I can show the editorial board and sales department or the deal is off."

"I thought that would be your misfortune, too."

"*Too* is the operative word. If this book doesn't look as if it's going to be written on time, I'll cut it before I leave here."

"Won't she sell it somewhere else?"

"Probably. But for less money, I'm sure."

"You don't give her much leeway."

Alicia shrugged. "Business is business."

"At Bette's expense?"

"I have some influence as Deni's editor. I'll do my best to see that doesn't happen."

"Thanks," Coop said, but he was thinking that with Alicia business really was business. "Bette's gone and can't be hurt, but I don't want her reputation damaged for no reason other than to sell books."

"I'll look out for her, and for you."

"Me?"

"Deni will also be writing about you."

Coop knew she was right, but he hadn't given it much thought. "When you get in bed with dogs you get up with fleas. With wolves, sometimes you get up bleeding or not at all."

"Deni and I aren't exactly in bed together," Coop said.

Alicia smiled. "I didn't mean it like that."

But as he left, Coop wondered if that was exactly what she did mean.

CHAPTER NINETEEN

The Sapphire Diner was crowded, but Coop had managed to secure a corner booth toward the back and near a window, where conversation would be reasonably private. He sat waiting and sipping a diet cola, watching the press and controlled turmoil of New Yorkers on their lunch hour maneuvering for takeout at the counter, or for booths or tables the instant they became free. Orders were shouted, miraculously remembered, only occasionally fouled up while on the way to or from the display case or kitchen. Noise, shifting motion, seeming confusion. Lunch out of chaos. Somehow it all worked, like the city itself.

Deni arrived and spotted Coop in the booth. She shouldered her way through the counter crowd and sat down opposite him. One of the waiters appeared, a handsome guy who looked as if he spent five hours a day in the gym, five in a hairstyling salon. He was the kind of waiter tourists figured would be making ends meet while waiting for a break in show business. Deni ordered a pastrami sandwich and a Heineken.

"I think he's an actor on one of the soaps," Deni said, watching the waiter walk away.

Coop doubted if she'd ever seen the man before. Deni liked to romanticize and feel connected to fame if only by beer and a pastrami sandwich.

"Wine of our Days, I think," Deni said, seeming to sense that Coop saw through her and understood her need for reflected celebrity. Her need for so many things.

That was when Willingham arrived. He shook hands with Coop, then with Deni as he was introduced. The waiter had noticed Willingham and returned, so Coop and Willingham both ordered turkey clubs, Willingham a Diet Coke like Coop's.

"Everybody in law enforcement trying to lose weight?" asked Deni, who was the only overweight one in the booth.

Willingham was even thinner than the rangy Coop, with squarish features and a bristly gray crew cut. Younger than Coop, in his early forties. He had blue eyes that looked into people with a steadiness that was unnerving. Coop could see that he was making Deni uncomfortable.

"You *can't* be sensitive about your weight," she told him with a smile.

"Could be but I'm not," Willingham said. Coop wished the agent had dressed differently today. He was wearing a blue suit, white shirt, red and blue tie with a miniature knot. Most likely person in the diner to be an FBI agent.

"Thanks for your willingness to listen to us," Coop said, trying to smooth the way.

"You made me curious on the phone," Willingham said. "And I heard about Bette. I'm sorry."

"You people are like a big family, right?" Deni said. "No matter what organization you're in. Just cops who come together when there's a problem."

"Pretty much like a family," Willingham said. "And like real families, we don't always get along."

She gave him her rapacious smile. "I hope we can all get along this time. There's something in it for all of us."

Willingham looked at Coop. "You said on the phone this is about Bette."

"Maybe more than Bette," Coop said. Pausing only when the food was brought to the booth, he recounted what had happened since he'd discovered Bette's body in the cottage.

Willingham listened carefully, absently eating his club sandwich and probably not tasting it.

When they were finished with lunch, everyone ordered coffee, Deni a cheese Danish. Coop handed Willingham the large yellow envelope containing information on the case, including the two footprint photos.

Over coffee, Coop and Deni watched while Willingham methodically examined the envelope's contents. He spent a long time studying the crime scene photos, then the shots of the two footprints.

When he'd replaced everything in the envelope, he handed it back to Coop. "The footprint photos are a questionable match," he said.

"You kidding?" Deni asked. "They had to have been made by the same shoe."

"Says in there the patterns haven't been matched with a manufacturer." Willingham nodded toward the envelope.

"That's why we don't have a definite match," Deni said in exasperation.

"The murder methods are different. Different weapons."

"That's this guy's thing, doing it different ways in different cities so the cops won't tie in the crimes and figure there's a serial killer operating. He's read the literature, knows how you people think."

"It'd make a helluva crime novel," Willingham said. "So what's the connection between the victims? I mean, what ties them together in this guy's mind?"

"The long hair, for one."

"Gotta be more than that," Willingham said. "You and Coop said yourself the victims seemed to have known and trusted their killer—killers."

"What about the fact they all seemed to have been sexually fondled with latex gloves?"

"What about it? Either of you got latex gloves at home?"

Deni and Coop exchanged glances and shook their heads no.

"Well, neither of you are worried about leaving fingerprints anywhere," Willingham said. "But if you were, you could probably find some place within a few blocks of here that sells latex gloves."

"You really think it's a blind alley, Fred?" Coop asked.

Willingham sat back and rippled his fingers on the table. "All I'm saying is, I'm skeptical. I don't think you've got enough here that I can take it to my superiors in the Bureau and trigger an investigation."

"What would make you less skeptical?" Deni asked.

"Mainly, I'd like to see some connection between killer and victims, something in their pasts that led to these women knowing and trusting this guy—if he exists. A few of these crimes, there've been arrests, trials, and convictions."

"People are wrongfully accused and convicted all the time," Deni said. "It's the American way."

Willingham showed a ghost of a smile. "Not *all* the time, I hope."

"I'm sorry," Deni said. "You know what I meant."

Coop had been watching Willingham. "There something else, Fred?"

Willingham looked at Deni. "Family members know how to read each other."

Deni sat back and crossed her arms. "You two guys gonna let me in on what's going on here?"

"You came to me at a bad time," Willingham said to Coop. "The NYPD is particularly sensitive right now about the feds usurping their authority. Bette's murder, the case is strictly local, belongs to a couple of detectives in Queen's South Homicide. Hell, they haven't even bucked it up to SID. The Bureau can't go charging into it and take it over. Especially right now."

"Shit!" Deni said. "A turf war. Just like in the movies."

"Call it a police action," Willingham said.

"I call it Bureau politics," Coop told him.

"It is that, Coop. NYPD politics, too."

"Shit!" Deni said again.

Coop and Willingham said nothing for a while.

Coop slid the envelope across the table toward Willingham. "I understand your position, Fred. Just do me a favor and keep the envelope, will you?"

"Even without the politics, Coop, I'd still be skeptical."

"I understand, Fred."

Willingham nodded, reached for the envelope, and laid it on the seat beside him.

"What now?" Deni asked.

"Now I go to my regular job at the Bureau." Willingham shifted his weight and reached for his wallet in a hip pocket. "That was a damned good club sandwich."

"It's on us," Coop said. "That was the deal, Fred. That way we own you."

Willingham grinned as he stood up, then rested his hand on Coop's shoulder. "You own me, then. Bye, Deni." He shook hands with her, then turned around and made his way toward the door, the yellow envelope clutched at his side.

Deni stared after him, scowling. "That went nowhere."

"Not yet," Coop said. "Maybe not ever. But he took the envelope."

Deni turned her scowl on him. "That mean something significant in guy talk?"

Coop finished his coffee in one long sip before answering. "Means he took the envelope."

CHAPTER TWENTY

Milligan's Lounge was on West 86th Street, near Columbus and the entrance to Central Park. Theresa Dravic worked at Vale's Jewelry on Columbus, three blocks away from Milligan's. More and more, she was walking those three blocks after work.

At quitting time at the large discount jewelry store, she said good-bye to the manager, Harv, and went out into the cold. Though it wasn't yet Thanksgiving, holiday shopping had increased business. Vale's had been crowded much of the day and evening with early gift buyers examining, shoplifting, and sometimes buying jewelry.

The cold felt good to Theresa after the overheated store. Always Harv insisted on turning the thermostat up. Always one employee or another sneaked over and turned it back down. Until Harv had a lock box installed around it. Now everyone sweltered all day, except Harv.

Theresa was an attractive woman in her forties, with long dark hair and a figure that still caused men to pause and look twice. Bitten by the cold at last, she buttoned her fur-collared coat all the way up and strode past her bus stop toward Milligan's. She held herself erect as she walked, aware of the male eyes fixed on her. She used to enjoy knowing she was the center of male attention. But it had gotten old, along with her. Like a lot of things.

Once or twice each week she phoned and told her roommate Vera that she'd be working late. But where she went was to Milligan's, and sat on a bar stool and drank dry white wine because it was a woman's drink, not an alcoholic's. She drank the same kind of wine at home, too, from bottles hidden where Vera wouldn't find them. When she was home and had company and she needed a drink, she'd go into the bathroom, where there was a bottle hidden among the towels in the linen closet.

Sometimes at night she'd sit watching TV, warm and comfortable. Vera, a flight attendant, would be with her if she wasn't on a date or working a flight out of La Guardia. On top of the TV was a framed photo of Theresa's daughter Jan, who was in Chicago, a student at Northwestern with an apartment just off campus.

Theresa had plenty to live for and wondered why she wasn't happy or at least contented. It wasn't cheap, keeping a daughter in college, which was why she'd taken the job at Vale's, but she really didn't mind working. She still missed her husband Vincent, who'd been dead for three years now. But she'd learned to survive without a man. And she loved Jan, who was doing well at school. With Theresa working, there was enough money if they watched how it was spent. So why wasn't she satisfied with her life? Why did she crave and need and have to go to the bottle?

Usually she drank too much at Milligan's and left walking unsteadily.

Lately she'd limited herself to three glasses of wine. She'd stopped wondering why she had to go to Milligan's at least once during the week and usually twice. It wasn't for the wine. Not since she'd met Chris.

A car slowed and the man driving blatantly leaned down so he could peer out at her, as if she were some kind of hooker. It wasn't that sort of neighborhood. Didn't the asshole know any better?

Theresa quickened her pace, gaze locked straight ahead.

"Hey, Terry! Theresa, it's me, Harv!"

She slowed and turned her head, and saw that the car's driver was indeed Harv, who must have closed the store early.

"You want a lift, Theresa?"

She shook her head no. "Thanks, but I'm meeting someone."

He smiled and looked at her as if he didn't believe her. He was always trying to get in her pants. One of those guys who figured a widow in her forties couldn't hold out for long.

Horns honked. Harv shrugged, waved, and drove on. Theresa knew what he was thinking: Maybe next time. Eventually. Inevitably.

There was Milligan's, half a block ahead. The board out in front said they were serving angel hair pasta tonight. She decided that if Chris wasn't there, she'd hang around and have supper. She would have wine with her meal.

Then later, as she often did, she'd walk down to the park entrance and venture just slightly inside to sit on her usual bench. There she'd give herself time to recover from her meal and her drink, so she wouldn't make a fool of herself on the bus. So Vera, if she happened to be home, wouldn't think she'd had too much to drink.

Then, if she found herself alone, she would relax in front of the TV and have some wine. And eventually she'd fall asleep.

CHAPTER TWENTY-ONE

The days passed while Coop and Deni went over and over what they knew. Coop talked to some of Bette's friends again and had dinner with the still disconsolate Lloyd Watkins. He found himself liking the young man, wishing again that Bette had lived and might have enjoyed a long marriage and motherhood. A father's dream for the dead.

Maureen had been stepping up the pressure, calling Coop at odd hours to harangue him and goad him to dig deeper into Bette's murder, to listen to Deni Green, who in Maureen's mind had taken on a sagacity and importance far beyond reality. Maureen had begun reading Deni's novels. Maybe that accounted for her heightened faith in the author's own detection skills.

When the jangle of the phone by his bed shattered the early morning hours, Coop emerged from sleep assuming Maureen was calling him again.

Then he realized the bedroom was still dark. This was too early even for Maureen to be on the phone.

He dragged the receiver over to him and said hello in a sleep-thickened voice.

"Better get on your horse, Coop." Deni's voice. "We got another victim that looks like the work of our killer."

He blinked and rubbed his eyes, thinking she sounded like a character out of one of her mystery novels. "You found this out on your computer?"

"No. One of my police contacts called to let me know about it."

Coop came all the way awake and switched on the bedside reading lamp. "You mean this murder was in New York?"

"Yep. Queens. On the campus of a community college out near Nassau County. Security guard came across the dead body of a woman laid out on her back beneath a tree. Her head was resting on one of the larger roots near the trunk as if it were a pillow, and her hair was carefully fanned out like with the other victims."

"So there's a police report on this?"

"Not yet. That's the best part, Coop! Why you and I need to get out there soon as possible and examine the crime scene before the police make their usual dumb assumptions or overlook something like a nearby footprint that doesn't seem to be connected to the murder."

"How long ago was this murder?"

"Only hours. That's what's great about it. Ann Callahan isn't even cold yet!"

Coop was surprised Deni already had the victim's name. Probably Ann Callahan's family didn't even know yet that she was dead. Deni's police contact must be a good one, to pass out that kind of sensitive information. Maybe one who had little choice. There were a lot of questions he wanted to ask Deni, but he knew this wasn't the time. "You know the exact location?"

"You bet I do."

"I'll get dressed," Coop said, "then swing by and pick you up outside your apartment."

"Don't loaf on me, Coop. This murder's a lucky break for us. We should make the most of it."

"I won't be long. Keep in mind I was sound asleep only a few minutes ago." He scooted sideways, then stood up from the bed as he spoke.

"Hurry!" Deni pleaded. "I've never been to a homicide scene and I want to get there before they move the body. Maybe I can even see the fatal wounds. You think that's possible?"

"It's possible," Coop said, and hung up on her, disgusted.

The sun had been up only minutes when Coop and Deni reached the community college. Ann Callahan's murder had taken place near the edge of the campus. Coop peered through the windshield and saw yellow police scene tape near some trees, and a knot of figures standing motionless around something on the ground. In the diffused, early morning light, the scene was hazy and unreal. He wished he were dreaming, but he knew he wasn't. The figures in the scene were real, all right, and were mostly cops. And the object on the ground was a dead woman.

"Park there, near that bus stop," Deni said, pointing through the windshield.

Coop braked and pulled to the curb beyond the bus

stop sign, parking behind an ambulance. The emergency vehicle's parking lights were on, but not its flashing roof-bar lights. The emergency here was over. A white cloud of exhaust from a car engine drifted to the side up ahead on the cold breeze. Coop glimpsed a police cruiser parked in front of the ambulance. He was glad the bus stop was there to prevent solid parking along the curb. An unbroken line of parked cars might have prevented him from noticing the somber scene beneath the trees.

Coop and Deni climbed out of the Honda and walked toward the knot of people gathered like early mourners around the body. The wind was blowing in off the campus, seeming to carry the scent of death and causing Coop to turn up the collar of his black topcoat. His throat was raw. He wasn't feeling terrific this morning and didn't like being up so early. Especially to visit a homicide scene.

A few of the people around the body had noticed their approach and were watching them.

Coop looked over at Deni, who was staring straight ahead intently, her chin thrust forward.

"We're going to play this low-key," he told her. "It doesn't take much for two civilians nosing around a murder case to be cut out of the loop by the police. We need to keep our lines of communication open."

Deni snorted, her fogged breath streaming from her nostrils in a way that reminded Coop of cartoon bulls about to charge. "I'm the one with the line of communication here. It was my informant who called me on a cell phone less than an hour after the body was discovered."

"Don't mention that to anyone here other than me," Coop said.

"You think I'm stupid?" Deni asked.

"No. I think you're too clever."

When they got to within about twenty feet of the body, one of the figures standing over it detached itself from the group and advanced to head them off while the others resumed talking among themselves. They would allow anyone only so close to the frozen zone, cop talk for a crime scene that needed to be preserved.

The man who approached was stocky, with thinning, rust-colored hair and a broad, weathered face. Though he was wearing a tan raincoat buttoned to the neck, his brown pants and black cop's shoes splattered with mud told Coop he was police and had been a while on the scene.

"Sorry," he said with a reluctant smile, "no media allowed."

"We're not media," Coop said, before Deni could answer and seize control of the conversation. "I'm Ezekiel Cooper, used to be with the NYPD."

The man sniffed several times as if he had a cold. "Used to be?"

Coop noticed that his eyes were red and swollen, either from the cold or lack of sleep. "I'm retired," Coop told him, "working independently on my daughter's murder."

The stocky cop's expression softened. "You're Lieutenant Cooper. I remember you from a long time ago at the Two-Four Precinct. You and Art Billard partnered in a patrol car."

"You know Billard?" Coop asked.

"Sure." *Sniff, sniff.* "Haven't seen him in a while though. I'm Don Quinones, got the squeal on this one." He shook hands with Coop, then looked at Deni.

"Deni Green," Coop said. "Partner of mine."

Quinones nodded at Deni, who smiled at him.

"I read about what happened to your daughter," Quinones said to Coop. "Heard you were working the case as a civilian. Can't blame you for that. You think there's some connection between this murder and your daughter's?"

"It's possible. Mind if we get closer?"

"C'mon, Lou," Quinones said. He sniffed and led the way toward Ann Callahan's body.

They ducked beneath the crime scene tape, but Quinones stopped them about ten feet away from the corpse. "The lab guys are still looking at the area immediately around her," he explained. "We don't wanna stomp around there."

"You guys were all standing around her," Deni noted.

"We figured out where to step."

"Are there any footprints?" Deni asked.

Quinones looked at her. "Not that we can see so far. The grass was dry, and we haven't had rain or snow for a while so the ground is hard."

Coop stared at Ann Callahan's corpse, the way it was laid out on the ground, the head resting on the tree root as if it were on a pillow, her red hair fanned out in a perfect, unbroken crescent. She was fully clothed, still wearing a gray coat with a white leather collar. There was a small dark stain near the pelvic area the coat covered. The coat wasn't twisted or bunched. Coop guessed she'd been moved, arranged carefully after her murder. Her hands were folded just beneath her breasts. Her eyes were closed. She'd obviously been attractive when alive, but didn't seem to bear any resemblance to Bette or to Marlee Clark. Yet something about her in a subtle way reminded Coop of when he'd found Bette dead in the cottage, and of the crime scene photos of Marlee Clark's body. There was an odd peacefulness about the dead woman, Coop thought. Someone had cared. The same someone who had killed.

"How did she die?" he asked Quinones.

"ME suspects she was knocked unconscious first, then stabbed in the back with a long, thin blade that pierced her heart. Gotta wait for the autopsy to confirm, though."

"Sure," Coop said, glancing again at the bloodstain on the victim's coat, wondering if it signified what he couldn't mention because he wasn't supposed to know it. "What *do* you know about her?"

"Only what we found in her wallet, which was still in her purse and still contained thirty dollars. Robbery didn't seem to be the motive here."

"That doesn't surprise me."

"We learned from her wallet ID that her name's Ann Callahan, twenty-nine years old, address in Flushing. And at this point that's about all we know about her. The ME's guess is she was killed sometime before midnight last night. Security guard found her about four this morning and called us. Oh, one other thing we know about her is she wasn't registered as a student here. The admissions office has already checked for us on their computer databases." Quinones looked at Deni, then Coop. "Any of this help you?"

"It might," Deni said.

That wasn't what Quinones wanted to hear. Coop knew it was time to be honest with the man, especially if they wanted more information on the Ann Callahan case.

"Here's how it might," he said. He told Quinones what they'd learned since Bette's murder.

Quinones listened quietly, then excused himself and blew his nose four times into a handkerchief. He shook his head and frowned to express his discomfort and the misery of the world in general, then folded the handkerchief and stuffed it into a side pocket of his raincoat. "You sure got a lotta maybes."

"I know," Coop said. "That's why we're here. It'd help if you found anything tying this in with the other homicides."

"Especially a matching footprint," Deni said.

"Gimme your number," Quinones told Coop. "I'll share with you what I can. It's gotta run both ways though."

"You'll get what we have. And you can always check with Billard. He'll be up to date."

Quinones tore a sheet of paper from a small leatherbound notebook and handed it and a pen to Coop, who wrote down his name and phone number, then gave them to Quinones. He didn't give Deni a chance to write her name and number, knowing it might be an affront to Quinones. This wasn't your usual arrangement between cop and civilian. Deni wasn't and never had been a cop. Coop knew it and didn't want to have to say it. Quinones could probably guess it anyway.

"I'll give you a call sometime after the autopsy report," he told Coop. He shook hands with both Coop and Deni, then turned back toward the body beneath the leafless tree.

As Coop and Deni trudged back toward Coop's Honda, Deni said, "We didn't learn a hell of a lot by coming here, other than we both better wash our hands when we get home. Quinones has a god-awful cold."

"Except for the part about the cold, I can't agree with you," Coop said. "We learned weapon and cause of death, approximate time of death, and that the victim probably wasn't sexually molested or mutilated. And there was something about the way she was laid out, the way her body was arranged . . . It reminded me of when I found Bette."

Deni was silent for half a dozen steps, then said, "That *is* sometbing."

When Coop dropped her off at her apartment, she climbed out of the car, then turned and leaned down so she could speak to him. "I'll call and let you know what the police come up with, long before you hear from Quinones."

"It won't hurt to hear it twice and compare it," Coop said. He doubted Deni's police contact was in tight enough to know about the plastic St. Augustines, or if he did know, he was too smart to pass on the information to her. Coop sure as hell wasn't going to tell her.

"I'm glad we drove out there this morning," Deni told him, then straightened up, shut the car door, and strode toward her building entrance.

Coop wasn't sure he was glad. He kept seeing again the woman lying peacefully on her back beneath the dormant, skeletal tree. The tree would be rejuvenated with spring. The woman would remain dead forever.

CHAPTER TWENTY-TWO

The Flushing address of Ann Callahan's parents was a shotgun apartment in a flat-roofed brick building with deadlooking vines clinging to one corner. It stood at weary attention in a block of nearly identical buildings. There was no elevator, and the Callahan unit was on the third floor. The stairwell smelled as if someone in the building was cooking something with every conceivable spice. Coop was annoyed by the fact that he was breathing harder than Deni when they'd finished the climb up the narrow wooden stairs.

They'd rung from downstairs and had been told on the intercom to come up, but the door to 3C, the Callahan unit, was closed. Coop knocked and immediately heard floorboards creaking on the other side of the door.

It was Mr. Callahan who opened the door and peered out at them tentatively, as if he feared they might be bringing him even more terrible news.

He was a small man, with hunched shoulders and his chin tucked in so that he was staring up at Coop and Deni above the dark rims of his glasses. His straight gray hair was combed to lie flat over a bald pate. He was wearing pinstriped pants, a white shirt, black tie, and blue suspenders. Coop had found out that his first name was Edward and for the last twenty-two years he'd been a clerk for various city agencies and was now with the New York Department of Environmental Protection. With his rounded shoulders, bleary eyes, and pinched look about him, he fit the role of bureaucratic hermit crab.

"Can we make this fast?" he asked in a tired voice. "We've already talked to you people for hours. My wife's exhausted."

Deni started to say something and Coop nudged her. Better to let Edward Callahan assume they were police.

"I know it strains your patience, Mr. Callahan, and we're sorry. But we very much want to find whoever killed your daughter."

Callahan screwed up his thin lips in a way that suggested he might start to cry. Coop felt an unexpected pang of pity. He knew exactly how Edward Callahan felt.

But Callahan didn't cry. Instead he composed himself, then stepped back and let them inside. The apartment's interior was comfortably if a bit shabbily furnished, with overstuffed furniture and an ancient TV against the wall opposite the sofa. Imitation oriental rugs lay on the hardwood floor. A glass of water with half-melted ice cubes sat on an AARP magazine on the coffee table. Coop guessed that whatever the Callahans' ages, they felt a lot older today.

A short, worn-looking woman in dark slacks and a wrinkled green sweater entered from a dim hallway that led to the kitchen and bedrooms. Her eyes were red, her face puffy. She was gripping a rosary tightly in her right hand, and she'd probably been crying moments before coming into the living room.

"My wife Louise," Callahan said. "I told you she was exhausted. We both are. God . . ."

"I know how you feel," Coop said.

Callahan shook his head. "Don't tell me that. I don't want to hear it."

"We only want to ask a few questions about Ann," Deni said. "Then we'll leave you to your grief."

Louise Callahan began to sob again but caught her breath in a series of gasps. It seemed to Coop that her frenzied inhalations took all the air out of the room.

"Do you or your wife have any idea who might have been angry or upset in any way with Ann?" he asked.

"Not enough to . . . do that to her," Edward Callahan said. "Like we told the other detectives over and over."

Coop ignored the comment. "Who were her close personal friends?"

"She didn't have any that we knew. Maybe at work. She was a good girl, a shy girl who minded her own business."

Coop thought that was a strange answer. "Ann wasn't a student at the college. Do you have any idea why she would have been on its campus last night?"

"None. She was overdue from work at the bank. She took the bus home every weeknight. She was supposed to show up around six-thirty to help Louise start dinner."

Louise made another gasping sound, barely under control. Everyone looked at her. She dabbed at her eyes with a wadded tissue, never loosening her grip on the rosary. "I'll be all right," she said, mostly to herself. She took a deep breath.

"We don't know why Ann stayed on the bus all the way to the end of . . . to where they found her." Callahan glared at Coop and Deni. "I told you I'm tired! My wife and I both are. Worn out with answering questions!"

"Edward!" Louise Callahan said.

"Shut up, Louise. This can wait until later."

"But it shouldn't—"

"I said shut up!"

Coop wasn't sure if Callahan was tired of answering questions, or mad at his wife. But in his grief and anger he was becoming intransigent. Coop had seen it before. Had felt it.

"If she'd done what she knew she was supposed to . . ." Callahan said bitterly. "What she'd been told. If she'd just got on the bus after work and come here without doing something that tempted fate . . ."

"We don't know if she tempted fate," Louise Callahan said. "Maybe whoever killed her made her stay on the bus and go with him to where no one would be around when they got off."

Callahan glared at his wife but said nothing.

"Isn't that possible?" Louise asked Coop.

"It's one of a lot of possibilities we're trying to sort out," he said.

"Had Ann taken a trip by plane recently?" Deni asked.

Now Callahan swung around to glare at Deni. "She wouldn't fly. Not anywhere. Had a thing about it."

So much for Deni's homicidal flight attendant theory, Coop thought. "Where was it you said Ann worked?" he asked.

"Mercantile Mutual Bank," Louise said.

Callahan clenched his fists. "Damn it, Louise. Didn't you hear me say the questioning was over?"

"No," she said in a confused voice. "What you said was—"

"That's it!" Callahan interrupted. "That's goddamn *it!* We're both done answering questions."

"Okay, we're sorry, Mr. Callahan." Coop began fastening the buttons on his coat. "We understand."

Callahan seemed not to have heard. "Done, over, finished," he said. He stalked to the door to the hall and opened it, then stood rigidly holding it, waiting for Coop and Deni to leave.

Coop put his hand on Deni's shoulder and guided her toward the door. When Callahan saw they were cooperating and there was nothing to hurl his silent rage at, he gave a choked sigh and covered his face with his hands. "I'm sorry . . . I want to help you, really . . ."

"It's all right," Coop told him. "This isn't the time. We're sorry, Mr. Callahan. Mrs. Callahan."

Louise managed to twist her mask of grief into a brave smile.

"We'll catch the man," Deni assured them as she stepped out into the hall with Coop.

Callahan closed the door without answering. The hall was cool after the apartment. The air seemed cleaner.

"You can't be in there with them and not breathe in their grief," Coop said, when they were going down the stairs. Thinking of his own grief immediately after

Bette's death, how dark emotion had engulfed him in a way he hadn't thought possible.

"I hope he doesn't start in on his wife now that we're gone," Deni said.

Coop looked at her as they reached the second-floor landing. "Why would you say that?"

"He impressed me that way, Coop. A tight-ass weakling who vents his anger on people even weaker than he is, especially if they live with him. Typical male household dictator."

"They're both heartbroken," Coop said. "Maybe that's why it looks that way."

"Maybe," Deni admitted, "but it'd surprise me if he wasn't a spouse abuser. I still bet he'll start in on that mousy little hausfrau if he hasn't already."

Coop was afraid she might be right.

Back on the street, a light, cold rain had begun to fall. Coop said, "Was there something else about the scene upstairs that didn't seem right?"

"Don't quiz me, tell me," Deni said, turning up her coat collar.

"The sister, Cara. Usually in situations like this a family closes ranks, its members comforting and supporting each other. Why wasn't Cara with her parents in their time of family grief?"

Deni grinned at him. "Why, indeed?"

"It's only quarter to eight," Coop said, "but I don't have her address."

"I do," Deni said. "I know all about her."

She was already lowering herself into the passenger seat of his car by the time he got in behind the steering wheel.

CHAPTER TWENTY-THREE

Cara Callahan lived in a prewar apartment building on the Upper West Side, not far from Columbus Circle. Its blackened stone facade, complete with chipped Roman columns flanking the entrance, suggested better times. There was no official doorman, but when Coop and Deni entered the lobby, an elderly guy in gray work clothes who might have been the super laid down a *Times* and got up from a small sofa to ask if he could help them.

"Cara Callahan," Coop said.

The man's expression changed.

"We don't like it either," Coop said, "but we have to see her. It's about her sister's murder."

The man looked at Coop and saw cop. "Hell of a thing," he said.

"Hell of a thing," Coop agreed.

"I'll call up, tell her you're coming."

"That'd be good," Coop told him.

In the elevator, Deni said, "What would you have done if he'd asked for identification?"

"I would have acted surprised he thought 1 was a

cop. But 1 wasn't too worried about it. I saw he was the kind of guy who could spot a cop."

"You're beginning to impress me," Deni said.

"Only beginning?"

Like her mother, Cara had obviously been crying recently. She was an attractive woman in her thirties, and she strongly resembled the old photo of her sister the TV news had been showing. Her hair was blond though, rather than red like her sister's, shorter and worn in bangs. She was barefoot and had on a tightly sashed blue silk kimono with a beautifully done gold dragon design. Coop saw no other sign of Asian art or decor in the efficiency apartment, which was furnished traditionally and tastefully. He thought the place had probably been rented furnished, then given the personal touches that made it more livable.

"We've been to see your mother and father," he told Cara, after declining her offer of coffee.

"How are they?"

"They were understandably tired and preferred not to answer many questions about Ann."

Cara waved for Coop and Deni to sit on the sofa, then sat in a small gray vinyl chair and curled her legs up beneath her. "I'm not surprised. We're all . . . Well, you know how it must be. With your job, you must have seen this kind of thing before."

"Unfortunately, yes," Coop said, sitting down next to Deni. He unbuttoned his coat but left it on, and Deni followed his lead. They didn't want to give the impression they were settling in for a long visit, imposing themselves on Cara Callahan.

Deni said, "Your father was angry when we left."

Coop felt like kicking her.

Cara gave a sad little smile. Coop thought there might be a gravity about her even on an ordinary day. She was attractive but not a giggler. "So what's new?" she said.

"He get mad a lot?" Coop asked.

"He gets frustrated," Cara said.

"What's he do about it?"

"Let's just say it wasn't a happy family situation in that apartment. Then let's leave it at that."

Coop thought Deni had called it right. If Callahan didn't beat up on the women in his family, he probably abused them in other ways. That would explain why Cara had chosen to grieve her sister's death alone.

Cara hugged herself as if she were cold, though the apartment was comfortably warm. "You mind if I go get a cup of coffee?"

"Not at all," Coop told her. "But maybe you shouldn't drink coffee. It might keep you from sleeping."

"Who can sleep anyway?" she said, and got up and walked to the small kitchen, her hips moving gracefully beneath the silk kimono.

They waited until she'd returned and was settled back in her chair, her legs tucked beneath her again, exactly as before only with a steaming white mug of coffee in her right hand. The strong aroma of the coffee began to permeate the living room.

"Instead of us asking the questions you've probably already heard," Coop said, "why don't you just tell us about Ann. Your own words, whatever you want to talk about, however you want to say it."

"Ann," Cara said thoughtfully. "She's—she was my

little sister, three years younger. The shy one. All her life. Our family . . . my father is a fine man in some ways, but not in others. He likes control. No, he craves control. I broke away and left home, got a job and this apartment five years ago. Ann, she never had a chance."

Coop looked at her. "You lived at home until you were twenty-eight?"

"Off and on, but mostly on," Cara said. "Dad wanted it that way."

"And your mother?" Deni asked.

Cara gave a sad laugh. "She never had a chance, either."

"Did he ever abuse you?" Deni asked.

Cara shot her a look that gave even Deni pause. "Is that the crime we're investigating?"

"No," Coop said quickly. "Murder. Ann's. Do you have any idea who—"

"No." Cara cut him off. "Do people need a reason these days to murder someone? Aren't people killed by strangers all the time?"

"All the time," Coop agreed. She looked directly at him and a silent understanding seemed to arc between them. Coop, surprised, wondered if she had somehow realized he wasn't a cop. Or that if he was, there was something different about him. Her look had suggested that if she did suspect he was there under false pretenses, for some reason she didn't care. She'd play along. "Did you and Ann have any common friends or acquaintances?" he asked.

"Only a few. Ann's life was about going to work, returning home, helping with meals and housework. She was going to take care of Mom and Dad in their old age. That was her fate and she was resigned to it. That's still the way it is in some Irish families, Detective . . . What was your name?"

"Cooper. And that's how it is in a lot of families. Old-fashioned but it persists."

"And Ann knew Dad was going to outlive Mom. She told me that."

"How could she know?"

"We both knew. He has the willpower. He's the force. Not much can kill him. Mom's the one who bends, and when you bend often enough, you break."

Coop was beginning to appreciate what it must have taken for Cara to leave, to be on her own. "Did you talk to your sister about leaving home? Try to help her?"

"We talked about it a lot. Then came a time when we both knew talk wasn't going to change anything. I even helped Ann to find a job. That was so she could get her own place. But she never did, just talked about it. Then talked about it less and less. She fell into her routine, taking the bus to work, then home, then up in the morning and repeat yesterday."

"What about weekends?" Deni asked.

"Housework. Activities with the folks."

"No dates?"

"Only occasionally. Ann was very shy. There was nobody special. I kept waiting for that to happen, hoping she'd meet somebody who'd give her strength. But it never did." She took a long sip of coffee as if she wanted to burn her tongue. "Now it never will happen."

"If Ann had been seeing someone, had a lover or intimate friend in her life, would she have confided in you?"

"I probably would have been the first person she told. There wasn't anyone like that. I'm sure of it."

Deni leaned forward on the sofa. "Your mom and dad said Ann was afraid to fly."

Cara's lipstick-smeared lips curved slightly upward. "Isn't that what I've been telling you?"

"Sure. But what I'm asking is, might she have just told them she was afraid? Did she ever go anyplace by air, maybe just for a day, without them knowing?"

"No, I don't think that was possible. She really was afraid to get on a plane. She was afraid of so many things. It was built into her; then more and more doubt was added."

"Did you two often get together here in the city?" Coop asked. "Go to lunch or anything?"

"Only occasionally. I work in the loan department of Longpoint Bank down in the Village. Ann was a teller at Mercantile Mutual on the Upper East Side."

The phone rang, and Cara excused herself and went into the bedroom to answer it. They could hear her talking, thanking someone for their sympathy. Coop didn't have to hear the words to recognize that sort of phone call. He remembered receiving them after Bette had died, people talking uneasily to each other, not knowing what to say over a thin wire stretched through the terrible void left by sudden death.

When she returned, her eyes were moist. She'd been crying again.

Coop couldn't take it anymore, what they were doing to her. "We'll leave you alone," he said, standing up from the sofa. "Thanks for taking the time to talk to us."

Deni stood up beside Coop, and Cara followed them to the door.

As they were leaving, Coop was surprised to feel

Cara's hand on his arm. He turned around and she was looking up at him with her red-rimmed eyes. There was something in them other than grief now, something bright and hard.

"I want my sister's killer caught," she said.

"Of course. He will be."

"I'm not talking about assurances," she said. "I mean I *really* want him caught. Ann and I were closer than most sisters, especially when we were younger. I feel guilty myself, as if I've let her down. And maybe I have." Her grip on his arm tightened. "I want this son of a bitch to pay!"

Coop saw what was burning in her, how constant and brilliant it was. He knew now why a bully like Edward Callahan was no match for her.

"I want him caught just as much as you do," he said, as he and Deni stepped into the hall.

"No, you don't. You can't."

"Don't you believe it," Coop told her, and closed the door behind him.

She couldn't know how he burned with her.

CHAPTER TWENTY-FOUR

Coop sat inside Seconds where it was warm and looked out the window at the dark waters of the cold bay. The wooden deck on the other side of the glass was closed for the winter, chairs and tables stacked neatly against one of the restaurant's outside walls and weighted down so the wind wouldn't claim them. After a vegetable plate meal that even Maureen would approve of, Coop was sipping coffee and observing the lights of passing ships, remembering sailing one summer in his youth. It was a different world for them out there away from shore, he thought, a dream between sea and sky, and when they returned to land it was like waking.

"You're getting to be a regular," Billard said, sitting down opposite him.

Coop shifted his weight so he was facing Billard. "I thought you were on duty tonight."

"On duty here," Billard said. "There was a schedule change at the precinct to accommodate higher brass. Somebody's daughter having an out-of-town wedding." Realizing his reference to a daughter might have been painful to Coop, or perhaps seeing something in his expression, Billard looked sheepish and said, "Sorry, Coop."

"Not your fault, Art. Happens all the time."

"But while we're on the subject," Billard said, "Quinones at the One-Oh-Five called me about the Ann Callahan murder."

"He didn't seem to mind Deni and me being at the crime scene," Coop said.

"He wasn't unhappy about that. But it didn't set too well with him that you and Deni talked to the family. It seems that Mom and Dad Callahan somehow got the impression you were with the police."

"We didn't tell them that."

"I'm sure you didn't." Billard smiled. "At least you didn't deceive the sister."

Coop said nothing, sipped his coffee.

"Would you rather have a beer?" Billard asked.

"Yeah. But I've gotta stay on my diet." He could hear in his mind Dr. Gregory urging him to appreciate the importance of exercise and diet. He'd told the doctor he was doing okay with the diet, but exercise was a different story. Some day soon, when he had the time, he'd start jogging. He'd told the doctor that. Dr. Gregory had smiled, knowing Coop was lying even if *he* didn't know it. "You'd be amazed how many of my patients have coatracks that look just like treadmills," he'd said.

"Coatracks . . ." Coop muttered.

"Huh?" Billard was staring at him.

"Nothing, Art. Thinking out loud. Go ahead with what you were saying."

"Quinones brought me up to date on the Callahan murder," Billard said, still looking at him a little oddly. "Cause of death was a thin blade to the heart, after the victim was knocked unconscious. No skull fracture, but enough of a blow behind her right ear to black her out. Also, it appeared her clothes had been unbuttoned so she could be fondled; then they were buttoned back up."

"Being there . . . it reminded me of when I found Bette," Coop said. "There was something about the way her body was positioned, with the hair fanned out, the hands folded, almost lovingly."

Billard was observing Coop somberly. "Whoever killed the Callahan woman came away clean," he said. "No fingerprints, tooth marks, or footprints."

"Deni's theory is we have a serial killer smart enough to do his murders in different cities and vary his methods, so the crimes aren't connected."

"Ann Callahan and Bette were both killed in New York," Billard pointed out.

"So was Ellen Banta."

"Five years ago," Billard reminded him.

Coop had to acknowledge that. He wondered if Deni had affected his judgment. Had he become partially blind? Was he screening out any information leading away from the longtime serial killer theory?

"You think it's possible a family member is responsible for Ann Callahan's death?" Billard asked. "As well as Bette's?"

As well as Bette's? Coop stared at him. "Why do you ask that?" But he knew. Billard must have seen the ME's report.

"The victim's mouth, anus, and vagina were clear of semen or anyone else's blood or saliva. Nothing that might provide a DNA sample. But there was St. Augustine."

"Oh, Christ!"

"Keep this one quiet, too, Coop. Only the cops and killer need to know. I just wondered what your instincts are telling you about the Callahan family. The kind of feelings you can factor in but we can't."

"Mom had no motive. Dad doesn't have the guts."

"And big sister?"

"Cara? I don't see a motive there."

"Lots of family chemistry under the surface," Billard said. "At least, that's what Quinones thinks."

"Then he's a good cop. But I still don't see Cara as the killer. She's got a fire in her, though. I think both sisters were abused by their father. Maybe not sexually, but abused."

Billard was silent for a while, staring glumly down at the table. Coop knew he was considering the dark possibilities of a three-way incestuous relationship in a family of four. What, for instance, would Mom think? How might she have reacted?

"Did Quinones ever figure out why Ann was on the campus that night?" Coop asked.

Billard looked up. "No. They don't know her at all out there. None of the students or faculty. It looks like that's where she just happened to be killed."

"Nobody just happens to be killed anywhere, Art."

Billard gave a humorless laugh. "That's the Coop I used to know. But I have to disagree with you. People do just happen to get killed, and in all kinds of places."

"Not when there's a widespread pattern."

"What pattern do we have here other than with Bette and Ann Callahan? A plastic saint. Two women."

"More than two women," Coop said.

"Sorry. Then we have to add different cities."

"They were all lying on their backs."

"Marlee Clark was in a chair," Billard said. "She and Bette were killed indoors. Ann Callahan died outside."

"What about their hair being fanned out?"

"Maybe they were dragged by their feet and that did it."

"And the shoe prints?"

"They don't provide a definite match. And there appears not to be a manufacturer of that particular shoe sole pattern. Not to mention that the prints were only found at two of the murder scenes—*if* they were made by the same shoe."

Coop sighed and stared back out the window. A large ship was passing by slowly in the bay, the reflection of its lights shimmering on the dark water. Overhead, a jet settled toward Kennedy, its lights descending in an arc traversing the ship's course. A galaxy of cross-purposes. Coop didn't like it, but Billard made sense.

But Billard was dealing only with the facts.

Hadn't even seen the bodies.

"You gonna have dessert?" Billard asked. *"Creme brûlée* this evening. It's terrific."

"I don't doubt it," Coop said, "but since I just finished a vegetable plate, I better pass on dessert and not let all my willpower go to waste." He wished Billard would quit trying out subtle ways to knock him off his diet, as if warming up to knocking him off the murder investigation.

"Nonfattening," said the corpulent Billard, "if you don't count sugar, butter, and cream."

People do lie to themselves, Coop thought, *even when they're staring at the truth.* Maybe in his grief that was what he was doing.

When the waiter appeared with the check, Billard reached out and snatched it before Coop could react. "Since we're pretending you're still a cop," he said, "dinner's on the establishment."

Coop was miffed enough at him not to argue.

He and Billard went to the restaurant bar and talked about everything but the murders, while Billard drank Chardonnay and Coop had club soda with lemon twists, all the time yearning for a Beck's dark. But while they were sitting in the dim, warm light, drinking and discussing the NYPD, sports, movies, a part of Coop's mind was considering everything Billard had said.

By the time he left the restaurant, Coop realized that, reasonable or not, he was becoming even more convinced that Deni was right—there was a serial killer out there clever enough to have been taking victims for years.

Call it tunnel vision, Coop thought. Or instinct. Or a subconscious shuffling of facts. Or simply thinking with the gut instead of the head.

Whatever it was called, it had served Coop well during his years on the force.

When he got home that evening there was a message on his machine from Fred Willingham. The FBI agent had gone over the information Coop had given him, even run the sole print photos through computer analysis. The impressions might have been made by the same shoe—only might. The other similarities in the murders were interesting but not yet fully developed as correlating factors. He was sorry, but the Bureau had no authority in local homicide investigations, and until more evidence accrued that definitively linked the murders, the FBI wouldn't intercede.

Coop wasn't surprised, but he went to bed disappointed.

The Night Caller lay in bed remembering.

His time. Night. Shadows. Rain not ready to fall. A slice of moon only for him.

A time when he knew it was time. When it had to happen.

His time.

He'd called Ann Callahan's name from the shadows, frightening her at first. But she'd soon been reassured by his softly modulated voice. He knew how to reassure people. To lull them.

Then he moved like fate from beneath the trees, and there in the moonlight was the puzzlement on her beautiful features, in her marvelous eyes. Then the recognition, the realization. Then the fear that came with the knowledge of not knowing. The force, the end's beginning, the mystery, the thing between them.

Magic.

He said her name and she gasped and turned to run. Of course she would.

He was ready. He had planned it. He had lived it. Like a dance remembered.

The blow he struck was just so. Perfect.

With a quick and satisfactory glance around, he bent over her, then dragged her into the darkness among the trees.

Some were of necessity.

This one was for pure pleasure.

His time and hers.

Later, when he was ready, he woke her to his liking.

CHAPTER TWENTY-FIVE

Cara got off the bus near East 57th and checked her reflection in a shop window. She was wearing her best business outfit beneath a long leather coat, black pumps with medium heels, hair still neat even after the cold wind that gusted down Second Avenue. Satisfied with what she saw, she worked her hands into her gloves, adjusted the maroon muffler at her throat, then walked toward the Mercantile Mutual sign at the corner.

It had been more than a week since Ann's funeral; Cara didn't feel she could wait any longer to do what she had in mind. The police were, or at least seemed, enthusiastic enough about tracking Ann's killer, but it hadn't taken Cara long to realize there wasn't really much chance of them finding the man. Cara had checked the statistics: The success rate was low in solving stranger-on-stranger homicides. Since no one in Ann's life seemed her likely killer—since there were relatively few people *in* Ann's life—Cara had decided to work on the assumption that her younger sister had been murdered by a stranger who'd developed a fixation on her. She'd read the literature and knew something of how psychosexual killers worked. And she had no doubt the motive was sexual even though the police hadn't mentioned vaginal penetration.

Near the blue and white Mercantile Mutual sign she stopped and stepped back into a doorway, out of the cold breeze.

She knew she had to play this just right, not seem like a monstrous relative trying to take advantage of a tragic situation. Cara trusted her negotiating skills, her ability to assess and manipulate people if it were necessary. She knew that if she presented herself in exactly the right way, this would work. And she was ready with her story of limited opportunity at Longpoint, her suspicion that the bank would soon be acquired by a larger savings institution in the Midwest. Ann had talked about how she loved working at Mercantile Mutual, and Cara, with experience in the mortgage loan department, would be willing to start at a low salary if there was an opening for virtually any job in the bank.

Even Ann's job.

The banking industry was in an uncertain state. Banks were merging, closing, losing customers to mutual funds and online banking. While this created unemployment in the industry, it also created high turnover at many banks. Jobs were available for applicants with Cara's degree of experience and skills. And if she had to use sympathy, even tears, to become employed at Mercantile Mutual, she would do it. Right now, it was the most important thing in her life.

* * *

Coop was alone when he knocked on Cara Callahan's apartment door three nights later.

She was fully dressed this time, wearing dark blue capri pants and a cream-colored sweater that looked like cashmere. Her hair was mussed, bangs combed to the side and a blond lock hanging down on her forehead and partly over one eye. She was much more attractive now that her eyes weren't reddened and puffy from crying. Her features had an interesting angularity to them, especially her slightly hooded blue eyes with their slanted upper lids. Again the strong resemblance to the photos of her sister Ann came through.

Coop glanced down and saw that she was barefoot, as on his last visit. He stared at her shapely ankles, her squarish toes with their red nail polish, and wondered if she always went around the apartment barefoot.

"Drop something?" she asked.

He looked up to see that she was smiling. A bit embarrassed that she'd noticed him assessing her intensely, he decided to regard her question as rhetorical. "I was near here and thought you might have a few minutes to talk some more about the investigation."

She nodded and stepped back so he could enter. "I have plenty of time, Detective . . . "

"Cooper."

"Of course. Sorry. I tend to forget names."

"But never faces?"

"Never faces."

He went past her and waited until she'd sat down again in the gray leather chair; then he sat down where he'd sat before on the sofa. The apartment still smelled like fresh-perked coffee, as it had on his first visit.

"You drink a lot of coffee?" he asked.

"Too much," she said. "Want a cup this time?"

"No, thanks." It was quiet in the apartment. The pre-war building's thick walls blocked street sounds entirely. The drone of the refrigerator motor in the kitchen seemed loud in the absence of other noises. It reminded Coop of the humming of the beach cottage's refrigerator the day he'd walked in and found Bette's body. He tried to block the sound from his mind, the way the thick walls of the building shielded residents from intruding noises. "I, uh, asked for you at Longpoint but they said you'd left early," he told Cara. "I also overheard some conversation to the effect that you've given notice."

"That's right."

"Not leaving town, I hope."

She cocked her head to the side and stared at him. "Is that a cop question?"

"Sure. What else?" He had a hard time looking directly into her eyes. A hard time looking away. He was aware that she knew about the unsettling effect she was having on him and still hadn't made up her mind what to do with it.

"I don't know what else," she said. "I do know I didn't hear you or the woman who was with you last time identify yourselves as being with the police department."

"I'm not exactly police," Coop said. "I'm conducting a parallel investigation, working with the department."

Cara continued regarding him with an expression he couldn't quite read. She said, "Time to drop the bullshit, Cooper."

"My friends call me Coop."

Her expression didn't change. "Maybe I'll call you Coop. Maybe I won't. Who are you? What are you? Why are you here?"

Coop knew when it was time to come clean. "My name is Ezekiel Cooper. What I am is a former NYPD cop. Why I'm here is a bit complicated. I think your sister was one of a long line of victims of a serial killer."

Cara leaned forward, interested. "Is that what the police think?"

"No. The FBI doesn't think so, either."

"FBI?"

"This is a killer who takes his act on the road, varies his modus operandi so the locals think his crimes are particular to their city."

"But you see a pattern?"

"I do. Deni does. We haven't convinced the police or FBI yet, because the evidence connecting the crimes isn't strong enough. But it's there. I believe in it."

"Deni's the woman who was with you last time?"

"Yes."

"Also a former cop?"

"No. She's a mystery writer. Has this series of novels about a cat that helps solve crimes. The Cozy Cat books. Ever hear of them?"

"No. I'm a dog person."

"Good. So am I. Do you have a dog?"

"No. So what's her purpose in this? Does she want to write a novel about this serial killer?"

"Nonfiction book," Coop said. "The Cozy Cat novels aren't selling as well as they used to, so she's branching out into true crime."

"Are you her collaborator?"

"I'm not a writer. We're only collaborating on the investigation."

"But you're in this for money, just like she is. Won't you get a percentage of the book's profits?"

"No," Coop said, "we haven't even talked about that."

Cara stared curiously at him. "Then what's your interest?"

Coop hesitated before answering. "My daughter Bette. She was one of the killer's victims. Just like your sister."

"Shit!" Cara said, sitting back. It was a reaction that surprised Coop.

"If you don't want to cooperate, I'll understand," he said.

"You want revenge," Cara told him.

"I want justice. And you?"

"Revenge," she said. She stood up from her chair and he expected her to ask him to leave.

Instead she said, "You want that cup of coffee now, Coop?"

As they sat and talked for the next hour or more, Cara felt her interest in this lean, determined ex-cop heighten. He seemed solid and true, someone who knew what he was and could recognize what he had to do and then do it. There were fewer and fewer such men.

Cara dated infrequently and was usually—no, always—sooner or later disappointed. *Maybe not this time,* an inner voice was telling her. This one really was different. Better. There was hope. Still there was hope.

Another inner voice urged her not to dare believe, not to listen.

" . . . You listening?" Coop asked. He was smiling.

She realized her mind had turned inward.

"I'm listening," she said.

CHAPTER TWENTY-SIX

At first Coop thought a wasp somehow left over from summer was in his apartment.

But it was the buzz of the intercom that was pulling him up from a deep sleep the next morning at—he glanced at his watch—five after eight.

He dragged himself out of bed and padded barefoot across cool hardwood floor and warm throw rugs to the living room and small foyer, then pressed the intercom button and asked who was there.

Maureen's voice; just what he wanted to hear.

He buzzed her in so she could get through the main door.

While she was elevatoring up, he put on a pair of pants, rinsed a stale taste from his mouth, then splashed cold water over his face to wake himself completely. He left his hands wet and was smoothing back his sleep-mussed hair as best he could when there was a knock on his door.

Carrying a towel and drying his hands as he went, he walked to the door and opened it.

Maureen looked grim. Since it was Saturday morning she was dressed for the weekend in a camouflage jacket, tan T-shirt, and khaki pants. She was wearing high-topped boots and her pants were tucked into them and bloused out paratrooper style. A black nylon fanny pack rode high on her left hip, and a small pair of binoculars had been slung around her neck by a thin strap to dangle just below her breasts. In her right hand was a folded newspaper. She was holding it as if prepared to swat a dog. Or Coop.

Without saying hello, she stalked past him and slammed the paper, opened, onto his desk that was pushed up against a living room wall. The resultant breeze caused several unpaid bills to flutter to the floor.

"Look at this!" she commanded, crossing her arms just above the binoculars.

Coop thought he'd better look.

Surprise, then anger, welled in him. The newspaper was opened to an inside page featuring a story captioned DISTRAUGHT DAD SEEKS DAUGHTER'S KILLER. There was a head shot of Deni Green, and another photo of Coop himself crossing a busy street. He realized it must have been snapped through the window of the Sapphire Diner.

Maureen was fuming. "I was on my way to go birding when I stopped to have some Evian and read the paper." She uncrossed her arms and slapped the paper, crinkling it and making a surprising amount of noise. *"This* is what I came across!"

Listening to Maureen's angry breathing, Coop quickly scanned the article, which contained only a brief account of his and Deni's actions in attempting to find

Bette's murderer. Deni was quoted as being convinced Bette was a victim of a serial killer.

When Coop turned away from the desk, Maureen said, "Isn't it rather questionable to alert a murderer to the fact that he's being pursued by a former policeman who's the father of one of his victims?"

"No argument," Coop said, not liking the article any more than she did. He walked into the kitchen to make a pot of coffee. Maureen followed. "I didn't know this was going to happen," he said, fitting a filter into the Braun brewer. "I'm as surprised as you are. It had to be Deni's idea."

That Deni might be entirely responsible for the article brought Maureen up short. "Then maybe there's a point to it. And you should use brown, recycled filters if you don't want to drink bleaching chemicals with your coffee."

"You'd have to ask Deni what was the point." Coop spooned ground coffee into the bleached white filter, then poured water into the brewer from a plastic quart jug.

"I'm glad to see you at least use bottled water for your coffee."

"It tastes better than tap water," Coop said, switching on the brewer. He realized he was too petty to give Maureen the satisfaction of admitting he was using something natural for his health. She had a way of drawing out his worst qualities.

"I don't think that article is a good thing," Maureen said.

"That was my impression. And you're right. It decreases the odds of an arrest."

"Don't tell me about odds. I'm in the insurance business. I deal with information and odds all the time."

"I said you were right," Coop reminded her, irritated by her hostility. "Weren't you going bird-watching?"

"We call it birding. There's a lot more to it than just watching. Probably Deni Green has an adequate explanation. If you were to read her books you might have a higher regard for her abilities."

"I don't know what was in her mind," Coop said. "Remember, you're the one who pushed me to link up with her."

"Because our daughter was murdered and you and the police were doing nothing. That's another reason why I have strong reservations about that news report."

"I don't follow you."

"It might cause the police to close ranks and protect someone."

"Someone?"

"Bette's killer. If he is someone in the NYPD, he now knows you're on his trail. He can work to cut off your sources of information, or even see that you're fed misinformation. He might plant the idea that you're interfering in police business. He has knowledge now. And options. He can hide behind his shield."

"Bette's killer isn't a cop," Coop told her.

"You don't know that!"

"But I'm ninety-nine percent sure of it."

"There's something else he might do," Maureen said, ignoring Coop's protestations. "He might get close to the investigation, monitor it. That way he can escape and go underground if he has to. I want you to promise you'll be on the alert for someone like that."

"I promise," Coop said, figuring it would cost him nothing.

"Not as if you mean it."

The brewer was gurgling now, and the kitchen filled with the scent of coffee. It reminded Coop of Cara Callahan. Was he always going to think of her whenever he smelled coffee? He decided not to offer a cup to Maureen.

"I'm leaving," she said. "Call Deni Green and ask her why she talked to that reporter. I'm sure she had a good reason. I expect you to let me know."

"I will," Coop said, taking the easiest course.

"I'll be in Central Park."

"Do you have a cell phone?"

"No. They give you brain cancer." If she saw Coop wince, she pretended not to notice. "Call me at home this evening, or I'll call you tomorrow."

She shifted the bulk of her fanny pack and started for the door.

For some reason he suddenly didn't want her to leave. They shared the same grief and pain, and reflexive anger. Coop had seen it before and now he fully understood it: the bond of a dead child. *Their* dead child of their creation.

"Maureen . . . "

"What?"

He didn't know what to say. "Isn't it a bad time of the year for bird-watch—for birding?"

"Not if you want to track their migratory habits," Maureen said. "Like you're supposed to track the migratory habits of that serial killer."

Coop didn't bother showing her out. Just before he heard the door open and close, she called, "I'll leave the paper so you can enjoy it with your caffeine."

He was glad she'd left it.

He wanted to read the Distraught Dad piece word for word.

CHAPTER TWENTY-SEVEN

Coop finished reading the Distraught Dad feature, then poured a second cup of coffee and decided to phone Deni.

He carried the newspaper and his coffee over to his desk, sat down, and punched out her number with the eraser end of a pencil. While he listened to the phone ring on the other end of the connection, he gazed out the window and saw by the streaks on the glass that the gray morning sky was delivering a light rain. The weather would interfere with Maureen's bird-watching, he thought. *Good.*

After the sixth ring, Deni picked up and muttered a hello.

"You woke me," she said accusingly, after Coop had identified himself.

Good, he thought again. He said, "It's not so early that my ex-wife hasn't already been here and gone."

"And? . . . " Deni asked.

"She left behind the newspaper she came to show me."

"Oh." Her tone had changed.

"The one with the piece on our investigation. Photographs of both of us."

"Oh. I, uh, took that photo of you when you were crossing the street outside the Sapphire," Deni said. "I thought it might be good for the book, the dust jacket. I meant to tell you. And I meant to call you and let you know about the article before you saw it this morning. Horseshit of me not to have. I guess I overslept."

"Then I suppose you haven't seen it."

"I read it late last night, actually. Alicia had a copy sent over to me. A courtesy thing."

"Alicia?"

"The article was her idea. She thought we could use the news media to aid in our investigation and get the book written."

"Just how does she figure something like this will help in our investigation?"

"The national press might pick up on the story. Maybe the police in other cities will finally realize there's a connection between the murders, that there's an incredibly successful and dangerous serial killer out there. Maybe even the FBI will finally get off their dead asses and do some investigating. I don't get you sometimes. Don't you want to see Bette's killer caught as soon as possible?"

"You knew this was going to happen and went along with it?"

"Of course. I need to get this book written, Coop." Getting defensive. All the way awake. The old Deni now, like a bear aroused in its cave.

"That wasn't the way to do it, Deni. All you'll do is

alert the killer and antagonize everyone who's helping us."

"Damn it, Coop, the killer already knows he's broken the law. And who's helping us that we're going to antagonize?"

"The police, the FBI, victims' family members, just to name a few. When people die violent deaths, there's no way to be sure how the folks they've left behind will react, or the people close enough to the case to have seen and smelled the blood. I know the story being published didn't make my ex-wife very happy."

"Maureen's upset about it? I don't know why she should be. Alicia had me talk to her. She gave me some of the information for the article."

Coop was astounded. "You've been talking to Maureen, too?"

"Of course. She was thrilled to meet me. Do you know she's read most of my Cozy Cat novels?"

"Did you tell her what she said might find its way into the news media?"

"Well, no. How could I? I was flying blind at the time, didn't know myself the piece was going to be written."

Coop sat pressing the receiver to his ear so hard that it hurt, staring furiously out the window at the rain.

"Coop," Deni said in a slow and reasonable tone, "I still don't understand why anyone would be angry about this being in the newspaper."

"Neither you nor Alicia cleared it with me."

"Why should we have to?"

"Don't you understand we're civilians walking the edge of an open homicide investigation?"

"Sure. But we're staying legal, aren't we?"

"It isn't so much a matter of legality as it is of having continued cooperation. There has to be a sharing of information, a mutual trust. That means no surprises."

Deni sighed into her phone. "I have a feeling, Coop, that you're overreacting and are going to be the only one upset about that story in the paper."

He slammed the receiver down and sat squeezing it in his frustration.

It rang beneath his hand.

He was sure it was Deni calling back, but he was at least calm enough to modulate his voice when he said hello.

The voice that came back at him sounded furious. "Coop, this is Billard. What the hell's with that Distraught Dad story in the paper this morning?"

Coop explained it to him, then gave him the phone numbers of Deni Green and Alicia.

Billard had still been plenty irritated when he and Coop were finished talking. Coop suspected that police cooperation would have ended with the conversation if he and Billard hadn't been old and good friends.

Watching the rain fall harder and at a sharper angle from low gray clouds, Coop tried to calm himself. It had been brought home to him that both Deni and Alicia were even less trustworthy than he'd thought. If Deni had talked to Maureen without mentioning it to him, and been a willing source for a reporter, who else might she have confided in? He looked at the story's byline: Earl Gitter. The name rang no bell in Coop's memory. He folded the newspaper and dropped it into the wastebasket in the desk's kneehole. If only he could do that with every copy.

The phone rang again. He picked up.

Deni.

"Have you calmed down by now, Coop?"

"No. I don't think Art Billard has, either."

"Billard?"

"He called here. He'll be calling you and Alicia soon."

"So let him. I don't think there's any reason—"

"That's because you don't realize what you've done, Deni."

"I think I do realize it. Why don't we wait and see what kind of fallout occurs before we get all excited?"

"Here's a bit of fallout I should remind you of," Coop told her. "Now the killer knows who is personally looking for him. He knows our names. He knows what I look like. He knows what you look like. And he might be even more upset than Billard."

He hung up on her again.

Before she could call back, he punched out the number of Whippet Books.

When there was no answer, he remembered it was Saturday and the publisher was closed.

Coop didn't want to wait until Monday to talk with Alicia Benham. Leaving the receiver off the hook, he pulled a phone directory out of the drawer and hoped Alicia Benham had a listed number.

She was the second A. Benham he called, noticing that her address was on West 82nd Street. Easy walking distance.

Like Coop, Alicia hadn't had breakfast. They agreed to meet at Morgan's on Amsterdam for coffee and pastry within the hour.

Morgan's was a small bakery that served mostly carry-out but had half a dozen tables across from its display case and serving counter. As usual, there were several customers around the counter and cashier, but only a few of the tables were occupied. The sugar and cinnamon scent of the pastry piqued appetites. Even the coffee smelled good, though Coop had already drunk three cups this morning and the taste of it still lay bitter beneath his tongue.

The weather cooperated. Rain had stopped falling shortly after he'd left his building, and the black umbrella he carried was folded wet and leaned now like a huge crashed bat against the wall by his chair.

Alicia, dressed in black as usual, even to the black raincoat she shrugged out of as she walked into Morgan's, saw Coop immediately and smiled and walked toward him. She was wearing a skirt today, short enough to reveal legs that were thin but nonetheless shapely.

She sat down opposite him at the table and they both ordered warm cinnamon rolls that were slightly larger than the plates they were served on.

"Having already read this morning's paper," Alicia said, "I bet I can guess what you want to talk about. I suppose you're angry."

"I am goddamn angry! And disappointed in you."

"I never pretended to be somebody I'm not. I want Deni's manuscript, and soon. I'll do most anything to get it."

"Pathetic."

"Did you pass any bag ladies on your way here, Coop?"

"I don't know."

"You might have looked right through them. I don't want to be one of them."

"What about your word that you'll try to protect Bette's reputation if Deni smears her?"

"I meant that. I'll do what I can. There's no reason why I shouldn't. Believe it or not, I like you, Coop."

While she cut her roll into quarters and spread rapidly melting butter on the exposed sides of one of the wedges, he told her about his conversations with Deni.

"She didn't express any reservations to me about sending her to give the interview," Alicia said.

"Maybe she doesn't trust you."

"Of course she doesn't. Deni doesn't trust anyone, because she knows no one can trust her."

Coop used a fork to take a bite of cinnamon roll. He'd never regarded any kind of sticky or greasy confection as finger food, even ate french fries with a fork. "What the hell kind of people did I get mixed up with?"

"That's an odd question for a cop to ask."

He thought about it. She was right. He'd certainly met even less scrupulous people than Alicia or Deni Green. Lots of them. "Let me ask you another question," Coop said. "Has Deni at least had conversations with you about the book?"

"We've talked about it," Alicia said, "but not in any way I find very revealing. I learned more from that newspaper article than I have from Deni herself."

"She doesn't seem to realize she's alerted the killer that we're dedicated to his capture. And she's revealed who we are, what we look like. She's put herself in mortal danger."

"But she's stirred up publicity to keep public interest from cooling off. That will pay, eventually. Anything to sell books, Coop. You've heard of the *New York Times* bestseller list?"

"Of course."

"If Deni gets a book on the list, it will give her career a rocket boost, and it will preserve my job at Whippet for a while, keep me from falling victim to consolidation and technology like so many other editors."

"Is it really that serious?"

"Oh, maybe not. I can always freelance edit or become an agent. But everybody in publishing knows it, feels it—the Internet'll get you if you don't watch out."

"Progress, huh?"

"'Fraid so. I'm simply being honest with you. And Deni knows what the interview can do for her. She's trying to flush the killer out, maybe even prod him into committing another crime and possibly making a mistake, so she can have something to write about."

"This isn't a goddamn writing exercise," Coop said, "it's a homicide investigation. These are real people. My daughter, Bette, was very real—is still very real to me. Don't either of you have enough humanity to understand that?"

"I told you, I'll try to protect your daughter's memory. And Deni, well, she's a writer."

"Do all writers think like that?"

"Not exactly. She possesses more of one characteristic than most writers."

"What's that?"

"She's an asshole. But I endure her for the same reason you do, and should continue to do: you need her. Or at least she's useful to you. And she's going to write her book, one way or the other. This way I stay employed and you have some knowledge of what she's up to, and maybe you can even influence what she's going to write. And most importantly, she might help you to solve the riddle of your daughter's murder."

"You're saying I need her more than she needs me."

"Or at least as much. And try not to worry. I'm sure she'll stop talking about the book and write it. She's working up to it. She told me she hasn't yet figured out quite how to deal with the subject matter. Doesn't even know yet who the main character will be."

"Meaning?"

"She hasn't yet decided who the story will mostly be about."

"I hope it won't be Bette."

"I can't promise you it won't be, Coop. Even though I'm Deni's editor, and I'll try to protect Bette's reputation for you, my options are limited. Who becomes the central character in her book mostly depends on what Deni learns, and how she decides to use it." Alicia buttered another wedge of cinnamon roll. "The book might be mainly about the killer, if he's interesting enough. Or it might be about one or another of the victims."

Coop stared at her and absently picked up a piece of his roll, not noticing he was getting icing all over his fingers.

Alicia smiled across the table, knowing what he must be thinking. "It even might be about you."

CHAPTER TWENTY-EIGHT

The Night Caller sat beneath the slanted skylight in his Manhattan loft apartment and used its diffused light to read the newspaper. He'd been at his work heavily much of the day and hadn't had time to catch up on the news. But he enjoyed his coffee and his paper, and had been glad to settle down with them to read in the fading evening light. He much preferred natural light, perhaps because he spent so much time in artificial or fluorescent brightness. An unhealthy glare. He was sensitive to such things. Because of his nature he was sensitive in many ways, and in some ways callous.

At first he paid little attention to a feature piece captioned DISTRAUGHT DAD SEEKS DAUGHTER'S KILLER. The usual gross sensationalism.

But when he started to move on to the next page, his gaze fell on a name buried in the text. Sue Coppolino.

He sat forward, concentrating now on the page before him.

Someone, this Distraught Dad, along with a woman who was apparently some kind of writer, had interviewed Sue Coppolino in prison about Marlee Clark's murder. Other names leaped out at him from the text. Some of them called to him. They knew him. They knew him still. There were faces. Faces. His thoughts scattered like roaches exposed to sudden light. He could hear them! Hear their insect legs and brittleness scurrying on concrete!

Terror locked him tight. Was he losing control? Was the center not holding? That was the darkest thought of all. More horrifying even than the roaches.

Start at the beginning, he told himself. *This concoction of fact and lie is written in organized fashion, so use it to organize your thoughts.*

After waiting for his heartbeat to slow, he forced himself to begin reading the first paragraph.

Ten minutes later he stood up and carried his untouched and cooled cup of coffee into the kitchen. After pouring the coffee down the sink and placing the cup in the small dishwasher, he opened a cabinet door near the refrigerator. He got a glass and poured into it two inches of Southern Comfort from a bottle he kept in the cabinet. Was he drinking more lately? Too much? *No,* he told himself. *Don't, don't.* Now wasn't the time to worry about *that.*

Seated again on his small leather sofa, he sipped from the glass while staring at the newspaper he'd left lying on the floor, staring at the photographs of former NYPD detective Ezekiel Cooper and the writer Deni Green. Ezekiel, he thought. A biblical name. Did this man fashion himself some sort of angel of vengeance? Of justice? And what about the woman Deni Green, who looked like a cruel man with a malicious glint in her eye? He knew that glint, had seen it in the mirror of the past. One thing he'd determined from reading the article was that these two hunters (as the journalist had called them) knew nothing about their prey.

Yet sitting here, their prey felt a twinge like something tiny but alive stirring inside him. The police weren't such fools that they spilled everything they knew to a cheap journalist at a second-rate newspaper. Why would these two hunters be so foolish?

And what could they know, anyway? Why should he even care about them? He was certainly their intellectual and spiritual superior, and he'd been careful.

He smiled and took another sip of Southern Comfort.

What *could* they possibly know?

Nothing, he decided. But he certainly knew a great deal about them. There it was, lying on his apartment floor in a newspaper. It often amazed him, how gullible people were. Gullible enough to underestimate him. People had underestimated him all his life. The reason why was obvious.

That they were wrong had always been obvious to him.

Well, not always.

But he had learned.

As they were learning. His enemies' confusion was his strength.

He thought that was somewhere in the Bible. Like Ezekiel.

Deni he was certain wasn't in the Bible.

God damn them both.

Lying back on the sofa, staring up at the shadows of

clouds moving like dark thoughts across the skylight, he sipped Southern Comfort and began drifting into sleep knowing God wasn't relevant.

The Night Caller found solace in the fact that he didn't need God. No need for God to damn them, after all; he could damn his own enemies. He could destroy them. They didn't know their fate. He did. *Cita mors ruit.* Swift death rushes upon us. He decided when.

He was their fate.

In time. In sleep. Sleep and time carne together and consciousness tilted and faded. The glass of Southern Comfort slipped to the floor, bouncing once on the carpet, then rolling in a wide arc and spilling its few remaining amber drops like scattered sequins among the coarse fibers.

Control went. Sleep came.

Sleep always came. For everyone. Prison and sanctuary.

CHAPTER TWENTY-NINE

Coop was sitting in his car with the engine idling and the heater on when Maureen left work at Allied National Insurance that evening.

There she was, walking with her head down, close to the building to avoid the biting wind. Maureen was wearing her drab brown coat buttoned tight all the way to her chin, its collar turned up. It didn't appear that she was wearing socks beneath her practical artificial leather shoes. She wore no hat or gloves despite the cold. Coop figured she thought the cold was natural, so it must be good for her.

She had to walk past him, and when she did, she noticed him and broke stride.

Coop leaned over and opened the passenger side door. "Come on in for a minute out of the cold," he said. "We need to talk."

She moved close to the door and leaned down to gaze sternly at him, the wind plastering her hair to the side of her face like a claw. "Need? I don't need to talk with you."

"Please, Maureen. It's about Bette."

She was motionless for a few seconds. He was getting cold.

Finally she lowered herself into the car, staying as far away from him as possible, but left the door hanging open.

Cold air swirled around his ankles. "Close the door, Maureen."

"No. This will do just fine."

Coop guessed it would have to. "I'm asking you to listen while I try to explain why you shouldn't talk to Deni Green again about Bette."

"Deni is working at solving Bette's murder, just like you're supposed to be doing."

"Deni and I are supposed to be working together," Coop said. "She didn't tell me she was going to talk with you."

"Why should she have to? Because she's a woman?"

"For God's sake, Maureen—"

"Do you tell her whenever you're going to talk with someone? Did you tell her you were coming here to talk with me?"

Coop said nothing. She had him in one of her conversational traps. And, he had to admit, maybe she had a point

Maureen was smiling at him triumphantly.

"It was Deni's sneaking behind my back that prompted this conversation," he said. "Otherwise I wouldn't be here."

"I wish you'd sneak behind somebody's back and learn something. Instead, you play your stupid games with your police friends. You don't have to do that. You're not bound to their code. You're no longer a policeman."

"But I need their cooperation if I'm going to find Bette's killer."

"It doesn't seem like cooperation to me. Deni said the police haven't been much help at all."

"She's wrong."

"So, is the suspect in jail? No. In fact, there isn't even a suspect."

"There will be. But what I want to impress on you is that Deni's writing a book, and she's being pressured to do it fast. She wants to make money out of this, Maureen. That's why she's pumping you for information. And believe me, when it comes time to use that information, she won't care who gets hurt."

"Her ulterior motives don't interest me, as long as she finds Bette's killer."

"But she doesn't know how to look. She's not a cop and she's never been one."

"In her way, she's probably solved more crimes than you. Her profession has prepared her for precisely this kind of investigation."

"That's absurd! She's a writer. She sits at a keyboard and makes things up. She commits crimes on paper, then solves them on paper. This isn't on paper, Maureen. This is life."

"It helps to have someone cerebral in this investigation. The police simply gather information until they might have enough of it for a solution to fall into their laps. They don't solve deductive puzzles the way Deni does in her Cozy Cat mysteries. They don't synthesize their information and extrapolate."

Coop could almost hear Deni talking. "Did she tell you that?"

"She didn't need to tell me. It's obvious to almost everyone but an ex-cop."

"She doesn't know as much as she thinks. Or as you think."

"Have you ever read a Cozy Cat mystery?"

"No. I tried but couldn't."

"Then how can you judge her capabilities as a detective?"

"I don't recall taking the Cozy Cat test at the police academy."

Maureen swung a leg out of the car. "You're being sarcastic now instead of reasonable. I'm leaving."

"I'm sorry. But if you continue to talk with Deni, you're putting her, me, and possibly yourself in danger."

Maureen twisted her body so she could look directly at him. "Me?"

"None of us knows exactly how a killer like this thinks. Deni and I pose an obvious threat to him, maybe even a challenge that will attract him and make him kill more often. And if Deni writes anything that gives him the impression you might know something, anything that could pose the slightest threat to him, he might make you a victim."

She snorted. "That's ridiculous! Anyway, what do you care?"

"I care, Maureen." He caught himself and said no more, knowing how she'd react if he told her that her pain was his and he felt sorry for her.

"Serial killers only murder certain types of victims," she said.

"Not necessarily."

"Yes, necessarily. That's the point of their murders to begin with."

"What makes you so sure?"

"Deni told me. She also said serial killers subconsciously want to be caught. That's why they kill more and more often and take more chances. And that's why somebody smart enough can get into their minds. You only need to help them be caught."

Coop felt like telling her what bullshit that was. Instead he said calmly, "We don't really know how all of these killers think. And I'm not so sure they kill more and more often because they want to take chances and be caught. It could simply be because they're coming unraveled and losing control."

"This one certainly seems to have control of the situation," Maureen said. She swiveled sideways to stand on the sidewalk outside the car. Coop watched the wind pluck at her coat, twist it where it had come unbuttoned to expose a knee that looked somehow obscene in its ruddy nudeness. Then she slammed the door hard enough to make something fall and tinkle loosely behind the dashboard.

Coop watched her walk away, her head bowed, advancing determinedly into the frigid wind. He thought back to their wedding day, then the early times with Bette. Happiness had seemed automatic for years. Then came the change, gradually at first, then with a rapidity that overtook everything. Had this Maureen always been inside the other, needing only time or some kind of catalyst in order to emerge? Maybe there was someone else inside all of us, waiting to meet challenges, climb to new heights, sink to new lows, surrender reason.

Strangers within strangers. Strangers who sometimes killed.

Coop could understand the medieval belief in demonic possession. It was an easy explanation for some people's aberrant behavior, and perhaps not so far from the truth. Sleeping demons awakened by who knew what?

Cara smiled at the last customer in line, adroitly counted out cash in twenties, then stuffed the withdrawal slip through the slot in the marble counter behind her teller's cage.

Mercantile Mutual was modeled on the old-fashioned savings institutions whose areas of wood paneling, brass, and marble lent depositors a sense of permanence and security. In Mercantile Mutual, however, the oak paneling was realistic treated plastic, the brass teller's cages were actually colored PVC pipe of the sort you might find beneath your sink, and the pink-veined marble was cultured. The decor seemed to have the desired effect on customers, though, and the money was real.

When she was finished closing down her station, Cara said good-bye to Bill Farrow, her fellow teller, then went to the employee's lounge behind the loan department and got her coat from the closet.

Loan manager Lou Morganstern, seated at the table drinking 7 UP from a can, nodded to her and smiled. "So, Irish, how do you like M-and-M so far?"

"Fine," Cara told him. She didn't particularly care for Morganstern, who was a short, balding man of middle age who had a way of staring at women until they turned around. Cara herself had felt the force of his attention, and turned her head just in time to see him glance away with a lingering kind of sly guilt in his eye and at the corners of his mouth. "It's just what I expected."

"You'll do well here, I'm sure," Morganstern said, "once you learn the ropes."

"The ropes are pretty much the same in all banks," Cara told him.

He grinned. "Yeah, different knots, is all."

Cara was aware she'd gotten her position at Mercantile Mutual because she was Ann's sister. Even with her experience, she had to start near the bottom, with the promise that she'd move up when a new, Long Island branch under construction was completed. Cara didn't care why she got the job, or what happened on Long Island, as long as it didn't interfere with what she had in mind in the here and now. She wrapped her red silk muffler, like Ann's, around her neck before putting on her coat. It was cold outside, with a threat of snow.

Morganstern finished his soda and casually kinked the aluminum can with one hand as if to show his strength. "We were all sorry about Ann," he said. "You kind of surprised everybody when you came in for work that first day, how much you resemble her."

Cara could see why they'd be surprised. She'd waited until she was hired to dye her hair red like Ann's. She had to use an artificial braid in back, since her hair was shorter than her late sister's. Then she'd bought a gray coat similar to the one Ann had been wearing when she was killed, a red silk muffler like Ann's. When she caught sight of herself in a mirror, she was sometimes startled by her resemblance to Ann. They wouldn't be mistaken for twins, but no one would be surprised that they were sisters. They were the same type. The type that attracted Ann's killer.

"You got any other sisters?" Morganstern asked, tossing the can at a trash receptacle. It bounced off the rim and clattered across the floor.

"No," Cara said, buttoning her coat. "No one. There's no one else."

She felt Morganstern's eyes on her as she went out.

On the street, she got her gloves from her purse and worked them on, then walked the block and a half to the bus stop Ann had used. That was the idea, to be the same type of woman as Ann, to adopt the same hairstyle and dress, to walk in her footsteps, eat lunch where she ate, ride the same buses and subways, board at the same stops.

In Queens, Cara would sometimes ride the bus all the way to the end of the line, near the college campus where Ann had been killed. More often, she would get off the bus after a few stops, cease being Ann, and take the subway back across the East River to Manhattan, then a bus to near her apartment on the Upper West Side.

At the bus stop, she stood outside the flimsy kiosk so she would be more visible, ignoring the two women inside who stood huddled against a poster advertising a Broadway show.

The killer might live or work in the area, or at least spend time here. Whatever quality it was about Ann that had drawn him to her, Cara wanted it to have the same effect again.

She hadn't told anyone what she was doing. She knew what they'd say, that it was a manifestation of her grief, that it was foolish and dangerous.

That she was bait.

She smiled grimly. Bait . . .

The raw wind kicked up around her, blowing bits of paper and cigarette butts in a tight circle at her feet, causing her nose to run. She removed her gloves, and as she reached into her purse for a Kleenex, her knuckles brushed the cold steel of the .25 semiautomatic handgun that she'd bought where a friend had told her to go in Brooklyn.

She didn't feel like bait.

CHAPTER THIRTY

That evening, Coop listened to his land-line answering machine message from Earl Gitter, the reporter who'd done the Distraught Dad piece, asking for an interview. Then came Deni Green's message:

"Coop, old buddy, I know I'm rash, a bad girl sometimes, but we need each other. Alicia called and wants some material on the book, says she's getting pressure from the managing editor. And sure, we want to find the asshole who killed Bette. But first things first, especially if both things are almost one in the same—that is, starting to outline the book, and finding the serial killer who offed your daughter. My book—"

The chip had run out of recording room and the machine cut her off.

Good, Coop thought, pushing the DELETE button.

He got a Beck's dark from the refrigerator, his one beer that he allowed himself every other day, and carefully poured it into a frosted glass he kept in the freezer. Making the beer the object of a ceremony seemed to improve its taste. Then he went back into the living room and sat down in the chair facing the television. Using his right hand to lift the glass to his lips, he used his left to work the TV's remote.

Channel One, the local news, flickered to life on the screen.

It was the top of the hour. The "bug" in the lower right hand corner of the screen informed him that outside temperature was twenty-one degrees. Glad he was inside, Coop watched the attractive anchorwoman take viewers through the news: Another subway pushing attack, a tourist from Omaha almost killed; three children dead from smoke inhalation in an apartment fire in the Bronx; another jogger beaten and raped in Central Park; a newborn infant discovered in a Dumpster in the Village . . .

Depressing. So much so that Coop pressed the mute button on the remote. Soundlessly before him appeared a steamy five-car pileup on the Queensboro Bridge, an old woman speaking frantically while a trickle of blood ran down her forehead from above her hairline, a guy in a suit and tie shielding his face with a newspaper as he was being led to a waiting police cruiser.

Coop switched off the TV and sat in silence, sipping his beer. It bothered him a bit that sometimes loneliness seemed like a friend. He rested his head against the soft back of the chair and closed his eyes.

The phone rang and he sat motionless, letting the machine answer. After his message, Deni's voice:

"Coop, pardner, we really should talk. Hey, Coop, I bet you're screening your calls. I do that a lot, myself. You'd be surprised, the loony phone calls a successful writer gets. My guess is you're sitting there reading the paper, trying to tune me out. Listen, Coop. Hey! Hey! Hey, fuck you, Coop!"

Feeling better, he grinned.

After sleeping late the next morning, he called Longpoint Bank, where Cara Callahan worked, to ask her if she'd thought of anything more that might be useful.

He was told that Cara had left the bank, and he was given the name of her new employer—another bank.

As Coop replaced the receiver, he realized it was the bank where Ann Callahan had worked.

He sat by the phone and thought about that for a few minutes. Then, instead of calling, he decided he'd talk with Cara again in person, maybe catch her during her lunch break.

At five minutes to noon he was parked on East 57th, across the street from Mercantile Mutual.

He was astonished when she emerged from the bank. The red hair, the gray coat and red scarf, even the shoes. They might have been removed from her sister's corpse. For a second he was looking at Ann Callahan.

She turned left and strode along the sidewalk toward Third Avenue. Coop climbed out of the car, turned up his coat collar, and followed on his side of the street.

When she went through a door under a sign reading DARBY'S DELI, he jogged across the street.

Before entering the deli, he peered in through the steamed window displaying fresh-baked bread and pastries. Cara was in line at a counter. Beyond the counter were tables and chairs, even an archway into another room with more seating. As he watched, the man in front of Cara carried a tray with food on it to one of the tables.

Coop walked a few doors down and stood as if studying books in a shop window, making sure she wasn't ordering food to go, giving her time to sit down before entering. He'd learned from experience that it was wise to approach people he wanted to question when they were in restaurants and had just sat down to a meal. They were far less likely to get up and walk away.

When five minutes had passed, Coop entered the deli.

There was Cara seated at a table near a window. If he'd continued walking past the door, she might have glanced out and seen him.

She sensed him standing there and looked up from spreading mustard with a plastic knife on a pastrami sandwich. Those green eyes—Cara's, not Ann's dead eyes staring up from the brown grass beneath the campus trees—fixed him where he stood. He couldn't help but notice that her new red hair suited her eyes and complexion.

He was relieved when she smiled and said, "Coop! Sit down, please. Have you had lunch?"

"No, but I'm not hungry." He sat on a wobbly chair across the table from her. "I called at Longpoint Bank and they said you'd gone to work here."

She smiled again in a way he liked. "At the deli?"

"At Mercantile Mutual, just down the street. Where your sister Ann worked."

She took a bite of sandwich and chewed, regarding him.

"I wanted to talk to you," he said. "See if you might

have thought of something else about Ann, something that might be useful."

"I don't think so, Coop."

"When I saw you on the street, I thought for a second you were Ann. The clothes, the new hairdo, everything . . ."

"People deal with grief in different ways," she said.

"I've seen a lot of those ways, Cara."

"Maybe I've always been jealous of my little sister, and now I want to live her life. Doesn't that give me a motive for murder?"

"It might, if you talked that way to the wrong people. And now you have what you always wanted. That isn't what's happening, though, is it?"

She gave him her beautiful smile again, warm sun in the gathering winter. "No," she said. She hadn't yet twisted the cap from her bottle of Diet Coke. She did so now, poured half into a paper cup, then slid the bottle over to Coop.

He thanked her and took a sip. "It isn't hard to figure out, Cara. The red hair, the way you're wearing your makeup. And the new gray coat and red scarf that are almost exact duplicates of Ann's."

"The coat and scarf don't really go well with the hair. Ann never did have the best color sense."

"They're distinctive together, though. That's what you want, isn't it?"

"Yes, that's what I want."

"Now you work where Ann worked. And I suspect she mentioned to you or you found out from some of the others at Mercantile Mutual that she sometimes ate lunch at this deli. You're even sitting by the window where you can be seen from the street."

"I think Ann's killer might have lived or worked, or at least spent time, in this neighborhood. If so, he's probably still in the area. He might have first seen her here, first gotten his idea to stalk her and kill her."

"It's possible he first saw her on the college campus where she died," Coop said.

"Sure. But I'm betting he saw her around here and then waited for his chance. He might even work in the bank."

"The police don't think any of the employees look good for her murder, Cara."

She sat back and looked directly at him. "The police can be wrong. I can be wrong that the killer spends time in this neighborhood, maybe even banks at Mercantile Mutual. But I could be right, and at least I'm doing something about Ann's murder. Aren't serial killers usually attracted to a certain type of woman, one who resembles their mother or a girlfriend who jilted them? Someone like that?"

"Very often they are," Coop admitted.

"Well, I'm now very much the same type as Ann, and I'm going to work and eat where she did, walk in her footsteps, ride the same bus and subway on the same route. I'm going to listen and ask questions at Mercantile, learn more about Ann's daily habits from the people she worked with. Her life and the killer's must have intersected somewhere before the night of her death, and Ann didn't have much of a life other than work and home."

"What you're doing might be successful enough to get you killed."

"Or to identify the killer. He probably got to know Ann. They must have talked somewhere sometime before he simply decided to murder her. Maybe he'll decide to get to know me."

"It doesn't always work that way. Sometimes serial killers prey on strangers."

"Not this one. It appears the victims knew him, even trusted him."

"Who told you that?"

"No one. It was in that newspaper piece a few days ago. Your friend Deni Green mentioned it to whoever wrote it."

Damn Deni, Coop thought. "I'd rather you didn't do this thing," he said. "You're trailing bait for a killer."

"That's not exactly what I'm doing. But what if it were? Bait sometimes catches fish that get fried."

"Sometimes the fish turns out to be a shark, and the bait turns out to be a meal. That's where you are now, Cara, in shark waters."

The smile again, but this time there was something different about her eyes, the same hard light he'd seen in them before.

"For a while," she said, "that's where I intend to swim."

CHAPTER THIRTY-ONE

Seattle Detective Sergeant Roy Lyons sat at his desk and stared glumly at the phone. Yesterday a woman had attacked a man with a long electrical device she'd been using to kill slugs in her garden, some kind of thin, heated, and sharply pointed metal rod. In the dank Washington climate, Seattle residents often had to deal with slugs that were a particular threat to plants. Unconventional and imaginative methods were sometimes used, as in this case. The Slug Slayer, as it was called by its manufacturer, looked to Lyons a lot like an electric dipstick heater used to warm and thin a car's oil in cold weather so the engine would start. Whatever it was, the Slug Slayer did slay slugs, and it could double as a heated sword. The woman's neighbor, one pesky Adam Adamski (Could that really be his name?), was hospitalized with punctured and singed intestines. The swordswoman was free on bond.

Lyons's partner, Marty Sanderson, approached the desk with a cup of coffee in one hand, a file folder in the other. He grinned at Lyons and extended the cup toward him. "Want a slug?"

"Shut up," Lyons said.

"Oh, ah, yeah."

"You don't fool me," Lyons told him.

"Any luck finding witnesses to the stabbing?" Sanderson asked, obviously suppressing another smile but sticking to business.

"Two men are canvassing the neighborhood. They're supposed to call when they find a witness. They've been at it for several hours and the phone hasn't rung."

"I'm here to change the subject," Sanderson said. "Remember that woman about a month ago who'd been worked over in her bathtub with a can opener?"

"I tend not to forget those things." He also couldn't forget what the ME had shown him at the morgue, how a plastic saint had been inserted in her vagina, deeply with the aid of a knife cut. After death, thank God. That information was still secret from press and public. Whoever knew it other than the authorities was the killer. The saint was a cheap plastic statuette sold in religious gift shops. It was also used by florists to embellish floral displays and funeral wreaths. The company that manufactured the things sold them by the thousands. St. Augustine was one of their most popular models.

"Georgianna Mason," Sanderson said anyway, as a reminder. "Remember we found a heel print in the bathroom?"

"Yeah. The killer was barefoot. He'd probably undressed so he wouldn't get blood or water on his clothes while he was . . . using the can opener." Lyons also remembered that the print of a bare heel was obscure enough that it wouldn't be useful in court even if they were sure they had the killer and that his heel had made it.

Sanderson tossed the file folder he was holding onto Lyons's desk. "After getting dressed, the killer must have walked back into the bathroom and stood for a moment to admire his work before leaving. Lab guys found another print with their forensic lights, not visible to the naked eye, this one made by a shoe."

"They think it was made by the killer?"

"There was blood on the shoe's sole. That's why they were able to bring out the print. It took them a while to do it; then the file got misplaced. It was found yesterday. There's a computer-enhanced image there in the folder."

Lyons opened the crime folder and looked at the image of a footprint. It was of a man's shoe, about size ten, he figured. Too bad it wasn't a jogging shoe; they usually had elaborate and distinctive sole prints, easy to match. This shoe was unusual in that the sole design was a simple crisscross pattern of straight lines running to the edges.

"Might this match the shoes of anyone who was in the apartment just after the body was discovered?" Lyons asked.

"Negative," Sanderson said. "That's been checked. And the lab says there are no signs of variation or clotting, so the blood had to have been fresh when the sole came in contact with it."

"Okay." Lyons was grateful for the new information, but he doubted that it would lead anywhere in and of itself. Another piece of a sordid puzzle. He left the file folder open and slid it across the desktop toward

Sanderson. "See if this print will show on a fax, and start contacting shoe manufacturers and wholesalers. Maybe we can get a match. It can't hurt to know what kind of shoes the sick bastard wears."

"Whatever kind they are, I'd like to use their laces to hang him by the neck," Sanderson said.

"Very unprofessional, Marty."

The phone rang as Lyons was sitting watching Sanderson walk away through the squad room with the folder.

"Sergeant Lyons?" said the caller. "This is Patrolman Eganer. You know, about the stabbing yesterday? . . ."

This was good, Lyons thought. Eganer was one of the cops assigned to canvass the neighborhood where the assault had occurred. He was fresh-faced and only a year in the department, but sharp and with a bright future despite the fact he'd probably only shaved once or twice in his life. "What've you got?" he asked the young patrolman.

"A neighbor whose backyard is on the diagonal with the one where the guy was stabbed. She says she heard loud voices arguing, looked out her kitchen window, and saw everything. The victim was just standing there, even had his hands in his pockets, when he was stuck with that snail thing."

"Slug."

"Oh. Sure."

"You get a statement?"

"Sure."

"Fine work, Egener. See what else you can find, then come back here before lunchtime."

"Sure will."

Lyons hung up the phone feeling only somewhat better. A man was in the hospital with cauterized stomach wounds, but at least he was alive. There was a good case against his assailant now, a strong possibility that she'd be convicted of assault with a deadly weapon. Trouble for both of them, but a chance for justice.

Trouble, Lyons thought; that was what his job was mostly about. It could be miserably depressing and leave indelible images that would haunt until death. He remembered Georgianna Mason—what had been Georgianna Mason—in her bathtub.

The guy in the hospital, the woman with the Slug Slayer, they only thought they knew trouble.

CHAPTER THIRTY-TWO

It didn't take Cara long to slip into her new routine.

While she was pleasant at work, she kept her distance from her fellow employees. She wanted to talk to them, listen and learn about Ann, but she didn't want to form new friendships. She knew Coop was right; what she was doing was dangerous. She had no right to make it dangerous for someone else.

So she took her lunches alone in nearby restaurants she knew Ann had frequented. When she heard where Ann had gone shopping sometimes during her lunch hour, Cara went there the next day. It was a clothing shop near the Citigroup Building on Third Avenue. Cara browsed through the merchandise for a while—even used the changing rooms to try on a blouse.

After leaving without making a purchase, she spent time in the nearby shops on the street, then the array of shops in the Citigroup Building. Though Christmas was still over a month away, there was a large model train exhibit in the building's lobby, featuring a detailed, miniature town and at least ten trains running on synchronized schedules. She watched for a while, fascinated, then began skirting the large exhibit and observing the other people watching the trains. So large was the model town that one side of it was daytime, the other nighttime, with windows glowing in the tiny houses, streetlights dotting the thoroughfares, and the trains running with beamed lights. No one appeared to be paying any attention to Cara except possibly a man standing opposite her, on the night side of the town, wearing a tan topcoat, checkered muffler, and tinted glasses. Because of the glasses, Cara couldn't be sure where the man was looking, but he seemed to be facing her directly and gazing over the level of the model town.

Odd that he should be wearing sunglasses in the building's lobby, she thought, pretending to ignore him.

She decided to walk away and window-shop among the indoor merchandise to see if he'd follow.

After a while, she turned around and looked back at the model train exhibit.

The man was nowhere in sight.

She thought she caught a glimpse of him pushing through one of the revolving doors to go outside, but she couldn't be sure.

Her heart was pounding. Take it easy, she told herself. This was only the first time someone seemed to be watching her, and she couldn't even be sure of that. It was the tinted glasses worn indoors that had spooked her, and the way his muffler was wrapped high and concealing his chin. As if he didn't want to be recognized.

But as she started toward the revolving doors herself, she noticed two more men wearing tinted glasses in the lobby. Maybe it wasn't so unusual. Lots of people wore sunglasses in the late fall and winter, and it was easy to forget to remove them indoors. In fact, they made glasses now with lenses that appeared darkly tinted from the outside, but didn't obstruct vision at all for the wearer looking the other way through them.

She went through the revolving door into the cold November air and walked to the Third and Lex subway station.

The platform was crowded, and everyone seemed rather subdued, possibly because down near the escalator a street musician was playing a mournful tune on a violin. It was Irish and familiar.

Pushing before it a cool wind that ruffled Cara's hair, the F train heading east toward Queens roared in and rumbled to a stop.

She boarded and was hit by the odor of crowded bodies and perhaps urine. Now mothballs, as someone in a thick wool coat crowded against her. Cara remained standing so she could survey most of the car. The train lurched and accelerated, causing a heavyset woman gripping the same vertical steel bar Cara was holding to bump into her. She didn't apologize. A ragged older man seated on the other side of the aisle stared blankly at Cara. As the car swayed, a bearded man glanced up from the Hebrew paper he was reading and momentarily locked gazes with her.

No one among her fellow passengers resembled the man with the tinted glasses and checked muffler.

Cara felt relief, and then guilt.

She shouldn't be relieved. Wasn't she doing this to lure the killer into the open? Wasn't she exactly what Coop had said, knowing and willing bait in shark waters?

Unexpectedly, fear washed over her like a cold wave. So powerful was the sensation that she became slightly nauseated. Gripping the steel bar tightly as possible, she began to tremble, flexing her knees and trying to maintain her balance in the speeding, swaying subway car.

The woman standing next to her noticed Cara's odd behavior and stared.

Her expression suggested she couldn't care less.

The train roared like blood through its dark artery beneath the city.

CHAPTER THIRTY-THREE

Deni Green picked up the phone in her apartment, then slammed it back down. The wind kicked up outside, rattling the windowpanes and causing the drapes to sway slightly. This apartment was too drafty, too small; it was becoming unbearable. She'd planned to move by now, but the royalty checks kept getting smaller. Her bank balance soon followed. Then the damned tech stocks her friend Midge had talked her into buying took a dive.

The windows rattled louder, mixed with the sound of light rain striking the glass, weather with claws trying to get in. Deni picked up the phone again and used a forefinger to peck out Coop's number. As soon as she heard his recorded voice, she hung up.

She stared at the phone. It had its features, but it wasn't a wireless or cell phone. Conversations on them could be prey to eavesdroppers with scanners. Technology. Who knew where it was going? Her stocks had plunged because they'd been leapfrogged by even newer technology. She wouldn't be surprised if soon all books were first published on the Internet. None of them would be hers, if the Cozy Cat series kept using. up its lives, if this true crime venture didn't work. Time was working against her. Alicia was getting more and more demanding and threatening. Where the fuck was Coop?

Deni stood up and began to pace. She was wearing her baggy red sweater and gray sweatpants, and two pairs of socks to protect her from the draft that flowed close to the floor. She ran her fingers through her mussed hair. What was Coop up to? Was he trying to punish her just because she was smart enough to stir public interest in his daughter's murder and he wasn't? Naive asshole! "What did you expect out of him?" she asked herself aloud. "He's just a dumb cop." They weren't paid to be imaginative. To be creative like writers.

She caught sight of herself in the wall mirror and grimaced. She'd never liked the way she looked. Her weight problem had plagued her even in high school. Dates had been nonexistent. In college there had been sex, but she'd known at the time that was all there was to it. And even the sex hadn't been all that good. She'd never felt the earth move, that was for sure. Except for those times with . . . Well, never mind, that had been an experiment. Goddamn men! Damned Coop!

Deni found herself about to cry, felt her features contort. This was happening more often lately because she was under stress. A weakness, fault lines being tested.

She took deep breaths and the sensation went away and she could think clearly again.

This killer, he had his sexual hang-ups, no doubt fed by his disappointments in himself and in others. That was why Deni thought she had a way into his mind.

Kindred spirits. Was she supposed to tell Coop that? What did he know, get on and get off kind of guy like him? She'd heard cops talk about women, knew how they thought. No worse than most men, only they didn't hide the fact. Not among themselves, anyway.

She glanced in the mirror again at her lumpy figure and doughy face, eyes seeming smaller and beadier now in pads of florid flesh. So everyone didn't have to be attractive. There was life without men. Happy, productive life, and without some guy drooling and pawing all over you. She had her electric boyfriend; he plugged in and vibrated at three speeds. That was all she needed in that department. And when they had a falling-out and he stopped performing, he could be replaced and with a manufacturer's moneyback guarantee that was more foolproof than a prenuptial agreement.

Deni walked back to where her computer monitor was glowing on her desk.

Alicia had phoned again, pushing her to get something to Whippet Books on the serial killer project. Deni had explained to her how it wasn't easy, what with Coop suddenly getting a burr up his nose and not cooperating. Alicia had said she was done listening to excuses, that Deni would just have to deal with the problem. Sure. What did editors know about writing books, anyway? What did they contribute? As far as Deni was concerned, Alicia was mostly in the way.

Deni had been at the computer, trying to block out a basic outline for the book. She would get something to Alicia, and it would have to be good enough. She tried to convince herself that Whippet Books wasn't about to tell the author of the Cozy Cat mysteries to take a hike. Plenty of publishers would line up to buy the series. Deni's agent Kate might not think so, but Kate had been wrong before. Kate hadn't even thought Cozy Cat was going to be successful at first. Now she was plenty enthusiastic about the series, glad to deduct her commission. Deni had known all along that women would love the Cozy Cat series. Single women struggling against the system, married career women beaten down and looking for an alternative world, married whores seeking escape from domineering husbands. What Kate and the rest of them didn't understand was that Deni was an outsider. She knew how women thought because she was one, but she wasn't born with what were sometimes called feminine wiles. And she understood men because she thought something like them only without the poisonous testosterone to cloud her logic. She understood the mistakes women and men made.

The man who'd murdered Bette Cooper and those other women only understood women, not himself. She understood the thought processes and weaknesses of both sexes. While the killer was sizing up potential victims, engaging in the foreplay of the hunt, then eventually the kill, Deni would be tracking him, getting closer to who and what he was, even though there had been blind alleys and would be more. She was confident she would eventually get inside this guy's sick mind, understand him as he'd never been understood, then find him. She already understood more about him than Coop could ever imagine. This killer, this sick, testosterone-saturated fuck, while he was following his dick, she'd be following him.

She decided not to try phoning Coop again. Screw

him. He needed her as much as she needed him. He'd come around.

Deni went into the kitchen, opened the refrigerator, and reached for a Diet Pepsi. Then she withdrew her hand, closed the door, and opened the freezer below. The hell with the diet soda, she'd have some chocolate Häagen-Dazs instead. She deserved it, with what she was going through.

She carried the bowl of ice cream into the living room and sat down with it before her computer at the desk. Deftly she moved the mouse and gave it a series of clicks, then leaned forward in her chair. Frowning as the first generous spoonful of ice cream made her molars ache, she studied the monitor screen.

After a few minutes, she exited her word processor and went to her bookmarked Web sites in her Research folder. She would continue her painstaking search through public records for parallels, cross-checking nationwide sources. Any problem with Alicia would disappear if she got a solid lead on the killer. So would any problem with Coop, if the prick would ever answer his phone.

Her own phone suddenly chirped beside her.

With her free hand, she lifted it and pressed it to her ear. "Deni Green here."

"Miz Green, this is Maureen Morgan."

Deni waited, poised to tell off whoever this idiot was who'd dialed a wrong number or thought she might sell her something.

"I'm sorry," the voice said. "Formerly Maureen Cooper. Bette's mother."

Deni brightened, smiling. She was sorting through her mental file cabinet now, trying to remember everything she'd learned from her previous conversation with Maureen, everything Coop had let slip about his ex-wife. Tree hugger, teetotaler, animal rights nut, vegetarian . . . "Oh! I was just thinking about you!"

"And I you," Maureen said. "Coop warned me not to talk with you again."

"Then that's something we have in common."

"I think we should get together and talk more, despite what my former husband says. You might learn something valuable from me, and I from you."

"Would this be without Coop's knowledge?"

"Of course."

"When would you like to meet?"

"What about tomorrow, if you're not busy?"

"Sure. We can meet somewhere for lunch. A restaurant near where you work, if you'd like."

"I guess that would be okay."

"It will have to be vegetarian," Deni said, spooning in a bite of Häagen-Dazs. "I don't eat meat or dairy products. Is that okay with you? Or if you'd prefer, maybe we could just get together for a nonalcoholic drink."

"That might be better," Maureen said. "Do you like virgin mango daiquiris?"

"I'm willing to try one," Deni said, licking the spoon. "In fact, they sound scrumptious."

CHAPTER THIRTY-FOUR

Coop expected Cara to turn into Darby's Deli, where she'd eaten lunch before. Instead she walked past its entrance, then around the corner off 57th Street, and entered Viva Trattoria, a small Italian restaurant with a lot of ferns in its front windows. This was apparently another place she'd learned her sister Ann had frequented.

It was a clear day but cold. Since Cara would be inside the restaurant for a while, Coop considered going back for his car and parking it across the street, sitting in it with the engine idling and the heater on. Then he decided against it. Maybe she'd change her mind and have lunch somewhere else, or she'd entered the restaurant simply so she might be noticed by whoever had killed Ann. It might be one of the waiters, or a customer sipping Chablis or about to take a bite of pasta. He'd glance up and there would be a flash of almost recognition, and then, if Cara had it figured right, the attraction that had made her sister a victim. *Look at me,* she was saying, *I'm Ann Callahan's type—your type.* Coop wondered again if Cara fully comprehended the danger she was placing herself in. How could she be so gloriously stupid or so brave?

He backed into a doorway of a small shop that sold watches and electronics and stood ostensibly looking at a display of refurbished antique timepieces. What he was actually doing was watching both sides of the street in front of the restaurant, taking note of people so he'd remember them if they appeared the next time he followed Cara. And he knew he would follow her again. Something about her attracted him with an almost palpable magnetism. Just as it must have attracted the killer, but for different reasons.

If she insisted on acting as bait, he would try to protect her. He obviously couldn't spend all his time shadowing and guarding her, but he could do so often. Maybe it was his smartest move, anyway. If Cara succeeded in putting herself in the same place at the same time as Ann's killer, Coop might be there along with them. Hunter, prey, and pursuer.

Then something that had nothing to do with the weather sent a cold tingle up his spine. If and when all three came together, he was the only one who'd be recognized instantly by the other two. He and Cara knew each other, and thanks to Deni and the interview she'd given the newspaper, the killer knew what Coop looked like.

Moving deeper into the doorway, out of the wind and out of sight from most of the street, Coop felt again his irritation with Deni, with her disregard for everyone in this case except herself. Aside from the usual request by Earl Gitter for a follow-up piece on the Distraught Dad article, there'd been an angry message, then several calls and hang-ups on his answering machine last night. All attributable to Deni, he was sure.

Coop wasn't planning on returning her calls, or telling her he was shadowing Cara in her attempt to attract the killer. Not yet, anyway. He'd let Deni stew and maybe learn a lesson in cooperation. Maybe, for a while anyway, she'd play straight with him.

Deni pretended to like her mango daiquiri, a cloyingly sweet concoction that made her long for her customary straight bourbon. The health drink lounge, an almost unnoticeable place on Broadway called Growing, Growing, Grown, was something bizarre, too. It sold herbs and houseplants as well as vegetable and fruit drinks, and it smelled strongly of saffron. She'd use it in a book, Deni decided. There was a small serving counter, and an array of tiny round tables and miniature chairs that looked as if they belonged in an 1890s ice cream shop. Everything in the place other than the drinks seemed to be in shades of white or green. A sign behind the bar read HEALTH, HERBS, AND HAPPINESS. Deni had noticed a crushed cockroach on one of the green tiles. She'd decided not to point it out to Maureen.

How Coop's former wife was dressed was really something. She'd removed her plain brown coat to reveal neutral-colored slacks and a sacklike long-sleeved blouse. She wore no makeup and had a sallow, slightly pitted complexion and drab hair. A photo negative had more color. Maybe she'd been a looker once, but not now. The most vivid thing about her was her choice of shoes, black and practical, sort of ankle-length boots made out of what looked like vinyl, with oddly pointed toes. Deni was glad when they were out of sight beneath the table so she wouldn't give in to her compulsion to laugh at them. They looked as if they belonged on a fucking elf.

Deni cast all that aside and told Maureen most of what she and Coop had discovered. She skillfully tilted it so it seemed that she'd done most of the work and achieved most of the results. And she didn't bother with worrying if Coop would want his former wife to know these things. He wouldn't bother to pick up his phone, so screw Coop. And this was information that should be cross-referenced, anyway. If he had any sense, Coop would thank her for talking with Maureen. At least Maureen would talk to Deni; according to Coop, all his ex wanted to do in his presence was throw verbal darts at him.

"I wanted to thank you personally for what you've done," Maureen said, sipping her disgusting mango drink, "and to let you know I stand ready to help you in any way possible. It seems obvious to me that you've been a lot more productive than the police."

"They've got a lot of crime to cover," Deni said, "and they have a short attention span."

"Not to mention tunnel vision."

"Funny," Deni said, "I accused your former husband of that not long ago. He got angry."

"He often gets angry at the truth. Wby do you even work with him?"

"He's a valuable line into the police department. I use him to get information; then I use the information my way. That's why I wouldn't want him to hear about this conversation and get in another huff."

"I suppose he's in a huff now about that newspaper article."

"That's right," Deni said. "How did you feel about the article?"

"I thought it was fine. At least it's something. Nothing else was being done. That's what Coop doesn't seem to realize. And I told you before, he won't learn about our conversations from me."

Deni caught the plural "conversations" and liked it. She faked another sip of mango drink and leaned closer to Maureen. "Is there anything Coop talked about with you that I didn't touch on?"

Maureen toyed with her plastic swizzle stick and looked thoughtful. "I don't think so. He's baffled and all over the map. Even told me once the killer might not know himself he'd done these terrible crimes. Told me psychotic murderers sometimes blank out the horror of their deeds and might even pass a polygraph test."

"That's ridiculous," Deni said. This time she actually did take a sip of her mango daiquiri and almost gagged.

"Of course. The notion that someone is wandering around not knowing he's the sort of person that could do these things is absurd. Magazine-stand psychiatry. Do you believe in psychiatry as a science?"

Deni knew she'd better be careful here. "As a science?"

"Have you ever been to a psychiatrist?"

"No. Never. You?"

"Once. After our marriage broke up. It was the biggest bunch of bull I ever heard." Deni smiled understandingly. "I think it can be just that. Only at a steep price."

"I'd just as soon talk to someone like you," Maureen said. "Someone with imagination and insight. I have a feel for these things, and I know that somehow you can get inside this killer's mind, know what he's thinking."

"I'm trying," Deni said.

"It's not a question of trying."

Deni wondered what she meant by that.

Maureen frowned and shook her head. "It was easier to talk to Coop, to trust him, before the cancer."

"Cancer?"

"Yes. It's in remission now. There's no telling how long he has to live."

Holy shit! Deni thought. That explained a lot of things. Such as why Coop was in such a hurry to find his daughter's killer. This was terrific for the book. "That's too bad. I hope he's out of the woods."

"He'll never be that, as I understand these things. And I know something about them, working for an insurance company that sells whole life. Statistically, I mean. I read that somewhere.

"There's no telling when the disease will resume its course." Maureen used her hollow swizzle stick for a straw and sucked on it until it made a gurgling sound as she finished every ounce of her drink. Then she looked up at Deni. "You mean Coop entered into a long-term business arrangement with you and didn't even tell you about his illness?"

"He mentioned it," Deni lied, "but he didn't go into any detail. I didn't want to pry, figured it wasn't any of my concern."

"I'd think it would concern you, under the circumstances. It was something you should have known." Maureen glanced at a wall clock that looked like a beer advertisement, only the beer was a brand of celery drink. "I'd better get back. You'd be surprised how busy the insurance industry can be. Not that it isn't interesting. It really is."

"I can imagine," Deni said.

Maureen smiled at her. "Yes, I believe you can."

Deni knew what she meant: they were both part of the sisterhood that tried to lose loneliness in their dedication to their work. And both knew loneliness was a persistent stalker.

Maureen tried again to use the swizzle stick to drain more daiquiri from the bottom of her glass, then stood up. "If I think of anything that might be useful, I'll call you. Will you do the same for me?"

"I'll keep you informed," Deni promised, realizing that this was the second reason for their meeting and maybe Maureen wasn't so dumb.

Maureen nodded, picked up her coat from where it was folded on a chair, and strode from the health lounge. She hadn't left money for her drink, leaving Deni to pay the check.

Cheap at the price, Deni thought.

CHAPTER THIRTY-FIVE

The Night Caller felt the need.

More often now. Wasn't that how the police and the amateur psychologists said it worked? The pressure built. The serial killer's compulsion to kill increased, his behavior became more irrational, his caution deteriorated, and the time separating his victims from one another decreased. A kind of Newton's Third Law of flesh and blood and bone—leading to a mistake.

Idiots all. The police, the TV talk show pundits, the FBI profilers, the fools who wrote books on the psychology of serial killers and on self-defense for women. . . . Yet this was the one thing they were right about: The waves of need, the essential points of release, did draw closer together.

Sooner and sooner, but not now. Not yet.

He looked out the window at the cold, dark night beyond his reflection in the glass, then went to the closet and got his coat and hat. After pulling the long, checked muffler from where it was tucked inside his coat sleeve, he wrapped it around his neck, then slipped into the coat. Using the windowpane for a mirror, he placed his hat on his head and adjusted its angle, wrapped the muffler tighter about his throat. Now his face was barely visible, the way he liked it.

Then he switched off the lamp, his reflection disappeared, and the city lay vulnerable before him. Lighted windows dotted its jagged skyline; headlights and taillights moved in an orderly glare below; rows of streetlights intersected madly like lives lived, each bright pinpoint starring in the crystalline night.

It was time to go out, to make his usual rounds. The walking did him good, calmed what lived inside him, what paced in his breast even as he lay still in his bed at night. He looked away from the galaxy below, and up through the skylight at the stars unobscured by clouds. "Julia," he said softly, a curse, a murmured prayer.

Then he moved toward the door, through the dark, liking the dark.

As he stepped outside the building, the city night struck him with cold and noise. He put on his lightly tinted glasses, made sure his muffler was tight around his neck, then began to walk.

Despite the hour, there was considerable traffic, and quite a few people on the sidewalk. No one seemed to be paying much attention to him, or even giving him a second look. He shouldn't be surprised. Any two people might pass on the street, preoccupied, not really looking at, much less recognizing each other. He might walk past the Distraught Dad and his cocksucking writer collaborator; he might know them but they wouldn't know him, since they had no idea what he looked like.

So how much danger did the Distraught Dad and the hack writer actually pose? A used-up cop, and a thick-necked scribbler who preferred cats to men? What could they do to him other than amuse him?

Possibly nothing would pass between him and them even if their paths crossed. Though he'd seen their pictures in the paper, he might not recognize them at a glance. People didn't always look like their photographs. He didn't himself. Didn't even resemble his reflection in the dark windowpane. Someone else looking out at him or in at him, right side left side, left side right side. Someone else entirely?

No, not entirely.

One person he invariably recognized when their paths crossed, definitely and forever, was the woman the police and news media would someday call his latest victim.

They had no idea how right they were.

She would be his latest, but not his last.

His latest, whom he'd already met.

Seattle was unseasonably warm but not unseasonably gray. During the late fall and winter, gray was what Seattle residents had learned to endure, and sometimes even came to miss if they left the area.

Detective Sergeant Roy Lyons, lying on the beach during the third day of his vacation on Topsail Island off the North Carolina coast, was for some reason wishing the glaring sun would cease so he could look at the sky without wearing tinted glasses or wincing. Next to him his wife Laverne was lying on her stomach, her bikini top untied so there would be no horizontal pale line on her back where the sun hadn't fried her. She was propped up on her elbows, alternately sipping Pepsi through a kinked plastic straw and reading a book. A mystery with a cat on the cover.

"Jesus!" Lyons said, and sat straight up on his towel.

"Huh?" Laverne asked, not looking away from her book.

"I forgot!"

"I checked everything before we left," she said. "At least try to relax."

"Nothing about the house. I forgot to notify someone about something."

"At work?"

"Yeah. And in the spirit of vacation, I didn't bring my cell phone."

"It'll wait, Roy."

Maybe, he thought, plopping back down.

Or maybe it would wait too long, give a killer enough time to claim another victim. A woman walking around now, smiling, loving, laughing, or crying, who might do none of that very much longer if Lyons continued to leave his lazy ass plunked down on a beach towel while he soaked up rays and thought vacation thoughts.

Lyons sat up again.

"For God's sake, lie down and relax, Roy! You're in my sun!"

"Hand me the beach bag," Lyons said.

Laverne sighed and complied.

Lyons took off his tinted glasses and let them dangle on their cord against his bare, perspiring chest as he rooted through the bag for his wallet. When he found it, he removed it and pulled out the prepaid phone card he'd bought at the airport.

He worked his feet into his rubber thongs and stood up. "I'll be back."

"Arnold Schwarzenegger said that in a movie a while back," Laverne told him, "and it wasn't long before he had a heart attack. You should relax, Roy, think about play, not work."

"Right after I do this," Lyons said.

"This what?"

"Phone call. There's a pay phone down the beach near a concession stand. You want me to bring you anything back?"

"Another Pepsi," she said, turning a page.

Ten minutes later he was at the concession stand. He must have walked too fast through the sand, because the cheap thong on each foot had created what would probably be a blister where the rubber tube was wedged between his big toe and the one next to it. He limped over to where there were two phones near some trash receptacles in the shade of a thatched roof. Bees buzzed around the receptacles, which were open fifty-gallon steel drums painted green. Lyons wondered briefly what it would feel like to be stung where he was sunburned from yesterday.

A woman in a bikini something like Laverne's was talking on one of the phones, standing with her bare shoulders hunched and trying to ignore the bees. Lyons went to the next phone and used his card to call the squad room in Seattle, then Marty Sanderson's extension.

Sanderson was out, but Lyons identified himself, then had the call patched through to his partner's cell phone.

"Roy!" Sanderson said, surprised, when the call had gone through. "How's the weather down there?"

"Not like in Seattle. You step outside and your clothes start to get wet from the inside here."

"It's not raining here," Sanderson said. "Beautiful day. Not a cloud."

"You're lying, Marty, but that's okay. I didn't call for a weather report." Lyons heard a car horn honk thousands of miles away. Sanderson must be outside, or in his car in traffic. "Remember that lab photo of the bloody shoe print that was found at the scene of the Georgianna Mason murder?"

"Yeah . . . Christ, the can opener gal with the plastic saint up her twat. Footprint wasn't visible to the naked eye, but the lab guys used their lights on it, brought it up so it could be photographed."

"That's the one." Lyons heard buzzing and swatted a bee away with his free hand. "Now remember those irritating phone calls we got some time ago from a writer in New York? Puts out some kinda cat mystery novels but she's working on a true crime book."

"Yeah. You talked to her, but I remember. She said her book was about the murder of a former New York cop's daughter."

"That's the one."

"Also said she'd put us in a book if we came up with something she could use. But we had nothing in our files that fit what she wanted."

"That's right, Marty. But that was quite a while before the lab brought us that bloody shoe print from Georgianna Mason's apartment, so I didn't make the connection right away. The writer asked about one a lot like it. 1 want you to fax a copy of that print to her."

"This all came to you on your vacation?"

"That's how memory works, Marty. Will you fax the

photo when you get a chance? I'm sure the woman's phone number and name, Denise or Deni something, is in the murder file."

"Sure will. Anything else?"

"No. Now I can go back and relax like Laverne said."

"Unless you think of something else."

"Yeah. You're right. Gotta go now and put on some sunscreen, get back to the beach."

"I thought you went down there for the sun."

"I did."

"Then why the sunscreen? That doesn't make sense."

"No," Lyons said, "it doesn't."

He said good-bye to Sanderson and hung up the phone. He thought he really might be able to stretch out alongside Laverne on the beach and relax now. It felt good, having done what he knew was the right thing. Satisfying.

He guessed that was why he was a cop. That and the high pay and frequent outpourings of public gratitude.

CHAPTER THIRTY-SIX

From his usual doorway across the street, Coop watched Cara leave Mercantile Mutual after work and stride toward the corner. There was confidence and alertness in her walk, but nothing suggesting wariness.

He knew that she'd put in an appearance at some of the shops or restaurants she'd discovered Ann had frequented before her death. Eventually she would walk or bus downtown, then at the 53rd and Lex subway stop she would take the F train across the East River to Queens. There she would either board the bus that ran to the turnaround point where her sister was murdered, or she would spend a little time walking, or in a shop, before taking the F train on its western run back to Manhattan and going to her own apartment on the Upper West Side.

He stayed on his side of the street and began tailing Cara. She was walking fast, and his heartbeat and breathing picked up. He could see his breath fogging before him. Exercise, yes. But Dr. Gregory might not approve of this kind of exertion.

It was a grueling routine, and it took all of Coop's

skills to keep from being spotted as he shadowed her. Not only this evening, but others. So far he thought all her efforts were in vain; no one suspicious seemed to appear regularly among the people she passed on the sidewalk, or who rode with her on the subway. Coop couldn't be so sure about the bus; there was no way he could board and ride with Cara and her fellow passengers without being noticed by her. Some of the time he managed to hail a cab and had the driver tail the bus. He would sit silently except for his instructions to the driver, watching whoever boarded the bus and got off, people's lives touching tangentially and usually without their awareness.

Following Cara, Coop realized how many people there actually were in the New York streets, on the city's subways and buses. It was no surprise that up to now Cara had been wasting her time.

Yet some nights as he walked behind her it came to him with a chill that the killer had probably walked behind Ann in much the same manner, maybe on these very streets. Cara looked so much like Ann, especially at a distance, that Coop might be virtually striding in the murderer's steps, seeing almost precisely what he'd seen, thinking some of the same thoughts. Some of them.

The sensation was uncomfortable. He stamped his feet and turned up his collar to the cold, his mind shying away from identifying so closely with a mass murderer.

And he was sure now, along with Deni, that a serial killer was out there. Aside from circumstantial evidence, only the murderer's "signature" linked the killings, and that itself was a tenuous connection. Clear prints of that distinctive crisscross-pattern shoe sole found at another of the murder scenes would go a long way toward proving definitively that a serial killer was operating nationwide, and obscuring evidence of his existence by varying cities and murder methods. Of course the last two victims—Bette and Ann—had been murdered by the same person. St. Augustine could attest to that. Coop tried to think of some connection between Bette and St. Augustine but couldn't. He didn't think she'd even attended church for years. But of course he didn't know everything about her. That was one thing that scared him, what he might find out. And he was sure it frightened Maureen, despite what she said.

Maureen had been right about one thing—serial killers usually were compelled to prey on certain types of women. The murderer could only to a degree vary the similarity of his victims, his preferred type.

And right now Coop was following a brave or foolish woman who had forged herself into that type by using her dead sister as a model. Was she an angel of vengeance, or a death wish walking?

Despite the cold, Cara walked a long way on Second Avenue this evening. Near East 61st Street, she turned west toward Third Avenue and trudged for a while with her head bowed against the breeze whipping between the buildings. Her pace was quicker now, more purposeful. Coop was unprepared when she suddenly turned and disappeared into one of the buildings.

As he approached where he'd last seen her, he realized she hadn't gone into the building at all. Instead she'd apparently entered a small cathedral set between two newer, taller buildings. It was a medieval misfit among modern structures, its stone darkened by age, its Gothic spires dwarfed by the soaring vertical planes on either side. Rusty downspouts had long ago bypassed leering stone gargoyles that were made even more hideous by chipped and worn noses and chins. A tarnished brass plaque set in stone near tall, arched doors identified the building as St. Alexius Cathedral.

This explained why Cara had walked such a distance this evening, Coop decided. She must have learned that Ann had come here at times, possibly to pray for a way out of her dreary existence. Cara had walked rather than taken a bus or cab because the frugal Ann might have walked—and been seen and made a target by her killer.

Coop marveled again at what Cara was attempting. It was an instant she sought, the briefest intersecting of lives that would bring a flash of remembrance and murderous desire. Nothing anyone watching would notice, but for two people a glance that would alter universes. Maybe, Coop speculated, church was where you might go to understand such things.

Small as the cathedral was, Coop knew he couldn't enter it without danger of being seen by Cara. He moved out of the biting breeze and took up his position near the side of a newsstand kiosk and watched for her to come out.

As he stood with his shoulders hunched and his fists jammed deep in his coat pockets, he thought things might have been made simpler, or more complicated, if Cara had entered St. Augustine Cathedral—if there even was one in New York.

He noticed a man walking along the sidewalk on the other side of the street. The man was of average height

and weight, wearing a tan topcoat, a voluminous muffler, and a broad-brimmed hat. Something about him
tickled Coop's memory, but he couldn't be sure he'd
seen him before. There were a lot of tan topcoats and
matching broad-brimmed hats in New York. But the
way the muffler was bunched about the man's chin, and
the hat was angled forward so the brim shadowed his
face, might have been what triggered something in
Coop's mind. And from here, it appeared that the man's
glasses might be tinted despite the low evening light.
Something else that played in Coop's memory.

He cautioned himself. As with the topcoat and hat,
there were plenty of people who wore glasses with
slightly tinted lenses all the time—if indeed they *were*
tinted. Or people who simply hadn't thought to remove
their sunglasses as the light dimmed. On the other
hand, the hat, muffler, and glasses made it difficult to
know what the man looked like. It would be impossible
to positively identify him later if called upon.

All of which of course meant nothing. But Coop
added the man to his mental list of people to watch for
in case their paths crossed Cara's.

After exactly fifteen minutes, Cara emerged from
the cathedral and strolled toward Third Avenue. She
usually got off the bus near Second Avenue and 53rd
Street before walking along 53rd toward Third and the
subway stop. Ann's path toward destruction. Cara did
this time after time, boarding the F train to Queens, sitting or standing, watching and not watching the other
passengers, avoiding direct eye contact as the train
lurched forward and picked up speed. Subway etiquette, like a mannered dance before death.

Her time in St. Alexius had warmed Cara, so she didn't seem to mind the walk to the subway stop. But Coop had been standing in the cold while she was inside. He was glad when they descended the steps to the token booth and turnstiles.

He watched Cara use her Metro Card to pass through the turnstiles, and he followed with the card he habitually kept in his pocket. He always carried one since losing someone he'd been tailing years ago for want of a fare. Along with a lot of irate subway passengers, his quarry had noticed him climb over the turnstile. It had been easy for the man to conceal himself in the throng of people on the platform, and board a train about to depart while Coop was still on the escalator.

Coop had his card out and timed it right this time. Cara didn't notice him as he followed her down to the crowded subway platform.

People were standing close together as if for warmth, now and then jostling one another as a breeze wafted from the dark tunnel and a train arrived. Some stood reading or pretending to read books or magazines or folded newspapers, while others stood as if in a trance. Another day in the life was ending. Coop knew that few of them realized how precious and fleeting those days were. At the far end of the platform, a street musician began pounding out a wild, loud rhythm on some paint bucket drums, as if the noise might frighten away what frightened, and bring surcease to those waiting and glancing now and then into the black tunnel.

Cara's evening walk must have tired her out. No visit to Queens this time. Instead she boarded a Brooklyn-bound F train that would cut crosstown to where she could transfer north or take a cab up Broadway to the Upper West Side.

She was deviating from the trace of her dead sister now, calling it a night.

Coop decided not to follow. He would walk back and take a bus up First Avenue to where his car was parked.

As he was striding toward the escalator, he glanced at an F train headed toward Queens. It was moving so fast the windows passed like shuffled cards. He thought he glimpsed through a window the man wearing the tan topcoat, broad-brimmed hat, and muffler, but he couldn't be sure.

CHAPTER THIRTY-SEVEN

Maureen hadn't been this cold for a long time, but she didn't mind. She shifted the sign propped on her shoulder and looked up at the patch of dark sky between the buildings. Low black clouds were scudding across a background of leaden gray, blown by a wind that found its way down her collar whenever she turned to walk the opposite direction on the sidewalk along with her fellow demonstrators.

Hank, the lead demonstrator and coordinator of Citizens for a Legalized Animal World (CLAW), stood off to the side near the curb, the wind pressing his luxurious gray beard to one side, his benevolent moon face beaming beneath his black knit watch cap. He raised his long arms and screamed, "More rat blood, lower ratings!" several times in succession.

Maureen and the other demonstrators took up the chant. Maureen's voice was loudest. She waved her sign that she'd carefully lettered herself: RATS HAVE RIGHTS!

This TV network whose headquarters they were picketing had dared to broadcast a series episode wherein impoverished children used rifles to hunt rats in a junk-yard. This did not conform to CLAW's view of how the world should work.

Most of the people streaming past on the sidewalk didn't seem to pay much attention to what CLAW was doing here. A few of them smiled or laughed out loud.

"Rats are social animals just like us!" Maureen would scream at the smilers. "They have families, look out for each other, even sacrifice themselves for the group! How would you feel if you were one of the rats in last night's episode of *Pizza for Five?*"

An older, gray-haired man dressed in black leather and wearing a gold hoop earring veered toward her, smiling. Despite the smile, he had an old, ruined face that could only be sad.

Maureen held her ground. "How would you feel, sir, to be hunted by sadists with rifles? Do you know they used real live rats for those scenes?"

"No, I didn't," the man said.

"Rats have rights!" Maureen screamed at him. "For God's sake, show some compassion for fellow living beings!"

"I'm with you, sister. I did a hitch in 'Nam. I was a rat."

"Then maybe you should join us," Maureen suggested, mollified.

He shook his head no. "They were rats, too," he explained.

"This is different."

"Maybe give the rats guns," he said.

Everyone around Maureen began to shout and jeer. She looked away from the man she was talking with and saw that three men in business suits had ventured down to the lobby and were standing just inside the building's locked glass doors. They were all sleekly groomed, well fed, and infuriatingly smug.

A large stone suddenly bounced off one of the glass doors, causing the executives inside to flinch and back away. Then another stone was hurled, harder than the first. With a loud cracking sound, the glass in one of the doors turned milky white.

More stones began bouncing off the shattered but cohesive safety glass. They weren't the sort of stones one found lying about on a Manhattan street; obviously they'd been brought to the scene for this purpose.

It was exhilarating, seeing and hearing the stones smash into the glass. Maureen was no longer the slightest bit cold. Her cause possessed and warmed her like a great internal firestorm welling from her heart. Let anyone else think what they might! She was doing right with the power of right. She was lending that power to lesser, helpless creatures whose own pain was mute. A woman screamed something Maureen couldn't understand, and a roar of agreement rose into the cold air.

Maureen waved her sign. "Rats have-"

A firm hand gripped her elbow.

She turned and found herself in the clutches of a large uniformed police officer. "We are a legal assembly!" she shouted.

"You're obstructing the flow of traffic," the officer said. "Not to mention inciting a riot."

She could barely hear him over the shouts of the crowd.

"This is America!" she shouted.

"Be that as it may, you're going to have to come along, ma'am."

She struggled only briefly, dropping her sign and accidentally stepping on it. "Rats have—"

"I know, ma'am."

"Stop it right now! My husband—"

"I know, ma'am," the cop said unsmilingly.

"I demand that you read me my rights."

The officer did better than that. He recited them from memory in a low monotone. As he did so, she saw from the corner of her eye Hank being led into a nearby white police van without rear windows.

She was aware that the cop who held her had stopped speaking and was guiding her toward the van.

Maureen kicked him in the leg.

He winced. "Now, ma'am . . ."

She kicked him again, and out of nowhere another cop had her. She was on the hard, dirty pavement before she knew it, her arms pinned behind her. Her right cheek was against the wet sidewalk. Cold handcuffs were applied to her wrists. They hurt.

"I demand—"

She was helped to her feet and dragged unwillingly to the police van, through the low-lying fog of its exhaust fumes.

"I demand—"

"Careful you don't bump your head, ma'am."

And she was in the dim interior of the van, seated alongside a woman who was quietly sobbing. Hank was seated opposite her, beaming triumphantly.

"Hot damn, we got arrested!" he said. "Did you see all the TV cameras?"

Maureen hadn't. She shook her head numbly. She'd never been arrested. The inside of the van seemed to be closing in on her and smelled awful. She was afraid. The sobbing going on next to her didn't help. The other CLAW members slumped in the van appeared merely saddened and resigned.

"We're under arrest," she repeated after Hank. "We're really under arrest . . . ."

Hank gave a loud whoop.

"Hank, stop it!" one of the women near him said sharply.

"Please!" Maureen said.

A man in a dark suit and not wearing a coat peered into the van, then disappeared. She'd noticed a fancy badge pinned to his lapel. The van's rear doors were suddenly slammed shut, and within seconds it began to move.

"What . . . happens now?" Maureen asked.

Hank grinned at her. "Do you know someone who can bail you out?"

Ignoring the cold, he followed her at a distance as he had before. After leaving her job at Vale's Discount Jewelry, Theresa Dravic walked not toward her bus stop, but along Columbus Avenue toward Milligan's Lounge.

The Night Caller kept pace, watching the sway of her long hair, the play of her generous hips beneath her coat, her neat, clipped strides in her black high heels. Would she be meeting Chris at Milligan's?

It hadn't taken long for the Night Caller to realize Chris was the potential problem. The potential lover.

The sin eater. Short, blocky, swaggering Chris. The potential. That potential had moved up the clock on the doomed Georgianna Mason. Chris was that, was the *that* this time.

But there was more than Chris. The Night Caller knew how certain alcoholics could remember nothing of when they were drunk—until those times when they were drunk again. Another world existing in an alcoholic dimension, with drink as its ticket to enter and reenter. But not only drink. Also certain drugs. The same world, the same dream, different gates.

It wasn't the Night Caller's concern that Theresa was becoming an alcoholic. He'd seen her certainly drunk more than once as she walked unsteadily out of Milligan's, often to sit on a park bench until she sobered up enough to continue her way home. That was all he needed to know. That, along with Chris's growing presence and influence, prompted him to act. That, and it was time anyway. He always knew when it was time. Time was what kept everything from happening at once. He understood time. Time was something he kept in his pocket.

Would she meet Chris this time?

CHAPTER THIRTY-EIGHT

Deni was smiling as she hung up the phone after talking to Detective Sanderson. At first she hadn't remembered him; she'd committed to memory instead the lead detective, Lyons. But Sanderson had explained that Lyons was vacationing, and had in fact called him from somewhere in North Carolina.

Then Sanderson told Deni what she so wanted to hear. In further examination of Georgianna Mason's apartment, the Seattle police lab had managed to detect a bloody footprint not visible to the naked eye. The killer, who apparently had undressed to prevent being bloodied himself by what he'd done to Georgianna, had dressed to leave after the murder and made a mistake. He'd stepped in some of his victim's blood, possibly without knowing it. Or maybe he had known it and thought he'd cleaned the sole of his shoe adequately. The footprint matched the ones found at the scene of Bette Cooper's murder, and Marlee Clark's. Marlee, Bette, Georgianna . . . Three victims in different parts of the country. That FBI prick Willingham would listen now. He'd have no choice but to believe.

Coop would listen, too.

Deni's fax machine beeped, indicating that a fax was about to be received. It had to be the one Sanderson promised to send.

She walked over to stand by the machine, and her smile broadened as she watched the fax paper emerge with a somewhat smudged but undeniable image of a shoe sole with a crisscross pattern identical to the others.

All she had to do now was hand the fax over to Willingham. Or to Coop.

As the machine continued its steady electronic grinding sound, Deni stared at the almost completed fax and gave this more thought.

No, not Willingham. That might be premature. Those FBI hard-asses tended to take over a case and become very secretive. They would not only be less cooperative than the police, they would put up a wall between her and what she needed to know to write her book.

It would have to be Coop.

But not necessarily now.

He needed her more than she needed him. She would keep the fax to herself for a while. Teach him who was most important in this project.

She was the one who'd intermittently called the Seattle police and made sure they would forward any new information. Screw Coop. Let him stew in his own sick juices.

The machine beeped twice, then was silent. Deni removed the fax and lovingly carried it across the room to her desktop copy machine.

She made two copies and placed them in a bottom

desk drawer. The fax sent by Sanderson she slid into an eight-by-ten yellow envelope. Tomorrow she'd place it in her safety deposit box.

A storm was blowing in from New Jersey, lightning but no thunder yet. The lamp on the desk flickered and wind rattled the panes in her apartment windows. How her mood had changed! The cluttered, tiny apartment seemed cozy now rather than stifling, the rattling windows emphasizing the bad weather beyond the walls. Warm in here. Comfy.

Deni went into the kitchen, located a clean glass, and poured herself two fingers of Crown Royal.

Carrying her drink, she returned to the living room and walked to the window. For a while she stood gazing outside at the rain that had begun to fall and was making the early evening suddenly dark.

She thought again of Coop and glanced at the phone on her desk. She should call him about the Seattle fax immediately, she knew. She felt a little guilty.

But only a little. He certainly didn't deserve any favors from her, after the way he'd been avoiding her. She was sure she felt any guilt at all only because she was basically a decent person.

"Screw Coop," she said aloud.

And toasted her wavering reflection in the windowpane.

Coop's phone rang at 10:30 that evening, just after he'd swallowed his pills and settled into bed. He was exhausted from shadowing Cara in the cold and had decided to skip TV news at eleven and get a good night's sleep.

He sighed and sat up in bed. Then he switched the reading lamp back on and picked up the phone.

"Coop?" said the voice on the phone, even before he had a chance to identify himself. Maureen's voice.

"Something wrong?" he asked, wondering if she was calling him for no reason other than to harass him. If that was her game he would simply hang up on her and disconnect the phone cord from its jack.

Silence on the line. He wondered if she'd hung up. "Maureen?"

"I need your help," she said.

CHAPTER THIRTY-NINE

Coop had to admit he was amused, but he did his best not to reveal it to Maureen. She was sitting beside him with her hands folded in her lap, staring straight ahead. As he drove through wet, reflecting nighttime streets toward her New Rochelle apartment, he sat silently, concentrating on the traffic. The only sound in the car was the relentless *thumpa-thumpa* of the windshield wipers.

Maureen's brush with the law hadn't taken all the starch out of her. "I suppose you're waiting for me to say thank you," she said at last.

"It wouldn't be out of line," Coop said, "considering I climbed out of bed and drove to the precinct house to bail you out so you wouldn't have to spend time in jail with your friends."

"You make it sound as if I deserted them!" she snapped.

Like a rat from a sinking ship, Coop thought, but said nothing.

"I wasn't the only one who got someone to obtain my freedom," Maureen said.

Coop braked the car and took a corner. "True. That guy Hank beat you out the door."

"He was glad to see the TV camera crews arrive."

"At the pro-rat demonstration or the police station?"

"Both. We were trying to be noticed so people would take the time to think about what's happening every day to animals on this planet. That was the purpose of our demonstration. Hank said the additional publicity surrounding our arrest furthered our cause."

"I suppose, Maureen. Though in most people's minds, rats have a lot of negatives."

"So do people themselves."

"Sure. But be honest, have you ever harbored any real affection for a rat?"

"Do you honestly want me to take advantage of what you just asked?"

He had to laugh. "I suppose I did set myself up."

Maureen responded with her own brief and strangled laughter. *Thumpa-thumpa,* said the wipers. "Thanks for bailing me out, Coop," she told him after another block.

It must have hurt her to say it, he thought, considering her feelings toward him. Must have taken a lot for her to phone him in the first place. But whom do you call when you get arrested if not your ex-cop ex-husband? "You're welcome." He shook his head. "Rats . . . ." He laughed again.

This time she didn't. "I did a lot of thinking while I was waiting for you to come for me," she said.

"About rats?"

"About Bette."

"Oh."

"I want you to do me a favor." The old Maureen was back.

"Another?"

"All right, another. I'm not asking for myself, but for our daughter. 1 don't think enough investigation had been done in Haverton."

"That's because the murder occurred in New York."

"But Bette's friends and coworkers were only talked to a few times. And what about Lloyd Watkins? He was almost her fiancé. Don't you think he might have some more information about her, be able to offer some insight?"

Coop thought she might be right about Watkins. He'd had a good story, a solid alibi. Coop had even come to like him. But maybe he'd been passed over too quickly and placed out of the frame. Geography could do that to the way cops thought. Distance worked in a killer's favor. Distance was one of the reasons why Coop and Deni were searching for a serial killer. One of the reasons other people were not.

"Will you do that for me and for Bette, Coop? Drive back to Haverton and ask some more questions?"

"I'll go back and talk to people there," he said, "if you'll do something for me."

"What's that?"

"Stop talking to Deni Green."

"I only talked to her because I thought it would help."

"It doesn't help. She's not a cop, she's a writer."

"But she writes mysteries. Detective stories. She understands the criminal mind and how to solve crimes."

"Writing about a detective doesn't make you one," Coop said. "She writes about killers, too. I doubt that she's ever murdered anyone other than on paper."

They'd arrived at Maureen's street. Coop turned the corner and drove to the middle of the block, then parked before her building. He left the engine idling, but the light rain had stopped so he switched off the wipers.

"All right," Maureen said, biting off the words. "We'll exchange promises. When will you leave for Haverton?"

"As soon as I can," Coop told her. "I have some things to do first."

"You would." She didn't say it as if she were angry, only defeated. Tears glistened in her eyes, about to spill over.

Before he thought, he reached out for her, partially drew back his hand, then caressed her cheek.

She sat stiffly, unmoving. Slowly he leaned forward and kissed her lightly on the lips. "Do you want me to—"

"No, please!" she interrupted.

"We shared a lot of years, Maureen. Some were good years."

"Some weren't."

"Don't be angry."

"I'm not." She stared ahead out the windshield for a moment. "Coop? . . ."

"What?"

"Nothing." She sighed hopelessly. "Always nothing."

Without explaining what she meant by that, she

opened the car door and sloshed through puddles toward her building entrance.

He sat in the idling car watching until she got inside, this good woman who loved rats and hated him.

He wondered why she couldn't love them both.

CHAPTER FORTY

Billard called Coop at four in the morning. "You awake, pardner?"

It was twenty years ago. They'd just made detective and were huddled up on a case where a guy in Brooklyn had chopped off—

It was now. Coop was awake and Billard was middle-aged and going to fat and Coop was middle-aged and might not get much older.

"Christ!" Coop said into the phone. "You took me back more than twenty years."

"You were asleep, dreaming." But something in Billard's voice made Coop believe he'd understood, had maybe felt the same way. "You were asleep."

"I usually am at four in the morning."

"Then you got a good prostate. Why I'm calling is we got a homicide on the edge of Central Park near the West Eighty-sixth Street entrance. Looks like your guy."

"Did he leave St. Augustine behind?"

"Sure did. On the ground this time. Deliberately, or

he mighta dropped it for some reason and was in too big a hurry to stop and pick it up."

Coop was already up and sitting on the edge of the bed. "You gonna be there?"

"Yeah, but not before you. The whip's name is Porter, lieutenant out of the Two-Oh. I already got word to him about you."

Billard was talking as if it were twenty years ago. Coop understood: Porter was the officer in charge, out of the 20th Precinct. "Thanks, Art."

"Not for nothing, I hope."

She was a brunette with long hair, lying on a park bench as if she were asleep. Porter led Coop to her, raising the tape so he could enter the frozen zone. Several people were moving carefully around her, bent over her. Coop didn't move too close. Professional courtesy. Also, the moon was bright in the cold sky and he had a clear view.

Porter, a hefty, swarthy man who badly needed a shave, had a lieutenant's badge pinned to his coat lapel. He watched as Coop stood staring at the woman.

"Too early for a time of death, I guess," Coop said.

"Yeah, but it's been at least a couple of hours, probably more."

Coop was disappointed. The woman had long hair, but it was mussed and not in the usual fanned pattern around her head. And now that he was closer he saw that her eyes hadn't been closed. She appeared to have been dumped on the bench rather than laid out carefully and lovingly.

Lieutenant Porter jammed his hands in his coat pockets. "Billard said the guy you're looking for varies his MO."

"Maybe not this much, Lou. How'd she make the trip?" Amazing. Only a few minutes at a New York crime scene and Coop was talking as if he were still in the Job. Billard was contagious.

"Big knife or hatchet or something to the nape of her neck. ME said it killed her instantly, like she was beheaded. Nerve ganglia or something."

Marlee Clark.

"Maybe he is my guy," Coop said. Playing dumb about the plastic saint. Porter wouldn't trust a civilian with the information and didn't know if Coop was tuned in to it.

"Something might have scared him off," Porter ventured.

"Something might have. Anything else on him? Or around the victim? Any footprints?"

"Nothing like that," Porter said. "All I can tell you is she was a reader. Or somebody was."

Coop looked at him. "Reader?"

"This was found under the bench, like she dropped it."

Carefully, by the page edges so as not to disturb any fingerprints, Porter held out a paperback novel.

Even in the dimness Coop saw the outline of a cat on the glossy cover, and the name of the author: *Deni Green.*

"Mean anything to you?" Porter asked, seeing the expression on Coop's face.

Coop told him that it did and told him how.

"Probably just coincidence," Porter said. "We got the victim's name from her purse. Theresa Dravic. And her address. Lives with a flight attendant—female—who's out of town working on the other side of the country. I already got the word the apartment's full of mysteries, lots of them by this author. We even found a Barnes and Noble membership card of some sort in her wallet."

"Kinda dark here to be reading," Coop said, "unless she sat down a long time before she died."

"Way it looks, the book fell out of her purse. Something else mighta, too. Some kind of plastic religious figure. A saint or prophet, maybe. But it was found a little way from the bench, like maybe somebody else dropped it there. Might not be any connection with the crime. Doesn't look like it's been out in the weather long, though."

Coop dummied up about the saint. "Anything taken from her purse?"

"Doesn't look like it. Wallet and money seem intact. And there's a pretty good Seiko watch on her wrist. No robbery here, unless the doer was scared away." Porter scratched his sandpaper jaw hard enough that it sounded like a rasp. "Coincidence," he said again, but not with much conviction.

Both men had been in the Job for a long time and thought the same way about coincidence.

A plainclothes cop approached, glancing at Coop, then focusing his attention on Lieutenant Porter. "Lou, we got a call for you in the radio car." Coop knew it would be on the detectives' special band.

"Go ahead," he told Porter. "And thanks."

"You got any more questions, you give me a call," Porter said.

Coop said that he would, but he saw a Channel One

van turning into the entrance to the park and figured there'd be a lot of information about Theresa Dravic in tomorrow's news.

As he was walking toward the street, an unmarked arrived and Billard's bulky form emerged from it. Coop decided to hang around a while longer, maybe go someplace with Billard and get coffee. They could pretend some more that it was twenty years ago.

CHAPTER FORTY-ONE

D arby's Deli served breakfast.

Cara had agreed to meet Coop there an hour before she had to go in to work at Mercantile Mutual. That was easy enough for him, since he'd been awake since four o'clock.

The deli was warm and welcoming with the scents of baking and fresh coffee. Most of the business was counter trade or carryout, the customers people who, like Cara, worked in the neighborhood.

Coop looked around and saw Cara already seated in the window booth she favored because she could be seen from the street. Her gray coat was folded on the bench seat next to her, and she was wearing dark slacks and a gray sweater. Her red hair was in a long braid down her back. She was drinking coffee from a large brown mug that was steaming as if it had just been topped off.

After confirming that she wanted breakfast, Coop got two toasted bagels from the counter, a coffee, black, for himself, and went to sit with her.

He liked the way she smiled at him, the way they

were comfortable with each other as if they were old friends from a lost world. Coop wondered again, should you fall for someone if you might have limited time left on earth? Did anyone have a choice? And who didn't have limited time left on earth?

"Thinking deep thoughts?" Cara asked over the rim of her coffee mug.

"The deepest. Have you had any luck acting out Ann's daily life?"

"I don't know. Maybe whoever killed her didn't approach her right away."

"I can almost guarantee that. Most serial killers stalk their victims before striking. It prolongs the sick fun."

"You really are sure Ann was the victim of a serial killer."

"I'm sure, but I can't prove it."

She gave him her smile. "Cop's instincts?"

"That, and the way evidence is accumulating."

She placed the steaming mug before her, the smile gone. "Do you have some new piece of evidence?"

"A dead woman in the park," he said, and told her about Theresa Dravic.

"That explains the bags under your eyes," she said. "The reason why you look like you've already been up for hours is that you have. Can we be sure this woman was the victim of the same killer?"

"Who's sure of anything? But I think the odds favor it."

She nodded and began spreading cream cheese on her bagel. A messy business. After laying the knife on her plate edge, she licked two of her fingers. "Since she died after we made this date, that can't be why we're here. Is there other new evidence?"

"No. If I led you to believe that, I'm sorry."

"Don't be. If we're here only because you wanted to see me, good." She was making it tough for him.

"It isn't only that. I was worried about you. And after seeing Theresa Dravic, I'm even more worried. I think I have a better idea than you do of what you might be taunting by walking around where Ann walked, wearing similar clothes, looking too much like her."

"I thought we'd already established that you disapproved."

"Yeah, we did. I'm not going to ask you to stop permanently."

"Oh?"

"Just for a few days."

She studied him, obviously trying to look into his mind. He was thinking how beautiful she was with her hair red. How he'd love to—*Idiot!* He interrupted his own thoughts. Middle-aged, doomed idiot!

But she didn't seem to see him that way. She appeared wary. "Why would you want me to stop for a while? What difference could it—" Realization widened her eyes. "Have you been following me, Coop?"

He couldn't answer right away, though he knew immediately that he wasn't going to lie to her.

"Coop?"

"Sometimes," he admitted. "I told you, you worry me."

"And you want to protect me."

"Of course I do. You're—"

"What?"

"You don't seem to know it, but you need protection."

She took a bite of bagel, dabbed her lips with her

napkin to remove nonexistent errant cream cheese, then sat thoughtfully, chewing. After chasing down the bagel with a sip of coffee, she said, "While you've been following me, have you noticed anyone?"

He knew what she meant—might he have noticed a man who had possibly killed her sister and would try to kill her? "I don't think so," he said. "But that's the point. Maybe he won't be so noticeable at first. Serial killers tend not to look like serial killers."

"But you have a trained eye."

"More trained than yours. That's why I've been shadowing you. To see who else might be doing the same thing."

"You're incredibly deft at your work," she said with a faint smile. "I didn't notice you."

"And you might not notice him until it's too late. That's why I'm asking you not to roam the sidewalks and shops, or ride the subway and bus that Ann rode. Only for a few days."

"Is this because you're taking a trip and can't be my protector?"

He nodded. "Driving to Haverton, where Bette lived and worked. I want to talk again to some of the people who knew her."

"And you'd be distracted if you were worrying about me."

"Exactly right."

She gazed fixedly at him; then something in her seemed to relax. "I'll stay off the subway and bus."

"And the shops and restaurants?"

"I need to eat lunch, Coop. And I'm going to assume you don't mind if I keep working and getting paid."

He grinned, realizing he was being quite the authoritarian. He had no right. "Okay. Thank you."

She touched the back of his hand and leaned slightly toward him. "It's nice to be worried about."

"I haven't known the feeling in years."

"Then get used to it," she told him.

He suddenly wasn't hungry. He felt terrific, but his appetite was gone. His appetite for food.

She read him easily. "I have to get up from here in a few minutes and go to work, Coop."

"We could go to my place instead. Or yours," someone else said. No, Coop realized it had been *his* voice! He wished he could reach out and snatch the words from the air before they got to her.

"The most I'd better take off work is this morning."

He was having trouble breathing. "There's a hotel near here."

She smiled at him. "I take it you've had enough coffee."

He kissed her before helping her off with her coat. And as soon as he felt the warm wedge of her tongue against his lips all doubt and awkwardness disappeared. Both their coats wound up tossed over the back of a chair. Their clothes were scattered on the floor.

In bed he started to speak but she kissed him again. Then she trailed her tongue down his chest, his stomach, used her mouth on him.

"Not yet," she said, and was on top of him, lowering herself onto him. He gasped, admired her breasts as she loomed over him with her arms straight. He sucked each breast, massaging the nipple softly with his tongue.

He was amazed by how all his reservations about any relationship had flown with his desire for her.

They were both perspiring now; the scent and taste of her made him want her all the more. She dropped her upper body down and began to move. He gripped her buttocks, for a few minutes feeling them flex and relax, then carefully, without hurting her, rolled her onto her back.

Coop had heard that the French referred to orgasm as "the little death."

There in Room 276 of the Atherton Hotel, with the cold morning and everything else on the other side of the walls and window, he thought it was exactly the opposite.

Afterward they showered together, then leisurely got dressed. Neither wanted to leave the room. Both knew they must.

Cara kissed him on the lips, then put on her gray coat, wrapped the red muffler about her neck, and folded it over her throat. For an instant Coop thought about the man in the tan topcoat and voluminous muffler, but only on the edges of his mind.

"Don't follow me to the bank," she said. "It's only a few blocks away. Stay here awhile if you feel like it. I'll be okay."

But he went downstairs with her, then stood with her outside the hotel as they buttoned their coats.

"Let me know when you're back in the city," she said.

"I will. I'll call to make sure you're all right."

As they parted he held her close and kissed her there on the sidewalk, in front of the doorman. Not like him at all.

Where is this going? he wondered. *Where in the hell is this going?*

When Coop got back to his apartment the phone was ringing. He locked the door behind him, then crossed the living room and lifted the receiver, still thinking about Cara.

When he said hello, the voice on the other end of the connection said, "Coop, it's Alicia. I'm calling to ask a favor of you."

He had a pretty good idea what it would be.

CHAPTER FORTY-TWO

"Deni called me," Alicia said over the phone. "She told me you're still angry with her—with us—because she talked to that reporter who wrote the piece in the paper."

Coop waited a few seconds for her to say more, but she didn't. The phone call she was referring to must have occurred yesterday. Either Alicia hadn't caught the news, or she hadn't made a connection between Theresa Dravic's death and Deni Green. The reports Coop had seen and read hadn't mentioned Deni's novel found near the body. Never mind, Deni would probably call her soon enough.

"It isn't only that," Coop said. "Deni's increasingly difficult to work with."

"She said you weren't returning her calls."

"True."

"That's *you* being difficult to work with."

"I'm not working with her at all," Coop said. "Not right now."

"She asked me to act as an intermediary." Alicia's voice remained calm and amiable. He could imagine her in her soft-tone office, with its book- and manuscript-lined shelves and wide window, the distant Statue of Liberty over her shoulder. Two hard women holding out for a future without guarantees.

Her reasonableness irritated Coop. "I thought you were the one who cautioned me about Deni."

"I was, but things have changed. This project has to be returned to the front burner."

"It's still on my front burner. I'm still investigating, just not with Deni."

"Even if you don't need her, she can help you, Coop."

"She hasn't so far." But he knew that wasn't true.

Alicia knew it, too, but she didn't press him on it. "I know the investigation's the most important thing to you. And let's face it, the book is Deni's top priority."

"Her goddamn career."

"Hers and mine," Alicia corrected. "And if you see it in that light, maybe you can understand why Deni's so obsessed with this project. I want the book to be a success, too. And that doesn't mean I don't want your daughter's murder solved. But the book has to become a reality before it can succeed."

"Has she mentioned Bette to you?"

Alicia's voice changed, became more concerned. "You're still afraid she's going to defame your daughter, is that it?"

"Can you guarantee she won't?"

"I can guarantee that I'll do what I can to prevent it."

He thought about his impending drive to Haverton, and what he might find if he made further inquiries. Especially if he leaned harder on Lloyd Watkins. He knew Maureen was right; he should have gone back there long ago, asked more questions. He'd been afraid of the answers. Everyone, he had come to realize, was afraid of certain answers.

"Do you believe me, Coop?"

"Yes."

"Then call Deni, get together with her so she at least puts something definitive on paper. When she does that, some of the pressure will be off and we'll have a better idea of where we stand."

"I'll call her, but I still don't trust her."

"Neither do I. But we could both use her efforts in our behalf."

"I'll get in touch with her in a couple of days," Coop said. "I've got some other problems that have to be cleared up."

"If it's your health—"

"Who talked to you about my health?"

"Deni mentioned it."

Coop felt tension build in him. He knew where Deni must have learned about his cancer. "I should have left her in jail," he muttered.

"What? Who?"

"My ex-wife Maureen. I posted bond for her. She was arrested in that animal rights protest in Midtown yesterday."

"That business about rats?"

"Yeah, human and otherwise."

"Jesus!"

"A couple of days," Coop said firmly.

"Enough said," Alicia told him, "except for be careful."

"Of what?"

"Humans and otherwise."

                    *   *   *

Deni had finished a late snack at the Internet Knish
on Amsterdam. It was past midnight, but she remained
seated at one of the Internet café's computers, sipping a
latte and cruising the Web.

Most of the other diners had gone. She and a guy
who looked like one of the homeless were the only
ones left. He was hunched over a table at the other end
of the restaurant, munching on a plateful of doughnuts
and drinking ice water while he worked his keyboard.
Might have been a dot com millionaire last month,
Deni thought with a smile, and here he was probably
trying to keep warm while he surfed for porn.

Or maybe he was at one of the genealogy sites,
searching for some relative he might put the touch on.

The thought suddenly depressed her, that the sad-
looking man might be seeking someone related, some
soul prevented by blood from ignoring him without
guilt.

She threw off the thought and concentrated on the
cold-case homicide site she'd found. The Web site was
run by some sort of club in Vancouver whose geek
members collected information on unsolved murders.
Pathetic but potentially useful.

She clicked on a photo of a dead woman seated in a
car and sipped her latte while the story behind the picture appeared on the glowing monitor. A domestic dis-
pute. The woman had died after a severe beating at the
hands of either her husband or her lover. Both were
missing. One might have killed the other. Intriguing,
Deni thought, but nothing she might be able to use.

The old Korean guy who managed the place was
wiping down a nearby table and glancing over at her

from time to time, obviously hoping she'd leave so he could shoo away Mr. Homeless and close shop.

Fuck him, she thought. To teach him not to stare at her, she deliberately spilled the rest of her latte on the floor and ordered another.

When the confusion of him bringing her a new latte and mopping up the old was ended and she turned back to the computer, she noticed that her purse on the chair next to her was unsnapped. She looked over and saw that the homeless-looking guy was gone. A screen saver, progressively larger fish devouring each other, was showing on his computer's monitor.

Had she left the purse unsnapped? Maybe, but it wasn't at all like her. Deni reached inside the bulky purse and as soon as she touched her wallet knew something was wrong. The leather wallet wasn't folded but open wide and jammed down along the side of the purse, as if it had been hastily returned there.

She yanked out the wallet and looked. There had been forty-seven dollars in it. The money was gone.

Knocking over her fresh latte, she leaped from her chair and sprinted toward the door. Her feet slid out from under her on the wet tiles of the just-mopped floor.

Deni had barely struck the floor, causing a hell of a pain in her left hip, when she was scrambling to her feet. She began running again, but more cautiously, holding on to chair backs and the corner of the counter for support. She had some trouble opening the door and bent back a fingernail getting out onto the sidewalk.

She stood with her fists on her hips and stared up and down the block.

The homeless creep was gone.

"Damn him!" she said aloud, and pushed back into the cafe, sucking her sore finger.

The Korean guy stood leaning on his mop and staring at her fearfully as she marched a circuitous route over the dry area of the floor to where she'd been sitting, snatched up her purse, and went back outside. She hadn't paid her check, but just let that bastard stop her and ask for money after hers had been stolen right under his nose.

When she got back to her apartment, still furious, she found that the thief had stolen not only her money, but her key ring.

Her door keys and the key to a locker at a gym where she sometimes worked out were on that chain. It would be easy enough to get another key from the building super, but the locker key might be a bitch to replace. There might even be a charge for having lost it.

She twisted and rattled her doorknob, but she knew it was no use. She never left her apartment without locking the door behind her. Who in New York ever did? It struck her that the locker key wouldn't be the only expense. To be safe, she'd have to change both her door locks, the knob lock, and the heavy-duty dead bolt. In the meantime, she couldn't get inside her apartment.

The pain in her left hip flared again, as if taunting her for her bad luck and her bad life. More pain! In her body and in her pyche. Just what she needed. She must have bruised the hip badly when she fell in the restaurant. A deep bone bruise that would hurt for a long time.

Too angry to think straight, Deni slapped the hard, flat surface of the steel-core door, stinging her palm.

Rubbing the sore hand on her thigh, fuming, she limped away to go downstairs and wake up the super so she could share her rage.

CHAPTER FORTY-THREE

The Night Caller smiled. This time things had gone right. Not as they had when he'd taken Theresa Dravic. He recalled her rigid shock, temporarily paralyzing her. It took seconds, eternal seconds, for awareness to fade, and the arc, the knowledge that he was fate and life and she was fated and dying, had been there, had arced between them eye to eye. How smoothly he'd struck so the wound was barely visible, tilting her back quickly as if dipping her at the end of a dance, and lowering her toward the bench so the blood would run away from him. With his latex gloves, he'd just begun to place the book in her right hand and turn to St. Augustine, when horns blared and a man shouted in a way that was almost a loud bark.

No time to think, only to react. The Night Caller bolted into the shadows, then in among the trees. Only later did he see that what he'd heard was simply an argument between two cab drivers. They hadn't seen him, but he could hardly go back now. The mood was broken and the ritual was ended prematurely, and the ache years wide inside him would soon return.

But this time his task went well because the woman was careless, sloppy in dress and action. It had been easy enough to reach in and lift Deni Green's keys from her purse as she stood at a crowded intersection waiting to cross the street. He'd used his old skills and his unbuttoned winter coat to shield his actions, and been so calm that he'd deliberately also taken her wallet. After removing her money from the wallet, he'd even had time to drop it back into her purse. He didn't need the wallet; he'd already found Deni Green's address in the phone book, and observed her leaving her apartment building. By the time the traffic light signaled WALK, Deni Green's future had changed.

He fell back but stayed behind her as she walked two more blocks. She seemed preoccupied as before, keeping her head down and charging bull-like so people approaching from the opposite direction veered out of her way.

The Night Caller was glad when she entered Internet Knish. He was familiar with the café, had eaten there more than once and used its computers. She'd be a while with whatever she ordered before approaching the cashier to pay her check and learning her money was missing. If she used one of the café's computers, as was likely, she might be there a long time instead of returning immediately to her apartment.

He watched her through the window for a few minutes as she settled at one of the tables that gave access to a computer. She placed her order with one of the white-shirted servers. That's when he made up his mind.

Not the pressure. That wasn't why he was doing this. But the pressure was building again, the ache and the demon, just as the literature predicted. Waking him at night, looking out of and into him, clawing at him, clutching his sex from the inside. Maybe there would be some relief, but that wasn't why he was contemplating this. He needed to know what Deni Green knew, thought she knew, didn't know, would never know.

It was only a short walk to Deni Green's address. The Night Caller kept his muffler bunched high around his throat and chin, adjusted his tinted glasses, and entered the building.

There was no doorman, and the small tile lobby was empty. With a quick but knowledgeable glance around, he satisfied himself that there were no video cameras covering the lobby, recording the comings and goings of tenants or their visitors. Video cameras, he decided, video cameras that might be anywhere, contributed to the paranoia in the world.

He rode the elevator up to Deni Green's floor, encountering only a young woman getting out at lobby level as he stepped in. She was carrying one of those insulated containers used to deliver warm carryout food and seemed to pay little attention to him. On her way back to make another delivery, he supposed, coming and going, in and out of people's lives, people's memories. Part of them forever without their knowledge. He'd seen people like the delivery woman suddenly and surprisingly appear, seemingly for no reason. Seemingly. Then they were forgotten again. But never gone. Waiting in amber.

Moments later he was inside the writer's apartment. It was tastelessly furnished and too warm. It smelled of spoiled food. And of course it was sloppy. Empty soda cans on the coffee table, magazines and newspapers on the floor, along with a throw pillow from the sofa. Despite the excessive warmth, he didn't remove his coat. Instead he went straight to the computer sitting on the desk. Deftly he took off his gloves to reveal latex gloves beneath, and booted the computer.

When the computer was up and running, he inserted a blank disk in its A drive. He didn't know Deni Green's ISP or password, so he couldn't get online, but he copied everything he could from her hard drive to the disk he'd inserted. Included in what he was duplicating were her temporary files and cookies that would reveal where her Internet roamings had taken her.

When the first disk ran out of space, he inserted a second disk, copying more files along with her download and e-mail logs, which at present he wouldn't be able to access.

As he worked he felt an almost overpowering desire to leave something behind so she'd know he had been here, something to frighten her so that she'd lie awake at night, suffer as he'd suffered. Fear, once it lived in you over time, never moved out completely. But fear could eventually become your ally. Then your friend. Even your servant. Fear could be loaned and borrowed. Loaned and called like a debt into bankruptcy.

He was tempted to push his luck. He could stay longer and risk Deni returning home, realizing her door key was missing, and calling for the building super, maybe even the police.

In that way fear was dangerous, even though it gave him great courage and the invisibility of daring.

The joy of fear could be the enemy of caution, the fear of joy the enemy of life.

When he'd copied enough files from the hard drive

of Deni's computer, he placed the disks in one of his coat pockets. From the other pocket he drew a wad of wax. Carefully he pressed the keys on Deni Green's ring into the wax, one side, then the other. The impressions could be used for obtaining his own keys. The writer would be searching for him, and they would soon be sharing an apartment without her knowledge. The idea of it made him even warmer, but in a way quite pleasant and in the core of him. Deni Green wouldn't know the power he held over her unless he chose to exercise it. But *he* would know. For now, that was enough.

When he had the impressions, he placed the wax in a plastic sandwich bag and carefully inserted it in a coat pocket.

It was time to go. He'd obtained what he wanted.

There was a small table near the door into the hall, lightly fuzzed with dust. *Clean me!* he felt like writing in the dust with his gloved forefinger. *Clean me, please!*

Instead he placed the writer's key ring on the table so she would think she must have set it down there on the way out and then forgotten. He would leave the dead bolt unlocked, as she might have done even though she remembered it differently.

When she was let into her apartment and saw the keys, she would have to admit it was possible that she'd absently placed them there before leaving, neglecting to key the dead bolt from out in the hall. Memory danced. People forgot. It could have happened that way. Which meant that a thief had stolen her money, but not her keys.

Before long, she would talk herself into thinking it

had happened that way. She wouldn't bother having her apartment's locks rekeyed. Why should she, since her keys were right there on the table where she must have left them?

He knew she'd think no one had been in her apartment or had keys to it, because she'd want to believe that. She'd want to believe she was safe and the demons were locked out and not in.

The Night Caller knew she'd convince herself of it.

He knew how they thought.

He knew them, all of them. Not just their minds but their hearts. Not just their hearts but their souls.

On the way out of the building, and for a while on the sidewalk, he encountered no one. He might as well have been invisible.

Keeping his head lowered, he wrapped his muffler tighter against the wind. The wind like time, time like wind, scouring away flesh to leaveth only bone.

Deni Green's new roommate was smiling. But anyone would have had to look closely to know it.

CHAPTER FORTY-FOUR

Light snow was falling when Coop drove past the new housing developments bordering the highway outside Haverton. Soon the houses were older, the bright dusting of snow making them look picturesque rather than run-down, as they had on his last visit.

In the town proper he passed homes that were more modern and expensive before reaching the downtown area with its steepled church and gray stone city hall facing each other across the square. There were only a few people on the snowy streets, walking fast and bundled against the cold. Only the war memorial Union soldier, huddled in his bronze cape, stood brave and motionless in the center of the square and seemed to observe Coop's passage.

Coop drove beyond the square to Main Street. He didn't stop today at the brick building with its white columns where Bette had worked. He'd phoned Prudent Stand Real Estate earlier asking for Lloyd Watkins and was told Watkins was on vacation but was still in town. Coop had decided to drop in on Watkins unexpectedly. The surprise of seeing Bette's father on his doorstep again might rattle him into saying something he'd rather keep secret.

Just east of town, Coop steered the car into the Beau Jardin condo development. Its white and tan brick buildings, with their low hedges and mansard roofs whitened by snow, looked postcard pristine.

Street signs and addresses were obscured by snow, so it took him a while to find Lloyd Watkins's condo on Rue de Montre. The Honda continued to slide for a few feet when he braked at the curb, making him wonder how the highway would be driving back to New York.

When he climbed out of the car, he noticed that the temperature had dropped considerably in the last few hours. Cold air bit at his nose and throat. The snow was still light, but persistent. A few inches had collected on the sidewalk, which no one had shoveled.

Coop pushed the doorbell button to the town house's private entrance and waited, feeling the gentle cold touch of snowflakes settling on his face and the backs of his hands.

What sounded like a chain lock rattled faintly; then Watkins opened the door. Though it was afternoon, he was wearing a robe and corduroy slippers, and his dark hair was mussed. When he saw Coop, his dimpled chin dropped, and his bushy eyebrows gathered in a frown. He tried to speak but could only stammer. Coop had expected something of a reaction, but nothing this strong.

Finally Watkins got out, "Uh, Mr. Cooper . . ."

"I was in Haverton and had a few more questions to ask about Bette," Coop said, as if he hadn't noticed Watkins's discomfort. "I thought I'd drop by and see if you were home."

"I, uh, am."

"Yes. You mind if I come in for a few minutes?"

"Well, no, but . . ."

A figure appeared behind Watkins.

Now it was Coop who was surprised.

"Come inside, Mr. Cooper," Hillary Bland said. She was wearing pajamas beneath a yellow silk robe.

Looking embarrassed, Watkins lowered his head and stepped back so Coop could enter.

The condo was a lot neater than the last time Coop had seen it. The magazines that had been scattered on the floor were now in a stack on the coffee table. Also on the table were two drink glasses on cork coasters. They contained ovals of melted-down ice floating in diluted amber liquid.

Watkins was still speechless. Hillary brushed back a strand of her long auburn hair and met Coop's gaze. "If you think something is going on between us here, you're right," she said. "If you think it was going on before Bette died, you're wrong."

Coop studied both of them, then nodded. "I'll take your word for it." He removed his coat, folded it wet side in, and laid it over the back of a chair. He motioned toward the glasses on the table. "Can I have a drink?"

Watkins seized on something to do, maybe to get him out of the room. "We were drinking single malt Scotch," he said. "Glenfiddich."

"My brand," Coop lied. "On the rocks."

Watkins picked up the two glasses from the coffee table and hurried into the kitchen.

Hillary didn't say anything until he returned only a few minutes later with three glasses of Scotch and ice. She accepted her glass and sat in a corner of the sofa.

Coop sat down in the chair where his coat was draped. Watkins sat as far away from Hillary as possible at the opposite end of the sofa.

Coop nibbled at the Scotch, not really wanting it. "I'm not here to play morality police or pry into your private lives. I only want to talk to you some more about Bette."

"She and I had broken up even before she . . . was gone," Watkins reminded him. "This might seem too soon to you, but it's one of those things that just happened. I'd phone Bette and she'd make up some excuse, tell me she wasn't feeling well . . ."

"No further explanation is necessary, Lloyd," Hillary told him. She fixed a direct stare on Coop. He was liking her more and more. "Ask any questions you choose, Mr. Cooper."

"Did Bette say how she wasn't feeling well?" Coop asked, looking from Hillary to Watkins.

Watkins appeared puzzled for a few seconds. "Oh, I see what you mean. No, she didn't. Tell you the truth, I doubt if she really was sick. I'm sure she didn't want to see me and was just making polite excuses."

"Had she taken any time off work because of illness?"

"No," Hillary said. "Bette was out of sick leave, and Prudent Stand doesn't take kindly to unscheduled absenteeism for any reason."

"Would you say she might have come to work sick sometimes because her job was in the balance?"

"No. But it soon would have reached that point."

"Some employer," Coop said. "Why do people stay there?"

"They pay well," Hillary said simply.

"If Bette was out of sick leave, she must have missed a fair amount of work."

"Her sick days weren't taken in succession," Hillary said. "Three in a row at most."

"Sick leave covered two weeks," Watkins said. "And you're right, she was off work a lot. It didn't seem like it, but the sick days must have added up. Soon they would have cut into her vacation time, but they hadn't. She took her two-week vacation just before she went into New York and stayed at your cottage."

"And she told no one where she was going or why?"

"Not that we know of," Hillary said.

"She also told me she wanted to spend some time at the cottage to relieve job-related stress," Coop said. "Either of you know what that was about?"

"No," Watkins said. "But I can believe she was under stress, like everyone else at Prudent Stand. And maybe she really wasn't feeling well and it was getting to her. Hell, I feel that way myself sometimes. After what happened to Bette, I had to take some of my own sick days. I could barely drag myself out of bed most mornings."

"Would you know the name of her doctor?"

"'Fraid not," Watkins said.

"It might be in her records at work," Hillary said. "I can make a phone call for you."

Before Coop could answer, she was on her feet and moving toward the kitchen, and presumably a phone.

Watkins simply looked ill at ease as Hillary's muted voice carried like the mutterings of his conscience to the living room.

When she'd returned and reclaimed her corner of

the sofa, she said, "They'll call me back as soon as they find it. They think I'm off sick today and I want to see Bette's doctor for myself."

"They'll be calling Lloyd's number," Coop said.

Hillary gave a slight smile. "I'm friends with the woman in Records. She knows about Lloyd and me."

A small town, Coop thought, and not that large a company. Probably everyone knew about Lloyd Watkins and Hillary Bland. What might they also know about Bette? The possibilities scared Coop, who had seen every side of human nature, everything human faces could conceal.

He took a second sip of Scotch and decided not to take another. "Is there anything else about Bette? Even if it doesn't seem important to you. Anything you might not have told me the first time around?"

Watkins shook his head "I'm afraid not. I'd give anything if I could help, but I can't."

"Any other friends she might have had outside your circle?"

"Yes! Maybe one!" Hillary said. She seemed genuinely surprised that she'd come up with something. "Bette did volunteer work at the east branch library sometimes, and she mentioned a woman named Stern. I can't recall her first name."

"Abigail!" Watkins said. "I remember Bette mentioning an Abigail Stern. She's a library employee, I'm sure."

Coop glanced at his watch. "What are library hours?"

"In this weather," Hillary said, "you can be sure they'll close at five."

"Only an hour from now," Coop said. He stood up and put on his coat.

"Aren't you going to wait for the name of Bette's doctor?" Hillary asked.

"I'll phone you when I'm done at the library. Will you still be here?"

She blushed and nodded.

Watkins jumped up to show him out. "I hope we've helped you, Mr. Cooper."

"Me, too," Coop said.

At the door, Watkins offered to shake hands.

Why not? Coop thought. *Life goes on.*

As he walked back to his car, he realized he might not have had that reaction only a few days ago. It had something to do with Cara Callahan.

No, it had everything to do with Cara Callahan.

After getting lost driving to the library, he arrived at five minutes to five and found it closed. The lights appeared to be off inside, and his pounding on the door raised no reaction.

Discouraged, he drove slipping and sliding to his motel and called Hillary Bland at Watkins's condo.

She gave him the name of Bette's doctor, a general practitioner who specialized in gastronomical disorders. A Dr. Scott Ferguson. Hillary even obtained the doctor's office address and phone number.

Coop dutifully wrote down the information, then thanked her and slogged through deepening snow to the motel restaurant.

The snow had put everything on hold until tomorrow.

If only it could put tomorrow on hold.

CHAPTER FORTY-FIVE

Cara paused near the entrance to St. Alexius Cathedral, then walked up the chipped concrete steps and went inside.

The cathedral was long and narrow, with a center aisle and pews that would seat only about ten on each side. Faint, tinted light filtered through a tall stained-glass window behind the pulpit, an image of St. Alexius himself with haloed head and a cross on the left side of his ornate vestment. Cara knew he was the patron saint to beggars, belt makers, nurses, pilgrims, and travelers. She thought that last part, pilgrims and travelers, made him the patron saint of just about everyone.

Though narrow, the cathedral had a remarkably high beamed ceiling, and gallery walls decorated with aged frescoes and darkened statuettes of the apostles poised high above in shallow grottoes. After the din of the New York streets, it was remarkably quiet. The warm light streaming through the clerestory windows seemed thick enough to touch.

Seated in one of the back pews was a woman with her head bowed so low that it wasn't visible from behind. Farther down, on the other side of the aisle, a ragged-looking man was kneeling between the pews, also with his head bowed. The cathedral seemed to be occupied by no one other than the two worshippers and Cara.

Cara and Ann had been raised Catholic. Long ago Cara had drifted away from Catholicism, then from organized religion entirely. But Ann had remained true to the faith, and Cara had learned that she often came to St. Alexius for solace and to pray.

Cara had kept her promise to Coop not to walk in Ann's footsteps while he was away, but she didn't think he'd mind too much if she came to St. Alexius. Her reasons didn't only center on Ann. Cara had always heard that those raised Catholic inevitably returned to the fold. She didn't think that was the case with her, but considering recent events, she was slightly surprised to feel the desire to pray. It couldn't hurt, and it might help her to understand, to better cope with her grief and anger, to sleep all night without waking.

She walked down the aisle toward the pulpit, her footfalls silent on the faded red carpet that ran through the nave of the church. The dust motes swirling in hazed, tinted light, the subtle smells of the cathedral, took her back to her first communion and long-ago Sundays she would rather have spent elsewhere. The light transformed by stained glass seemed an artist's idea of heavenly illumination. Ancient polished wood, mustiness, centuries-old stone, lingering incense, all converged in a single scent that found its way through pain and time and soothed her. She wondered if it might be the only thing now that could soothe her.

In the front of the church she knelt and crossed herself, something she hadn't done in years, then moved to sit in one of the pews. She placed her purse beside her on the wooden pew, then lowered the padded kneeler on the pew in front of her and kneeled again.

She thought of Ann, how as young girls they'd sat beside each other so many times at Mass, how Ann was always eager to get in line to accept the host while Cara had to be talked into it, sometimes elbowed into it by their mother. She saw Ann at home with their mother and father, with their father.

Something was spotting the front of her coat. She was surprised that it was her own tears. She hadn't realized she'd begun to cry.

Cara bowed her head farther, squeezed her eyes tightly shut, and let herself cry almost soundlessly, hearing only her own labored breathing.

She stayed that way, motionless, reconciling herself with the past and fighting her way out of it.

It was only when she thought of Coop that her tears lessened and she regained control of herself. She wondered if their time at the Atherton Hotel was another reason she'd come here, a good Catholic girl again, burdened by carnal guilt

But she didn't feel like confessing, because there was no guilt in her after what had happened with Coop, only joy and the memory of joy. And hope.

She did say a silent prayer in the wish that he shared her hope. He'd told her about his illness, and she'd answered that it made no difference. Remission could last years, and who knew how much future anyone had? She hoped she'd made it clear to him that he'd turned his despair inward so it grew out of proportion and threatened to consume him even if the cancer didn't. If only he could realize that!

Eventually she stopped crying.

She didn't know if she felt better, but she was exhausted, purged of at least some of her tension and agony.

She scooted back up to sit on the pew, swallowed, wiped her eyes with her hand, then reached over to get a tissue from her purse.

That's when she discovered her purse was gone.

CHAPTER FORTY-SIX

In the morning, Coop went first to the library.

The snow had ceased falling, leaving about three inches on lawns and roofs. As he drove through the streets of Haverton, people were out scraping their windshields, shoveling snow from sidewalks, seeming not at all troubled by the inconvenience of winter weather. Some were even putting up Christmas decorations. The streets themselves had been snowplowed early. He encountered no delay on his drive to the library where Bette had been a volunteer worker.

Her library work was something else she hadn't told her parents. It bothered Coop how far the three of them had drifted apart in the flow of time. Was it that way with most families?

In the Job he'd come to believe that no one really knew anyone. After a while, being related didn't seem to make much difference. He again felt uneasy about what he might learn. It was like a body hunt in a homicide case, digging for something he wanted to find but dreaded.

He parked in a cleared section of the lot near the low

brick building, then trudged inside, wiped his feet on a large rubber mat, and set out to find Abigail Stern.

The library smelled like all libraries, a combination of old paper, glue, and printer's ink, mingled with the wood and varnish of rows of tables. The scent of sanctuary.

Abigail Stern was in the stacks, replacing returned books.

As Coop rounded the steel shelves he saw a thin, middle-aged woman standing on a rollable stool and replacing an armful of books on a top shelf. She reminded him of his old high school librarian, the same scraggly gray hair, thick-rimmed glasses, dowdy dress, even skinny legs heavily criss-crossed with varicose veins. She had the visual part of the stereotype down pat. He wondered about the rest of it.

"Ms. Stern?" he asked, though the woman at the desk who'd directed him here left little doubt as to whom she'd described.

Abigail Stern looked down at him and nodded, favoring him with a smile that could only be described as beautiful. Behind the thick lenses, her blue eyes sparkled with life and amiability.

Coop told her he was Bette's father and she agreed to speak with him. Her voice was softly modulated, her elocution precise. Coop blanched at the thought that people like her were being replaced by computers.

At a secluded table near Periodicals she sat across from him and folded her hands on a copy of *Ellery Queen's Mystery Magazine* that someone had left there. Coop hoped his quest would reach the kind of neatly wrapped and satisfying ending found in the magazine's pages.

After expressing her sympathy for his grief, Abigail Stern told him what a sweet and helpful volunteer Bette had been.

"Did she have any kind of conflict with anyone in the library?" Coop asked. "Maybe even a regular patron when he came in to take out or return books?"

"Nothing that I can recall," Abigail Stern said. "And frankly I can't imagine Bette getting into much of an argument with anyone. Not that she was a wet noodle, she simply understood people and got along with them. She told me once that if it weren't for the money, she might try to make library work her career."

Coop found that difficult to believe. Or maybe it was Bette exercising her understanding and ability to get along with people.

"She was never out of sorts," Abigail Stern said, "even during the time when she wasn't feeling well."

"When was that?" Coop asked, recalling the sick leave Bette had taken before using part of her vacation to relieve stress.

"Well, the last several weeks leading up to . . . when she went to New York City."

"Did she tell you she was going to be staying for a while in the family beach cottage?"

"No. Bette wasn't one to talk much about herself. She was a great listener."

"But she told you when she didn't feel well."

"Only some of the time. Other times I could tell by looking that she was under the weather, but she didn't complain."

"Did she say what was wrong with her?"

"Never. I would find her sometimes in the lounge, seated at the table and looking terribly depressed. Once

I even thought she'd been crying, but I can't be sure. I can tell you that the last time I saw her, just two weeks before the tragedy, she didn't look well. It was obvious that she was forcing herself to be cheerful with patrons. And she was uncharacteristically pale. I put it down to possible stomach flu that was going around Haverton at the time."

"Did you notice her taking any kind of medicine?"

"No. Not even an aspirin."

"Do you know the name Lloyd Watkins?"

Abigail Stern bowed her head in thought, then looked up at Coop. "I believe that was her young man; then they broke off their relationship. She mentioned it only once. After that she apparently decided not to share her discomfort. I didn't press her on the subject."

No, you wouldn't have, Coop thought "Who else might she have mentioned her illness or romantic life to?"

"No one else at the library, I'm sure. She and I were almost always the only ones present. That was why she was temporarily put on staff, to assist me. We're converting to a completely computerized system, complete with e-books."

"That's a shame. Will your job be affected?"

"I spend three nights a week in computer class, Mr. Cooper. The times will not plow me under."

He smiled. "I wish more people felt the same way. Did Bette ever mention a Dr. Ferguson?"

"Not that I can recall. Was he her physician?"

"So I've been told."

"Then he'd be the one to tell you about her physical state."

"Of course." He stood up. Through the windows on the other side of the library, he saw that a light snow had begun to fall. He didn't like highway driving in the snow; he would see Dr. Ferguson, then begin the trip back to New York.

"I didn't mean to push you toward the door," Abigail Stern said. "We can talk about Bette some more if you so choose."

"I think you've already helped me," Coop said. "And thanks for your time."

"Time's a valuable commodity, but I give it gladly if it helps to find Bette's murderer."

Coop believed her on both counts.

After Coop had identified himself on the phone, Dr. Scott Ferguson agreed to find a few spare moments that morning and talk with him. Someone else who put a high value on time.

The doctor's office was in a medical building half a block away from Haverton's small hospital. Ferguson's office was on the third floor. Coop found himself in a well-appointed waiting room with green carpeting and comfortably upholstered chairs. The walls were festooned with brightly colored impressionist art prints, Renoirs, Manets, Cezannes. On a table was an art deco sculpture of a woman in a position suggesting she was about to dive into water.

Coop pressed a button that caused a sliding frosted glass window to open and a brightly smiling young woman in a white uniform to peer out. He told her his name and that he had an eleven o'clock appointment just to talk to Dr. Ferguson, and she said, "Oh, yes!" as if she were overjoyed that he'd reminded her.

The window slid closed, a door opened, and she led Coop down a hall with doors leading to various rooms for various medical procedures. She ushered him into Dr. Ferguson's office, told him the doctor would be in as soon as possible, then left, closing the door behind her.

Coop looked around. More artwork. The usual framed certificates. Photos of an attractive blond woman and two small children, he assumed the doctor's family. Bookshelves stuffed with leather-bound medical tomes, except for a space at the end of one shelf that contained paperback best-sellers. Nothing by Deni Green. The doctor leaned more toward Grisham and King. The single window was bordered by thick beige drapes. Not much noise penetrated the office.

The door opened and a man in his early forties bustled in, smiling. He had very dark hair and eyes, and was average height and already putting on middle-aged weight at the belt line. He'd shaved so close this morning that he'd nicked his chin several times.

He introduced himself to Coop, shook hands, and sat down behind his desk. The air he stirred with his motion carried the faint smell of iodine. A green fountain pen lay near the desk pad. He picked it up and toyed with it with both hands.

No longer smiling, he said, "I was sorry to hear about Bette."

Coop thanked him for his concern, then said, "What I was wondering about was the state of her health."

Dr. Ferguson cocked his head sideways, then gave a hint of a smile that had nothing to do with humor.

"Unfortunately she's gone, Doctor, and the subject

of a homicide investigation. Not to mention that I'm her father. Doctor-patient confidentiality hardly applies here."

"I suppose she hadn't decided to tell you yet."

"Tell me?"

"You, the rest of her family, whomever she confided in. Bette was going to be operated on, Mr. Cooper. She had cancerous cysts on one of her kidneys."

Coop felt his breath rush out of him.

"Sorry to surprise you."

He decided not to tell Ferguson about his own cancer. "Was it life threatening?"

"Not yet. Tests determined that it hadn't metastasized. The problem was that the cancerous growths were close to her spleen. That's why she agreed to the operation."

"What kind of operation?"

"Something very new. There was a way to remove part of the kidney without damaging the spleen, but it would require a cellular transplant."

Coop thought about this. "Are you talking biogenetics here? A way for her to regrow the missing part of her kidney?"

"Not exactly *her* kidney. The purpose of the operation was to replace missing kidney tissue with other live tissue. Recent experimentation indicated that tissue from the kidneys of a donor animal, in this case a pig, would be accepted by the host organ. If you care to refer to a recent article in the *New England Journal of—*"

"You're saying part of a pig's kidney was to be implanted in my daughter?"

"Simply put, yes. She volunteered for it, on my approval. To do otherwise would have meant an unacceptable risk of permanent damage to the spleen and perhaps an accelerated rate of cancerous growth, or a long but sure wait for the cancer to claim her. The surgeon who was to perform the operation had done so successfully three out of three times during the past six months."

"Was this operation going to be performed here in Haverton?"

"Oh, no! We don't have the facilities here. New York City, at Mercy Hospital. That's where Bette had the diagnostic tests. She'd gone into New York for preparatory procedures, some of them quite invasive, then . . . the operation itself. She'd kept her illness secret from everyone here in Haverton, fearing word would get back to her family in New York. She was going to tell you after the operation was successfully performed."

"But why? . . ."

"I asked her but she wouldn't say. I suppose she simply didn't want you or her mother to worry."

That's why she wanted to stay at the cottage, Coop thought. A quiet, private place where she could prepare for invasive medical tests, then a major operation. And he knew why she'd kept the operation a secret. It was apprehension, caused by knowing what her mother would think about living tissue from another species becoming part of her own daughter. Apprehension on top of what she was already feeling. *Why didn't you come to me, Bette? Why didn't you ask your father for help?*

He told himself that she would have eventually. Possibly just before the operation.

He would continue to tell himself.

"The autopsy report didn't mention cancerous growth in one of her kidneys," Coop said.

"I'm no medical examiner, Mr. Cooper, but the cause of Bette's death was fairly obvious. And it took a long time for a battery of top diagnosticians to detect the cancerous cysts. Without biopsies being performed, they might be mistaken for simple and harmless anomalies. The condition might easily have been overlooked during an autopsy after a homicide."

Coop stared out the window for a moment at nothing but blank sky. "What would have been her chances?" he asked.

"If the operation had been performed? I wouldn't want to quote odds, but good, I'd say."

"She would have lived?"

"I think so."

Coop stood up, feeling dizzy.

"Are you all right, Mr. Cooper?"

"Fine. Okay. Thanks for taking the time to see me, Dr. Ferguson."

The doctor stood up behind his desk. "I sincerely hope I haven't caused you any further grief. . . ."

"No," Coop said, "I'd already reached my limit."

As he turned and left the office, the doctor was staring at him with more compassion than doctors usually revealed.

CHAPTER FORTY-SEVEN

Coop drove through deepening snow all the way back to New York. By the time he left his car at the curb, where it would almost certainly be buried by the snow's natural fall or by a snowplow, some of the largest snowflakes he'd ever seen were dropping almost straight down. Vehicle and pedestrian traffic had almost entirely ceased by now. An unbroken white plane was developing fast on the streets and sidewalks. Feeling snow work its cold way between his socks and black Florsheim dress shoes, he made his way to the entrance to his apartment building.

Dave the super had shoveled the steps and the walk directly in front of the stoop. Coop stomped his feet in the inch or so of snow that had fallen since then and told himself to remember to add ten dollars to the cost of Dave's Christmas gift this year.

The apartment was warm and had never seemed so comfortable. But even before he'd removed his coat, the phone began to ring.

It was Alicia. Coop explained that he'd just come in

from outside and asked if he could call her back in a little while. She said that would be fine, then surprised him by giving him her home number.

Fifteen minutes later, wearing clean, dry socks and with a mug of microwaved instant hot chocolate in his hand, he sat at his desk and played the messages on his machine. Two hang-ups, a pitch for a donation to the Police Benevolent Fund, Earl Gitter asking for the third time if Coop would please call him regarding the newspaper article he'd written on the search for Bette's killer—and two messages from Alicia simply asking him to return her calls.

When he'd done so, she said, "I've been trying to get in touch with you off and on most of the day."

Coop decided not to tell her where he'd been. "Good news or bad?"

"I'd say good. Have you called Deni yet?"

He said he hadn't.

"I think you better. She's got some new information."

"What is it?"

"She insisted I promise not to tell you."

Coop felt irritation along with the hot chocolate warm him. "Are you serious?"

"I know it's infantile, but she'll get totally pissed off and unmanageable if I say anything. In fact, you better not even mention that I called you."

"What the hell's the game here?" Coop asked.

"She wants to tell you herself. She wants—no, she needs—the satisfaction."

"This kind of bullshit," Coop said, "is exactly why I don't like working with her." *Or with you,* he might have added.

"Can't blame you for that. But I made a promise to her."

"Are you the sort that keeps promises?"

"Only certain kinds. This kind, because it's in my best interest. It helps maintain a necessary bond with a writer. But I didn't promise not to call you, and I thought I should do that so you'd know what was going on and not wait too long to contact her."

Coop felt even less like getting in touch with Deni. He knew that what seemed important to her, and to Alicia, might be of no practical value in solving the case. "Is this about Bette?" he asked.

"No. I will tell you that much."

He had no choice but to go along with the game. "Okay, Alicia, I'll get in touch with Deni."

"Soon?"

"Soon is relative." Whatever this new information was, it would probably keep. Possibly Deni had found out about one of her novels being discovered at the Theresa Dravic crime scene. Or it might well be something made up by Deni in order to get his attention. No need to rush to phone her. And things would continue to slow or downright stop because of the deep snowfall. The city that never slept would at least nap.

"You're angry. I don't blame you. Will you try to understand my position?"

"Sure."

"Be the good guy I know you are, Coop."

"Okay, Alicia. I'll get in touch with Deni soon."

"How are you feeling?"

"Feeling? Oh." He didn't want to discuss his illness. "I'm going to have some supper, then sleep for about ten hours."

"You been doing something exhausting?"

"Driving through the mess outside for most of the afternoon."

"I'm not going to pry, Coop."

"Thanks, Alicia."

He took the opportunity to hang up the phone.

Wondering again, what kind of people was he involved with here?

He would call Deni, as he'd told Alicia. But whatever she had to say would wait. There was someone else he had to talk to first.

Cara met him for breakfast again at Darby's. She wasn't able to get a booth by the window this time. Instead they were seated next to an array of framed celebrity photos on the wall. Each photo was signed, usually with a complimentary remark about Darby's Deli. Coop thought the handwriting on all of the photos except the one of Barry Manilow looked remarkably similar.

The morning outside was crisp and cold, with a bright sun already starting to melt surface snow despite the low ambient temperature. The direst snowfall predictions had fallen short, but not so short that a snowplow hadn't banked icy slush against Coop's car and left it curb bound. It never snowed in the subway, and Coop, like many New Yorkers that morning, took advantage of the fact to get where he was going. It surprised him, as it always did, how soon after a heavy snowfall the sidewalks were cleared to at least create narrow paths, and the streets were clogged with traffic that was nonetheless moving. New Yorkers were tough. They took no bullshit off of anyone or anything, including snowstorms.

Cara looked beautiful. Coop leaned down and kissed her cheek before sitting opposite her. "You're still here," he said.

"In the deli?"

"In the world. For me. Care to go into work late again today?"

''There's nothing I'd like more, lover." She looked across the table, into his eyes, drawing him into her eyes. "But I'm afraid tomorrow I wouldn't have a job to go to."

"Do you need a job to go to?"

"Of course."

"Am I ahead of myself?"

She touched the back of his hand. "Not too far ahead."

What he wanted to hear. What he wanted.

She took a bite of her bagel with cream cheese and finished chewing and swallowing before saying anything more. How could a woman look so sexy eating a bagel with cream cheese? "I didn't think you'd mind if I went to church while you were gone," she said.

Coop put down his coffee mug and smiled. "Church? Do you attend regularly?"

"Hardly ever."

"You trying to be cryptic?"

She didn't return his smile. "No. I did as you asked and suspended my walking in Ann's footsteps while you were out of town. Except that I went to the church where she used to go sometimes."

"Why?" He was irritated and it was in his voice.

"Because I wanted to go to church." A bit defensively.

"Ann's church?"

"That was part of it," she admitted. "Do serial killers usually hang around churches?"

"More often than you might think. My former wife even suspects they hang around police stations." Then he wondered why Cara was telling him this. If she'd simply kept silent, he wouldn't have known she'd attended Ann's church. Why was this an issue? "Did something happen in church?"

"Yes, but I doubt if there's a connection with Ann's murder. My purse was stolen."

"You mean snatched?"

"No. More like pilfered when I wasn't looking."

"Did you see the thief?"

"No. I was kneeling and praying. Crying. And when I looked up and reached for my purse to get out a Kleenex, the purse was gone from where I'd set it down on the pew."

"What was in it?"

She shrugged. "My credit cards, expired driver's license, key to the apartment, about fifty dollars in my wallet. And of course my identification and address, in case I ever misplaced my purse."

Coop sat back, angry and alarmed. "He might have been sitting right behind you."

Cara tried to take a sip of coffee but her hand was trembling and she gave it up and put down the cup. "Don't you think I realize that? Whoever took my purse had to have reached over the back of the pew where I was kneeling." She tried again, and with exaggerated movements sipped coffee and set the cup back exactly where it had been before she'd picked it up—like a drunk trying to pass for sober. Cara was trying to pass for unafraid. "The thief might not even be the killer," she said, trying to convince herself as well as Coop.

He wanted to take her hand, comfort her, but his anger was still in the way. "That's a pretty big *might*. Whoever stole your purse knows your name, where you live."

"Callahan's a fairly common name."

"Are you serious? You think the killer won't make the connection? You and Ann look almost enough alike to be twins, thanks to your new hairdo and wardrobe."

"Then maybe he will make the connection. I've notified the credit card companies that my cards were stolen, and I'm going to have the apartment lock rekeyed."

"Thank God!"

She reached across the table and clutched his sleeve with a kind of desperation. "I find I don't like it when you're upset with me. I'm sorry. Can't we go on from here?"

"I guess I am upset," he said. "I'm also afraid for you."

"And I'm afraid. This isn't the way I planned it I wanted to spot him watching me, then lead him into a trap."

"What church was it?" Coop asked.

"St. Alexius on East Fifty-seventh Street."

"Not that far from the bank."

Cara looked uneasy. "Meaning he might have followed me there from work?"

"It's a possibility."

"It's also a possibility the thief never killed anyone. That he carried the purse outside where he wouldn't be noticed, took the money from my wallet, then tossed everything else down a storm sewer or into a trash can. You can probably tell me approximately how many purses are stolen every day in New York. Mine might simply have been one of those."

She was right, Coop knew. But he also knew she didn't understand what cops thought about coincidence. "We have to assume the killer took your purse," he said flatly. "He noticed your resemblance to Ann, too strong a resemblance perhaps, and he was curious."

She sighed, giving up arguing with him. "If the thief is the killer and knows I'm Ann's sister, won't he sense a trap and back off?"

"He might. Or he might consider you a challenge he can't walk away from. He may be smart, but compulsion trumps intelligence. And if that's what happens, he's locked on to you like a radar-guided missile."

She bowed her head, unable to hide a twinge of fear.

Wasn't this what you wanted? he almost asked. But while he wanted to impress upon her the danger of her circumstances, he cared about her and didn't want to frighten her even more.

Coop looked across the deli and out the window. Even on snow-narrowed sidewalks, hundreds of people streamed past the deli every hour. It was the same way outside the bank where Cara worked. What were the odds that one of them had murdered her sister, noticed their similarity, then followed her to St Alexius and taken her purse? They were long. But long shots won horse races often enough to keep people betting. "Your phone number is unlisted," he said. "Was it in your purse with the rest of your identification?"

"Yes. I'm going to call from work and see if I can get it changed."

"Don't," he said.

She looked surprised. "Why not?"

"It could answer our question. If whoever stole the purse calls you, we might learn if he's Ann's killer."

She swallowed hard. "My God, that's a call I'd rather not take."

"It will help us to know where we stand. Leave your answering machine hooked up; maybe he'll leave a message."

She managed a wan smile. "I'd prefer that."

"Something else you should know," Coop said, "is that he might be calling to make sure you're home."

She looked down at her quaking hands and folded them together to keep them still.

"Do you want me to stay with you? I mean, over-night?"

She stared at him while he hoped she'd say yes.

"No," she said. "Whoever killed Ann doesn't stalk couples. Besides, I still think it's likely the theft of my purse hasn't anything to do with Ann's murder."

He nodded, admiring her stubbornness despite himself. "If you change your mind . . ."

She grinned at him. "Who should I call?"

"That better be a rhetorical question."

"It is."

"Do you have a gun?"

Her jaw muscles clenched. "No. It was in my purse."

"Christ!" He sat back.

"I'm sorry, Coop." She looked as if she might begin to cry. He didn't want that. Might not be able to stand it.

"In the grand scheme of things," he said, "that probably doesn't matter. I have a gun in the trunk of my car. I'll give it to you when we leave here. You ever hear of the Sullivan Act?"

"Yes."

"Good. I just wanted to make clear to you that you'll be breaking the law walking around New York with a gun, and I'm helping you." He glanced at the new-looking purse she'd put on the seat next to her. He was glad to see it had a zipper and a long shoulder strap. "Carry the gun in your purse, and run the purse strap from your left shoulder to your right hip, across your body. It might not be as stylish that way, but it discourages purse snatchers." He studied her. She was obviously apprehensive, but her squarish jaw was set, her green eyes glowing with determination. Beautiful. "Another possibility," he said, "is for you to stay at my place until this is all resolved."

She smiled slightly and shook her head no. "Sounds like the same possibility. I'd love to, but I'll take a rain check. I haven't come this far just to frighten the killer away when he's finally gotten interested in the bait."

"That bait analogy," Coop said, "scares the hell out of me."

"Me, too. But it's apt enough, and I'm stuck with it."

He finished his coffee and left his bagel untouched, trying to digest this new development. After giving her the gun, he'd walk her to the bank. She should be safe there. "We should meet for lunch," he said.

"No, I'll be okay, lover. Really. I know how to be cautious."

"Eat here again, then. After you leave the bank, stay on the crowded sidewalks, don't take any detours. Have lunch with another employee if possible."

"I promise." She raised her chin and met his gaze directly. "But there's something you should know. I'm not giving up on this no matter what happens. There are still some people who knew Ann who I want to talk to."

"I thought she led a more or less reclusive life."

"She did. But she had a knee operation at Mercy Hospital last year, and she took therapy and was an outpatient there for several months."

Mercy Hospital. More coincidence. Or was it? Mercy was one of the largest hospitals in the city. "She was a jogger?"

"Ann? Not hardly. She wasn't into sports or much of any kind of physical activity. She wrenched her knee stepping down from a bus."

"Good," Coop said. "At least I don't have to jog to keep up with you."

The stubborn expression gradually left Cara's features. She'd been expecting more of an argument. But Coop figured it would be worthless to try talking her out of whatever she'd decided might reveal Ann's killer. He was getting to know her; determination was her long suit.

He leaned across the table and kissed her cheek. "I hope it works."

"Works?"

"Your prayer at St. Alexius. I hope you get whatever you were praying for."

"I already did," she said.

He lifted her hand from the table and kissed it. Very gallant. *Look at you,* he thought, surprising himself yet again.

"Was this a lovers' quarrel?" she asked, caressing his cheek.

"Definitely," he said.

"If I'm only a few hours late for work," she said, "maybe I can explain it away."

This time, in the same hotel room, they made love less desperately, taking their time, getting used to each other. There was a lot to learn and every turn was a delight.

She lay on top of him when they were finished, her head resting on his bare chest. The room was warm and smelled of sex—he would always associate this hotel with that scent. He had been stroking her hair, but now his hand was still in it, his fingers intertwined with it as if captured there.

"Have you noticed," she said without moving, "that we're compatible?"

"Some," Coop told her.

She bit his chest hard enough to get a reaction. He could feel her cheek crinkle in a grin.

"I want you," she said. "Jesus, I want you!"

"Again?"

"No, not that. I mean I *want* you."

"It seems," Coop said, "that you've got me."

"Do you want me?"

"I want you," he said, "and I don't want anything to happen to you."

"Like lose my job?"

"Not like lose your job," he said, and rolled her off him, then pinned her against the soft mattress. He held both her wrists over her head and leaned down so his face was close to hers. He almost said, *Like lose your life.*

Instead he kissed her.

CHAPTER FORTY-EIGHT

If she hadn't learned it from one of her police contacts, Coop decided that when he phoned Deni he wouldn't talk about the Theresa Dravic murder, or Deni's paperback novel found at the scene. Especially the novel. That was one Porter might be holding back from the press and public to use as his ace when they found a suspect. And it was possible the killer's prints were on the glossy cover. If he knew, there was no telling what he might do. Coop remembered a guy in Brooklyn who cut off the tips of his fingers to avoid a murder conviction after he'd choked his—

Deni picked up on the second ring, and she didn't mention the Dravic murder. Maybe she hadn't heard about it yet or made any connection. Or maybe she was focused and excited about what she was telling him, what she recognized as the break in their hunt for the serial killer—the fax of the shoe print found at the Georgianna Mason murder scene. Coop wished he'd phoned her sooner. He'd been wrong; this wasn't some wacky idea like her airline attendant theory. This was something solid.

If it was as she described.

The shoe sole print in Seattle would all but confirm that there was a devious and prolific serial killer operating in different cities, and smart enough to alter his MO so that even the FBI wouldn't connect the crimes— if the locals even thought to bring the FBI in on the case.

This new evidence would bring the FBI running. Fred Willingham should be notified and given a copy of the Seattle print as soon as possible. And maybe the NYPD would decide it was time to share the plastic saint information, if Georgianna Mason had suffered the same posthumous humiliation as the other victims. Coop was sure they hadn't shared it yet. The kind of territorial imperative in law enforcement the killer counted on was working for him.

But Coop had been misled by Deni before. The smart thing would be to see the shoe print himself before calling Willingham. He told Deni he'd drive over to her apartment and look at the fax image.

"You don't trust me?" she asked over the phone.

"Don't make me answer that, Deni. I'm on my way as soon as I hang up."

"You'll see you should have trusted me all along. And had more respect for my investigative abilities." If gloating could ooze through a phone line, it would be all over Coop. "You don't have to apologize to me, Coop, but I do expect congratulations for breaking the case."

"I wouldn't describe it as broken, Deni. We don't know what connects the victims. And we don't know the identity of the killer."

"That'll happen."

"We're a lot closer to it, if you're telling me the truth and this fax is what you say it is."

"It's a clear image, and with expert witnesses to back it up in court."

Coop had been here before; he knew Deni would tell anyone anything in order to work her will on them. "When I get to your place," he said, "I don't want to hear the dog ate the fax."

"I don't have a dog," she said huffily. "I have a cat."

"Since when?"

"I'm thinking about getting a cat."

He'd forgotten his car was locked in by snow and ice.

The subway again. This time slower, more crowded. New Yorkers were out and about in force, flaunting their ability to shrug off any weather. Throwing out a dare to everything from Godzilla to nuclear attack. It was an attitude Coop had always admired.

Almost an hour had passed before he pressed the intercom button for Deni's apartment and she buzzed him in.

The first thing he noticed was that the place smelled like too much perfume or deodorant not up to the job of disguising body odor. And the living room was a mess. A pillow and tangled quilt filled a corner of the sofa. Empty soda cans stood guard around a pizza crust on the coffee table. Deni was in wrinkled slacks and what looked like a flannel pajama top. Obviously she'd been holed up against the storm here and stayed in this morning. The TV was on but muted, Oprah silently exhorting viewers to buy a book. Maybe some-day she'd be hawking Deni's book.

"How was driving in this mess?" Deni asked, as she ushered him inside.

"Nonexistent for me. A snowplow has my car locked to the curb."

"Fucking New York," she said, sending a whiff of terrible breath his way. The pizza, he guessed.

Without further conversation, she swaggered over to her desk, picked up a sheet of white paper, and re-turned to show it to Coop.

When he reached for it, she held it clamped between thumb and forefinger hard enough to turn her nails white. "I'll make you a copy," she said with her fierce grin.

He examined the fax without touching it. The shoe print was as advertised. Once the Seattle techs had found it and brought the bloodstains up, they had a complete sole print that looked identical to the others, with the same irregular crisscross pattern. In this print it was obvious that most of the pattern was on the por-tion of sole that covered the ball of the foot. The sole's toe was apparently smooth leather or rubber.

"Lyons in Seattle faxed you this?" Coop asked, making sure.

"Not Lyons, Sanderson. Lyons was on vacation in some happy, healthy place where the sun is shining. He remembered the print and called Sanderson, told him to fax it to me. That's what I get for bugging them about looking for a shoe print. They thought I was a pain in the ass, I could tell."

Coop agreed with Lyons and Sanderson, but he said, "Congratulations, Deni."

She grinned wider, not so much joyfully but with a sadistic pleasure. Coop had said uncle.

"Make my copy," he told her.

He watched while she went to her desktop copy machine and ran off a duplicate. When she'd handed it to him, he said, "I'll get this to Fred Willingham."

"Willingham? The FBI?"

"Sure."

"Maybe we oughta wait a while," Deni said. "See where this leads us. Maybe we can tie the victims together somehow."

"That's what we've been trying to do," he reminded her.

"Not entirely. We've also been trying to establish they were killed by the same person. I think we pretty much covered that one, so why don't we start from where we are now and get the jump on Willingham and the FBI?"

"Nobody's better at closing down serial killers than the FBI, Deni."

"That hasn't been the case here so far. Hell, we couldn't even get them interested in our serial killer theory."

Coop waved the fax. "They'll be plenty interested now."

"Not if we don't tell them now."

"It's a crime, you know, withholding evidence in a homicide."

Deni glared at him. "Sounds like a threat. You gonna rat on me, Coop? Send me up for the big fall, shweetheart?" Not a bad imitation of Bogart.

"It wasn't a threat, Deni."

"So it's some more of your macho crap? Some fucked-up sense of duty?"

"We don't turn this over to the FBI, the killer has more time to take another victim. Maybe more than one."

She shook her head and laughed at him as if he were hopeless. "Two things, Coop: The FBI couldn't catch a cold even on a day like today. And the FBI isn't writing a goddamn book."

"The FBI nails somebody every now and then. And the book takes a backseat to catching a killer."

"Not my backseat!"

"You're obsessed."

"Oh? With what?"

"Your book. Your career."

Her expression was one of anger and aggression, but her lower lip trembled. "You're damned right I'm obsessed. I'm a celebrity, a successful writer. And I intend to make it even bigger than I have." A tear tracked from the corner of her eye down her cheek. "Try to understand, that's all the fuck in this world I've got! Everything! Without it, I'm . . . scared . . ."

"I'm sorry for you. I mean that, Deni." He headed for the door.

"A little time, Coop. Just so I have a chance to work my computer, jump on the Web, check my sources. You'd be surprised, the cybermagic I can work. A little time. Please!"

"A little," he agreed, on his way out. "I can do that."

"Days?"

"Hours."

He slammed the door hard behind him with the force of pity and anger. He was disgusted with himself for what he'd just agreed to. If another woman was murdered . . .

Cara . . .

CHAPTER FORTY-NINE

Coop stopped at a FedEx two blocks from his apartment and made two copies of the fax Deni had given him. Then he trudged toward home, glad to see that the sky was clear and no more snow was likely. The fresh-fallen snow had been beautiful; the gray slush it had become was not. Snowplows were still beeping and growling about, widening the lanes in side streets. As Coop was walking past his parked Honda, he saw that a plow's blade had scraped away much of the snow that was blocking it. Maybe he had wheels again.

He got into the car to see if he could free it, but it was still locked in tight. The snowplow blade must simply have shoved and packed more slush beneath the undercarriage and against the tires. Hopeless, he decided. Maybe it would be spring before he drove again.

He climbed out of the low-slung car, relocking it to protect the radio, then continued on his way.

Standing inside the door to his apartment, he peeled off his gloves and coat. He was tired, probably from the rarified cold air, but he couldn't be sure. His heartbeat seemed slightly rapid, too. That scared him, and he removed his shoes and stretched out on his back on the sofa for a while.

From outside came the muffled rush and hum of traffic, the distant blaring of horns, something hard banging away on concrete, the chatter of a jackhammer, faraway construction and destruction. Close by, a man shouted something unintelligible and a woman answered; a bus roared and rumbled away from the stop near the corner. It was all a vivid dream. Coop didn't want to lose any of it, and he became aware that his eyes were moist.

Self-pity. God, he hated self-pity! When he was a rookie and had tromped all over evidence at a crime scene and been chewed out, an older cop had told him he might as well not waste time feeling sorry for himself, because nobody cared if he did. The antidote for self-pity was to do your job. Harsh but true, Coop had discovered. It was advice he'd carried with him ever since.

He sat up, swinging his legs over the edge of the sofa, and put his shoes back on. He wasn't so weary now, and his heartbeat had evened out. Even a perfectly healthy man might have felt as he had, after spending time with Deni, then trekking long city blocks through arid cold

Thirsty, he briefly considered a beer, then instead went into the kitchen and ran cool tap water into a glass. He carried the glass back into the living room, sat down at his desk, and addressed an envelope to FBI agent Fred Willingham at the Bureau's New York field office. In it he slid a carefully folded copy of Deni's fax, along with a brief note explaining to Willingham what it was. This way Coop would have mailed the information to Willingham only hours after he received it,.and the postal service would give Deni the time she wanted so badly.

Then he phoned Billard and told him about the faxed shoe print and that he'd mailed a copy to Willingham. Covering his ass, and he hadn't promised Deni he wouldn't notify Billard immediately.

Billard asked for a copy, as Coop knew he would, and after hanging up he addressed and stamped another envelope.

He bundled up in coat, muffler, and gloves again, then walked to the mailbox at the end of the block and dropped in both envelopes, noting that the next pickup was at five that evening. Then he returned to his apartment.

This time when he lay down on the sofa, he fell asleep.

Cara roused him from a deep sleep with a phone call a few minutes after six.

"Did I wake you, lover?" she asked, after hearing his sleep-thickened hello.

"Stretched out on the sofa a while ago," he said, "next thing I knew it was now. Are you all right?"

"I'm fine. Are you more awake than you sound? I want to tell you something."

He ran his tongue around the inside of his mouth, not liking the taste or the enormous size of his fuzzy teeth. "Sure. Tell away."

"I thought I should call you right away and let you know I got my purse back."

He sat up straighter. "How?"

"It was sent to me anonymously in a big padded envelope. I found it in my mail when I got home from work."

"Are you sure there was no note with it?"

"Positive. I checked carefully."

"Was there a return address?" But he already knew the answer to that one.

"No. And the envelope had a Grand Central Station postmark. I'm sure whoever did it didn't want to get involved. In fact, my guess is that whoever stole it felt guilty and had second thoughts."

"Cara, you're not cynical enough."

"You're cynical enough for both of us, Coop. And the thief did remove the money from my wallet before he or some good Samaritan returned it."

"What about your credit cards?"

"Well, they're gone, too. But that's all."

"Some guilt. Some second thoughts."

"So whoever took my purse was simply a sneak thief, maybe somebody desperate for money who gave in to temptation."

"In a church," Coop said.

"The big thing is, this suggests the theft had nothing to do with Ann's murder."

Coop figured she was probably right.

"I miss you," he said. "You want to go to dinner?"

"The weather's still too lousy to go anywhere tonight. Besides, I already called out for pizza."

Still stubborn, he thought Still determined. Maybe obsessive. *Like me?* "You're not going to invite me over? I can afford some red wine without a metal cap. Goes well with pizza."

"Not tonight, lover. Too many things have happened. I need to do some thinking."

He decided not to press. "Me, too, I guess." He wondered if he should tell her about Georgianna Mason's murder and Sanderson's fax to Deni. Better not, he decided. It would be best if nobody was informed before Willingham got his copy. He had to smile at himself. Department politics. Cover as you move. Old habits hard to break.

"Sleep well," she told him.

"I already have." He heard the yearning and suggestion in his voice.

She laughed softly. "I guess it's the cop in you. You never give up."

"Never."

Another old habit.

While he had the phone in his hand, he made another call, long distance to Seattle.

He was prepared to track down Marty Sanderson and wake him in his bed if necessary.

But it wasn't necessary. Sanderson was on duty and took Coop's call within a few minutes.

Coop identified himself and established his authenticity, then confirmed that Lyons was indeed on vacation in North Carolina and Sanderson had sent the fax Deni showed him.

"Anything else I can help you with?" Sanderson asked, after giving Coop the information he requested.

"I've got a question," Coop said.

"If I can answer it, I will."

"Two words, actually. St. Augustine?"

"Yeah," Sanderson said, after a while.

"A few more questions, then," Coop told him.

CHAPTER FIFTY

First he made sure that she was out. Then, carrying his brown leather briefcase, the Night Caller let himself into Deni's apartment with her key and was greeted by a large, startled cockroach on the floor just inside the door. *Sloppy, unclean bitch!* He scooped up the roach with his free hand an instant before it made it to a dark space beneath the molding, then hurled it against a wall hard enough to kill it.

He sat down at the writer's computer. It didn't take long for him to render it blank and without threat or meaning, as she herself would soon become.

When he was finished, he sat and thought the old thoughts, waiting until he heard her key rasping in the lock. He snatched up his briefcase as he rose from the chair, and went with cat silence to the closet where he assumed she would hang her coat.

He knew from experience how she would react when she opened the door and there he was. There would be a long, long moment of shock and horror and seeping dread, in which he had all the time in her world to act, because his time was different from hers. She would gasp, hold her breath as something dearer to her than she knew. Maybe she'd faint. The point was, once she opened the closet door, she would know the abyss.

But she didn't open the door.

Not this time.

Fate was patient as stone. He waited and watched as she removed her coat just inside the apartment door, then tossed it on the sofa. She was a slob with no predictable habits. But he'd known that about her by her apartment. What did it matter, how she veered this way and that as she moved toward her moment?

She disappeared down the hall and he removed from his pocket the heavy wool sock filled with finely grained sand, then placed the briefcase on the floor. In less skilled hands the soft sap would have been ineffective. Not in his hands.

Just as he was about to leave the closet, he heard water running. The unmistakable hiss and whisper of it splashing hard in a column into the old cast-iron tub. If he waited a while longer she would be in the bathtub, like Georgianna Mason. That was all right. He could improvise. He was the future and knew the future and could mold it to his purpose.

Unpredictable again, she strode into the living room wearing a large pink bath towel wrapped around her and sat at her desk. She switched on her computer and tried to boot it up, but it didn't respond. The erasure of its operating system had already preceded hers.

She was still staring, puzzled, at the glowing monitor, when he silently opened the closet door, rapidly closed the distance between them, and struck her just so with the sap.

The bitch somehow moved as he'd swung his arm.

Only a few inches, but it had been enough to inconvenience him.

He raised the sap again and rained blow after blow on her head and shoulders. She tried to grip his arm, then finally slumped down and rested her head on the desk.

By the time he'd gotten his briefcase from the closet and removed from it the Manhattan phone directory and twelve-inch length of heavy iron pipe, she was seated straight up again in her desk chair, but in a daze. Her fingers fluttered as she raised her hands before her eyes.

He wasn't surprised by that. He'd rather expected it.

In one smooth motion he rested the phone book squarely on top of her head and smashed down on it with the pipe. He'd struck four or five quick, violent blows before she slumped again over her desk, her head resting in the crook of an elbow as if she were asleep.

But she was tough, this one. Tougher than any of the others, who certainly on some level understood and cooperated in their dying.

The Night Caller leaned over her, felt for a pulse, and found none. Casually, he reached out and snapped one of her fingers. No response to extreme surgical stimulus, he thought, smiling.

He'd come prepared for what was to be next. Earlier that evening, while Cara Callahan had been down in her building's well-lighted and safe laundry room, the Night Caller had used his duplicate of her door key to let himself into her apartment. He'd browsed about as he always did at first, getting to know her better, and found the gun.

No need for her to have *that,* he thought, and slipped the gun into his pocket. He wondered how she'd obtained a replacement so soon for the one that had been in her purse and was now in his apartment.

Later, when he got back to his apartment, he saw the words *Police Special* engraved in the second gun's blue steel, and he knew where she'd gotten the gun. That had given him the idea. The cop. The Distraught Dad. Old Testament bastard. The Night Caller would make sure he had something more than a crude concept of justice to occupy his mind. The idea had come unbidden, like a revelation from the Book.

Still keeping an eye on the surprisingly resilient Deni Green, he placed the revolver in the fold of the phone directory, using the bulk of its pages to muffle the shot as he pulled the trigger and fired a round into the nice soft back of an upholstered chair so the bullet wouldn't be misshapen.

It was doubtful that anyone had heard the muffled shot, but it was possible. The explosion had been louder than anticipated, so he'd have to hurry.

The Night Caller quickly stuffed phone directory, pipe, and sap into the briefcase. The gun he slipped into his pocket.

He glanced around him, satisfied, then hurried from the apartment. Aside from three preschool children playing on the stairs in the vestibule, no one noticed his passing. He smiled as he stepped carefully around a scattering of toys and upraised faces fresh as spring blooms. *In the midst of death we are in life.*

Upstairs, at the sound of a car horn honking in the next block, Deni Green stirred, raised her head, then dropped it back down.

* * *

The next morning, Coop was glad to see that the weather had further improved. Brilliance from a cold sun in a clear sky illuminated his kitchen window that looked out on an air shaft. He'd already showered and was seated at the kitchen table, having a breakfast of buttered rye toast, coffee, and orange juice, when the phone rang.

It might be Deni. He decided to let it ring and call her back after breakfast. But the voice on his answering machine in the next room was Billard's:

"Coop? You there? If you are, you better pick up."

Coop put down his toast on the paper towel he was using for a plate, wiped his buttery fingers on the towel, then reached over and lifted the receiver from the wall phone by the sink.

"Hold on, Art." He punched the pound key and the loud whine in the receiver ceased as the machine switched itself off.

"Coop?"

"Yeah. Something up?"

"Deni Green's been badly beaten. Hit on the head with a blunt object, also been worked over on the back, shoulders, and arms."

It took Coop a few seconds to take in what Billard had said. "How bad is she?"

"Hospitalized. Critical condition. It happened sometime last night, apparently. Water was running over in her bathtub, leaking into the apartment below, so the super let himself in and found her."

Coop flinched at a mental image of Georgianna Mason lying dead in the blood Jell-O of her old claw-footed tub. Had Deni somehow avoided that grisly fate?

"She wasn't in the tub," Billard said, "though she was wearing nothing but a towel. Like she was getting ready to take a bath, then remembered something and sat down at her desk. Her computer was on. Looks as if she struggled a bit, maybe fought her attacker long enough that he gave up, or maybe got scared off by something."

Blunt object . . . Coop wondered if Deni's attempted murder might have no connection to the other victims. None of them had suffered multiple blunt object trauma.

He caught himself. Of course she was probably the latest in a long line of victims of the same serial killer. His MO had been altered; that was, after all, his MO. And the killer knew Deni's name, so it would have been simple to learn her address. Maybe she'd been getting too close. Maybe the killer figured she had to be stopped, tried for her, and was interrupted, frightened away.

Maybe Coop would have to be stopped.

"Where's Deni now?" he asked.

"Mercy Hospital. In the ICU. Doctors say she has a fighting chance, but we shouldn't be surprised if she doesn't make it."

Coop gave the receiver a squeeze hard enough to whiten his knuckles. Maybe the killer hadn't failed after all.

"She isn't conscious," Billard said. "They say she might never be, and if she does regain consciousness, she might not be able to remember what happened even if there isn't permanent brain damage."

"Where are you calling from?"

"Deni Green's apartment," Billard said "The techs are still going over it. When I heard the squeal I drove in here, knowing you'd want whatever there was on this one."

"Mind if I come over?"

"I thought you'd ask that," Billard said "Come ahead."

"1 can leave here in a few minutes. You still gonna be there?"

"Sure," Billard said. "Why would I leave a party like this?"

Coop hung up the phone, took a final searing sip of coffee, then hurried into the bedroom to get dressed. He put on a clean white shirt, a tie that he'd left looped and knotted, then a dark sport jacket. Best to look as much like a working cop as possible. Then he wet his hair and smoothed it back with his fingers. After giving his mirror image a final check, he left his apartment to join the party in Deni's.

"From what I heard," the chief tech on the scene said, "this is likely to become a homicide, so be extra careful what you guys touch, where you step." He was a bandy rooster of a redheaded guy in his sixties. Coop remembered him from years ago. Garrity, he thought his name was. Techs seldom talked that way to cops on the scene, but Garrity always had. Nobody told him to shut up, so Coop figured he must have an angel high in the department. Or maybe Garrity was simply smart and had gotten everyone to think that.

"Looks like she was taken by surprise while she was concentrating on her computer," said Billard, who was standing back against a wall, out of the way. She was found slumped over her desk, her head resting in the crook of one arm."

Coop looked at the desk, the empty office chair on rollers. Deni's computer monitor was still glowing, a screen saver showing cats bounding soundlessly across cyberspace.

"Maybe she was about to get in the tub, then ran in here to answer the phone," Coop speculated.

"There's a phone in the bathroom," one of the plain-clothes detectives who'd overheard him said. Then he continued writing with a ballpoint pen in a black leather notepad. "It's working fine."

"More likely," Billard said, "she remembered something she wanted to do on her computer, came in here to do it before she forgot, or while the water was running to fill the tub, then was attacked after she sat down."

"Attacker could have been hiding in that closet," said the detective with the notepad. He was a tall, lanky guy about forty, wearing a brown suit that looked as if it were tailored by the Salvation Army.

Coop thought he was probably right about the closet, which was on the opposite side of the living room directly across from the desk chair. He'd seen Deni hang her coat in there; it was used only for coats and a vacuum cleaner she seldom used, a few assorted junk items.

"Anything stolen?" he asked.

"Don't know yet," the detective said, not looking up from his notes.

It was the answer Coop expected to hear. This was a fresh crime scene; there hadn't been much time to develop hard information.

"I know who tried to kill her," Coop said, trying to get the lanky detective to at least look up from whatever he was writing. "I just don't know his name."

"Or how to get in touch with him," the detective said. Then he did look up and gave a sad smile. "Lieutenant Billard filled me in."

"I don't suppose you know if she was on the Internet when she was attacked."

"Couldn't say. Hasn't been time for any of that yet." He looked at the computer glowing on the desk, the endless parade of cats crossing the monitor screen. "She's a writer, I understand."

"Right. Cat mysteries." Coop waved a hand toward a bookcase displaying several of the Cozy Cat novels.

"Cat solves the crimes?"

"Cat helps. The main character is fashioned after Deni Green herself."

"She own a cat?"

"No, I don't think she likes them. Or they don't like her."

"Way it is with cats," the detective said. "Finicky."

"Way it is with people who write about cats that solve crimes."

"If I may play human detective," Garrity said, "I'd guess the assailant was frightened away abruptly. I saw the victim just before the paramedics removed her. Her wounds were inflicted with power and viciousness, all of them. Whoever was beating on her didn't simply get tired or lose enthusiasm. He was trying to kill her and was interrupted."

Ignoring Garrity, the detective flipped his notepad closed. He walked over to Coop and extended his hand. "I'm Dickerson," he said, "One-Nine Precinct. I'm the whip on this one. After talking to Lieutenant Billard, I can guess what you have to say, but I need your statement."

"Of course," Coop said, shaking the oversize hand. Pianist's fingers, he thought. Extraordinarily long and strong.

"When we've had time to learn more here," Dickerson said, "I'll call you, or you can call me, and I'll bring you up to speed."

"You all better clear out of here for now," Garrity said. "Let us do our work so you can do yours. Unless of course you want one of your fingerprints to turn up in the wrong spot and make you good for the crime."

"There's a coffee shop down the block," Dickerson said to Coop, still tuning out Garrity. "We can have a little privacy there while you give me your statement, maybe even get some breakfast."

Cop-to-cop talk, Coop thought. In what other profession would two people stand near bloodstains at the site of a severe beating and consider going to breakfast?

"I already ate," Coop said, "but the rest of it sounds okay."

"We can make it short," Dickerson said. "There's no point in you going over to Mercy yet to see your friend, anyway. Indications are she won't regain consciousness for quite a while."

Coop didn't insult him by asking if cops were assigned to stand by and get Deni's statement if and when she regained consciousness and could speak.

As everyone other than the crime photographer and lab techs, who'd been working mostly in the bathroom and bedroom, filed from the apartment, Billard said, "I notified the FBI, Coop. Fred Willingham. After this came down, I didn't see that there was any choice."

"That's fine, Art. I'd have done the same."

"Agent Willingham sounded excited when I told him about the fax."

"Like fireworks after a home run," Coop said.

After Billard parted from them down in the street, Coop and Dickerson walked toward a Starbucks in the next block. Coop knew it didn't have to be this way. He could be standing in Deni's bedroom giving his statement, or down in the building's vestibule.

He decided he liked Dickerson. liked his professional courtesy.

Maybe identified with him and envied him for the life he was living. The life Coop loved and hated and would never stop missing.

Two young girls, one of them standing on a chair, were winding strands of miniature Christmas lights around the supporting pillars at Starbucks. Dickerson and Coop went to a table in the back, where no one else was sitting and the tiny clear lights were already glowing.

The questions Dickerson asked were the ones Coop would have asked in his place. Amazing how smoothly a police interrogation went if both parties knew the rules, and the one being questioned had nothing to hide.

Then Dickerson drained the last of his espresso and handed Coop a folded sheet of paper. "This was found tuck to the bottom of the desk pad on Deni Green's desk. What's it mean to you, if anything?"

Coop looked at the list of names, all women, followed by dates and cities. Among the names were those of the women he and Deni had pegged as probable victims of the serial killer. The cities were where they had died, the dates were when.

Coop explained the list to Dickerson. "Deni was using her computer to trace other possible victims," he continued. "My guess is that's what the rest of these names represent. Her killer didn't realize she'd printed it out, and he missed it or had to get out before conducting a thorough search." Coop pulled a pen from his pocket. "You mind if I copy this?"

Dickerson gave his okay, and Coop copied the information onto a paper napkin.

He offered to pay for the coffee, and Dickerson accepted but left a tip before leaving Starbucks.

Coop sat for a while, sipping ice water and studying the women's names on the list. All murder victims, he was sure, as the cities and dates opposite the names of known victims were those of their deaths.

Two things about the list struck Coop. Though there were three gaps of inactivity in the dates, generally the time between murders was decreasing. Typical of the increasing need and madness of a psychosexual serial killer. The other thing was the appearance of a particular date—August 28—three times. The three death dates immediately after the gaps of inactivity.

Coop decided he needed to learn more about that date.

CHAPTER FIFTY-ONE

Back in his warm, tiny apartment that had felt cozy but now seemed stifling, Coop called Alicia and gave her the news about Deni.

"My God!" Alicia said. "What happens to the book now?"

The words had obviously leapt from her lips before she could stop them; he didn't like that reaction from her. Publishing must do things to people. Some people, anyway, who were playing out of their league for high stakes. Maybe police work wasn't as callous and diminishing as he'd thought.

"And poor Deni! You say she's in critical condition?"

"Critical," Coop confirmed.

"This is awful! Do you think there's a connection between what happened to her and what you two were working on?"

"I think so," Coop said, "even though there's no direct evidence pointing to it."

"Cop's intuition?"

"More than that. The thing about our killer is he

reaches into his trick bag and leaves various clues meant to mislead. He's apparently studied the literature on serial killers. It's his different guises that protect him."

"But Deni said he always left what she referred to as 'his calling card.' She said all serial killers do that."

"This one does, too, but not enough to create much of a pattern." He thought about the long hair fanned out around the victims' heads. Only some of the victims. But Deni had been assaulted, and Theresa Dravic had been killed, hurriedly and perhaps with interruption. And of course Deni's hair was short. Georgianna Mason's hair was long, but wet and tangled from her involuntary bath of blood and tap water. Aside from Deni, the victims were all lying or reclining on their backs in relaxed positions, laid out with an undertaker's care. But how many murder victims everywhere were found lying on their backs? Probably more than half, as they sought their final breaths and good-bye look at the world they were leaving. At least two of the victims—Marlee Clark and Ann Callahan—had red hair. Bette's natural hair color had been auburn, maybe with streaks of red. Georgianna and Theresa Dravic he wasn't sure about. Possibly a pattern there.

But there were the shoe prints with their distinctive crisscross pattern. And now there were the shoe prints from Seattle.

And of course, St. Augustine. Beginning with Bette, then Georgianna Mason and Theresa Dravic. The last three known victims, murdered closer together in time, more brutally. Deni hadn't been mutilated and sexually violated, but Coop was sure that was a clever killer's diversion or there simply hadn't been time. Or maybe it

was because Deni was attacked not out of psychosexual compulsion, but simply to stop her investigation
and upcoming book. The plastic saints would work
well in her book, Coop thought, the calling card she'd
talked about. The killer was now more firmly in the
tightening grip of compulsion, boasting of his grue-
some work, taunting the police because he must, even
though it increased the odds of him being caught.

". . . Is Deni conscious, Coop?"

Alicia was talking.

"No," Coop said, breaking out of his reverie. "The
doctors aren't sure she'll regain consciousness."

"From what you say, she might have seen her attacker."

"It's probable that she saw him. There was a brief
struggle."

"You always say *him,* as if you know the killer is a
man."

"Didn't Deni tell you they usually are? Women
don't kill women that way, not unless there's some motive other than violent sexual compulsion."

"Like, say, a best-selling book?"

Coop was jolted. He actually held the phone away
from him for a moment and stared at it, as if he were in
a schlocky television scene. "What are you saying,
Alicia?"

"Nothing, actually. I know I should be ashamed, but
before this happened, I was . . . well, speculating."

Say it, Coop thought. *Come right out and say it.*
"That Deni was the killer? Involved in a grisly plot of
her own in order to write a true crime book?"

"Don't think too poorly of me, Coop. I told you, it

vas only idle speculation. The dark side of my mind, I
uess."

"I think we can throw that kind of speculation out
he window now."

"Yes. Thank God for that, anyway."

He was sure she didn't mean it. Probably she was
hinking that if Deni were the killer it might make a
ıell of a best-seller—written by another of her authors.

"How did you suppose she was going to end the
ıook?"

"I did wonder about that," Alicia said, after a pause.

Steam pipes clanked and rattled in the old, thick
valls, reminding Coop of the cold outside. "Does Deni
ıave any family that should be notified?" he asked.

"I'm sure she doesn't. At least, no one she'd want to
ıe notified. A stepfather she absolutely hated, and she
old me her mother was dead and there were no sib-
ings."

Coop felt a pang of sadness for Deni. Almost the
vay he'd felt after Bette was gone forever. Deni wasn't
.uch a bad sort, really, only someone who carried bag-
ʒage and deep pain from the past, like so many people.
ʒhe was alive, but maybe as close to death as a person
:ould get, and dying could be so damned lonely. "It
.eems somebody other than you and I should care
ıbout whether she lives or dies," he said.

"I'll phone her agent."

"Fine. That's something. Maybe he'll know some-
ıody to call."

"There isn't any point in visiting her if she isn't con-
:cious. Sometimes they don't even let you near some-
ıody in intensive care. You have to stay on the other

side of a window. And you can't even bring them flow
ers. They might contaminate the air."

"I'll drop by the hospital later on and check on her,
Coop said.

"God!" Alicia said. She sounded genuinely appalled
"We're going to have to figure something out here. W
need to have some editorial meetings, maybe hire an
other writer. . . . Well, you know. This is an unpre
dictable, tough business, Coop."

"I'm getting the idea," he said.

"I've got to get busy here. Will you do me a favo
and keep me posted on Deni's condition?"

He said that he would and hung up.

"Guess what I just learned!" he heard her call excit
edly to someone just before the connection was bro
ken.

Coop called Cara next at Mercantile Mutual. H
told her Deni had been badly beaten and urged her to
exercise special caution.

"I hope she pulls through," Cara said immediately.

"I'm thinking of *your* safety."

"And I'm thinking of yours, Coop. It seems obvious
that if the killer saw Deni as a bigger threat to him than
I am, he'd also see you that way."

"Are you always so infuriatingly logical?"

"No," she said. "You'd be the one to know that." She
paused a few beats. "I don't want to lose you, lover
Not ever."

"You won't. We won't lose each other."

"Are you sure it was the killer who attacked Deni?
mean, he didn't kill her."

"He tried. Or maybe he was satisfied knowing he'd

damaged her capacity to think clearly for the rest of her life. Or testify against him, if it came to that."

"Is she hurt that badly, that she's permanently brain damaged?"

"I don't know. It's possible. Will you be extra careful? For you and for me?"

"I will, darling, if you promise the same."

"I promise," he lied. At least it felt like a lie, even though he meant it. The reply was so automatic. Part of the job. Though he was no longer a real cop.

As he was replacing the receiver after talking with Cara, he glanced down and saw that his hand was trembling. He realized his stomach was roiling, and he was suddenly very tired.

Coop knew it was the stress of the investigation, of his obsession to find Bette's killer. Dr. Gregory was right in advising him to avoid stress, in pointing out the close relationship of stress and disease, partners in destruction. One consolation was that the killer must be feeling the same stress, or worse. Coming unraveled. Unless he was incredibly strong, he was coming unraveled.

The hiss and clank of the old steam radiator system was somehow soothing. Coop pushed himself up from where he was sitting and walked over to the sofa. He intended to lie down and relax, calmly think over recent events and what they might mean. But even as he was removing his shoes and arranging throw pillows for his head, he knew he was kidding himself.

He was asleep within minutes.

*   *   *

That afternoon, Billard called.

"There's no change in Deni Green's condition," he said. "If she does survive and remember what happened, we should have an ID on whoever attacked her. The doctors at Mercy say she's suffered massive blunt-object trauma to the head. Something like a phone book interrogation."

Coop knew what Billard meant. In rougher times, cops would place a phone directory on top of a suspect's head and beat on it with their nightsticks. The energy of the blows was transferred to the skull through the phone book, causing pain and massive damage, but leaving very little external evidence of a beating. Even if the suspect died, sometimes an ME or coroner in earlier years couldn't or wouldn't determine the exact cause of death.

"The other damage to Deni, contusions, even a broken finger, are relatively incidental," Billard said. "It's the injury to the head that's life threatening."

"Is her skull fractured?"

"No. But it might not be if a soft sap was used on her, or if something was used to transfer and radiate the shocks of the blows. The doctors are still trying to determine the extent of brain damage. You know how it works, Coop, it's the brain bouncing around inside the skull that causes the real injuries. And CAT scans and MRIs show a lot of internal bleeding. They've drilled into her skull to relieve the pressure."

"Christ!"

"If her attacker is the guy you're looking for, he's mixing up his techniques again."

"That's his game," Coop said. "It was him. He go

on to her because of that newspaper article, found out what she looked like and where she lived. He must have been scared away, or thought she was dead, or he would have killed her." *And maybe he has killed her.*

"I hope Deni got a good look at him, Coop. I hope she can describe him, maybe even ID him."

"Has it ever been that easy, Art?"

"Never that I can recall," Billard said. "And it probably won't be this time, either."

"There's a new piece of information you should know, Art. The victim in Seattle, Georgianna Mason, who was killed less than a month ago. St. Augustine."

"I know. I got the information when I called Marty Sanderson. He told me you'd asked about it."

"I figured it had reached that point. Somebody had to make the connection."

"Yeah. You did right. Same cheap plastic statuette, same slice to the vaginal tract to facilitate entry."

Coop told him about the list of names found in Deni's apartment. "One date appears more than any other on the list. August twenty-eighth mean anything to you, Art?"

"Sure does. I went to a Catholic school. Why am I not surprised?"

"So what's August twenty-eighth?"

"It's the Feast of St. Augustine. Celebrated all over the world."

"I think our killer has a unique way of celebrating," Coop said. He felt anger growing in him and fought it down.

"This fucking world!" Billard said.

Coop didn't have to remind him it was the only world they had.

After assuring Coop that he'd keep him informed Billard hung up.

It was too warm in the apartment now and Coop was sweating. He could feel the dampness of his shirt beneath his armpits, at the back of his collar. He'd lain too long in one place, so exhausted he hadn't moved For a moment he thought of opening a window; then he told himself that was the way to pneumonia.

He sat for a long time on the edge of the sofa, staring at the snow banked on the window ledges across the street. A scraggly gray pigeon that looked as if it might be freezing to death was perched on one and seemed to be staring forlornly back at him. A bleak scene for a bleak time.

CHAPTER FIFTY-TWO

It wasn't all that terrible, the Night Caller thought. To kill out of practical necessity had always been a tolerable act and weighed lightly on the conscience. Somewhere people did it every day, politicians, generals, cops. Killing the writer had been that way—that she wasn't yet officially dead wasn't of much concern. It was only a matter of time, and that part of her that could do him harm was already in blood and ruin.

There'd been no need to take time for the complete ritual. Those murders were different, solemn acts of mercy and infinite understanding for both parties. Giving and taking and knowing at last.

But he hadn't really minded that much eliminating the threat of Deni Green, and it gave him additional ways to mislead the authorities. After all, she didn't fit any pattern or definition—other than pest.

Dangerous pest

Survival, that was why they killed, the politicians, the generals, the cops. And that was why he'd killed the writer, removed her and what she knew from the world. Her future could no longer intersect with his, because now she had no future. It was all simple and amazingly complicated.

The cop was still a threat. The Night Caller knew that. He'd seen his photograph, and later the man himself. But even in the grain of black and white newspaper photography, there it was in his eyes. It had risen from the paper and struck the Night Caller like a revealing electric shock. *He is my opposite side. He will never stop, because he can't.*

The Distraught Dad.

Time enough for him. Time will take care of him. The special policeman, the romantic, the Police Special.

Time will take care of us all, every one, the detritus of fate, sleeping in the cradle of eternity. Everyone beautiful at last.

Some will rest easier. Knowing forever.

Everyone beautiful at last.

The air was cool and smelled of Pine-Sol disinfectant. Coop sat in a green plastic chair and stared at the scuffed black leather toes of his shoes.

He was on the third floor of Mercy Hospital, in a waiting room that was really more of an alcove with a sofa, several chairs, a coffee machine, and a red vending machine that dispensed canned soda or bottled water. The hall was wide, with teal carpeting. Near the waiting alcove and nurses' station, the carpeting gave way to a tile floor that had a waxed, dull gleam to it. The nurses' station was about fifty feet away, a busy hub with three nurses inside a circular counter. They were consulting computers, taking phone calls, studying or marking charts on clipboards. Every five minutes or so, one of them would raise a section of the counter and escape the circle to scurry down the hall in response to a flashing call light, or to make a patient force down a pill or endure some minor medical procedure. Angels of kindness and discomfort.

The duty nurses on Three weren't the only hospital personnel striding back and forth in the hall off the waiting alcove. The intensive care units were down the hall to Coop's right. To his left was a set of swinging doors that hissed and opened automatically when anyone approached them from either direction. White-clad nurses, green-clad doctors, people in business suits and casual clothes, came and went, some of them pushing gurneys or linen carts, most of them looking preoccupied. Near the nurses' station, many of them made a right-angle turn toward the elevators. Others walked the straight line between the ICUs and whatever lay beyond the wide swinging doors.

Coop had been allowed to look in on Deni. And that, literally, was all he could do. He had to stand behind a large window so he wasn't breathing and contaminating Deni's purified air.

She lay in a bed with her head heavily bandaged, a clear oxygen tube coiled up to her nose. Another clear tube dangled from a corner of her mouth. Her eyes were closed and her face wore no expression. Were it not for the bruises on her right cheek, she would have seemed a wax figure not yet given identity and personality by its maker. A plastic packet dangled from a steel pole next to the bed, feeding a tube that led to a needle in the back of her left hand, life a drop at a time.

One of her doctors, a tall guy a nurse had identified as Dr. Lewellyn, Deni's primary physician, entered the room and glanced over at Coop behind the window. Then he studied the chart at the end of the bed, made a notation on it, and left the room. Coop thought maybe he'd come to the other side of the glass and talk to him, but he continued on his rounds.

Coop saw a uniformed cop slumped reading a magazine in the main waiting room, but he chose not to sit with him and make strained small talk. Instead he drank a bitter cup of coffee in the waiting alcove near the nurses' station. Then he took up his position on the hard plastic chair where he would be easily visible, in case there was a change in Deni's condition.

Hospital personnel continued to pass in both directions, their footfalls making no sound on the tile floor. He was aware of their passing only because of the faint, flickering shadows created by the overhead fluorescent lighting. Or now and then someone whose shoes squeaked would stride past.

Something made Coop look up. The cop who'd been in the waiting room was turning the corner near the nurses' station, heading toward the elevators. One of the nurses was staring in Coop's direction.

The atmosphere changed. Time seemed to slow down. A sad-looking man in what looked like a gray maintenance uniform strode past Coop, his shoes squealing like anguished mice on the waxed tile floor. Coop would always remember the sewn-on name tag above his shirt pocket: *REV.* Curious. What might the letters stand for? Revere? Reverend? Revelations? From the opposite direction a tall, tired-looking man in green scrubs approached. Deni's physician, Dr. Lewellyn. He was wearing rubber-soled shoes much like

Rev's, only his footfalls made no sound at all. He might as well have been a ghost.

A suspicion, a possibility, grew in Coop like embers stirred to flame.

"Mr. Cooper?" the doctor asked. "Denise Green's friend?"

Coop said he was. *Denise.*

"I'm afraid she's gone," Dr. Lewellyn said. He reached out and gently touched Coop's shoulder. "I'm sorry. There really never was much of a chance."

"Did she regain consciousness? Say anything?"

Lewellyn shook his head no. "She was never even close to being able to do that."

Coop nodded. "Thanks for your efforts, Doctor."

"The nurse said you weren't a relative. . . . Is there anyone the hospital should contact?"

"Her agent, I guess."

"Agent?"

"She was a writer. Her agent, her editor at Whippet Books . . ."

"I'll tell the nurses."

The nurse who'd been staring at Coop had followed the doctor but stayed at a discreet distance, where she stood very still with her hands folded in front of her. Now, sensing their conversation at an end, she approached.

"Mr. Cooper?"

"Yes."

"There's a phone call for you. You can take it at the nurses' station."

Coop thanked Dr. Lewellyn again, then followed the nurse.

Another nurse, seated behind the circular counter, lifted a phone on a long cord and set it on the counter-top.

Coop said hello into the receiver, turning away from the seated nurse.

"It's Art Billard, Coop. I have some more information on Deni Green."

"Art, she just—"

"I'm calling you as a friend, Coop. But I'm still a cop, so be careful what you say."

What the hell was *this* about?

"Everything on the hard drive of Deni's computer was deleted," Billard said. "Really deleted by someone who knew what they were doing. Our tech heads say there's no way to recover anything."

"Like Georgianna Mason's computer," Coop said. He remembered Bette's notebook computer was never located.

"That might help."

What did Billard mean by that?

"You were in New York when the Mason murder occurred, weren't you?"

"I believe so, sure."

"What about when Deni Green was attacked?"

"Why?" Coop asked, moving cautiously now.

"The lab boys discovered a bullet imbedded in the back of an upholstered chair by her desk. It appears whoever beat her also shot at her but missed."

"The bullet couldn't be too misshapen. Have it run through the FBI computer, find out what kind of gun fired it. Maybe the barrel pattern is even on file with them and we can identify the individual gun and its owner."

"No need to check the FBI files. We had the pattern the NYPD computer database. It fits the barrel of a mith and Wesson thirty-eight Police Special. Your un, Coop. The one you kept when you were pensioned ff."

Coop said nothing. He was trying to grasp what he'd ıst heard. The purse stolen from Cara had been re-ırned minus cash and credit cards, and her gun. Coop ad given her his gun to replace the one that had been tolen. Now it had been used by whoever attacked)eni. Coop was sure the shot had been fired into the hair precisely so the police would run their ballistics :sts and suspect him.

"You still got that gun, Coop?"

"No." He could hear Billard's hard breathing.

"If Deni comes to, she can ID her assailant, set this traight."

"Deni just died."

More ragged breathing. "We've got murder, then."

"You didn't make this call, Art."

Coop hung up.

He turned to the nurse who'd told him he had a phone all. "Humor me on something?" he asked.

She put down her pencil and smiled. "Sure."

"When I was sitting there waiting for word from the octor, I noticed that most of the medical people here vear shoes that don't squeak on the tile floors. Is there reason?"

"Other than it drives us nuts, it can be very distracting ı the operating room. And it can cause what someone ays beneath a surgical mask to be misunderstood."

"So you buy special shoes?"

"Soft-soled shoes, usually. For comfort."

"But they squeak worse than leather on a tile floor.

"Some of them do. But you can cut the soles s
they're sectioned and won't squeal on tile."

"Really? Is that fairly common in hospitals?"

"It is here at Mercy, so I'm sure it's done in othe
hospitals. Especially among operating room personne
You in the shoe business or something?"

"Sort of."

Coop thanked her. Then he left Mercy Hospital a
fast as he could without actually breaking into a ru
The rubber soles of his shoes squealed on the waxe
tile floor with every step, as if in agony.

CHAPTER FIFTY-THREE

There was risk now in everything. Coop didn't pause outside the hospital to hail a cab. He wanted to walk, anyway. To think. Finally he found a phone booth on East 57th, fed it a cold coin, and called Cara's apartment.

He stood with the receiver to one ear, a finger in the other to block the sounds of traffic, and listened to the phone ring over and over on the other end of the connection.

By the tenth ring he knew she wasn't going to answer. He told himself she'd worked late, or gone somewhere after leaving the bank. Or maybe she'd simply gone somewhere for supper.

A siren warbled shrilly and a police cruiser turned the corner and immediately got bogged down in traffic. Dirt-crusted gray snow was banked on one side of the street, narrowing it. As the patrol car sat and the driver worked the siren for repeated soprano howls, Coop hung up the phone and walked on.

* * *

The Night Caller finished showering and began dress
ing carefully, almost ritually. Jockey shorts, then pants
belt buckled before seating himself on the foot of the
bed. One sock and shoe on, shoe tied, before slipping
on the next sock and shoe. The day's bright sun and the
heat from the loft apartment had melted all the snow
on the skylight, and the resultant glare lay harsh on
everything it touched. So much so that after combing
his hair he avoided glancing into the mirror, knowing
and loathing what he would see.

Time to look ahead, the Night Caller decided, choos
ing a tie from the many in his closet.

He settled on a red silk Moschino with a subtle woven
pattern.

He stood still for a few seconds, the tie draped over
his extended forefinger.

A Windsor knot, he decided.

He could tie one without looking in the mirror.

Cara took a cab to Mercy Hospital and had the driver
let her out in front of the nearest entrance to the physical therapy wing.

She paid the fare, then wearing her new purse
strapped across her torso as Coop had suggested, strode
through one of the revolving glass doors into the lobby.

It was warm in there. A large rubber mat had been
laid just inside the door and was puddled with melted
snow from people's shoes and boots. In the center of
the lobby was a tall artificial Christmas tree with only
red ornaments and an aluminum stepladder nearby. A
woman at the reception desk directed Cara to the floor

where Ann had been treated as an outpatient for several months after her knee operation.

Cara walked past a line of newspaper machines and a small gift and flower shop to the elevators. With a man wheezing laboriously and a young volunteer tending a woman in a wheelchair, she rode the elevator to the seventh floor.

Cara had helped Ann during one of her first visits here, accompanying her in a cab and aiding her as she used crutches to enter the hospital and limp on and off the elevator. After that visit, Ann had quickly become more proficient with the crutches and insisted on coming alone for her therapy sessions.

None of the nurses looked familiar to Cara, until she glanced into an employees' lounge and saw a heavyset dark-haired woman sitting at a table drinking a cup of coffee.

Cara stuck her head into the room and looked around. The nurse was alone. Cara saw a large mole on the side of her nose and was sure she was the one who had greeted Ann on the visit when Cara was along.

"Mind if I come in?" Cara asked. "I'd like to talk to you for a minute about my sister."

"They'll help you at the nurses' station," the woman said. "Just down the hall and around the corner, near the elevators."

"I know. It's you personally I want to talk to. I think we met the time I brought Ann in for a therapy session."

The nurse sipped coffee, wondering how to deal with this. "We treat a lot of Anns, ma'am."

"Ann Callahan. Her knee had been operated on."

Now the nurse looked interested. "The Ann Callahan who was . . ."

"Yes."

"Come in and sit down. Pour yourself a cup of coffee."

"I'll skip the coffee but I'll sit," Cara said, and settled into one of the molded plastic chairs across from the nurse.

"I'm Justine," the nurse said.

"Cara Callahan."

"You said. Did they ever catch the man?"

"No. That's kind of why I wanted to talk. Was there anything about Ann's visits here that you remember as being unusual?"

"You a cop?"

"No. Just a sister."

Justine smiled. The mole made her nose crinkle. Her round face was tanned except for her forehead, as if she'd recently returned from wearing a hat on a Florida vacation. "Nothing unusual I can recall. I helped train and monitor Ann for her exercise regimen. She was always cheerful. Nice person."

"Am I the only one who ever accompanied her here?"

"Yes, as far as I know. And you only that once. Ann was the independent type that didn't want to be a bother. She came here alone by cab. Later, when she was off the crutches, she said she rode the bus."

Cara jotted down her phone number on a napkin for Justine and gave it to her, in case Justine remembered something that might prove useful. Then she thanked the nurse and stood up.

"Come to think of it," Justine said, when Cara was at

the door, "I do recall something. But you oughta talk to somebody in surgery, where they did the knee operation."

"Why is that?"

"I don't exactly recall what the deal was, but there was talk over there about something odd happening in the recovery room."

"Something odd?"

"Well, not all that odd. Don't get your hopes up. This was just some of the normal hospital gossip. And not very interesting at that, or I would have remembered."

"Is there anyone in particular here at the hospital I might ask?"

"Eileen Dampp, with two *Ps*. She's an OR nurse. That's if she's on duty this evening. You know where surgery is?"

Cara listened to Nurse Justine's directions to turn this way and that, take this elevator, those stairs, follow the signs . . .

She thanked the woman and left her to her coffee break.

After stopping twice to ask directions, Cara found surgery on the sixth floor of the opposite wing, in a newer-looking part of the building constructed above the parking garage.

Hospitals, Cara decided, had more twists and turns than the mind of a madman.

CHAPTER FIFTY-FOUR

Most surgery is done in the morning. Afternoon and evening are for stabilization and recuperation. There were a few patients' rooms on the surgery floor at Mercy, and an occasional visitor carrying packages or flowers. But when they left recovery, most patients were taken to rooms on the floor above.

There was only one woman behind the circular counter of the nurses' station, a sandy-haired, efficient-looking nurse wearing curiously dated horn-rimmed glasses. She listened to Cara's request, told her yes there was an Eileen Dampp with however many *Ps* on duty, and asked Cara to have a seat in the waiting room. As Cara walked away, she saw the woman begin to make a phone call.

The waiting room, scene of daily impatience and angst, was now unoccupied. It was furnished in plush black vinyl, a sofa and two matching recliner chairs. A TV mounted high on the wall was playing CNN soundlessly. Sensitive Judy Woodruff looked highly offended and wracked with sympathy. There was the usual coffee brewer in a corner, a rack of dog-eared magazines next to it.

Cara sat down, picked up a *Newsweek,* then scanned meaningless words about a new biogenetic breakthrough. It mattered not at all what words were on the pages before her. She wasn't concentrating on the text.

She didn't move for the full ten minutes it took for Eileen Dampp to arrive.

She was a small, attractive woman who had bright blue eyes and an Irish face that another Irishwoman would recognize. There seemed about her a frenetic energy, even though she was standing still.

"Cara Callahan?"

Cara started to stand, but Eileen Dampp waved her back down and sat down herself on the arm of one of the recliners. "I'm Eileen Dampp. They told me you had some questions about your late sister Ann." She had a nice voice, businesslike but kind. Cara guessed she was an exceptional nurse, one of those rare people born to the job of caring for others.

"I was told that something odd happened during Ann's knee operation here nine months ago," Cara said. "Were you assisting in the operating room?"

"Yes," Eileen Dampp said, "but I'm guessing that what you were told about happened in recovery. When Ann was coming out of anesthetic she began to scream. She claimed she saw a horrible wooden mask staring down at her. Rather, the mask itself wasn't so horrible. It was even handsome and pleasant. But she kept screaming about the eyes. Said the mask had malevolent, terrifying eyes. An unfavorable reaction like that isn't all that unusual, but it was difficult to quiet her down. It seemed real to her, and for whatever reason it scared her a great deal."

"Did anyone ask her what she thought the dream meant?"

"No, we assumed it meant nothing. People recovering from heavy anesthesia are liable to dream anything. The subconscious is a jumble for quite a while after a lengthy operation under general. You'd be surprised at some of the things we hear in recovery. It was the screaming that made this particular instance stick in my mind, because one of the doctors on staff happened to hear it and chewed out some of the duty nurses for not controlling the noise."

"Ann never mentioned anything like that," Cara said.

Nurse Dampp shrugged. "She probably realized it was like a simple childhood nightmare and put the incident out of her mind."

"Probably," Cara said.

Nurse Dampp started to stand up, then settled back down. "I'm sorry about your sister. I hope they catch whoever did it."

"Thanks," Cara said. "Catching whoever did it is the reason I'm here."

The nurse looked at her as if about to say something. Instead she did stand up. "If I can help you any other way, just call and ask."

Cara thanked her.

"Callahan. That's obviously Irish."

"Very obviously," Cara said.

"As is Cara. In Gaelic it means *friend*. And here you are still trying to be a friend to your lost sister."

"I suppose that's true."

"My maiden name was Reilly."

Cara smiled. "It shows. Thanks again for your help."

Nurse Dampp returned her smile. "I'm going to a wake in Brooklyn after I get off work tonight. I'll raise a glass to your success."

And I to yours, Cara thought, watching the compact, energetic woman hurry away to return to work.

She hadn't felt so Irish since her last confession. *Say three Hail Marys and an Our Father.* For some reason, that made her think of Ann, and she held back tears.

The Night Caller took the elevator to surgery on the sixth floor of Mercy Hospital. There were three other people on the elevator. One woman smiled, but they all glanced at his face and looked quickly away, pretending not to notice the gift from his father.

It had happened long ago and yesterday.

The grotesqueness (though they hadn't called it that) was not as noticeable as he thought (they'd told him yesterday and long ago). It was natural for him to exaggerate it in his mind, to assume heightened reaction in others. In time he would understand.

They were wrong but they were right. In time he understood everything. The simplicity beneath the complication. Horror and liberation. Always a price.

Two of the other passengers got off at lower floors. The Night Caller and a small, nervous man the lighted panel indicated was going up to eight, blood and radiology, were the only occupants by the time the elevator reached six.

As the doors slid smoothly open, The Night Caller stepped out and barely glanced at the knot of people on his right, about to board the adjacent elevator going down.

His step faltered and he did a double take.

Cara Callahan had just boarded the down elevator with half a dozen others!

He wasn't imagining it! He was positive! Earlier he'd seen her with the Distraught Dad. Now at Mercy! Cara Callahan!

She must have been talking to people here—on the sixth floor!

Instead of continuing on his way to recovery, he spun quickly in a U-turn and entered the down elevator.

He made it just before the doors slid closed, cutting off the view of the duty nurse at the counter about to greet him, now staring curiously.

CHAPTER FIFTY-FIVE

Coop walked the streets, head down, shoulders hunched, hardly feeling the cold. The shoe prints had finally yielded their meaning. He was sure now the killer was some kind of hospital worker. A doctor?

He had a hard time believing this one. Though most of the fatal wounds *had* been skillfully inflicted. He recalled the medical report in the Marlee Clark case describing how the deep hack at the back of her neck, just beneath the skull, had severed the ganglion, in effect separating body from brain as neatly as a guillotine blade. Theresa Dravic had been killed the same way. Ann Callahan had been taken with a precise knife thrust. And Georgianna Mason had been alive most of the time in her bathtub while the can opener was used on her, yet little blood or water had been splashed from the tub. That had to require some kind of skill, to render her alive but helpless to resist such a thing. And there was apparent skill in the knife cuts to allow deeper insertion of the plastic stints in the vaginal tracts. Medical skill.

Bette had gone into Mercy for diagnostic tests. Ann Callahan had gone there for her knee operation.

Coop stopped at another public phone. He looked around, realizing he was on Riverside near the park. He dug in his pocket for more coins, stuffed them into the phone with cold fingers, and called Maureen's home number.

Her phone rang seven times before she answered.

"What do you want?" she asked gruffly, after he'd identified himself.

"A favor. For me and for Bette."

"Describe it," she said, sounding dubious.

"Can you go into your office at the insurance company tonight?"

"Tonight? At this hour? Why would I want to do that?"

"To check on something for me. For us. Using your company computer and software."

"What about Deni Green? Doesn't she have a computer?"

"Deni is dead."

"Dead . . ." Maureen repeated numbly.

He told her what had happened, then said, "You're the only one who can help now. And Deni wouldn't have been able to get into the confidential information I—we need, anyway."

"What kind of confidential information?" she asked weakly. Obviously Deni's death had shaken her badly.

"Medical and insurance records. If you have access to the computer and databases, I need you to check the names of women I think might be victims of the same man who killed Bette. I need to know if they had any insured medical procedures performed on them during the last several years. Can you check through their medical insurance?"

"It would be easy if my company insured them. Possible if they had other insurance, but it would take a little longer. What specifically are you searching for?"

"I want to determine if they had hospital stays, at which hospitals, and who were the attending physicians and other medical personnel."

"That last might be difficult. I'd have only the billing records to work with."

"Will you try?" Coop pleaded. "Will you please go into the office and try?"

"No."

He held his temper. "Why not?"

"I won't need to go in. My home computer gives me access to the one at work. I can do what you want right here at my desk in my living room. Or at least I can try. I don't guarantee results. Do you want me to phone you when and if I find out anything?"

"No," he said hastily. "I'll check back with you every hour or so. I'm going to be moving around. Do you have a paper and pencil handy?" he asked, before she could question him about his whereabouts.

She told him to wait a moment, then returned to the phone.

He gave her the names and exact spellings of the victims, working from memory, even supplying her with some of the addresses. He would have added the names Dickerson had given him, but the napkin he'd copied them on at Starbuck's was in his apartment.

"I'll get back to you," he said when he was finished. "And thanks, Maureen."

"I'm doing it for Bette," she said, and hung up.

* * *

What Maureen hadn't told Coop was that the last time she'd talked with Deni, in the writer's apartment, Deni had shown her a list of several other probable victims in different parts of the country. While Deni was in the bathroom, Maureen had taken the opportunity to run off a duplicate of the list on her office copy machine. She'd planned on using the list to goad Coop into more aggressive action.

She turned away from the phone and switched on her computer, then began rummaging through her desk drawers to find the list. Along with the names Coop had supplied her, it would be interesting to match its names with online insurance claim files.

Standing behind and very near to Cara in the crowded elevator, the Night Caller studied her slightly distorted reflection in the gleaming steel sliding door. Her image was dreamlike, wavering with her slightest movement as if she were underwater. Perhaps the dream image was accurate. There were Eastern religions that considered God real and life an illusion, a dream.

She hadn't noticed his face, he was sure, when he'd crowded onto the elevator. Her back had still been turned and she was apologizing to someone, perhaps for stepping on his toe. Now, in the reflecting door, his own distorted features seemed much like hers. Only he knew the distortion was more than simply reflection. Yet only he saw the distortion. In reality his cosmetic surgery performed years ago had been as effective as possible. The scars, the nerve-damaged, droopy eyelids that made him appear always weary, the jagged discol-

ration along the edge of his jaw that pulled one corner
f his mouth sideways, lending him a sardonic, smug
xpression even in his sleep, all had been repaired. The
roblem was that such extensive surgery had left his
ace handsome to perfection, but with a masklike
vooden quality that drew stares. It was as if the per-
ectly carved head of a puppet had been fitted to a
uman being. Pinocchio, but with a perfect nose.

He'd heard about Cara's sister Ann's terror and
creaming in the recovery room while under anesthetic
or a simple knee operation to remove loose cartilage.
Though a local would have been acceptable, on his ad-
ice she'd opted for general anesthetic. First the relax-
nt and amnesiate to dispel anxiety and ensure she'd
ave no recollection of the procedure, then the De-
nerol—more than required—all administered intra-
enously. Perhaps he'd somehow underdosed the
mnesiate. The Night Caller was sure the grotesque-
iess of his face, magnified in the anesthetic haze, was
vhat had frightened Ann Callahan so in the recovery
oom.

Now he strongly suspected that Cara Callahan had
ieard about Ann's terrible vision. It would be remem-
iered because several of the nurses had been chewed
iut by that asshole Evans for not controlling Ann. The
lreamworld attempting to influence yet another dream.

The elevator descended toward hell and the lobby.
Elevator etiquette was still being observed, everyone
staring straight ahead or upward at a slight angle.
Would Cara glance in his direction as passengers got
iut?

At the fourth floor the elevator stopped and three
people got out. At three, two more departed. The re-

maining passengers spread out, seeking the natural
space around them that made fools feel safer. They
thought the elevator was getting larger when it was ac
tually getting smaller, warmer.

When the elevator stopped at two, four people piled
in, two women and two men. One of the men was im
mense, so heavy he was having difficulty breathing and
the bellows sound of his ongoing struggle filled the el
evator. Everyone already on the elevator moved to the
rear. The Night Caller edged away from Cara, toward
the opposite steel wall, so he could continue standing
slightly behind her.

The elevator plunged to the lobby, slowed, found its
level, and the doors slid open. Those last to board go
out first. The obese man laughed and slid his arm
around the shoulders of one of the women. A nurse
whose name might have been Amanda stood aside and
let an older man and woman file out, then got out herself.

That was when Cara glanced over at the Night
Caller.

Looked at him again, then quickly away.

But he knew. He knew them all and had seen the di-
vine spark in her eyes.

She knew who he was. From the street, the cathedral, the description of her sister's vision, the mating of
minds in space, she knew they'd met before.

In a brief suspension of time the Night Caller took it
all in. No passengers were waiting at lobby level to
board the elevator. A woman had just pushed through
the revolving doors, noticed the elevator, and was picking up her pace across the lobby so she might get in.

ara Callahan, studiously not looking at him, was step-
ing forward to get out.

To do what? Scream? Hurry to a security guard?
hone the police?

We know each other too well for that, the Night
aller thought, and reached for her.

CHAPTER FIFTY-SIX

Cara almost made it. Her right foot was almost o
the lobby tiles when she felt a powerful arm enci
cle her waist from behind. She tried inhaling to screar
but couldn't as she was yanked back into the elevator.

Immediately the arm was up around her throa
keeping her silent while she struggled. As she got
hand into her purse and felt around for her gun, sh
saw the man's other hand reach forward, his finge
press the CLOSE DOOR button. A woman had bee
hurrying across the lobby toward the elevators. Car
had seen her at an angle, observed her delay as the fou
people who'd gotten off the elevator crossed her path
momentarily blocking her from view. She would com
into sight soon, see what was happening.

Then the door began to slide closed.

She thought she caught just a glimpse of the hurryin
woman's dark coat as the view into the lobby was nar
rowed to a thin vertical slit, then disappeared altogether

Cara was alone with the man she was sure had mur
dered her sister. The man with the face Ann must hav
dreamed about in the recovery room. He was incredi

ly handsome—too much so to be real, as if he'd been created by art photographers and air-brushed. His improbably serene face was immobile and unreal, like a mask. The mask Ann must have seen while momentarily drifting up from under anesthetic in the operating room. The mask with the malevolent eyes, fixed on her with a gaze he didn't think she'd return.

Cara saw his free hand reach out and his forefinger firmly press the bottom elevator button lettered *S*. That caused him to shift his balance and loosen his grip slightly. She knew she still had a chance! This one chance!

Her hand was deeper inside her purse, fumbling through wadded tissue, comb, ballpoint pen, pack of chewing gum. With a horror that numbed her completely, she realized the gun Coop had given her was missing from her purse. She must have somehow forgotten it at the apartment, but she couldn't remember even having removed it.

She was jolted by a sharp stinging sensation in the side of her neck, as if she'd been bitten by an insect.

Or had the man with the marionette face leaned over and very delicately bitten her? A vampire? Was that why he appeared so artificially human? Absurd!

Then she was falling.

The elevator was descending.

Her terror remained above, drifting away from her.

The Night Caller was sure that what happened at the elevator hadn't been noticed. The woman who'd just entered the lobby didn't have the angle of vision to see them. And it had all been done quickly. Quickly and

neatly. Arm, pocket, button, needle. Animal instinct
Flash of fang, slash of claw. The impulse to surviv
lent economy of thought and motion.

He could be reasonably sure no one would be nea
the elevator in the surgery wing subbasement. Th
maintenance men, if they were in the lower level at al
stayed at the other end, well away from where the ca
davers were stored. And almost always they used th
service elevator.

As the elevator dropped, he glanced down at Cara
slumped on the floor unconscious from the powerfu
soporific he'd injected in her. He'd felt the disposabl
needle he always carried in his jacket pocket in case a
patient got violent, and with one hand removed it
plastic guard and readied it even before the elevato
reached the lobby. He hoped that in his necessary hast
he hadn't injected any air that might cause an em
bolism. But he doubted that had occurred, and it wa
seldom as serious as laymen assumed from watching
TV and reading mystery novels.

Cara's beautiful face was still, her expression un
troubled. He was glad. He bent slightly, extended hi
hand, and lifted her long red braid. After running i
gently through his fingers, he draped it softly over he
shoulder.

His fear, his panic, had been momentary. A meteoric
flash of flame across a sky where otherwise the heav
ens were in balance.

Pattern, darkness, light, and shadow, voices not hi
own.

Then fate transcended chance.

Control had been maintained.

"Julia."

CHAPTER FIFTY-SEVEN

"Nighklauer," Maureen said, when Coop called her apartment later that night. He was surprised by the vibrancy in her voice. The excitement.

"You were right," she went on. "All the names you gave me, the murder victims, had medical procedures performed at two hospitals in the city, and two in Seattle and Miami. All different procedures, some minor, some serious. Ellen Banta, Bette, and Theresa Dravic in New York. Marlee Clark in Miami, and Georgianna Mason in Seattle."

"So who's Nighklauer?" Coop asked. "The doctor who performed these procedures?"

"No, they were mostly different doctors. One at Greater Dade Hospital in Miami, one at St. Bartholomew in Seattle; the others, including Bette's diagnostic tests, were performed by two different surgeons at Mercy Hospital in Manhattan."

"Then who's Nighklauer? A nurse?"

"An anesthesiologist," Maureen said. "They often bill separately, kind of the freelancers of medicine, so it took me a while to find it. Dr. Victor Nighklauer was the attending anesthesiologist in each procedure. He practiced for years in the New York area, but he was re quested by a surgeon in Miami to perform an operatio on Marlee Clark the tennis star. Her surgeon specia ized in sports injuries and was on staff at Mercy th previous year before moving to Florida. After that, h moved to the West Coast, California and Washingto before returning eleven months ago to New York. N only that, I checked by phone with someone I know Mercy, and Nighklauer still practices there. He has handsome but masklike face from a childhood accide he never talks about. The nurses refer to him as th Night Caller, because that's what his name sounds lik when you say it fast, and because of his insistence o visiting his patients late at night after the morning o their operations, to check on them. Most anesthesiolo gists don't do that."

A masklike face. Coop had a vision of the man i the long coat, collar turned up, muffler bunched hig and tight around his throat, hat brim pulled low i front. Concealing most of his face.

Mercy Hospital.

Cara had said she was going to talk to the nurses Mercy Hospital about Ann.

"Something else, Coop. I had some names of proba ble other victims Deni gave me, going back over th last five years. They were from Florida, California, an Washington state. They all had insurance claims fo medical procedures during that period, and Dr. Nighk lauer was the attending anesthesiologist."

Coop knew these must be the names that were o the list Dickerson had found in Deni's apartment "Thanks, Maureen! Now do me another favor. Call Ar

Billard and tell him what you just told me. Then tell him Cara Callahan and Nighklauer might be at Mercy Hospital. Will you do that?"

"Cara Callahan?"

"Please, Maureen!"

"If you say."

He gave her Billard's home and department number. "Don't forget, Maureen."

"Listen, be—"

But he'd already hung up the phone and had stepped off the curb, looking desperately up and down the street for a cab, ignoring the cold wind that plucked at his collar.

Folded gurneys, collapsible wheelchairs, worn mattresses, empty oxygen bottles. The Night Caller knew no one would enter the subbasement storeroom. In a corner leaned half a dozen obsolete wheelchairs. Soon, when late visiting hours were over and the night shift arrived, and the hospital upstairs was teeming with people coming and going, he would tie Cara into the wheelchair, cover her with a blanket, and wheel her from a side door. From there it was only a short distance to where his car was parked. He was wearing street clothes and had left his coat, hat, and muffler on four in an employees' lounge closet. That was all right; he would remove his tie, turn up his shirt collar to conceal the scars on his jaw and neck, keep his head down as if concerned for the patient. Hospital employees would assume he was a volunteer wheeling someone to a waiting car or taxi. Necessary for insurance purposes.

The Night Caller smiled.

Thank God for medical insurance.

Cara lay sleeping now on her back on some crates he'd butted up against one another, limbs flung loosely to the sides. As if she were a willing offering to the gods. Like Julia.

He couldn't complete the ritual here. He hadn't attempted it with Deni Green, hadn't needed it. Had been interrupted with Theresa Dravic. Cara was perfect. He'd been almost ready for her anyway. He would take her to the privacy of his apartment and perform the ritual in his time, his own sweet time, then dispose of the body on the other side of town.

He rested a hand on Cara's still wrist, her pulse faint but steady, blood and life, and closed his eyes. His own sweet time.

Julia. When he was twelve, and Julia was ten and so perfect and beautiful. Her long red hair was worn always in a braid. She took such pleasure undoing it at night and brushing it, then rebraiding it each morning. Her ritual. When he passed her open bedroom door he would look in on her asleep, her hair no longer braided, fanned like spun red honey on her pale pillow.

And one night he couldn't walk on, had to enter her room. He lay beside her, stroking her hair, caressing her, exploring her wonders, knowing she was pretending to sleep, as they all pretended. Women pretended everything.

He returned to her the next night and the next and the next, until finally he probed too deeply and she screamed.

Her father had burst into the room, then stopped and stood still like a statue of an ancient warrior in a mu seum, wielding a baseball bat he always kept beneath his bed rather than a sword.

Then the sword fell. The Night Caller clenched his eyes shut, remembering the beating, the heavy blows, then the blade, the scars, what his father had done to him so no woman would look at him twice again.

His crime was never mentioned, something that had happened in another, darker world. But he was sent away to a strict boarding school, St. Augustine. The saint who had been a carnal sinner. He would never be alone with Julia again. He'd been filled with shame, spent nights contemplating suicide, eventually run away and supported himself on the streets by learning the art of the pickpocket and petty thief. But he'd been caught, escaped the machinery of the courts because of his youth, and had to be institutionalized.

He was held in the place of the roaches, huge ones peculiar to the region that actually hissed quite audibly. At night he would hear them, and sometimes feel them dart across his bare flesh with astounding speed. Though they were the size of a man's thumb, they were like the brief touch of quill feathers on his soft cheek.

Eventually he'd gotten used to them, learned to endure their touch. Like him, they were part of the dark.

The shame and the scars bored in. The stains spread. It was a time he kept locked away in a deep, distant part of his mind.

Four years later a nun came into his room and told him the news. His father had beaten Julia to death and then committed suicide. Hanged himself from a rafter in the garage of the family's suburban tract house.

Afterward the Night Caller had learned the details of the incestuous relationship his father and Julia had kept secret from him. The nuns and the doctors didn' know he felt relieved—he wasn't so sick and repulsive after all. His father hadn't been punishing him, bu eliminating him as a rival.

Though he still mourned and missed Julia terribly he began to feel better about himself, smarter. Eventu ally he was released from the institution and continued his education, this time at St. Alexius Academy. St Alexius, defender, helper, patron saint to nurses and pilgrims. It was after his time at St. Alexius, during medical school, that he'd had the so ineffectual cos metic surgery performed. The operations had been like a series of dreams that had only a temporary impact on the real world. The past had been cut away but had grown back.

He'd never known sweeter moments than when Julia had lain still and allowed him to touch her. He'd neve known such trust and acceptance since. Those mo ments in that long ago quiet bedroom determined his choice of career. He still was compelled at intervals to relive those moments. But only after making sure the woman would never cry out as Julia had, that she would never belong to another man or be harmed by him.

Georgianna Mason had been a precaution, Theresa Dravic an interruption, Deni Green a practical neces sity. Not again, he thought. Not this time. Not with this Julia. Destiny had touched destiny. Choice had become fate.

The Night Caller had denied himself the complete and unhurried ritual long enough. The careful, detailed recreation of his nights with Julia.

To deny himself longer would be unbearable.

CHAPTER FIFTY-EIGHT

There had been an accident on Roosevelt Drive, and traffic was backed up for blocks.

Coop sat stiffly in the back of the cab, eyeing the long line of vehicles before him, listening to the cacophony of blasting horns that accompanied every New York traffic jam. A cluster of three miniature Christmas ornaments tied together with a red bow hung from the rearview mirror. The cab smelled as if someone had recently smoked a cigar in it. Probably the driver.

"Try the side streets," he instructed the driver. "They'll be faster."

The man simply ignored him.

"The side streets!" Coop repeated. "Cut over to First Avenue!"

"This is shorter," the cabbie said, not turning his head. "Much faster."

"This is important, damn it!"

"Everything is important, my friend. Put your trust in me. I know my job." The cabbie turned up the volume on his radio, which was playing some sort of music Coop didn't recognize. Like jazz blown through crude reed instruments.

The cab braked again and was totally motionless.

Coop dug a ten-dollar bill from his wallet and stuffed it into the swivel tray in the Plexiglas panel separating the passenger compartment from the driver. He opened the door and climbed out

"C'mon back, my friend. This is fastest. Put your trust in me."

Coop couldn't. He was going to jog to First Avenue and try to catch another cab uptown.

"You forgot your change!" the cabbie yelled behind him. "Here's your change, my friend!"

Ignoring him, rushing away, Coop wondered, should he have put his trust in the man?

Cara could hardly move her arms and legs. Someone was helping her across a dim room. Her feet were dragging. One shoe came loose, was left behind. Then the other.

She tried but couldn't wake up all the way. Something was odd here, very—

She remembered. Her heart leaped in her breast.

Still she couldn't clear her head. She felt herself forced down, into a sitting position in a chair, felt cool metal against her wrists. Something was wound around her midsection, pulling her tight to the chair back. She tried to struggle but remained detached from everything that was happening. It felt as if her arms and legs were moving, but she couldn't be sure.

Then she heard a ripping sound. When unyielding strips of material were wrapped around her arms, fix-

ng them to the chair arms, she knew the ripping sound
ad been tape being torn. Duct tape? Surgical tape?
Again her heart pounded with fear.

She was aware of who was doing this to her, but he
vas shadow that came and went, bending over her, not
ouching her himself, using tape, other materials to
ind her tightly to the chair. Her feet were forced against
ach other, her detached feet, and her lower legs were
ound together. Then her thighs. She could move noth-
ng now but her toes and fingers. *Riiiiip!* Tape was
vound around her fingers. Cara tried to cry out but
here was a numbness in her throat, at the base of her
ongue. She wasn't even sure if she was shaping her
nouth to form a scream. She heard no sound.

She did feel in the back of her right hand a sharp
ain. She knew what it was this time. A needle going
n. A burning sensation as whatever was in the hypo-
lermic syringe surged into her bloodstream.

She heard a voice like hers say, "No." Off in the dis-
ance. "Please, no . . ."

Everything was fading, going away. She tried to
ight it, struggled to remain aware. Was she falling
sleep again? Dying? Was there a difference?

Soon she didn't care.

The Night Caller withdrew the needle from Cara's
vein and checked the transparent syringe, making sure.
He didn't want to inject her with too much secobarbi-
al. Not yet.

Cara was already back in her state of semiconscious-
ness, drifting in and out of sleep, not caring, faintly
aware. The Night Caller knew her twilight condition

precisely. She would be somewhat cognizant but help-less and manageable.

After dropping the syringe back in his pocket, he untaped Cara's now limp right hand and placed a cot-ton wad on the needle mark, securing it with a thin strip of adhesive. He would leave that hand exposed, marking her as a patient who'd recently received intra-venous medication. That would explain her semicon-scious state to anyone who might be curious. He felt the slackness of her neck and jaw muscles, massaged her throat for a moment. She wouldn't be able to speak, he was sure, even if she somehow thought of some-thing to say.

He took a long, last look around. It might be appar-ent that someone had been in the storage room, but there was nothing to indicate the trespasser's identity.

He had only to remove Cara from the hospital with-out detection. And he was sure he could accomplish that. She would soon be where they wouldn't be dis-turbed.

Soon now.

He did wish he could have gotten to know this one more thoroughly before the final recognition. But he knew her sister Ann. He'd administered the relaxant and amnesiate in the pre-op room and asked Ann the usual questions about her medical background, family, medications she might have taken. As she lost control he asked her more personal questions, about her pri-vate life, her password to get online, finances, love life. He would remove her house key from her purse in the wire basket that would be placed in a locker, make a wax impression of the key, then return it.

He wouldn't touch the patient after that. Not then.

When the OR nurse arrived he would accompany the patient as she was wheeled into the operating room. It was all a routine with him, with certain female patients. Always he would have recommended general anesthesia and MAC—monitored anesthetic care—so he could minister to them in the operating room, so he could make sure they wouldn't say anything revealing. After the operation he'd visit them that evening, talk with them, make sure the amnesiate had done its job. Invariably they remembered nothing of the operation. Nothing of any conversation beforehand.

Then he would enter their lives like a shadow. Become intimately acquainted with them though they'd virtually forgotten him. He would become a part of them they didn't know, like the dreams and memories they couldn't touch.

And when he knew them well enough, as if they were a sister, there would come the recognition and the final bonding.

He was thinking clearly through his anticipation. He could do that.

Because he knew, because he understood, there wasn't much he couldn't do.

He'd already removed his tie, using it along with surgical tape and strips of worn sheets to secure Cara. He turned up his collar, ducking his head so his grotesqueness wouldn't show.

This would work, he assured himself. People would only glance at his face, then look quickly away. It would be as if they hadn't looked at him at all. And why should someone entering or leaving a hospital—visitor or employee—pay particular attention to a patient being transferred to a car? Checking out. Only if the Night Caller encountered someone he knew might there be a problem. But his route would be a short one, and Mercy Hospital was immense, so there was little chance of that.

Little chance, but some. A chance he would have to take. A lie he would have to tell. A circumstance he could deal with later if questions arose, if anyone guessed that Cara Callahan had disappeared from Mercy, if anyone even connected her to him. And even if someone—the Distraught Dad?—did make a connection, he could only suspect. All any of them could do was suspect. Shadows left no trace, not even a scent. They were here, they were gone, had they been here?

Confidently, he pushed the wheelchair toward the door.

CHAPTER FIFTY-NINE

To the police and FBI, Coop was still a wanted man. He knew that. Maureen's phone call to Billard might raise serious questions, and he prayed it would bring help in time at Mercy Hospital. But it wouldn't mean Coop was in the clear, or that Cara was out of danger.

When he reached busy First Avenue, he kept his head down and walked close to buildings, watching for a cab with its service light glowing. He thought about Nighklauer. Coop had gained plenty of experience in medical and hospital procedure during the past few years, even if it had been only from the patient's point of view. He understood how an anesthesiologist could take advantage of his profession to learn more than he should about his patients. They usually saw you in your room or a cubicle where there was privacy. There they asked you a lot of precautionary questions, smooth-talking you to make you more at ease while they inserted the IV needle. Soon something to relax you was flowing through your veins, loosening your tongue along with the rest of you. Then something to make you forget; doctors didn't want patients recalling painful or gory details of any medical procedure, or any embarrassing conversation by patient or medical personnel.

Coop remembered two nurses talking about whether operations were painful. If the patient didn't recall the pain, one argued, then in effect there had been no pain. Coop didn't see it that way. He'd seen too many crime or accident victims block memory of horror from their minds completely, and without the use of anesthetic. They had experienced plenty of pain.

As he strode he became incensed again that a doctor would take advantage of his patients, learn intimate details about them while they were sinking into unconsciousness, medicated so they wouldn't remember. He could imagine Nighklauer wheedling everything he needed to know from them, bank account numbers, names of lovers, computer passwords. He must have stolen their keys and somehow had duplicates made and returned them before they recovered from the anesthetic he'd administered. That was why he visited them later that night in recovery, not because he was compassionate and diligent, but so he could be sure they wouldn't know, that they didn't remember what he'd asked, what he'd done.

Another terrible thought entered Coop's mind. Had Nighklauer taken physical liberties with his future victims when they were unknowing and helpless? An initial indignity before stalking and killing them because something about them triggered his murderous impulse. Seeing Bette in his mind, recalling her from childhood on, made him grit his teeth with rage.

Very near him, water splashed and brakes squealed.

Startled, he jumped aside as a car with a light on its roof, lettering on its side, pulled to the curb alongside him, its front tire in a deep puddle of melted snow.

Police car?

No. A taxi! And without a fare!

Coop's heart slowed and relief washed over him.

The driver was leaning down to see out the side window, staring at him expectantly. He was wearing a turban and smiling broadly. Coop was still standing motionless, getting over his surprise and instinct to bolt, as the cabbie used a forefinger to draw a question mark in the air, then pointed to the backseat.

Coop nodded and quickly climbed into the cab.

"Mercy Hospital! It's—"

"I know exactly where it is, sir," the cabbie said in flawless English.

As the cab accelerated, Coop buckled his seat belt.

The first two blocks were fast.

Then they were in slowed traffic again.

The cabbie on Roosevelt Drive had been right. Coop stared out the mud-stained window in frustration, listening to the same discordant symphony of blaring horns, waiting for traffic to break loose and the cab to surge ahead.

Right now, he could be crawling faster to the next intersection.

CHAPTER SIXTY

Billard had met FBI Agent Fred Willingham before. He'd never liked or trusted the man. But he had to admit that now his distrust was heightened because of his fondness for and faith in his friend. Billard knew Coop was innocent of murder. He also knew that what Willingham was doing was proper and prudent. Still, he couldn't make himself like it.

The FBI had arrived at Mercy Hospital moments after the NYPD and had virtually taken over the operation. Billard, standing in the lobby near the gift shop and elevators, had to admire how quickly and smoothly things were going. It was enough to give a city department cop an inferiority complex, like a bush leaguer suddenly finding himself part of Major League baseball.

No one at Mercy other than administrators knew what was happening. Not only would that be safer for patients, Willingham said—that was how he'd sold the idea to the chief of surgery—but it was imperative that the suspect not notice anything unusual. Unobtrusively agents assumed the roles of attendants and nurses. A few of them were even roaming the halls in pale green OR scrubs, complete with plastic booties over their shoes and stethoscopes draped around their necks.

Willingham had instructed Billard where to station NYPD personnel. The FBI SWAT team was present. Billard thought that was, to put it succinctly, overkill. Yet what choice did Willingham have? What they were dealing with here, the Bureau had finally decided, was the most desperate and dangerous kind of serial killer. So trained marksmen walked the hospital halls, and snipers were stationed on the roof over the main entrances.

Billard glanced at his wristwatch. The orders had been issued to everyone involved in the operation only a few minutes ago, but he imagined that by now most of them were in place and on the alert.

Late visiting hours were over, and the elevators were mostly full when they opened onto the lobby. There was also some kind of shift change going on, uniformed nurses and other medical types leaving and arriving. A man in his thirties, wearing work clothes and carrying a teddy bear, emerged from an elevator trailed by a woman and two small kids. Billard saw that there was a third child, an infant in a kind of sling arrangement backpack, peeking over the woman's shoulder. *Get your family out of here,* he shouted silently to the man as they leisurely strolled past on their way to the exit.

Billard caught sight of Willingham striding across the lobby toward him. Nice-looking guy in a neat suit and tie, might have been one of the doctors. He seemed calm, expectant, and exhilarated as a game show host. On the hunt. For Coop. Billard felt himself getting irritated again.

"Everything okay?" Willingham asked.

"As instructed," Billard said.

Willingham must have noticed the coldness in his voice. "Remember, I'm also a friend of Cooper's. But we've got no choice here. This has got to be done."

Billard nodded, not liking being wrong. Not appreciating the lecture.

"Undercover cops on floors five and seven?" Willingham asked.

Billard said his men were in place. FBI agents were patrolling six, the surgery and recovery floor. "What about Nighklauer?" he asked.

"He's not due in tonight, but the nurses say he often shows up to check on patients. We'll detain him when he comes in."

"And if he doesn't show?"

"We'll deal with Dr. Nighklauer after we deal with Cooper, if *he* shows."

"Do you think it's a good idea to wait?"

"You know Cooper's wife, Lieutenant Billard. She says the same anesthesiologist was present during medical procedures involving a variety of victims. That's not actually the kind of evidence to march on."

What Willingham was actually saying, Billard knew, was that Coop was still a stronger suspect than Nighklauer. Billard almost asked Willingham about the plastic saints; then he remembered that the NYPD hadn't shared that information with the Bureau. *And why should we have shared?* Billard asked himself. The

'BI only deigned to join the case hours ago. "What
'bout the footprints, identical sole patterns?"

"We inquired," Willingham said. "Dr. Nighklauer's
ιot the only one who does that cutting business to his
'hoes."

"And Cara Callahan?"

"Whatever her involvement is," Willingham said,
'she's apparently left the hospital."

Billard was getting the idea and not buying into it.
'You think Nighklauer is something Coop tossed out to
nislead us, don't you?"

"I'm not sure, but it's possible. If Dr. Nighklauer
ιrns up here, fine. If after we talk to Cooper he gives
ιs more to work on, then we'll move hard on the doc-
or."

"You have to know you've got something solid be-
ore you tangle with a solid citizen like Nighklauer,
ight, Agent Willingham?"

Willingham arched an eyebrow. "Exactly right,
⌐ieutenant. Is the parking garage below this wing cov-
⌐red?"

"There's a security guard there."

"Better send one of your men down there, too."

"If Coop is guilty, he's not likely to drive right up
ιnd park in the hospital garage. Besides, the men we
ιave watching his apartment say his car's still parked
lown the street from where he lives. And we're short
⌐n personnel—it's a big hospital."

"I know how big," Willingham said, "to the square
foot. Send a man down, Lieutenant." He walked away
⌐efore Billard could reply.

Billard watched Willingham disappear around a cor-

ner, then reached for the two-way clipped to his belt s
he could pull a man off the cafeteria watch and assign
him to the garage.

What a shit night this was turning into, he thought
Whatever the deal was with Coop or that nutcake ex o
his, he hoped Coop wouldn't show up any time soon a
Mercy Hospital.

Cara was rushing smoothly through translucent water
First she had sped through patterns of blackness and
light. Then she was sure she'd been in an elevator. Al
most sure. Difficult to know, when you're weightless.

How long ago had it been? Forms of people walk
ing, towering rectangles of shadowed doorways, glided
past on either side. People talking, sometimes laugh
ing. She tried to say something, anything, to them, bu
her tongue wouldn't budge in her mouth; then they
were past, in the past.

A long hall, cooler than before, then a door and even
colder air. The drop in temperature made her more
alert, but only for a moment. Pressure on her limbs was
released. She could move her arms and legs now
Someone was working over her, bending, straighten
ing. She could hear him breathing. Smelled oil or gaso
line. A car? Motion before her. Car door opening?

She was rising, her head tilted back. Above her was
darkened concrete, very near, dots of wavering light.

Then she was sitting down again, became stuck to
wherever it was she was sitting. In the car! Yes! Safety
belt. Good.

Hands folded in her lap. Like a good girl. Touch
One wrist on top of the other. Something holding them

together. Softness, a blanket settling over her from the neck down. For some reason she couldn't make out its color. It felt very warm. She almost smiled.

Then she remembered. This was wrong. She shouldn't be here.

But she couldn't recall why not. Was there a problem? She closed her eyes and tried to think about the past, but there was only the delicate present, so soon gone.

She heard a car door slam shut, very near. Then another.

The Night Caller hadn't passed anyone who might have recognized him as he'd wheeled Cara from the service elevator, then on the brief journey through the parking level halls to the garage.

His black Mercedes was parked nearby. Not the only black Mercedes in the garage. Many of the staff doctors drove them and had reserved spaces.

There was Eddie the security guard way at the other end of the garage. Old black guy, pensioned-off cop, friendly and with glasses with lenses so thick they made him look fish-eyed. Even with perfect eyesight, Eddie wouldn't be able to recognize him from such a distance, and not being on permanent staff, the Night Caller didn't have a reserved parking space.

He gave Cara a final check to make sure she was sitting up straight enough. Her eyes were open now staring about vaguely, but that was okay. Plenty of patients were driven home while still in an anesthetic daze.

Eddie had glanced toward him, but now the old man was ambling back toward his heated kiosk.

Excellent. The Night Caller could leave by the far exit, away from the kiosk, using his courtesy card so the wooden gate would rise and let him pass.

He twisted the ignition key and the big car's motor growled to life. Its power and smoothness lent the Night Caller confidence. He was the one doing the thinking here, the one who was real and moving in a dream of a dream.

This was going to work. Everything was going to be wonderful. Soon, soon he would have his world back.

Soon.

CHAPTER SIXTY-ONE

Traffic bogged down the cab only blocks from Mercy Hospital, so Coop again paid his fare and got out to walk. He thought God must have put New York traffic on earth as some kind of test.

When he was half a block away from the looming hospital, he began thinking about the best way to enter. It was possible that Maureen hadn't gotten her message across accurately to Billard. But even if she had, Coop knew he was still a wanted man. They might be waiting for him at the hospital, and he didn't want to be taken into custody and spend the next several days trying to extricate himself from the system.

If they were waiting for him here, surely they'd also be staked out near his apartment. They'd know his car was still parked nearby. Maybe he should enter Mercy through the garage, where he might be least expected.

The traffic light changed to red, and he stopped at the intersection and waited for the walk signal. He didn't want to barge out in front of traffic, didn't want to do anything that might draw attention.

That was when he saw the black Mercedes sedan

emerge from the hospital garage. It accelerated to make the green light, then glided past him only to be stopped by traffic down the block.

Coop stood stunned, trying to grasp what he'd just seen. Had he wanted so badly to see it that he'd formed the image in his mind?

He didn't think so. He was sure he'd glimpsed Cara in the passenger seat of the Mercedes. Her eyes were half closed and there was a dazed expression on her face, pale as bone against the black leather upholstery.

He whirled to run after the car, then saw that traffic was moving again. Brake lights dimmed and the Mercedes moved with the traffic.

Coop hurried across the street with the WALK signal and strode into the parking garage where the Mercedes had emerged.

A tall, slender black man in a security guard uniform stepped out of a lighted kiosk and ambled toward him. There was a gun on his hip, not one of the 9mms but an old service revolver like the one Coop had given Cara after hers was stolen.

The guard smiled, squinting at Coop through thick-lensed glasses. "Help you?"

"Do you know who was in the car that just left here? Big black Mercedes?"

"Couldn't rightly say. One of the doctors, most likely. Seems they all drive that kinda car."

Coop could feel time rushing around him, past him. He had to do something fast, had to act.

"You got a car like that?" he asked.

The guard grinned wider. "Sheeeit, no! I drive that old Dodge over there."

"Blue one?"

"Don't see no other."

"Listen," Coop said, smiling and stepping closer. He punched the old man hard in the stomach, feeling a metal belt buckle sting the knuckle of his little finger.

The guard folded up, air rushing out of him in a fog in the unheated garage.

Coop had the gun out of the man's holster even before he was on the ground. Then he was rummaging in the guard's pockets for his keys. Found them!

The guard had lost his glasses and was staring up at him, unable to breathe and terrified, thinking he was going to be shot.

But Coop was already sprinting toward the parked Dodge. The old car started at once. Coop tromped the accelerator and steered toward an exit. The wooden drop barricade splintered and gave easily, and the car was out in the street.

Coop spun the steering wheel and made a hard right, accelerating to catch up with traffic. A tiny cutout pine tree deodorizer swung like a pendulum below the rearview mirror. Something was rattling like crazy, and there was a lot of play in the car's front end. He tried the headlights. At least one of them still worked after the crash through the gate.

In the mirror he glimpsed someone running toward him, then giving up and standing bent over with hands on knees. He didn't have time to wonder who it was.

The theater crowd was still wending its way to hotel or home, or to late night dinner or drink. Traffic on West 54th Street was jammed almost solid. Cara remained upright but slumped in the passenger seat of

the Mercedes, her eyelids occasionally fluttering. Sof
sighing sounds occasionally wafted from her lips. Alon
the canyon of the avenue, horns blared and frustrate
drivers lowered their windows and shouted futilel
Pedestrians bustled ahead on the sidewalk, only to b
caught up with when a light changed or an obstacle o
some sort was removed, and traffic lurched forwar
half a block or so before getting bogged down again
The narrow cross streets of New York.

The Night Caller didn't mind. Everything was agai
under control, and there was the anticipation living an
coiled in the core of him. He had let the hospital blar
ket slip down to Cara's waist and could feel heat ema
nating from her. Her scent lay on his tongue like necta

He wasn't concerned with the delay. Seated so nea
to Cara, listening to her breathing, his body and hi
senses were one with hers. He could feel the interna
movement of her heart and lungs, know the rush an
calm of her respiratory system and the tense and re
lease with the silent hammering of her pulse. It was a
if her blood were running in his veins; that ability, tha
total empathy, was the rare quality that made him on
of the best at his profession. Cara wouldn't regain ful
consciousness a minute before he intended.

Though it was irritating, the traffic delay was actu
ally a gift of good fortune; enough time had to pass fo
Cara to be marginally aware and remain upright an
walk with his support. He knew he couldn't park in hi
usual spot in his apartment building's undergroun
garage. Security cameras covered the garage from ever
angle. It would be better for him to park on the stree
then walk a semiconscious Cara into the lobby, wher

ere was only one security camera mounted just inside
e door to record people as they entered or left. That
amera he could disable long enough so it wouldn't
:cord his and Cara's passage—at least not in any way
lat would make them recognizable. Although there
·as a security code used by residents to enter, there
·as no doorman, and there was seldom anyone in the
)bby this late at night. If anyone did happen to see
iem, it would appear that Cara had drunk too much
nd needed his support. A couple of lovers. It wasn't
ie kind of building where people knew their fellow
:nants, or cared much about them.

A small gray car tried to edge its right front fender
1 front of the Mercedes, gaining a few feet of valuable
avement. The Night Caller played the steering wheel
) the right, tapped the accelerator, and the intruding
ar was left behind. Its driver angrily leaned on the
orn. The well-insulated Mercedes muffled the sound.
he furious driver in the gray car couldn't touch the
Jight Caller in the world that was real. None of them
ould touch him. Beside him, Cara seemed to smile
long with him.

Faintly, but he was sure she'd smiled.

Coop was sure the Mercedes containing Cara was in
he block ahead. He considered leaving the security
,uard's old Dodge and sprinting the half block or so to-
vard the Mercedes, but he knew it wasn't a good idea.
`raffic might decide to move, and the gleaming black
ar would move with it, out of Coop's reach forever.

Good decision. The snow-crusted Buick a few feet

ahead of Coop suddenly lurched and picked up spee
Half a block this time before traffic began to cra
again, almost coming to another complete stop.

But steady movement continued, even picking up
about five miles per hour. Coop was passing pedest
ans he'd seen stride past him several minutes before.

Continuing this slow progress, stopping complete
only now and then, they drove past Fifth, Madiso
Park, Lexington . . . Coop kept a careful eye on cro
streets ahead to make sure he'd know if the Merced
turned a corner. He figured the old Dodge must have
exhaust leak. Fumes were finding their way into the i
terior. The little cardboard pine tree deodorizer da
gling from the rearview mirror had no effect. He crank
down his window a few inches.

By now the fact that he'd taken the security guard
car would be widely known. Its description and licen
plate number would have been transmitted to NYP
patrol cars. Coop wasn't too worried about that. It wa
a nondescript car, and locked as it was in heavy traff
on a one-way street, there wasn't much likelihood th
a police car would appear behind it. The situation wa
tense and precarious, but so far nothing he couldn
handle. As long as he knew where the Mercedes wa
and had the wheels to follow, Cara was alive and so we
her chances.

Despite the window he'd cracked to let exhau
fumes escape, the old Dodge's heater worked so we
that Coop unbuttoned his coat. He touched his fore
head and discovered he was perspiring heavily.

The car ahead moved forward again. Coop nudge
down on the accelerator and the Dodge gained a fe

yards, then shuddered. Its engine began to clunk and sputter.

Alarmed, Coop tightened his grip on the steering wheel and his eyes scanned the dashboard.

The fuel gauge needle rested on empty.

There were still several yards between the Dodge and the car ahead. With what remaining gas there was, probably only fumes, Coop managed to maneuver the old car to the curb and park it illegally in a loading zone. There was no need to kill the engine. He switched off the lights and turned the ignition key only out of habit.

He climbed out into the cold. He had no choice now. Unless he could somehow find a cab, which seemed impossible, Coop had to try to keep up with the Mercedes on foot.

He rebuttoned his coat and turned up his collar as he walked. Here and there he had to be careful crossing patches of ice or snow, sidestepping slushy puddles too impregnated with rock salt to melt. Once he did step in a deep puddle and felt icy water penetrate his shoe and sock.

But following the Mercedes this way was possible. Traffic moved ahead intermittently, sometimes as much as a block, and he had to pick up his pace. But invariably the long line of cars resumed a crawl or stayed motionless long enough for him to catch up.

He was within half a block of the black Mercedes when he saw it turn right on Second Avenue, where traffic was moving swiftly.

I'm going to lose it! Lose everything!

He clenched his teeth and ran, almost slipping on a patch of ice. Elbowing aside a woman walking a dog, he momentarily became entangled in the leash. "Easy! Take it easy, for Gawd's sake!" she implored, helping him to free his left leg. Then he was running again toward the intersection, weaving among knots of pedestrians. His heart was booming in his chest, his ears ached from the cold, and the back of his throat was raw from breathing icy air. This had to be bad for him, but he wouldn't slow down. He wouldn't give! He couldn't!

When he reached the intersection he stopped, slipping and almost falling again. Leaning against a building and huffing fogged cold air, he peered down Second Avenue.

Traffic was stopped at the next intersection for a red traffic signal. Neat rows of cars spanned the wide street as if it were a race track and they were waiting for the starter's green flag.

But the Mercedes wasn't among them. It had made the light and was lost to Coop, along with Cara.

CHAPTER SIXTY-TWO

The Night Caller had to circle the block several times before finding a parking space several buildings down from his own. After maneuvering into the tight space, he sat with the engine idling and waited until it was unlikely he and Cara would walk past anyone between the car and the building entrance.

Two teenage boys in quilted jackets, bulky gloves, and Yankees watch caps loped past, talking animatedly and loudly and not seeming to notice they were sometimes traversing ice and snow. ". . . Said I was gonna twist off her fuckin' ears!" one of them proclaimed loudly enough to be heard plainly inside the Mercedes. When they were past, the Night Caller switched off the engine, got out of the car, and walked around to open Cara's door.

He was about to reach inside the car to unfasten Cara's wrists and seat belt beneath the blanket, when a woman with a wire grocery cart emerged from the closest building. The Night Caller leaned into the car, hiding his face and listening to a squeaky wheel, until the woman had pushed the cart well down the street.

Then he quickly unwound the tape from Cara wrist, hit the button on her seat belt, and dragged h out of the car. ". . . Too much to drink," he said in conversational tone, in case anyone might by chan overhear.

Cara helped him, standing unsteadily and stari about in bewilderment.

"I'll take care of you," the Night Caller said gent He wrapped his arm around her back and held her u right, then moved ahead so she had to walk. The Nig Caller's eyes moved from side to side as they ma slow progress toward the entrance to his building.

"Where . . ." Cara murmured in confusion.

"Daiquiris," the Night Caller said, forcing a smile.

She slipped on ice near the door and almost too him down with her. He grunted, and with difficulty haul her back to an upright position.

With one hand he held her up against him. With th other he punched the tenants' code number out on keypad, then scooped a handful of gray slush from th concrete ledge beneath an iron railing. He deposite the icy nugget in a side pocket of his sport jacket, fee ing it immediately begin to melt coldly against his hi A buzzer sounded and he pushed through into a sma vestibule, dragging Cara along with him. Then he fish his keys out of his pocket and used one to open th doors to the main lobby. Before entering all the way, l got the partially melted glob of slush from his jack pocket and held it as he might a snowball. Staying we back so his features wouldn't be recorded, he reache up where he knew the security camcorder was mounte just above the doorway and stuck the icy gray mass ov its lens.

"Warm in here," Cara remarked, as they entered the rpeted lobby and staggered to the elevator.

"Feels good," the Night Caller said, thinking that his ck was holding, no one had seen them. And even if e slush over the camcorder lens melted fast and slipped f, the video would be hopelessly blurred from rivu-s of water. No one could be positively identified, es-cially viewed from behind.

He pressed the UP button and held his breath as the evator descended, hoping there would be no one on The digital indicator above the paneled door flick-ed from number to number, suggesting the car wasn't pping on the way down, no one else was boarding.

The elevator arrived, the oak-paneled door slid open, d no one was inside. Wonderful! The Night Caller ickly maneuvered Cara inside and pressed 7, the top tton. Except for the unlikely possibility that some-e would board on the way up to go to a higher floor, ey should be able to reach the top floor without being en. The Night Caller had the entire floor for his loft artment, so no one would see them in the hall.

They made it all the way to seven without anyone se boarding the elevator. Perfect! Fate and luck and stiny and death, all were watching over him like an-ent Greek household gods. Those who dared, won.

His door key was in his right hand, Cara clasped ghtly to him with his left arm, even before the eleva-r door glided open.

No one would see them now. There were only a few ort steps across the private entry hall, a few seconds hile he worked the key and got the door open, a few ore seconds for him to drag Cara inside and close d lock the door behind them.

She was his!

He led her deeper into his apartment and settled h
on the sofa. During the afternoon the sun had melt
most of the snow from the skylight, and soft illumir
tion from the surrounding city found its way into t
spacious loft.

The Night Caller checked Cara's pulse, then be
lower and examined her pupils in the dimness. Then
removed his sport coat and laid it neatly folded ove
chair back.

With a glance at Cara, he made sure all the blin
were closed. He walked into the kitchen and switch
on only the appliance light over the stove. He want
additional illumination in the loft, but not more th
there was outside. It was unlikely that anyone in a di
tant, taller building might be peering with binocula
or a telescope into the loft through the skylight, b
why tempt luck that had so far been kind? He kne
that as long as it was slightly brighter outside the som
what translucent skylight than inside the apartment, r
one with a long lens could see in.

He gathered a pair of scissors and a roll of duct ta
from one of the drawers beneath the counter, a sha
knife from another. Leaving the appliance light glov
ing, he carried these items to one of the closets at t
far end of the loft. From the closet he pulled out
folded gurney of the sort paramedics used, quickly a
adroitly unfolded it, then rolled it to a smaller clos
that held linens. It took him less than a minute to cov
the gurney with a clean white sheet.

He placed the items from the kitchen on the she
and rolled the gurney across the loft and situated it se

al feet off to one side, where the light filtering from
ɔove was brightest.

Then he went to a console near the locked door and
ɔt out a cobbled black leather bag of the sort some-
mes carried by doctors. From a cardboard box on a
ielf, he drew out a plastic figurine.

After placing the bag and figurine at the foot of the
urney, he went to get Cara.

Coop kept walking, knowing it was hopeless. Finally
e had to sit down to catch his breath. He let himself
ump on the concrete steps of a brownstone apartment
uilding, not caring that no one had shoveled them and
e was seated in snow. For a few minutes he listened to
imself breathe, watching the heat of his life fog and
rift away before his eyes. What would it be like to die?
or Cara? For him? Would the soul depart the body
ke the light gray spirit of his breath dancing away on
ιe breeze? Would the demon that possessed Nigh-
lauer reluctantly leave his body when he died?

Coop had run, then walked around the neighbor-
ood desperately, looking up and down blocks as he
rossed intersections, hoping he could spot the dark
Iercedes still in traffic or parked at the curb.

Now he was exhausted.

He was finished in strength and almost in spirit.

He felt drained of hope and health.

He clutched the iron rail to pull himself to his feet,
nd saw the black Mercedes.

It was only after he'd reached it that he knew there
/as still no hope. It was certainly the same car; like

any ex-cop he'd memorized the license plate numbe
But every parking space was taken on the block. It wa
unlikely the car was parked directly in front of th
building Nighklauer had entered.

Nighklauer and Cara might be in any building o
the block. Or even one of the adjoining blocks.

Every building would have to be checked, and Coc
knew there wouldn't be time, even if he somehow ge
in touch with Billard or Willingham and convince
them to come here and help. Convinced them to be
lieve him. Coop knew what was happening, where th
long struggle would lead. He could feel it. He was a
expert on diminishing time.

He stood by the funereal black Mercedes and gaze
about hopelessly, looking at too many brightly lighte
windows, too many darkened windows.

Behind any one of them might be Cara and Nigl
klauer. And Nighklauer's demon.

CHAPTER SIXTY-THREE

Gently, very gently, the Night Caller laid Cara on her back on the sheeted gurney, then shifted the gurney's position slightly so the light fell brighter on her.

For a moment he merely stood and admired her. She was so beautiful, her head resting on the white linen, her breasts straining against the material of her blouse. Her shoes had come off, and her manicured toes were enameled the same bright red as her fingernails. The nail on the ring finger of her left hand was broken raggedly. He felt bad about that and wondered how it had happened. He'd taken such care with her.

He began carefully exploring her beneath her clothes, sliding his palms sensually, probing and manipulating with his fingers the points of her breasts beneath her bra, so like her sister's, the mound of pubic hair, so surprisingly soft. She drew a deep breath, stirred. Her eyes opened and she looked up at him listlessly, wondering what was happening, aware and unaware, like everyone else, only more so.

He couldn't wait. His heart was racing, singing in

his chest. He withdrew his hands, noticing that the
were trembling. He rested them firmly on her breas
and they were still. "Julia?" She tried to focus her eye
on him and failed.

He decided to delay the final injection of secobarb
tal. She had smiled slightly in her confusion, he wa
sure. It would be better, for him and for her, if he le
her in twilight for now so she would be remotely awar
of what was happening. He did tape her wrists to th
gurney's steel frame, in case she somehow regaine
sufficient strength to change position.

After bending down and kissing her cool forehea
he began using the surgical scissors to cut away he
clothing. She didn't struggle or object, only stared ur
comprehendingly at him. The softened light illum
nated her face like an angel's. *Julia.*

It was time now for the hair; then she would receiv
the injection that would deepen her sleep to eternit
Lovingly, he moved her head to the side and bega
adroitly undoing her long red braid. It only amuse
him to find the braid wasn't her own but was wove
skillfully into her real hair. The effect would be th
same.

She moaned and tried to move, the dawn of fear an
knowing in her eyes. But she hadn't the strength or wi
to resist. He knew that even if her wrists weren't boun
to the gurney, she would barely have been able to mov
her arms.

The long red braid was almost undone now, and h
would soon fan the long hair carefully, like a hal
around her head, as Julia's hair had been when sh
slept. And Cara would sleep.

Soon nothing, no other man, would ever have c

harm her. He would let her regain almost full awareness before the final injection, so that she understood
when their gazes locked that nothing before mattered
and there was nothing more, she would be his forever.
The arc of perfect possession would make them one.
The final, massive dose of secobarbital would envelope
her soul as it shut down her body. She would sleep with
Julia.

As he began to arrange her fanned-out hair, she
stared numbly up at him, beyond him, and the translucent light that so transformed her beautiful still features darkened. Something changed in her eyes—there
was a comprehension in them that shouldn't have been
there.

The Night Caller paused and felt his own icy comprehension. Still bent over Cara, he swiveled his head
to look up at the skylight.

He sucked in his breath in disbelief.

The Distraught Dad! Cooper! On the roof and standing with his legs spread wide, like a dark colossus,
staring down at him through the skylight. Something—
a gun! In his right hand! Aiming a gun!

The Night Caller flung himself to the side at the roar
of thunder. The hand of the colossus slapped him to the
floor and fire erupted low in his back, on the right side.

The powerful hand tried to keep him pinned to the
floor, but he struggled to a kneeling position, then to
his feet, swallowing his pain.

With terror but no plan, with only instinct for direction, he ran.

*   *   *

Coop had mentally flipped a coin to decide which direction away from the parked Mercedes he'd try first.

He'd trudged slowly along the sidewalk, hoping to be able to enter buildings or peer into lobbies at tenant directories, scanning for the name Nighklauer. Dr. Nighklauer.

But New York buildings weren't set up that way. And all but one of the lobbies were locked and had card slots or coded keypads for tenants to enter, intercoms to identify visitors.

He was about to give up when he noticed the footprints in the snow near the entrance to the second building down from the parked Mercedes. Coop got down with one knee on wet pavement to make sure.

The crisscross pattern of the soles that had left the footprints was unmistakable. Beside one of them was what might have been a blurred print made by a bare foot. Or a nylon-clad foot that had lost a shoe.

He tried the lobby door and wasn't surprised to find it locked. There was a keypad, but he knew how long it would take to press buttons until he chanced upon the right code. What he did see was the bank of mailboxes and intercom buttons in the foyer between the street and lobby doors. There were names above the mail slots but he couldn't make them out. He *could* make out the *Dr.* above the mail slot of the top box, and the apartment number engraved in the dull brass.

Backing away on the sidewalk, he saw a narrow walkway between the building and the one next to it. There was no fire escape in front, so there should be one on the side or rear.

It had taken him only minutes to find the steel gravity ladder, leap, and pull it down, then ascend to the roof.

At the elevator the Night Caller paused. Cooper would expect him to race to the lobby, try to get out of the building. And maybe he wasn't—

The sound of a distant siren penetrated his thoughts. Then another. Coming for him? Of course he had to assume that! If Cooper was alone now, he soon would be joined by others, wolves joining the pack.

And wouldn't Cooper also hear the sirens? Wouldn't he be concerned with Cara. wonder if she were dead or dying? Wouldn't he enter the loft apartment as quictly as possible? No dropping through a shattered skylight like a movie superhero. The middle-aged Distraught Dad must have climbed the fire escape to reach the roof—now he would go back down it to one of the windows and find the blinds drawn so he couldn't see in. But he'd know Cara was alone. He would shatter the window, raise it, and enter.

The Night Caller pressed the elevator button. It was still at his level and the door immediately slid open. He threw himself inside and hit the button for the floor below.

He'd anticipated not this but something like it. Taken the precautions of wisdom. On the roof was a heavy two-by-ten construction board, twelve feet long, that he'd placed there over a year ago. It could be laid across the narrow walkway between the buildings, allowing access to the adjacent roof. By the time the elevator reached the ground floor, the building might be surrounded, but his enemies would wait in vain.

As the elevator sank, he probed the gunshot wound in his side with trembling fingers. The bullet seemed to be lodged in his right external oblique muscle. Though there was bleeding, it probably had missed any vital organs.

The elevator stopped, and he withdrew his hand and wiped bloody fingers on his pants leg.

Here was the delicate time. Alternate worlds. If Cooper had climbed the fire escape to reach the roof, he was indeed probably using it to descend to a window and gain entrance into the loft apartment.

If he'd somehow gotten into the building at ground level and used the service stairs to reach the roof, he'd have to use the stairs to descend to the floor below the loft, to where he could use the elevator to get back up to loft level. When the elevator door opened, he might be standing waiting to board. But the service stairs door only opened from the inside; probably Cooper hadn't used them. Or if he had, he might not have blocked the door to the roof so it wouldn't close and latch, trapping him up there unless he resorted to the fire escape.

The Night Caller held to the most likely, fire escape scenario. But he tensed his body, prepared to knock the surprised Cooper aside and rush past him if he was waiting for the elevator. The pain in his side flared, trying to bend him, trying to break him.

The elevator door hissed and slid open.

The hall was empty.

It took the Night Caller less than a minute to open the service stairs door and scamper up onto the roof.

e was sure he wouldn't encounter Cooper now. By
is time the Distraught Dad would be in the loft apart-
ent with Cara, or waiting for the elevator so he could
ursue his quarry down to the lobby and street.

But like the tiger, wounded but wily, his quarry had
oubled back and was now where least expected. The
ight Caller was sure now that his luck, his survivor's
tuition, would pull him through. He became even
ore confident when he stood surveying the roof and
as sure he was alone. On top of things again.

He realized he was smiling. He was actually smil-
g! He, not Cooper, was the movie action hero. It was
mple the rest of the way. He would escape again! It
as within his reach, his grasp, his destiny! Was he ac-
ally enjoying this?

Yes! he thought, yes, he was!

Until he saw that the board was missing from where
had lain for more than a year, wedged against the low
ick wall of the parapet.

The Night Caller leaned forward cautiously and
oked down.

And there was the board lying on the pavement
low. Thick as it was, it had broken.

Anything that fell from such a height would break.

Cooper had tossed out into space the long board
e'd found. It would be the only way off the roof other
an the fire escape, since the door to the service stairs
cked from the inside. He wanted to block means of
cape behind him the way a seaman might secure the
atertight bulkheads of a ship that could sink.

After descending the fire escape to one of the loft apartment windows, he used his elbow to shatter the glass, then began picking shards of it from the frame.

He worked the latch and raised the heavy wooden frame. With gun drawn, he pulled the closed drapes aside. He was sure Nighklauer had fled. He might even be wounded. But Coop also knew he wasn't dealing with anyone predictable.

He climbed through the window and found himself in a spacious, dimly lighted apartment.

And there was Cara, still as a white marble sculpture, lying on the small bed or gurney he'd seen through the skylight. The sight of her made him pause, grabbed his breath. The pale, smooth expanses of her flesh frightened him. Was she breathing? He still wasn't sure there was no one else in the apartment, but he rushed to her anyway.

She was alive, dazed. A gleaming knife and scissors lay on the sheet next to her. On the floor was a doctor's black leather bag, a hypodermic kit lying on top of it near the handle. Next to the bag lay the plastic figure of St. Augustine. Cara gazed up at Coop, seemed to know him, tried to say something but couldn't. He scanned her flawless pale body with his eyes. She seemed to be uninjured. On the outside. How could he know what kind of drug or how much of it was in her?

He hurriedly went to a phone and called 911, then barked his message to the operator loudly and clearly. Only once because that was all the time he had.

With a backward glance at Cara, leaving the phone off the hook, he dashed to what he thought must have been the door to the hall.

CHAPTER SIXTY-FOUR

When Coop flung open the door, he found that it led not to a hall, but a small foyer with a marble floor and bench next to an elevator.

He immediately saw something else—blood on the veined white marble. He pressed the elevator button and had to wait only a few seconds. It must have been on the floor below.

Hoping he'd shot Nighklauer and would find him dead in the elevator, Coop waited for the door to open, his gun aimed, finger tense on the trigger. God help anyone other than Nighklauer who happened to be in the elevator.

But when the door glided open, the elevator was empty.

There were a few spots of blood on its carpeted floor.

Coop got in and pushed the button for the lobby. The sirens he'd heard earlier were louder now—Billard, Willingham, the blues closing in. Nighklauer, wounded, might not get very far unless he got out of the building and away in a hurry.

But two floors down, Coop realized something was wrong here. Why so much blood on the white marble, and only three—no, four—drops on the elevator floor?

Then he remembered the elevator rising from just below when he'd pressed the buttons, remembered the board on the roof, and knew why Nighklauer might only have ridden one floor down.

The section of hall made into the foyer of his loft apartment had meant walling off the entrance to the service stairs when the building was remodeled. Nighklauer would have had to descend one floor to make his way back up to the roof using the stairs!

Coop didn't want to ride all the way down to the lobby, then back up. He punched the button for the next floor, left the elevator, then ran to the end of the hall and shouldered open the heavy steel door that would lock behind him.

Every breath a struggle, he began climbing the service stairs.

As Coop edged open the roof door, cold air hit him fogging his breath and biting hard at the back of his raw throat.

But it also cleared his mind. The cold, the adrena line, made him remarkably alert. He had never felt s ready.

He stepped the rest of the way out onto the roof.

And it was so sudden it startled him.

A dark figure, not much more than a shadow, darte across the roof near the opposite edge. Nighklauer Coop thought so, almost aimed and fired in that in tant. But he couldn't be sure of his target's identity. Only a shadow figure.

In flight!

Without a hint of hesitation, the dark figure launched itself and was hurtling in silhouette toward the adjacent roof, arms and legs spread wide and extended like an Olympic long jumper's.

For a moment Coop thought the jumper might make it, even felt a twinge of guilty admiration.

Then gravity worked its antimagic. Momentum suddenly slowed, and forward became downward.

Close. The jumper had come so close!

It had all been so quick and silent, a cold dream in the night.

His shoes crunching on the graveled tar roof, Coop slowly walked to the edge and looked down, to make sure what he'd seen was real.

He expected to see a twisted dark shape on the pavement below, near where he'd dropped the board.

Instead he saw Nighklauer a story below against the wall of the opposite building, clinging desperately to the square dark bulk of a covered air conditioner protruding from a window.

Nighklauer must have sensed Coop staring at him. He craned his neck awkwardly in order to return Coop's gaze. The planes of his face were serene but his wide eyes shone with horror and certainty. There was no way Coop could save him even if he so chose.

Would that have been his choice?

The deep and secret knowledge, the arc, bridged the dark space between the two men. But this time there was something more. They were both dying and each knew it about the other. The Night Caller couldn't understand that and wished he could ask Cooper about it. But he couldn't. He forced his eyes closed and pretended to sleep. He was lying beside Julia. They were both asleep.

The cloth or vinyl air conditioner cover began to slip from the unit, coming undone first on one side, then the other, a few inches at a time. On the other side of the window, someone parted the curtains to see what was happening, form and face barely visible in the dimness behind the reflecting glass. A woman with long hair. She didn't seem surprised by what she saw.

Bette! Coop realized with a leap of the heart. He almost said her name. She looked so much like Bette!

The air conditioner cover slipped all the way off.

The curtains swung closed.

Nighklauer was silent as he fell.

CHAPTER SIXTY-FIVE

Coop sat with Cara at one of the outside tables at Seconds, feeling the spring breeze blow cool off the bay. He was sipping a Beck's dark, his one beer for the day. On the table before them lay the remains of a good meal, one Art Billard had personally recommended.

Cara's hair was back to its original blond and cut short, stirring in the ocean air currents. At times, from particular angles in a certain light, she looked like her sister Ann. From any angle, in any light, Coop thought she was beautiful.

Sometimes he found himself wondering if it was his cancer, in remission but still there, that made her seem so wonderful. She was time and beauty and life, and all of it was precarious but he still possessed it. He wasn't immortal. That his time was limited made the bounty of his life all the more precious. And who knew how much time anyone had? Months? Years? Even decades were possible.

Far out on the bay, a boat with a triangular white sail tacked toward shore. The bright sun made its sail luminous against a sky that was the deepest blue Coop had ever seen.

He was staring out at the boat when Billard approached the table. Billard had put on weight and was wearing more expensive suits, looking more and more like a restaurateur than a cop. He was planning on full retirement in September.

He stood near their table, his hands folded in front of him. "Everything good?"

"Everything's wonderful," Cara said.

Billard smiled. "Maureen told me she was going to the wedding."

"We invited her," Cara said. "She helped save my life."

"She's well aware of it," Coop said to Billard. Maureen hadn't exactly turned over a new leaf, but the role she'd played in ending Nighklauer's string of victims seemed to have changed her, made her more contented with herself and her situation. It was because of her that women lived, and that one she knew, Cara, had a chance for happiness. Coop thought sometimes that Maureen didn't even begrudge him his second chance.

The waiter came and placed the check on the table. Billard immediately scooped it up. The waiter gave a little half bow and turned away.

"Wait a minute," Coop said to him. "We're going to have dessert."

Turn the page for an exciting preview of the next
Frank Quinn thriller

TWIST

Coming from Pinnacle in Fall 2013!

CHAPTER ONE

Medford County, Kansas, 1984

Abbey Taylor trusted to God and Ford to get her into Medford so she could buy some groceries. She was driving the family's old pickup truck. It was harder and harder for her to get around, much less into town, so she figured she should take advantage of feeling good on a nice sunny day and load up on whatever she could afford.

Billy had stayed home from work again today and was sleeping off another night out with his buddies. That involved plenty of meth, which was why he was in no condition to go in to work as an auto mechanic in Medford. All he wanted was to lie on the old vinyl couch and listen to some natter-head on the radio railing about how crooked the government was. Hell, everybody knew that already.

So Abbey, in her ninth month of pregnancy, left Billy to his anarchist dreams and waddled out to the old truck parked in the shade.

The truck was black, so it soaked up the sun, and as

soon as she managed to climb inside, Abbey cranked down the windows. That let a nice breeze in, scented by the nearby stand of pine trees.

She turned the ignition key one bump, and needles moved on the gauges. The gas gauge, which was usually accurate, indicated over a quarter of a tank. Abbey knew from experience that would carry her into town and back.

The engine stuttered once and then turned over and ran smoothly enough, though it did clatter some. She released the emergency brake, shoved the gear shift lever into first. The truck bucked some when she turned onto the dirt road, but she got it going smoothly in second and kept it in that gear so she could navigate around the worst of the ruts and holes. One particular bump was so jarring that she feared for the baby.

Soon she was on blacktop, and she put the truck in gear and drove smoothly along. The ride into town was pretty, the road lined with conifers and old sycamore trees and cottonwoods. The warm breeze coming through the open windows whisked away most of the oil and gas odor seeping up through the floorboards.

About halfway to town, on a slight hill, the motor began to run rough and seemed to lose power.

Abbey stomped down on the clutch and jammed the truck into a lower gear. That got her more power, but only briefly.

Then the engine chattered and died, and she steered the truck to the slanted road shoulder.

Abbey cursed herself for trusting the old truck. And she was worried about how Billy was going to react when he found out she'd run out of gas on the little traveled county road to Medford.

She heard a hissing sound and saw steam rising from beneath the hood. A closer look at the gauges showed that she hadn't run out of gas at all. The truck had simply overheated. She thought of Billy at home on the couch.

Where's a mechanic when you need one?

At least it had happened where she'd been able to steer the balky vehicle into the shade.

Abbey tried to judge just where she was stranded. It was almost the halfway point, and a far walk for anyone, much less a woman in her ninth month of pregnancy.

What if . . . ?

But Abbey didn't want to think about that.

She opened the door and kicked it wide with her left foot, then wrestled herself sideways out from behind the steering wheel. It was less trouble than it might have been because the truck was on a slant to the left, and her real problem was to catch herself when her feet contacted the ground and keep her balance so she wouldn't go rolling down the grade. Despite her problems, her thought of what that might look like made her almost smile.

Abbey stood with her hand against the sun-heated metal of the front fender for a moment, gaining her balance, then waddled around to the front of the truck.

Steam was still rolling out from underneath, but the hissing had stopped.

She knew then that she'd screwed up. She wanted to see what the problem might be, but she'd forgotten to release the hood latch in the truck's cab. Keeping both hands on the truck to help keep her balance, she made her way back to the open door on the driver's side.

She was halfway there when she heard the sound of a motor.

So there was another vehicle on the county road!

Abbey felt like singing with relief.

Then she realized she might have a problem. There was no guarantee the driver of whatever was coming would notice the truck pulled well off the shoulder like it was.

She tried to make her way back to the road side of the truck, all the while listening to the approaching car or truck motor getting louder.

Damn! It went past her. A dusty white van with tinted windows, rocking along faster than was lawful. Its radio or cassette player had been on. Abbey had heard a snatch of music as it passed.

Wait! She heard music now. A rock band. Sounded like the Stones' "(I Can't Get No) Satisfaction."

Abbey thought, *Ain't that the truth?*

Then she heard the motor, growing louder.

She *had* been seen! The van was backing up.

She glimpsed it between the trees, then saw it roll backward around the shallow bend and slowed.

It parked only a few feet from the truck. Mick Jagger shouted, "*I cain't get no— I cain't get no—*" as the van's door opened and a heavyset smiling woman awkwardly got down from behind the steering wheel and slammed the door shut behind her.

She was tall as well as bulky, and stood with her thick arms crossed, looking at Abbey, then the truck and the puddle beneath its front bumper, then back at Abbey. Her smile widened, showing bad teeth with wide spaces between them. Though badly in need of dental work, it was a kind smile and Abbey was glad to return it.

"Hell," the woman said, "you got yourself a problem, sweetheart. But it ain't hopeless." Her voice was highly pitched but authoritative, each word abrupt.

"The engine just stopped on me," Abbey said. "Overheated."

"I'll say. I'm familiar with these things." She strode over to the truck, the soles of her faded gray tennis shoes crunching on the gravel. "You know where the hood latch is?"

Abbey shrugged.

The woman went around to the driver's side door and opened it, reached inside and did something. The hood jumped upward a few inches. She slammed the truck door shut then walked around and raised the hood all the way, exposing the engine and the steaming radiator.

"Don't s'pose you carry any water," she said.

Abbey shook her head no. "Maybe we oughta take the cap off the radiator. It might make it cool down faster."

"Burn your hand, sweetheart. Maybe your whole damn arm. Gotta let these things run their course." She propped her fists on her hips and glanced up and down the road. "Ain't what you'd call heavily traveled."

"Never is."

"And you, in your delicate condition, oughta be someplace outta the sun."

"Couldn't argue that."

"My name's Mildred," the woman said.

"Abigail Taylor. Or just Abbey."

"You was headed for Medford?"

"Was."

"I'm goin' that direction, Just Abbey. How about I drive you there, you do whatever it is you gotta do, then we can come back this way with a jug or two of water? That might be all you need to get back home. You got a husband?"

Abbey was taken slightly aback by the question. "Sure do. He's home sleepin' now. Had hisself a rough night."

"Men!" Mildred said. "Still tryin' to get at you, I bet."

"Uh, no," Abbey said. "It's close enough now, that's stopped till after the baby."

"Baby good an' healthy?"

Abbey had to smile. "Doctor says so."

Mildred held her arm to balance her as they walked over to the van, then she helped Abbey up onto the passenger seat, next to the driver's.

Abbey settled into the seat while Mildred climbed up behind the steering wheel and got the van started. It rode kind of bumpy, but Abbey was glad to be moving.

"Gotta stop by my place and pick up somethin' on the way into town," Mildred said. "You mind?"

"Not at all," Abbey said.

Mildred turned the air conditioner on high and aimed one of the dashboard vents directly at Abbey.

"Too much?"

"Just right," Abbey said.

The day wasn't turning out to be such a disaster, after all. And she'd made a new friend.

She couldn't have been more wrong.

CHAPTER TWO

ew York City, the present

Some people thought it would never rain again in New York. It had been almost a month since a drop f moisture had made it to the ground. The sky re-ained almost cloudless. The brick and stone build-gs, the concrete streets and sidewalks, were heating p like the walls and floor of a kiln that didn't cool all e way down at night.

Quinn was fully dressed except for his shoes. He as asleep on the sofa in the brownstone on West Sev-nty-fifth Street, lying on his back with an arm flung cross his eyes to keep out the sunbeam that seemed to e tracking him no matter which way he turned.

The sun had sent a beam in beneath a crookedly losed drape, and an elongated rectangle of sunlight y with geometric precision in the middle of the car-et. The brownstone didn't have central air, and the owerful window units were running almost con-tantly, barely holding the summer heat at bay.

Quinn was a big man, and solid. He took up most of

the sofa. Ordinarily he'd be working this afternoon, but business was slow at Quinn and Associates Investigative Agency.

Quinn knew Pearl was holding down the office. Fedderman was talking to a man in Queens whose car kept being stolen again and again. Sal Vitali and Harold Mishkin were down in the Village, keeping close watch on a wayward wife, whose husband had hired Q&A to see if she was cheating on him, and was himself cheating on her. Quinn knew the parties were, most likely, more in need of a marriage counselor than a detective agency.

He'd seen this before. Harold Mishkin would probably wind up consoling and counseling. He was a friend and mediator to all humankind, and probably should never have been a cop. The NYPD, the violent streets of New York, hadn't seemed to coarsen him or wise him up over the years. It was a good thing his partner, Sal Vitali, looked out for him.

Maybe because of the heat and drought, crime seemed to be taking a break in New York City. Legal chicanery was no doubt still going strong, but only a small percentage of the illegal was finding its way to Q&A. The cheating married couple, the guy with the stolen and stolen car. That was about it for now.

Quinn stirred. He knew someone had entered the living room. Jody Jason, Pearl's daughter, and Quinn's ersatz daughter, who lived upstairs. He didn't move his arm or open his eyes. "'Lo, Jody."

"How'd you know it was me?"

"Your perfume."

"I'm not wearing any."

"The distinctive sound of your shoes on the stairs."

"I'm in my stocking feet."

"Okay," Quinn said, opening his eyes and scooting to a sitting position. "You and I are the only ones in the house, so it had to be you."

"Not exactly a Sherlock moment," she said.

Jody, skinny, large-breasted like her mother, with stringy red hair *un*like her mother's raven black hair, grinned at him. Pearl was in the grin, all right. "Occam's razor," she said. She was kind of a smart ass. That attitude could help her in her work. She was an associate attorney with a small law firm, Prather and Pierce, that fought the good fight against big business, big government, big anything that had deep pockets. The average age of the attorneys at Prather and Pierce was about twenty-five.

"I didn't know Occam needed a shave."

"Always." She headed for the kitchen. "Want some coffee?"

"No, it might make me vibrate."

"Something cool?"

"Makes more sense."

He heard her fidget around in the kitchen, then she reappeared with a mug in each hand. "Don't worry," she said, "yours is orange juice."

If it moves, sue it, was lettered on the mugs. She handed him his orange juice and then settled down across from him in a chair, tucking her jeans-clad legs beneath her slender body. "Business will pick up," she said.

"Not if some guy's car stops getting stolen."

"Huh?"

Quinn tilted back his head and downed half his orange juice. It was cold and tasted great. "This case

Fedderman's on. Guy's a graffiti artist, uses spray paint, dolled up his car so good it keeps getting stolen."

"He should take some color photos of the car, leave them stuck under a wiper blade. Maybe the thieves will be satisfied with a picture and leave the real thing at the curb."

"I'll suggest that to Fedderman."

"Feds will understand."

"Like Occam."

Jody looked off to the side and thought for a moment. "No," she said, "like Feds."

"Sometimes," Quinn said, "you are eerily like your mother."

"That a compliment?"

"A warning."

She took a long sip of her coffee. "Business will pick up," she assured Quinn. "In this city, with all the dealing and stealing that has to be set right, Q&A will get its share. Maybe something by way of your friend Renz."

"I'd rather Renz not be involved. He complicates things."

"Still," Jody said, "he's the police commissioner."

"Occam with a beard," Quinn said. "And unshaven scruples."

"Yeah," Jody replied. "That's more like normal life."

"If there is such a thing," Quinn said, finishing of his orange juice. He licked his lips. "Any more of thi in the fridge?"

"Nope. Nothing cold except beer and bottled water."

"Let me think," Quinn said.

CHAPTER THREE

ew York City, the present

He was real.

There he was again. He must know she got off
ork at Gowns 'n' Gifts at five o'clock, because shortly
hereafter she would see him.

Though he kept his distance, he didn't seem to mind
hat she saw him.

Bonnie Anderson was sure she was being stalked. It
ad been going on for over a week. Each time she saw
im she'd be more afraid. She *wasn't* imagining him—
hough in truth she'd never gotten a clear look at him.
Often his head was bowed so the bill of the cap he usu-
lly wore blocked or shadowed his face. But there was
omething about him, in his movements. A resolute-
ess. A man with something on his mind.

With me on his mind.

Bonnie shuddered and crossed the street.

He followed, of course.

She stopped.

He stopped.

Bonnie was a beauty, with long blond hair, a slender, shapely body, and a face whose planes and angles had intrigued a college art class almost as much as the rest of her. That was all too apparent with the male students, which always amused Bonnie.

No doubt the man following her was similarly aroused, but he didn't amuse her. He scared her in a subtle way that made her body seem drugged.

She was sure he wanted her to see him, wanted her fear to grow. For some reason, he was nurturing her dread.

She glanced back over her shoulder, and there he was.

He stood now about a hundred feet behind her on the crowded sidewalk, statue still, and stared from beneath the shadowed arc of his ball cap bill. It was odd how she couldn't see his eyes but she *felt* them on her.

Her fear expanded, and with it her anger.

You want me to be afraid, you bastard!

She spun on her heel and walked directly toward him. *Cope with your fears by facing them.* He seemed to smile—she couldn't be sure—as he leisurely entered a nearby deli.

Without hesitation she followed him into the deli.

It wasn't much cooler in there than outside.

A gondola with steel trays of heated food ran down the middle of the deli. Shelves of packaged food were along one side wall. A series of glass-doored coolers ran along the opposite wall, stacked with bottled and canned drinks and dairy products. Beyond the coolers

ore shelves of groceries. People were milling about
the counter and among the shelves and coolers. A
w of them were carrying wire baskets.

Bonnie looked around for the blue ball cap and didn't
e it. Didn't see the bastard. She went to the back of
e deli and walked along the heads of the aisles, paus-
g to stare down each one.

He was gone. Somehow he was gone.

Had he been the product of her imagination? A mi-
ge, maybe, from the heat.

Probably he wanted her to think that. Actually, he
ight have slipped back outside when she had her
ack momentarily turned and she was striding along
e cooler aisle. He'd had time to manage that. Just.

Charging back out onto the sidewalk, Bonnie
umped into a woman hard enough to make her stag-
er.

"I'm sorry, too," the woman snarled.

Everybody was irritable. The weather.

A male voice behind Bonnie said, "Bump into me,
weetheart."

She turned and saw a boy about sixteen leering at
er. He wilted and backed away as she glared at him,
en he walked past her and over by the curb without
lancing back at her.

If only they were all so easy to discourage.

A dry breeze was blowing, turning the city into a
onvection oven. Bonnie wished to hell it would rain at
east enough to cool down all the damned steel and
oncrete in the city. She looked up at the sky, not ex-
ecting to see a cloud. There were two small ones.
hey looked as dry as cotton.

Bonnie was only a few blocks from her apartment. She walked them uneasily, unable to keep her head still, trying to catch another glimpse of the man who'd been dogging her.

But she knew she wouldn't see him. He was through with her for now.

She hoped.